KILLING ME SOFTLY MEANS—

An out-of-body romance—with slow hand
A vampire lover seeking a red-blooded replacement
A woman double-dating with her stillborn twin
All your old girlfriends coming back from the dead—
at once!
A dancer calling to his partner from the grave
Two cross-dressers on the last train to Hell
A two-headed man with two of everything!

*A gourmet collection of Necromantic Erotica featuring
today's most compelling authors:*

Ursula K. Le Guin • Lucius Shepard • Pat Cadigan
Mary Rosenblum • Robert Silverberg • Nancy Kress
Robert Sampson • Kristine Kathryn Rusch
Maureen F. McHugh • Michael Swanwick • Tanith Lee
Michael Bishop • Nancy A. Collins • Mike Resnick
Nicholas A. DiChario • Parke Godwin

KILLING ME SOFTLY

Erotic Tales of Unearthly Love

Edited by

Gardner Dozois

HarperPrism
An Imprint of HarperPaperbacks

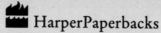 HarperPaperbacks
A Division of HarperCollins*Publishers*
10 East 53rd Street, New York, N.Y. 10022-5299

Individual story copyrights appear on pages 419-420.

A trade paperback edition of this book was published in
November 1995 by HarperPrism.

ISBN 0-06-105611-1

HarperPrism is an imprint of HarperPaperbacks.

HarperCollins®, ▲®, HarperPaperbacks™, and HarperPrism®
are trademarks of HarperCollins*Publishers,* Inc.

Cover photographs of cemetery/Lisa Katz/Photanica
Cover photograph of woman/Colin Samuels/Photanica

First mass market paperback edition: September 1996

Printed in the United States of America

Visit HarperPaperbacks on the World Wide Web at
http://www.harpercollins.com/paperbacks

❖ 10 9 8 7 6 5 4 3 2 1

Acknowledgments

The editor would like to thank the following people for their help and support:

Susan Casper, who did much of the scut-work and provided computer expertise; Ellen Datlow; Virginia Kidd; Vaughn Hensen; Ralph M. Vicinanza; Arthur B. Greene; Carol Christiansen; Marilee Heifetz; Marvin Kaye; Sheila Williams; Scott Towner; Kristine Kathryn Rusch; Pat Cadigan; Chris Fowler; Mary Rosenblum; Michael Swanwick; Michael Bishop; Maureen F. McHugh; Mike Resnick; Lucius Shepard; Nancy Kress; Caitlin Blasdell; and special thanks to my own editor, John Silbersack.

Contents

UNCHOSEN LOVE
Ursula K. Le Guin

Ursula K. Le Guin is probably one of the best-known and most universally respected SF writers in the world today. Her famous novel *The Left Hand of Darkness* may have been the most influential SF novel of its decade and shows every sign of becoming one of the enduring classics of the genre—even ignoring the rest of Le Guin's work, the impact of this one novel alone on future SF and future SF writers would be incalculably strong. (Her 1968 fantasy novel, *A Wizard of Earthsea*, would be almost as influential on future generations of High Fantasy writers.) *The Left Hand of Darkness* won both the Hugo and Nebula Awards, as did Le Guin's monumental novel *The Dispossessed* a few years later. Her novel *Tehanu* won her another Nebula in 1990, and she has also won three other Hugo Awards and a Nebula Award for her short fiction, as well as the National Book Award for children's literature for her novel *The Farthest Shore*, part of her acclaimed Earthsea trilogy. Her other novels include *Planet of Exile*, *The Lathe of Heaven*, *City of Illusions*, *Rocannon's World*, *The Beginning Place*, *The Tombs of Atuan*, and the controversial multimedia novel (it sold with a cassette tape of music and included drawings and recipes), *Always Coming Home*. She has had four collections: *The Wind's*

Twelve Quarters, Orsinian Tales, The Compass Rose, and *Buffalo Gals and Other Animal Presences.* Her most recent books are the novel *Searoad* and a new collection, *A Fisherman of the Inland Sea.*

Here she returns to the star-spanning, Hainish-settled interstellar community known as the Ekumen, the same fictional universe she used in her famous novels *The Left Hand of Darkness* and *The Dispossessed,* for a thoughtful and lyrical story that demonstrates that love can cross all barriers of class and age and gender— and even the ultimate barrier of them all.

Unchosen Love

INTRODUCTION

*By Heokad'd Arhe of Inanan Farmhold of Tag Village on the
Southwest Watershed of the Budran River on Okets on the
Planet O.*

Sex, for everybody, on every world, is a complicated
business, but nobody seems to have complicated marriage quite as much as my people have. To us, of
course, it seems simple, and so natural that it's foolish
to describe it, like trying to describe how we walk,
how we breathe. Well, you know, you stand on one
leg and move the other one forward . . . you let the air
come into your lungs and then you let it out . . . you
marry a man and woman from the other moiety. . . .

What is a moiety? a Gethenian asked me, and I
realized that it's easier for me to imagine not knowing
which sex I'll be tomorrow morning, like the
Gethenian, than to imagine not knowing whether I
was a Morning person or an Evening person. So complete, so universal a division of humanity—how can
there be a society without it? How do you know who
anyone is? How can you give worship without the
one to ask and the other to answer, the one to pour

and the other to drink? How can you couple indiscriminately without regard to incest? I have to admit that in the unswept, unenlightened basements of my hindbrain I agree with my great-uncle Gambat, who said, "Those people from off the world, they all try to stand on one leg. Two legs, two sexes, two moieties—it only makes sense!"

A moiety is half a population. We call our two halves the Morning and the Evening. If your mother's a Morning woman, you're a Morning person; and all Morning people are in certain respects your brother or sister. You have sex, marry, have children only with Evening people.

When I explained our concept of incest to a fellow student on Hain, she said, shocked, "But that means you can't have sex with half the population!" And I in turn said, shocked, "Do you *want* sex with half the population?"

Moieties are in fact not an uncommon social structure within the Ekumen. I have had comfortable conversations with people from several bipartite societies. One of them, a Nadir woman of the Umna on Ithsh, nodded and laughed when I told her my great-uncle's opinion. "But you ki'O," she said, "you marry on all fours."

Few people from other worlds are willing to believe that our form of marriage works. They prefer to think that we endure it. They forget that human beings, while whining after the simple life, thrive on complexity.

When I marry—for love, for stability, for children—I marry three people. I am a Morning man: I marry an Evening woman and an Evening man, with both of whom I have a sexual relationship, and a Morning woman, with whom I have no sexual relationship. Her sexual relationships are with the Evening man and the Evening woman. The whole marriage is called a sedoretu. Within it there are four submarriages; the two heterosexual pairs are called Morning and Evening, according to the woman's moiety; the male homosexual pair is called the Night marriage, and the female homosexual pair is called the Day.

Brothers and sisters of the four primary people can join the sedoretu, so that the number of people in the marriage sometimes gets to six or seven. The children are variously related as siblings, germanes, and cousins.

Evidently a sedoretu takes some arranging. We spend a lot of our time arranging them. How much of a marriage is founded on love and in which couples the love is strongest, how much of it is founded on convenience, custom, profit, friendship, will depend on regional tradition, personal character, and so on. The complexities are so evident that I am always surprised when an offworlder sees, in the multiple relationship, only the forbidden, the illicit one. "How can you be married to three people and never have sex with one of them?" they ask.

The question makes me uncomfortable; it seems to assume that sexuality is a force so dominant that it cannot be contained or shaped by any other relationship. Most societies expect a father and daughter, or a brother and sister, to have a nonsexual family relationship, though I gather that in some the incest ban is often violated by people empowered by age and gender to ignore it. Evidently such societies see human beings as divided into two kinds, the fundamental division being power, and they grant one gender superior power. To us, the fundamental division is moiety; gender is a great but secondary difference; and in the search for power no one starts from a position of innate privilege. It certainly leads to our looking at things differently.

The fact is, the people of O admire the simple life as much as anyone else, and we have found our own peculiar way of achieving it. We are conservative, conventional, self-righteous, and dull. We suspect change and resist it blindly. Many houses, farms, and shrines on O have been in the same place and called by the same name for fifty or sixty centuries, some for hundreds of centuries. We have mostly been doing the same things in the same way for longer than that. Evidently, we do things carefully. We honor self-restraint, often to the point of harboring demons, and are fierce in defense of our privacy. We despise the outstanding. The wise among us do not live in solitude on mountaintops; they live in houses on farms, have many relatives, and keep careful accounts. We have no cities, only dispersed villages composed of a group of farmholds and a community center; educational and technological centers are supported by each region. We do without gods and, for a long time now, without wars. The question strangers most often ask us is, "In those marriages of yours, do you all go to bed together?" and the answer we give is, "No."

That is in fact how we tend to answer any question from a stranger. It is amazing that we ever got into the Ekumen. We are near Hain—sidereally near, 4.2 light-years—and the Hainish simply kept coming here and talking to us for centuries, until we got used to them and were able to say Yes. The Hainish, of course, are our ancestral race, but the stolid longevity of our customs makes them feel young and rootless and dashing. That is probably why they like us.

UNCHOSEN LOVE

There was a hold down near the mouths of the Saduun, built on a rock island that stands up out of

the great tidal plain south of where the river meets the
sea. The sea used to come in and swirl around the
island, but as the Saduun slowly built up its delta over
the centuries, only the great tides reached it, and then
only the storm tides, and at last the sea never came so
far, but lay shining all along the west.

Meruo was never a farmhold; built on rock in a
salt marsh, it was a seahold, and lived by fishing.
When the sea withdrew, the people dug a channel
from the foot of the rock to the tideline. Over the
years, as the sea withdrew farther, the channel grew
longer and longer, till it was a broad canal three miles
long. Up and down it fishing boats and trading ships
went to and from the docks of Meruo that sprawled
over the rocky base of the island. Right beside the
docks and the netyards and the drying and freezing
plants began the prairies of saltgrass, where vast flocks
of yama and flightless baro grazed. Meruo rented out
those pastures to farmholds of Sadahun Village in the
coastal hills. None of the flocks belonged to Meruo,
whose people looked only to the sea, and farmed only
the sea, and never walked if they could sail. More
than the fishing, it was the prairies that had made
them rich, but they spent their wealth on boats and
on digging and dredging the great canal. We throw
our money in the sea, they said.

They were known as a stiff-necked lot, holding
themselves apart from the village. Meruo was a big
hold, often with a hundred people living in it, so they
seldom made sedoretu with village people, but married one another. They're all germanes at Meruo, the
villagers said.

A Morning man from eastern Oket came to stay in
Sadahun, studying saltmarsh grazing for his farmhold
on the other coast. He chanced to meet an Evening
man of Meruo named Suord, in town for a village
meeting. The next day, there came Suord again, to see

him; and the next day too; and by the fourth night
Suord was making love to him, sweeping him off his
feet like a storm-wave.

The Easterner, whose name was Hadri, was a
modest, inexperienced young man to whom the journey and the unfamiliar places and the strangers he
met had been a considerable adventure. Now he
found one of the strangers wildly in love with him,
beseeching him to come out to Meruo and stay there,
live there—"We'll make a sedoretu," Suord said.
"There's half a dozen Evening girls. Any, any of the
Morning women, I'd marry any one of them to keep
you. Come out, come out with me, come out onto the
Rock!" For so the people of Meruo called their hold.

Hadri thought he owed it to Suord to do what he
asked, since Suord loved him so passionately. He got
up his courage, packed his bag, and went out across
the wide, flat prairies to the place he had seen all
along dark against the sky far off, the high roofs of
Meruo, hunched up on its rock above its docks and
warehouses and boat-basin, its windows looking away
from the land, staring always down the long canal to
the sea that had forsaken it.

Suord brought him in and introduced him to the
household, and Hadri was terrified. They were all like
Suord, dark people, handsome, fierce, abrupt, intran-
sigent—so much alike that he could not tell one from
the other and mistook daughter for mother, brother
for cousin, Evening for Morning. They were barely
polite to him. He was an interloper. They were afraid
Suord would bring him in among them for good. And
so was he.

Suord's passion was so intense that Hadri, a mod-
erate soul, assumed it must burn out soon. "Hot fires
don't last," he said to himself, and took comfort in the
adage. "He'll get tired of me and I can go," he thought,
not in words. But he stayed a tenday at Meruo, and a

month, and Suord burned as hot as ever. Hadri saw too that among the sedoretu of the household there were many passionate matings, sexual tensions running among them like a network of ungrounded wires, filling the air with the crackle and spark of electricity; and some of these marriages were many years old.

He was flattered and amazed at Suord's insatiable, yearning, worshipping desire for a person Hadri himself was used to considering as quite ordinary. He felt his response to such passion was never enough. Suord's dark beauty filled his mind, and his mind turned away, looking for emptiness, a space to be alone. Some nights, when Suord lay flung out across the bed in deep sleep after lovemaking, Hadri would get up, naked, silent; he would sit in the window seat across the room, gazing down the shining of the long canal under the stars. Sometimes he wept silently. He cried because he was in pain, but he did not know what the pain was.

One such night in early winter his feeling of being chafed, rubbed raw, like an animal fretting in a trap, all his nerve ends exposed, was too much to endure. He dressed, very quietly for fear of waking Suord, and went barefoot out of their room, to get outdoors—anywhere out from under the roofs, he thought. He felt that he could not breathe.

The immense house was bewildering in the dark. The seven sedoretu living there now each had their own wing or floor or suite of rooms, all spacious. He had never even been into the regions of the First and Second Sedoretu, way off in the south wing, and always got confused in the ancient central part of the house, but he thought he knew his way around these floors in the north wing. This corridor, he thought, led to the landward stairs. It led only to narrow stairs going up. He went up them into a great shadowy attic, and found a door out onto the roof itself.

A long railed walk led along the south edge. He followed it, the peaks of the roofs rising up like black mountains to his left, and the prairies, the marshes, and then as he came round to the west side, the canal, all lying vast and dim in starlight below. The air was soft and damp, smelling of rain to come. A low mist was coming up from the marshes. As he watched, his arms on the rail, the mist thickened and whitened, hiding the marshes and the canal. He welcomed that softness, that slowness of the blurring, healing, concealing fog. A little peace and solace came into him. He breathed deep and thought, "Why, why am I so sad? Why don't I love Suord as much as he loves me? Why does he love me?"

He felt somebody was near him, and looked round. A woman had come out onto the roof and stood only a few yards away, her arms on the railing like his, barefoot like him, in a long dressing gown. When he turned his head, she turned hers, looking at him.

She was one of the women of the Rock, no mistaking the dark skin and straight black hair and a certain fine cut of brow, cheekbone, jaw; but which one he was not sure. At the dining rooms of the north wing he had met a number of Evening women in their twenties, all sisters, cousins, or germanes, all unmarried. He was afraid of them all, because Suord might propose one of them as his wife in sedoretu. Hadri was a little shy sexually and found the gender difference hard to cross; he had found his pleasure and solace mostly with other young men, though some women attracted him very much. These women of Meruo were powerfully attractive, but he could not imagine himself touching one of them. Some of the pain he suffered here was caused by the distrustful coldness of the Evening women, always making it clear to him that he was the outsider. They scorned him and he avoided them. And so he was not perfectly certain which one was Sasni, which one was Lamateo, or Saval, or Esbuai.

He thought this was Esbuai, because she was tall, but he wasn't sure. The darkness might excuse him, for one could barely make out the features of a face. He murmured, "Good evening," and said no name.

There was a long pause, and he thought resignedly that a woman of Meruo would snub him even in the dead of night on a rooftop.

But then she said, "Good evening," softly, with a laugh in her voice, and it was a soft voice, that lay on his mind the way the fog did, mild and cool. "Who is that?" she said.

"Hadri," he said, resigned again. Now she knew him and would snub him.

"Hadri? You aren't from here."

Who was she, then?

He said his farmhold name. "I'm from the east, from the Fadan'n Watershed. Visiting."

"I've been away," she said. "I just came back. Tonight. Isn't it a lovely night? I like these nights best of all, when the fog comes up, like a sea of its own. . . . "

Indeed the mists had joined and risen, so that Meruo on its rock seemed to float suspended in darkness over a faintly luminous void.

"I like it too," he said. "I was thinking . . ." Then he stopped.

"What?" she said after a minute, so gently that he took courage and went on.

"That being unhappy in a room is worse than being unhappy out of doors," he said, with a self-conscious and unhappy laugh. "I wonder why that is."

"I knew," she said. "By the way you were standing. I'm sorry. What do you . . . what would you need to make you happier?" At first he had thought her older than himself, but now she spoke like a quite young girl, shy and bold at the same time, awkwardly, with sweetness. It was the dark and the fog that made them both bold, released them, so they could speak truly.

"I don't know," he said. "I think I don't know how to be in love."

"Why do you think so?"

"Because I—It's Suord, he brought me here," he told her, trying to go on speaking truly. "I do love him, but not—not the way he deserves—"

"Suord," she said thoughtfully.

"He is strong. Generous. He gives me everything he is, his whole life. But I'm not, I'm not able to . . ."

"Why do you stay?" she asked, not accusingly, but asking for an answer.

"I love him," Hadri said. "I don't want to hurt him. If I run away I'll be a coward. I want to be worth him." They were four separate answers, each spoken separately, painfully.

"Unchosen love," she said with a dry, rough tenderness. "Oh, it's hard."

She did not sound like a girl now, but like a woman who knew what love is. While they talked they had both looked out westward over the sea of mist, because it was easier to talk that way. She turned now to look at him again. He was aware of her quiet gaze in the darkness. A great star shone bright between the line of the roof and her head. When she moved again her round, dark head occulted the star, and then it shone tangled in her hair, as if she was wearing it. It was a lovely thing to see.

"I always thought I'd choose love," he said at last, her words working in his mind. "Choose a sedoretu, settle down, someday, somewhere near my farm. I never imagined anything else. And then I came out here, to the edge of the world. . . . And I don't know what to do. I was chosen, I can't choose. . . . "

There was a little self-mockery in his voice.

"This is a strange place," he said.

"It is," she said. "Once you've seen the great tide. . . ."

He had seen it once. Suord had taken him to a headland that stood above the southern floodplain. Though it was only a few miles southwest of Meruo, they had to go a long way round inland and then back out west again, and Hadri asked, "Why can't we just go down the coast?"

"You'll see why," Suord said. They sat up on the rocky headland eating their picnic, Suord always with an eye on the brown-gray mudflats stretching off to the western horizon, endless and dreary, cut by a few worming, silted channels. "Here it comes," he said, standing up; and Hadri stood up to see the gleam and hear the distant thunder, see the advancing bright line, the incredible rush of the tide across the immense plain for seven miles till it crashed in foam on the rocks below them and flooded on round the headland.

"A good deal faster than you could run," Suord said, his dark face keen and intense. "That's how it used to come in around our Rock. In the old days."

"Are we cut off here?" Hadri had asked, and Suord had answered, "No, but I wish we were."

Thinking of it now, Hadri imagined the broad sea lying under the fog all around Meruo, lapping on the rocks, under the walls. As it had been in the old days.

"I suppose the tides cut Meruo off from the mainland," he said, and she said, "Twice every day."

"Strange," he murmured, and heard her slight intaken breath of laughter.

"Not at all," she said. "Not if you were born here. . . . Do you know that babies are born and the dying die on what they call the lull? The low point of the low tide of morning."

Her voice and words made his heart clench within him, they were so soft and seemed so strange. "I come

from inland, from the hills, I never saw the sea before,"
he said. "I don't know anything about the tides."

"Well," she said, "there's their true love." She was
looking behind him. He turned and saw the waning
moon just above the sea of mist, only its darkest,
scarred crescent showing. He stared at it, unable to say
anything more.

"Hadri," she said, "don't be sad. It's only the moon.
Come up here again if you are sad, though. I liked talking with you. There's nobody here to talk to. . . .
Goodnight," she whispered. She went away from him
along the walk and vanished in the shadows.

He stayed a while watching the mist rise and the
moon rise; the mist won the slow race, blotting out
moon and all in a cold dimness at last. Shivering, but
no longer tense and anguished, he found his way back
to Suord's room and slid into the wide, warm bed. As
he stretched out to sleep he thought, I don't know her
name.

Suord woke in an unhappy mood. He insisted that
Hadri come out in the sailboat with him down the
canal, to check the locks on the side-canals, he said;
but what he wanted was to get Hadri alone, in a boat,
where Hadri was not only useless but slightly uneasy
and had no escape at all. They drifted in the mild sunshine on the glassy side-canal. "You want to leave,
don't you," Suord said, speaking as if the sentence was
a knife that cut his tongue as he spoke it.

"No," Hadri said, not knowing if it was true, but
unable to say any other word.

"You don't want to get married here."

"I don't know, Suord."

"What do you mean, you don't know?"

"I don't think any of the Evening women want a
marriage with me," he said, and trying to speak true,
"I know they don't. They want you to find somebody
from around here. I'm a foreigner."

"They don't know you," Suord said, with a sudden, pleading gentleness. "People here, they take a long time to get to know people. We've lived too long on our Rock. Seawater in our veins instead of blood. But they'll see—they'll come to know you if you—if you'll stay—" He looked out over the side of the boat and after a while said almost inaudibly, "If you leave, can I come with you?"

"I'm not leaving," Hadri said. He went and stroked Suord's hair and face and kissed him. He knew that Suord could not follow him, couldn't live in Oket, inland; it wouldn't work, it wouldn't do. But that meant he must stay here with Suord. There was a numb coldness in him, under his heart.

"Sasni and Duun are germanes," Suord said presently, sounding like himself again, controlled, intense. "They've been lovers ever since they were thirteen. Sasni would marry me if I asked her, if she can have Duun in the Day marriage. We can make a sedoretu with them, Hadri."

The numbness kept Hadri from reacting to this for some time; he did not know what he was feeling, what he thought. What he finally said was, "Who is Duun?" There was a vague hope in him that it was the woman he had talked with on the roof, last night—in a different world, it seemed, a realm of fog and darkness and truth.

"You know Duun."

"Did she just come back from somewhere else?"

"No," Suord said, too intent to be puzzled by Hadri's stupidity. "Sasni's germane, Lasudu's daughter of the Fourth Sedoretu. She's short, very thin, doesn't talk much."

"I don't know her," Hadri said in despair. "I can't tell them apart, they don't talk to me," and he bit his lip and stalked over to the other end of the boat and stood with his hands in his pockets and his shoulders hunched.

Suord's mood had quite changed; he splashed about happily in the water and mud when they got to the lock, making sure the mechanisms were in order, then sailed them back to the great canal with a fine following wind. Shouting, "Time you got your sea legs!" to Hadri, he took the boat west down the canal and out onto the open sea. The misty sunlight, the breeze full of salt spray, the fear of the depths, the exertion of working the boat under Suord's capable directions, the triumph of steering it back into the canal at sunset, when the light lay red-gold on the water and vast flocks of stilts and marshbirds rose crying and circling around them—it made a great day, after all, for Hadri.

But the glory dropped away as soon as he came under the roofs of Meruo again, into the dark corridors and the low, wide, dark rooms that all looked west. They took meals with the Fourth and Fifth Sedoretu. In Hadri's farmhold there would have been a good deal of teasing when they came in just in time for dinner, having been out all day without notice and done none of the work of it; here nobody ever teased or joked. If there was resentment it stayed hidden. Maybe there was no resentment, maybe they all knew each other so well and were so much of a piece that they trusted one other the way you trust your own hands, without question. Even the children joked and quarreled less than Hadri was used to. Conversation at the long table was always quiet, many not speaking a word.

As he served himself, Hadri looked around among them for the woman of last night. Had it in fact been Esbuai? He thought not; the height was like, but Esbuai was very thin, and had a particularly arrogant carriage to her head. The woman was not here. Maybe she was First Sedoretu. Which of these women was Duun?

That one, the little one, with Sasni; he recalled her now. She was always with Sasni. He had never spoken to her, because Sasni of them all had snubbed him most hatefully, and Duun was her shadow.

"Come on," said Suord, and went round the table to sit down beside Sasni, gesturing Hadri to sit beside Duun. He did so. I'm Suord's shadow, he thought.

"Hadri says he's never talked to you," Suord said to Duun. The girl hunched up a bit and muttered something meaningless. Hadri saw Sasni's face flash with anger, and yet there was a hint of a challenging smile in it, as she looked straight at Suord. They were very much alike. They were well matched.

Suord and Sasni talked—about the fishing, about the locks—while Hadri ate his dinner. He was ravenous after the day on the water. Duun, having finished her meal, sat and said nothing. These people had a capacity for remaining perfectly motionless and silent, like predatory animals, or fishing birds. The dinner was fish, of course; it was always fish. Meruo had been wealthy once and still had the manners of wealth, but few of the means. Dredging out the great canal took more of their income every year, as the sea relentlessly pulled back from the delta. Their fishing fleet was large, but the boats were old, often rebuilt. Hadri had asked why they did not build new ones, for a big shipyard loomed above the dry docks; Suord explained that the cost of the wood alone was prohibitive. Having only the one crop, fish and shellfish, they had to pay for all other food, for clothing, for wood, even for water. The wells for miles around Meruo were salt. An aqueduct led to the seahold from the village in the hills.

They drank their expensive water from silver cups, however, and ate their eternal fish from bowls of ancient, translucent blue Edia ware, which Hadri was always afraid of breaking when he washed them.

Sasni and Suord went on talking, and Hadri felt stupid and sullen, sitting there saying nothing to the girl who said nothing.

"I was out on the sea for the first time today," he said, feeling the blood flush his face.

She made some kind of noise, mhm, and gazed at her empty bowl.

"Can I get you some soup?" Hadri asked. They ended the meal with broth, here, fish broth of course.

"No," she said, with a scowl.

"In my farmhold," he said, "people often bring dishes to each other; it's a minor kind of courtesy; I am sorry if you find it offensive." He stood up and strode off to the sideboard, where with shaking hands he served himself a bowl of soup. When he got back Suord was looking at him with a speculative eye and a faint smile, which he resented. What did they take him for? Did they think he had no standards, no people, no place of his own? Let them marry each other, he would have no part of it. He gulped his soup, got up without waiting for Suord, and went to the kitchen, where he spent an hour in the washing-up crew to make up for missing his time in the cooking crew. Maybe they had no standards about things, but he did.

Suord was waiting for him in their room—Suord's room; Hadri had no room of his own here. That in itself was insulting, unnatural. In a decent hold, a guest was always given a room.

Whatever Suord said—he could not remember later what it was—was a spark to blasting powder. "I will not be treated this way!" he cried passionately, and Suord firing up at once demanded what he meant, and they had at it, an explosion of rage and frustration and accusation that left them staring gray-faced at each other, appalled. "Hadri," Suord said, the name a sob; he was shivering, his whole body shaking. They came together, clinging to each other. Suord's small, rough, strong hands held Hadri close. The taste of Suord's skin was salt as the sea. Hadri sank, sank and was drowned.

But in the morning everything was as it had been. He did not dare ask for a room to himself, knowing it would hurt Suord. If they do make this sedoretu, then at least I'll have a room, said a small, unworthy voice in his head. But it was wrong, wrong. . . .

He looked for the woman he had met on the roof, and saw half a dozen who might have been her and none he was certain was her. Would she not look at him, speak to him? Not in daylight, not in front of the others? Well, so much for her, then.

It occurred to him only now that he did not know whether she was a woman of the Morning or the Evening. But what did it matter?

That night the fog came in. Waking suddenly, deep in the night, he saw out the window only a formless gray, glowing very dimly with diffused light from a window somewhere in another wing of the house. Suord slept, as he always did, flat out, lying like a bit of jetsam flung on the beach of the night, utterly absent and abandoned. Hadri watched him with an aching tenderness for a while. Then he got up, pulled on clothes, and found the corridor to the stairs that led up to the roof.

The mist hid even the roof peaks. Nothing at all was visible over the railing. He had to feel his way along, touching the railing. The wooden walkway was damp and cold to the soles of his feet. Yet a kind of happiness had started in him as he went up the attic stairs, and it grew as he breathed the foggy air, and as he turned the corner to the west side of the house. He stood still a while and then spoke, almost in a whisper. "Are you there?" he said.

There was a pause, as there had been the first time he spoke to her, and then she answered, the laugh just hidden in her voice, "Yes, I'm here. Are you there?"

The next moment they could see each other, though only as shapes bulking in the mist.

"I'm here," he said. His happiness was absurd. He took a step closer to her, so that he could make out her dark hair, the darkness of her eyes in the lighter oval of her face. "I wanted to talk to you again," he said.

"I wanted to talk to you again," she said.

"I couldn't find you. I hoped you'd speak to me."

"Not down there," she said, her voice turning light and cold.

"Are you in the First Sedoretu?"

"Yes," she said. "The Morning wife of the First Sedoretu of Meruo. My name is An'nad. I wanted to know if you're still unhappy."

"Yes," he said, "no—" He tried to see her face more clearly, but there was little light. "Why is it that you talk to me, and I can talk to you, and not to anybody else in this household?" he said. "Why are you the only kind one?"

"Is . . . Suord unkind?" she asked, with a little hesitation on the name.

"He never means to be. He never is. Only he—he drags me, he pushes me, he . . . He's stronger than I am."

"Maybe not," said An'nad. "Maybe only more used to getting his way."

"Or more in love," Hadri said, low-voiced, with shame.

"You're not in love with him?"

"Oh, yes!"

She laughed.

"I never knew anyone like him—he's more than— his feelings are so deep, he's—I'm out of my depth," Hadri stammered. "But I love him—immensely—"

"So what's wrong?"

"He wants to marry," Hadri said, and then stopped. He was talking about her household, probably her blood kin; as a wife of the First Sedoretu she was part of all the network of relationships of Meruo. What was he blundering into?

"Who does he want to marry?" she asked. "Don't worry. I won't interfere. Is the trouble that you don't want to marry him?"

"No, no," Hadri said. "It's only—I never meant to stay here, I thought I'd go home. . . . Marrying Suord seems—more than I, than I deserve—But it would be amazing, it would be wonderful! But . . . the marriage itself, the sedoretu, it's not right. He says that Sasni will marry him, and Duun will marry me, so that she and Duun can be married."

"Suord and Sasni"—again the faint pause on the name—"don't love each other, then?"

"No," he said, a little hesitant, remembering that challenge between them, like a spark struck.

"And you and Duun?"

"I don't even know her."

"Oh, no, that is dishonest," An'nad said. "One should choose love, but not that way. . . . Whose plan is it? All three of them?"

"I suppose so. Suord and Sasni have talked about it. The girl, Duun, she never says anything."

"Talk to her," said the soft voice. "Talk to her, Hadri." She was looking at him; they stood quite close together, close enough that he felt the warmth of her arm on his arm though they did not touch.

"I'd rather talk to you," he said, turning to face her. She moved back, seeming to grow insubstantial even in that slight movement, the fog was so dense and dark. She put out her hand, but again did not quite touch him. He knew she was smiling.

"Then stay and talk with me," she said, leaning again on the rail. "Tell me . . . oh, tell me anything. What do you do, you and Suord, when you're not making love?"

"We went out sailing," he said, and found himself telling her what it had been like for him out on the open sea for the first time, his terror and delight. "Can you swim?" she asked, and he laughed and said, "In the lake at home, it's not the same," and she laughed and said, "No, I imagine not." They talked a long time, and he asked her what she did—"in daylight. I haven't seen you yet, down there."

"No," she said. "What do I do? Oh, I worry about Meruo, I suppose. I worry about my children. . . . I don't want to think about that now. How did you come to meet Suord?"

Before they were done talking the mist had begun to lighten very faintly with moonrise. It had grown piercingly cold. Hadri was shivering. "Go on," she said. "I'm used to it. Go on to bed."

"There's frost," he said, "look," touching the silvered wooden rail. "You should go down too."

"I will. Goodnight, Hadri." As he turned she said, or he thought she said, "I'll wait for the tide."

"Goodnight, An'nad." He spoke her name huskily, tenderly. If only the others were like her. . . .

He stretched out close to Suord's inert, delicious warmth, and slept.

The next day Suord had to work in the records office, where Hadri was utterly useless and in the way. Hadri took his chance, and by asking several sullen, snappish women, found where Duun was: in the fish-drying plant. He went down to the docks and found her, by luck, if it was luck, eating her lunch alone in the misty sunshine at the edge of the boat-basin.

"I want to talk with you," he said.

"What for?" she said. She would not look at him.

"Is it honest to marry a person you don't even like in order to marry a person you love?"

"No," she said, fiercely. She kept looking down.

She tried to fold up the bag she had carried her lunch in, but her hands shook too much.

"Why are you willing to do it, then?"

"Why are *you* willing to do it?"

"I'm not," he said. "It's Suord. And Sasni."

She nodded.

"Not you?"

She shook her head, violently. Her thin, dark face was a very young face, he realized.

"But you love Sasni," he said, a little uncertainly.

"Yes! I love Sasni! I always did, I always will! That doesn't mean I, I, I have to do everything she says, everything she wants, that I have to, that I have to—" She was looking at him now, right at him, her face burning like a coal, her voice quivering and breaking. "I don't *belong* to Sasni!"

"Well," he said, "I don't belong to Suord, either."

"I don't know anything about men," Duun said savagely, still glaring at him. "Or any other women. Or anything. I never was with anybody but Sasni, all my life! She thinks she *owns* me."

"She and Suord are a lot alike," Hadri said cautiously.

There was a silence. Duun, though tears had spouted out of her eyes in the most childlike fashion, did not deign to wipe them away. She sat straight-backed, cloaked in the dignity of the women of Meruo, and managed to get her lunch bag folded.

"I don't know very much about women," Hadri said. His was perhaps a simpler dignity. "Or men. I know I love Suord. But I . . . I need freedom."

"Freedom!" she said, and he thought at first she was mocking him, but quite the opposite—she burst right into tears, and put her head down on her knees, sobbing aloud. "I do too," she cried, "I do too."

Hadri put out a timid hand and stroked her shoulder. "I didn't mean to make you cry," he said. "Don't cry, Duun. Look. If we, if we feel the same way, we can work something out. We don't have to get married. We can be friends."

She nodded, though she went on sobbing for a while. At last she raised her swollen face and looked at him with wet-lidded, luminous eyes. "I would like to have a friend," she said. "I never had one."

"I only have one other one here," he said, thinking how right she had been in telling him to talk to Duun. "An'nad."

She stared at him. "Who?"

"An'nad. The Morning Woman of the First Sedoretu."

"What do you mean?" She was not scornful, merely very surprised. "That's Teheo."

"Then who is An'nad?"

"She was the Morning Woman of the First Sedoretu four hundred years ago," the girl said, her eyes still on Hadri's, clear and puzzled.

"Tell me," he said.

"She was drowned—here, at the foot of the Rock. They were all down on the sands, her sedoretu, with the children. That was when the tides had begun not to come in as far as Meruo. They were all out on the sands, planning the canal, and she was up in the house. She saw there was a storm in the west, and the wind might bring one of the great tides. She ran down to warn them. And the tide did come in, all the way round the Rock, the way it used to. They all kept ahead of it, except An'nad. She was drowned. . . . "

With all he had to wonder about then, about An'nad, and about Duun, he did not wonder why Duun answered his question and asked him none.

It was not until much later, half a year later, that he said, "Do you remember when I said I'd met An'nad—that first time we talked—by the boat-basin?"

"I remember," she said.

They were in Hadri's room, a beautiful, high room

with windows looking east, traditionally occupied by a member of the Eighth Sedoretu. Summer morning sunlight warmed their bed, and a soft, earth-scented land-wind blew in the windows.

"Didn't it seem strange?" he asked. His head was pillowed on her shoulder. When she spoke he felt her warm breath in his hair.

"Everything was so strange then . . . I don't know. And anyhow, if you've heard the tide . . ."

"The tide?"

"Winter nights. Up high in the house, in the attics. You can hear the tide come in, and crash around the Rock, and run on inland to the hills. At the true high tide. But the sea is miles away. . . ."

Suord knocked, waited for their invitation, and came in, already dressed. "Are you still in bed? Are we going in to town or not?" he demanded, splendid in his white summer coat, imperious. "Sasni's already down in the courtyard."

"Yes, yes, we're just getting up," they said, secretly entwining further.

"Now!" he said, and went out.

Hadri sat up, but Duun pulled him back down. "You saw her? You talked with her?"

"Twice. I never went back after you told me who she was. I was afraid. . . . Not of her. Only afraid she wouldn't be there."

"What did she do?" Duun asked softly.

"She saved us from drowning," Hadri said.

THE GARDENER
Mary Rosenblum

Here's a bittersweet, compassionate, and eloquent story that suggests that loneliness may be the hardest thing we have to deal with, no matter which side of the grave we're on. . . .

One of the most popular and prolific of the new writers of the 1990s, Mary Rosenblum made her first sale, to *Asimov's Science Fiction*, in 1990. She has since become a mainstay of that magazine and one of its most frequent contributors, with almost twenty sales there to her credit; her linked series of "Drylands" stories have proved to be one of the magazine's most popular series. She has also sold to *The Magazine of Fantasy and Science Fiction*, *Pulphouse*, *New Legends*, and elsewhere. Her first novel, *The Drylands*, appeared in 1993 to wide critical acclaim, winning the prestigious Compton Crook Award for Best First Novel of the year; it was followed in short order by her second novel, *Chimera*. A third novel, *The Stone Garden*, has just been released, and she has finished a fourth novel. Coming up soon is her first short story collection, *Synthesis and Other Stories*. A graduate of Clarion West, Mary Rosenblum lives with her family in Portland, Oregon.

The Gardener

He started seeing her during rose-pruning season. Lin watched her through the hedge of leafless canes as he snipped away the excess stems. He wasn't close enough to see her face—she wore a green rain jacket with the hood up against the cold drizzle, so he couldn't even tell what color her hair was. But her drooping shoulders and curved back gave her mood away.

Sad.

She sat on the wet black arch of a fallen maple top at the edge of the pond. He watched her as he gathered up the scattered rose canes, thinking he should go speak to her, let her know that she was trespassing on private property. Mr. Wright didn't like trespassers. But the roses had overgrown badly and it was going to get dark before he got all the clippings picked up, so there wasn't really enough time to go bother her. And she wasn't doing any damage. She was just sitting there, tossing bits of bark into the still gray water.

He wondered what had made her so sad.

She came back a week later, on a soft gray evening that breathed a promise of spring. Sitting on the same log—he had meant to get out the saw and cut it up, but hadn't gotten around to it—she propped her hands on her knees and stared at a mallard duck that was swimming along the far side of the pond. Lin had been raking dead leaves from the flower beds. He would have to push the wheelbarrow along the path right behind her to get to the compost bin. The ground was too soft to take a shortcut across the grass. And he hesitated, thinking that he could go check the buds on the apple trees and dump the barrow later.

The woman lifted her head at last and took something from her pocket. The mallard perked up at the gesture and came swimming over, quacking hopefully. She laughed.

The hair lifted on the back of Lin's neck. There was bitterness in that laughter, a darkness that made the garden seem suddenly chilly. He grabbed the handles of the barrow and leaned into its precarious weight. The wheel squeaked badly—he had meant to oil it this morning—and she looked up, her eyes widening.

"Hello," he said, and his tongue stumbled to silence. She was younger than him—in her early twenties maybe. She had black hair and very white skin, as if she never went out in the sun. It made her eyes look enormous, shadowed with the sadness he'd seen in her shoulders last time. Not beautiful—not at all. But striking. "I . . . did you know that this is . . . a private estate?" he managed to say.

"No." She got up quickly, annoyed now. "I thought it was just like . . . land, you know? It looked pretty wild from the street. Like nobody cares."

"It's natural landscaping," Lin said stiffly. "The roses and the orchard are on the other side of the forest garden. You can't see them from the street. It takes a lot of work to make woods look natural."

"I'm sorry." She looked startled. No longer angry. "I didn't know. I'll leave. The pond—all this—it's beautiful. Really private. You can almost forget that there's a sidewalk out there, a city, hunger, pain. You can forget it all." She looked down at her cupped hand, shoved it back into her pocket. "When you do a good job you know it's good," she said softly. "And you know when you fuck up. You're lucky to work out here."

Her hand had been full of pills—red-and-white capsules. Lots of them. "Yeah, I guess I am." He looked up. "I want to show you something. I don't know if anybody else has ever seen it except me," he said quickly. "I'd just . . . like to show you." And fell silent again, not sure at all why he'd said this, a little angry at himself.

She blew a breath that lifted her bangs on her pale forehead, studying him for silent moments. Maybe she would leave, he thought hopefully.

"Why not?" she said at last. "Show me."

Still annoyed with himself, he parked the wheelbarrow on the level path so that it wouldn't tip over, and started her up the slope, beneath the big leafless maples. She followed him slowly.

"What are those?" She nodded.

"Wild rhododendrons." Lin studied the twisted stems and thick leaves. "They bloom in the spring— pink and white. But I like them best in the winter. Everything else is bare and they kind of stand out. You don't really see them when they're in bloom. Just the petals. Which is too bad, because they're beautiful." He pressed his lips together tightly because he had never said anything like that out loud before.

"They are," she said softly. "They're wild and elegant." She paused for a moment, and her profile was stark and beautiful against the fading light. "You have an eye for beauty, gardener."

"My name's Lin." He waited a moment, and then, when she didn't say anything, he trudged on.

They reached the top of the hill just as the sun sank behind the big firs that fenced the western side of the slope. He had never figured out why they hadn't built the house up here. Sometimes he thought that maybe the builder had understood something. You had to walk up here to see. The view wasn't easy. Nobody from the house bothered anymore.

"This way." He led her across the tussocky winter grass, following the winding path that he shared with the rabbits. The rock outcrop emerged gently from the sod, thrusting west and south above the rhodies and firs. Creviced with pockets of soil, it was scattered with needles from the tall pine whose roots pried it slowly from the soil.

You could see the city from up here, but it was softened by distance and the veil of winter branches, transformed into a scatter of diamonds on a velvet cloth, a galaxy of stars from a dream. They sat down together on the needles and rock, and her rapt silence banished the last of his irritation. He pointed out an early violet blooming in a crack filled with soil formed by decades of rotted needles. You don't have to let it hurt you, he wanted to tell her. You can stand back from the world— let yourself see the beauty instead of the pain.

She touched one of the violet's petals, and her eyes were full of tears. "I try to do this with my holos," she whispered. "Make this mood happen. And . . . I can't."

"You're an artist?" He wasn't sure what a holo was.

"I thought I was." She took her hand away from the violet, shoved it into her pocket.

He heard the rustle of the pills. "This is my favorite time of day." He looked out into the deepening twilight. "Sometimes I come up here just to listen to the wind. If you listen long enough, you can . . . almost understand. I don't think anyone else ever comes up here. But *you* can. Anytime you want. I won't bother you."

She was looking at him sidelong, her face curtained by her dark hair. "Why?"

"You see them." He fumbled for the words he needed, blushing again because words were so hard. "The rhody. The violet. You really *see* them." He shrugged helplessly.

For a moment, she frowned, her eyes full of the deepening twilight and the diamond glitter of the city. Then her hand stole over to cover his. Her fingers were cold, slender, and white against his weathered skin. "Thank you." She looked him in the face at last, gave him a tentative smile. "I think I may come up here." She stood up, brushed her hair back from her face. "I'm Carey." Then she turned and ran lightly down the path through the thickening darkness.

He followed slowly. He still had to dump the wheelbarrow. It was dark, but that didn't matter. He knew the paths well enough that he didn't need light. He closed his hands around the worn wood of the wheelbarrow handles, remembering the touch of her fingers on his, and wondered if she would really come back.

She did. He caught glimpses of her as she followed the path that led around the pond or climbed the hill beneath the firs. She always came in the evening, her face a pale glimmer in the shadows beneath the trees. And each time he saw her, he paused, full of a restless yearning like spring inside him. But he had promised not to bother her, and it was always late, and there was always work left to do, or tools to gather up. So each time he turned his back and went back to pruning, or weeding, or cleaning up.

The garden got so overgrown during the long winter.

But one soft evening, he found himself at the foot

of the path, the wheelbarrow emptied, his tools put
away. He began to climb, breathing the scent of spring,
his heart light in his chest. She wouldn't be there, of
course. He hadn't seen her come this way. He merely
wanted to enjoy the dusk, watch the city lights twin-
kle into existence.

But when he reached the base of the outcrop and
caught sight of her profile against the deepening blue
of the sky, his heart surged. He stood silently, just
watching her, one hand on the pine's sticky bark. She
was wearing a sweatshirt and jeans, and her long hair
lifted in the breeze. A wild jonquil bloomed near the
base of the pine, and he bent slowly to pick it. She saw
him as he straightened.

His face burned because she had caught him looking when he had promised not to bother her, and he
turned quickly away.

"Wait!" She ran over to him, brushing hair impa-
tiently out of her face. "Don't leave. I . . . I've been
looking for you, you know. When I come here. I never
see you. I decided that you were a ghost, or maybe an
angel. Are you an angel?" She tilted her head and
smiled into his eyes. "I never believed in God, but
maybe I could believe in an angel."

"I'm just a gardener." He looked down at her,
dizzy with her nearness. Her smile softened the planes
of her face and made her beautiful. Like the wild
rhodies were beautiful. "I saw you," he blurted. "I didn't
want to bother you."

"You don't." Her hand had tucked itself into the
crook of his arm and they were walking out to the lip
of the rock, as casually as if they did this every evening.
"I don't know how to . . . tell you. How much you did
for me when you showed me this place." She sat down
on the gritty stone, tugged him down beside her. "I do
holoture. I get gallery slots and the critics love me. My
stuff sells. But they're not *getting* it—the people who

like it so much." She looked down, her hair hiding her expression but not the bitterness in her tone. "They think it's pretty—all those images and scents and snatches of music and wind sound. They don't really *feel* it. I don't want to do pretty pictures." She looked up suddenly, her dark eyes wide. "I was . . . ready to quit."

"I saw," Lin said gravely.

She looked away. "Up here . . . this place gave me a different perspective, I guess. And partly . . . it was you. Saying that I saw what you did in the rhododendrons and the violet. You're so *alive.* It made me . . . ashamed of what I was thinking of doing." Her face tightened briefly. "I thought maybe . . . you'd let me garden with you sometimes?" It was her turn to blush. "Would you mind? I'd just like to hear you talk, and feel the dirt, and the day." She sounded shy, as if she expected him to refuse.

"Carey." He said her name softly, the way you'd touch the petals of an unfurling bud. "Sure," he said. "You can help." And that wasn't what he wanted to say at all, but the words flew away like sparrows. He looked at the jonquil in his hand, leaned forward to slip the delicate yellow cup behind her ear.

She caught his wrist before he could take his hand away. Her lips brushed his and he shivered, wanting to flee, wanting to put his arms around her and crush her to him at the same time. He combed his fingers into the heavy weight of her hair as she opened her mouth to him, all sensation contracting to the taste of her lips and tongue, the clean scent of her skin, and the sweet shiver that ran through his flesh. After a long time, they leaned away from each other, fingers twined together. It was dark now, and the waxing moon turned her hair into a river of shadow.

"I'll come help you tomorrow," she said softly. "Is that okay?"

He could only nod as he pulled her to her feet.
The firs brushed their faces gently with their fine-
needled twigs as they made their way down the path.

Dawn broke gray and misty, with a fine drizzle that
settled into Lin's clothing and hair and soaked him
inexorably. She wouldn't want to work in this
weather, he told himself as he pruned an unruly
cherry. And told himself that it didn't matter. But the
weight in his chest made that into a lie. He was raking
dead twigs and leaves from the new shoots of the cat-
tails at the east end of the pond when she arrived.
"Boo!" she said from behind him, and he nearly
dropped the rake, because he had been watching the
path in spite of himself and he hadn't seen her.

The drizzle had turned into brief showers. A hesitant sun peered through the new leaves of the maples,
sparkling in the droplets of water that clung to her
bangs. "I didn't think you'd come today." His smile felt
as if it was going to split his face.

"I told you I would," she said matter-of-factly. She
was wearing the rain jacket she had worn the first
time he'd seen her. "So, what are we going to do?"

We. The word hummed in his bones. "I . . . we
could clean up the birch copse," he said shyly. "A lot
of dead wood came down this winter."

"Sounds good." She tossed her head and laughed,
scattering crystal drops of rain. "I even brought a
lunch. And these." She held up a pair of new gloves.
"I don't think my hands are as tough as yours."

They worked hard together in the sun and brief
showers, stacking the fallen limbs, raking up the
twigs, and loosening the soggy rotting leaves around
unfurling crocus buds. Daffodils and narcissus already
were thrusting green spears above the ground, and
even tulips were peeking through. Then she steadied

the fallen branches for him while he cut them into neat lengths.

"Why don't you use a chain saw?" she asked as the stack of cut rounds slowly grew. "It would go a lot faster."

"Chain saw?" He shrugged and wiped sawdust from the rakers of his bow saw. "I don't know. I guess they never bought one, up at the house."

"That's shitty." She shoved damp hair back from her face and planted her fists on her hips. "Do you know how much this property must be worth? This huge and so close to downtown?" She blew out an exasperated breath. "And the cheap jerk can't even buy you a chain saw? I hope you don't mow the lawn with a push mower!"

"I don't mow the lawn." He wasn't sure why she was angry. "I just take care of the woods garden and the orchard. This works okay." He patted his saw. "We're almost done. We can stack it by this tree and I'll get it later with the wheelbarrow."

"He should buy you a garden tractor, too," she said as she gathered up an armful of wood. "Then you could pull a cart with it."

"I like doing it this way," he said.

"I'm not mad at *you*." She piled her armload carefully on the neat stack he had started and straightened, one piece of wood still in her hand. "It just seems unfair, but hey—no gas stink, no noise. You know . . . it feels *good* to do this. My muscles are tired, and that kind of fits with the rain and the branches . . . with everything." She traced the black limb scars on the papery white bark of the birch. "I wonder if I could make this work on a stage," she murmured.

"What exactly do you do?" He hadn't heard of holoture before, but then, he didn't pay much attention to art and that sort of stuff.

"I project images of things—I use landscapes mostly."

She frowned at the limb in her hand. "I project it above a holo stage, you know? And then I add other stuff—heat or cold. Wind. And scents. Scent is very important. Too many artists ignore it. I want people to . . . feel a certain emotion when they walk onto that stage. I want that scene to connect—to say something. I don't want them just to admire the view." She tossed the wood onto the pile. It bounced and tumbled to the ground.

"It sounds wonderful." He picked up the piece, put it neatly on top of the pile.

"I . . . I've started working on something." Her eyes sought his. "If I get it into a local gallery . . . would you come see it?"

It wasn't a casual question. "Yes," he said softly. "I will."

A single crack of thunder made them both jump, and rain began to fall in sheets. Carey yelped and grabbed the saw, pulling her hood up over her already-streaming hair. Lin picked up the rake and caught her hand, tugging her into a run toward the pond and the shelter of the firs beyond.

"I'm soaked." She laughed as they ducked beneath the relative shelter of the trees. "You're *more* than soaked. Can we go somewhere and dry off a little? Without getting you in trouble with your boss? And it's way past lunchtime. Don't you ever get hungry?"

"We could go to my place," he offered tentatively. "Mr. Wright never comes there. I have a towel you could use."

"Let's go." She grabbed his hand, tugged him out into the diminishing rain. "I'm freezing!"

They ran together through the firs and along the slope to the small shelf of flat ground occupied by the toolshed and the old greenhouse and the compost bins. His room had originally been one-half of the toolshed, but sometime in the past someone had added glass windows and a small woodstove. He felt her hesitation as he ushered her inside, and he looked around the spartan room as if he had never seen it before. Single bed with a faded patchwork quilt, table in front of the window, one straight chair, and one rocker with a broken arm. The naked bulb in the ceiling light looked ugly.

"There's water." He nodded at the blue pitcher that stood on the table, took an extra glass down from the shelf. "I'll get you a towel."

"You *live* here?" Her voice was hushed, incredulous. "All the time? You don't even have running water. Or a refrigerator. Or *any*thing! This is criminal!"

"There's a toilet through that door. And a sink. I don't *have* to live here." He handed her a towel, his shoulders stiff. "I like it."

"I apologize," she said in a subdued voice. "I'm glad you do it because you want to." She began to towel her hair. "Don't mind me, okay?"

"I don't." He touched her shoulder lightly, because her anger had been for him, and, he wasn't sure why, but it warmed him. "Would you like some tea?" He filled the pot from the teakettle simmering on the woodstove.

"Great." She combed her damp hair with her fingers, smiling. "I brought lunch. We can share it." Fumbling in the pocket of her jacket, she pulled out a bag. "I brought a wedge of brie, and some baguettes."

They ate bread and cheese. She sat cross-legged in the straight chair, her jeans tight on her slender legs. He poured the dark fragrant tea into two mugs, and, while they sipped it, she told him about holoture, how it worked. He told her about the seasons, how they segued from snowdrops to irises, from roses to asters, then falling leaves, and snow, and finally snowdrops again. Outside, rain beat against the window, and the kettle hissed softly on the stove.

Then for a while they simply sat, not talking, just listening to the music of rain, and fire, and simmering water. Abruptly, Carey got up, wrapped the bread loaf in its bag, and put it on the shelf with the cheese. Then she leaned her hands on the arms of his rocker, her hair falling in a shower around his face. "You have made me feel alive," she said soberly. "I don't think I was ever really alive before." She put one finger on his lips when he started to speak, then pulled him from his chair.

His arms went around her, and he kissed her, lost in the touch of her, the scent of her. "You're wet," she said, laughing, her lips against his cheek. And she was tugging at his shirt, working the damp fabric off over his head. The air felt cool on his flushed skin, and she had taken off her shirt, too. Her breasts pressed against his ribs, full of animal heat. He held her so tightly against him that he could feel the bones of her rib cage, her hips, and her pelvis pressing against him. His erection was pleasure that came close to pain, and then she was tugging him toward the bed, her jeans unzipped, sliding down her legs like water running over stones.

He was naked, too, although he had no memory of taking off his pants. And she was beneath him, her skin hot against his, pale as marble, and he was kissing her, drunk with the scent and touch of her, and a little afraid, too. Clumsy, he fumbled his way into her, and then her breath was a hot wind against his ear and he wasn't afraid anymore, was simply drowning in her, inside her, part of her, drowning. . . .

He drowsed, his legs still twined with hers, felt her pull the quilt over them both. Woke drowsy and dreaming to find her watching his face, her hair veiling them both. "I . . . I'm sorry." He blushed fiercely.

"Why?" Her eyes widened, and he buried his face against her neck.

"I haven't . . . done this . . ." He shook his head, felt her surprise in the movement of her body against his, and blushed more deeply.

She didn't answer him with words. The touch of her fingers and tongue made him shiver, but it had nothing to do with fear. He took his time, touching her, exploring her, making her laugh softly, deep in her throat. Laughed with her. And, after a while, he didn't feel clumsy at all, and she stopped laughing and made other noises, even deeper and more guttural.

They dressed in the fading light of sunset. The clouds had thinned, and the western sky was a blaze of orange and purple. Lin moved slowly, filled with a warm lethargy that made him smile. "Want to go have a beer?" Carey reached for his hand as they left his room. "Or coffee, or whatever?"

"Sure." He didn't want this evening to end. Hand in hand, they strolled around the pond, taking the path that led to the side gate. The sun had gone down, and the sky was a clear pure blue that made him want to weep, made him want to hold her hand forever, stretch this moment into eternity.

The side gate blocked the path, set into the tall hedge that he had trimmed last week. Rust blotched the iron bars, and leaves had drifted against the stone posts. He stopped as she swung it open. The shriek of the rusty hinges sounded like the cry of an injured rabbit. Beyond, the path turned into leaf-clogged stairs that led down between overgrown bushes whose branches nearly touched. "You can see why I thought nobody lived here." She laughed and tugged at him.

"It's the side gate," he said automatically. "Mr. Wright doesn't use it anymore." Beyond the branches, he could see the glimmer of a streetlight, caught a glimpse of concrete sidewalk. "I . . . can't." He pulled his hand free, took a step backward.

"Lin?" She searched his face, worry in her voice. "What's wrong?"

"I . . . don't want to go out there." He took another step back. "I don't have to." Memories moved like creeping shadows in the back of his brain. That streetlight would shine in through his eyes, and he would have to see them. "I . . . it's *safe* in here. It always has been." He was pleading, couldn't help himself. "I *can't*. I'm really sorry."

"Lin, wait." She caught his hand as he backed away, and her strength surprised him. "Lin, it's all right. We don't have to go out there." She wouldn't let him go, came close and tucked her arm around his waist.

They went back to his room. It looked so small and barren now, and, for a moment, as they climbed into the bed together, Lin wished that he hadn't spoken to her that day by the pond. She had opened that gate and let the light from the streetlamp in here.

But she didn't ask him any questions. She just lay close against him, the warmth of her body and the soft rhythm of her breathing relaxing his tense muscles, making the room his again. "I . . . don't remember much," he said finally into the midnight silence. "About my childhood, I mean. My dad worked in a sheet-metal plant. There were a bunch of us kids. He got drunk at night, beat us, beat my mother. I went to work for Mr. Wright's gardener, Patrick, when I was fourteen. This place . . . it was like heaven. And the plants—they grew for me. It's so beautiful here, and I keep it that way, you know? Nobody minds. I was twenty-one when Patrick died. Mr. Wright gave me his job." He shrugged, aware of her breathing silence beside him. "It's all I want—to keep it beautiful. I don't know. . . . Can you understand?"

"Yes," she said softly. "I really can."

That sad note was back in her voice. He hadn't heard it since her first visit here. He hugged her close, and she burrowed against him, and they fell asleep together.

He dreamed he heard her crying in the night, but when he woke up, she was asleep.

In the morning, she helped him divide clumps of flag iris along the pond. Then she kissed him and told him that she had to go back to her studio for a while. He wondered if she would ever come back, and, for the first time, that wondering was a knife in his heart.

She came back the next evening, appearing like an apparition from the shadows that veiled the pond. She was smiling, laughing, and she had a cloth carryall slung over her shoulder. "I'm scheduled for a show at the Epyx Gallery just a few blocks from here. I went in with the model and the manager signed it on right there!" Her eyes sparkled. "It feels good, Lin. It really does. It's going to do what I want it to do. We're going to celebrate!"

She brought out food in his room—fancy cheeses, smoked fish, and cold sliced meats that he had never tasted. There were smooth-skinned green fruits that she said had been created in a lab. She laughed at his surprise. They tasted like tart raspberries. And there was wine—pale gold champagne full of bubbles that tickled his tongue. They drank the wine out of his two mugs. It flushed her skin pale rose and made her giggle. He laughed with her, happy for her happiness, happier than he had ever been in his life.

"My exhibit opens in a month," she said. "I want . . . I hope you can come see it."

"I . . . want to." He concentrated on slicing one of the green fruits.

"You can do it, you know." She put a hand on his arm. "There are people who can help you get over it—being scared."

"Carey, I *like* it here," he said. Her touch had such a pleading feel. He stroked the back of her hand gently. "It's all right. I'm happy. I don't want to leave here, or do anything else."

"You wouldn't have to." She took his hands in hers. "But you wouldn't be trapped. It would be a *choice*, to stay here. You could leave and come back. The streets wouldn't scare you anymore. The past wouldn't scare you. And you could . . . come see my exhibit."

"I will," he said, and he pulled her close, kissed her gently, slowly, so that she could feel the promise in his flesh.

They made love, and it was like the champagne, tart and bubbly with her happy excitement. When he woke to the dawn, as he always did, she was already gone. A note lay beside the neatly wrapped remains of last night's picnic:

I have to work my butt off for the next month. See you later. —Carey

He put the empty champagne bottle on the windowsill so that it caught the sunlight in deep sparks of emerald. And then he went out to work on the bulb plantings beneath the maples, weeding out the creeper and grass that were growing up among them. And the sun was out, and the wind sang to him.

And he missed her.

She came to him every evening—sometimes with food, sometimes needing his arms around her and silence as they sat together on the rock. He showed her the first crocuses, free of weeds now, drifts of purple and white that made her face light up. And he showed her the bright new spears of the flags they had planted, the swelling buds on the rhododendrons. Days drifted by, and she didn't say anything more about getting someone to help him.

Then, one evening, she didn't come. Lin worked until full dark, teasing morning glory roots from the old rose hedge. If he didn't get them all, the fast-growing creeper would cover the old bushes entirely by midsummer. It was only when he could no longer see the pale roots in the dark soil that he stopped. She had to work on her exhibit, he told himself as he trudged up the slope to his room. It was due to open at the end of the week. She didn't have to come here every night. It wasn't a rule. Nothing had happened to her.

He didn't even know where she lived. Or her last name. It was as if she existed only here. In a way, that was true. He lay down on top of the quilt in his clothes, too tired to undress or get the cheese down from the shelf. And as he turned over, he caught a hint of her scent on the pillow. Tomorrow, he told himself. She'll come tomorrow.

But she didn't. Or the day after.

Over and over again, he found himself at the old side gate, staring through the screen of branches at the concrete sidewalk beyond. One afternoon, he even went through the gate and pushed his way into the thorny tangle. But what was the use? How would he find her out there? Who could he ask?

He turned back, closed the rusty gate behind him. He didn't go there again.

She came on the evening of the fourth day, appearing behind him on the rock, where he had gone alone to watch the end of day. It had turned cold, and she was wearing a heavy black jacket. Her hair fell in a river over her shoulders and her face looked thin, even paler than it had been, although he wouldn't have thought that possible. Her eyes were full of shadows as she sat silently down beside him. She didn't try to take his hand, and as he reached for hers, she drew away.

He put his hands in his lap, a slow chill filling him.

"I'm crazy," she said softly. "I come here, and I talk to you. We eat cheese, and drink wine, and I get my hands dirty. They're dirty when I get home, you know. I have to wash them. I have to use special soap to get the dirt out. And when I take my clothes off, I smell your scent on my skin." Her voice had been rising, and she gulped a breath, struggling visibly for calm.

"Carey," he said softly.

"I spent the night here. I have . . . made love with you." Her voice trembled. "Oh God . . . I love you! And you don't *exist*."

"No!" The word burst from him, torn from some center of himself. It left a gaping wound behind and he seized her by the shoulders. "How can you say that?" Frightened, not sure where the fear came from, he shook her. "How can you sit here and *say* that to me? What did I *do*?" He shook her again. She didn't resist, raised her eyes slowly to his face. "It hurts," she said wonderingly. Then her face hardened. "Come with me." She scrambled to her feet, throwing off his hands as if he had no strength at all. "Right now. I want you to see something."

Lin grasped for anger, wanting to tell her to go to hell, wanting to walk away and go prune cedar limbs or clean the stone benches below the rose terrace. But it was already too dark, and his anger ran through his fingers like water. She was walking away into the darkness, and all he could do was go after her.

"What are you going to show me?" he asked. But he already knew, because she was heading south along the firs. Toward the house. "You can't," he said, and grabbed her arm. "You're trespassing, and Mr. Wright is really strict about that. You'll get me fired!"

She shook him off and walked faster, hugging herself as if she was cold in spite of her jacket. The last of the fading light glistened on her face, and he realized that she was crying. He dropped back, let her go ahead as they descended the brick path that led down from where a gazebo had once stood. It was badly overgrown, the grass on each side uncut and matted from the winter rains. It shocked Lin, how Mr. Wright had let things go over here. A copse of paper birch marked the top of the broad brick stairs that led down to the house and yard, blocking his view of the grounds. Carey stopped at the top of the stairs and waited for him.

He rounded the birch clump and stood still on the scummy bricks. Below, a wide terrace separated them from the distant street. Cars streamed along it on the far side of the ancient boxwood hedge. The shrubbery had grown into huge mounds. Morning glory draped them, and blackberry canes choked the flower beds. The house was gone. Only a burned and blackened foundation remained.

No, he wanted to cry. This is a bad dream—*your* bad dream, not mine. Because it was there, and Mr. Wright was there, and tomorrow Lin should prune the apple trees between the pond and the side gate. . . .

"I couldn't find a personal access for Mr. Wright, so I came to see him. To talk to him about you. At first, I thought it was the wrong place—that there was a new house on the property, that I had missed it. Only I hadn't." She shivered beneath her coat. "Then I thought maybe you came in here from the street and made up this thing about a job, security, all that kind of stuff. And maybe believed it, now. Or . . . you might have been lying to me," she said in a low voice. "I accessed the local newsnet data files and paid a gofer to search the Wright family. The house burned down twenty-five years ago," she said in a thin, clear voice.

"The gofer found it right off—it got big coverage because Emmanuel Wright owned pieces of half the industry in the city. Two people died—a fireman who was up on the roof when it collapsed. And the twenty-nine-year-old gardener. He had helped Wright's grandson out of a window, and . . . a brick chimney fell on him." Her voice trembled. "Mr. Wright never rebuilt the house. His grandson owns the property now."

"I don't know what you found." Lin closed his eyes, fists clenched so that his nails bit his palms. "I don't know anything about any of this, and it wasn't *me*, if that's what you're saying." He opened his eyes, laughed a cracked note, and held out his hands to her, palm up. "Do I seem like a *ghost*?"

She looked at him, shuddered, and looked away. Lips pressed together, she reached slowly into her jacket pocket, pulled something out. Lin took the small sheet of paper she handed him, unfolded it.

"I had the gofer do a hard copy of one of the newspaper photos. It looks like a high school graduation picture." She drew a deep breath. "His . . . name is Lindon Jones. Was it . . . is it your high school graduation picture, Lin?"

Lin stared into the face that looked up from the sheet of paper. The picture wasn't glossy like a photo, but it was clear for all that. They'd stood in line for hours in the school hallway, waiting for their turn in front of the camera. He had been seventeen. He shook his head, but the memory didn't go away. There was no mirror in his room. But sometimes he looked at himself in the pond when it wasn't windy. You change some in twelve years. Not a lot, but some.

How much do you change in thirty-eight years?

"That's not me," he said flatly. "It can't be. Carey?" He took a step toward her and halted as she retreated, his heart twisting inside him. "You're saying I'm *dead*. How can you think that? I've *touched* you. We've made love!" He took another step, a fast one, grabbing for her this time, needing to touch her, to feel the warmth of her flesh beneath his hands, her lips against his.

She turned and ran.

"Carey!" He ran after her, down the overgrown and buckling brick walk that led past the gaping foundation and down to the street full of glaring, speeding cars. "Carey, don't! Come back, please. I'm not dead! I'm not a ghost! Don't be scared of me. Please?" She didn't look back, had squeezed between the halves of the loosely chained main gate and was running down the sidewalk. Lin halted, grasping the rusted bars, face pressed against cold iron. "I love you!" he cried, and his voice cracked and broke finally. "I *love* you. How can I be *dead*?" She stumbled, and for one heart-searing second he thought she would stop. Then the overgrown hedge hid her from his view, and he almost shoved himself between the bars to run after her.

But he didn't. The cars roared by like a flooding river and the streetlamps came on suddenly, blinding him with pitiless light. For a moment longer he clung to the ironwork, trying to count back the seasons—spring bulbs, summer pruning, leaf-raking, winter . . . It hadn't been that long. Surely. And the house . . . when had he come down here last? He had vague memories of Mr. Wright's florid face, a pale blue paycheck handed to him every Thursday in a clean white envelope. . . .

The images had the same dusty feel as that memory of waiting in line in the high school hallway.

Strangled to silence by the sobs that wouldn't come, he fled up the old path and across the crest of the hill. The toolshed waited for him, and, for an instant, he saw it with her eyes—a neglected weather-beaten building. Inside, the room jeered at him—a single room that nobody really lived in—sagging bed, a cracked toilet. No kitchen, no pictures, just bare floor, curtainless windows. Who would live here?

A ghost.

"No," Lin whispered. He shuddered, and the room became familiar again—home, no matter what *she* thought. He yanked the sheets and quilt from his bed and threw himself down on the bare mattress, burying his face in musty cotton that bore no trace of her scent.

He got up with the dawn and went out to prune the sucker shoots from the ancient apple trees. It was windy and gray, but the wind had a warmth that promised summer soon. When summer arrived, he would have to work hard to keep up with the morning glory that tried to climb the fences and young trees, with the quack grass that invaded the paths. His shears snipped through the slender shoots that sprouted from the mossy apple limbs, as he ticked off the jobs that had to be done. He would pick dead blossoms off the rosebushes and the irises. Snip, snip. Then fall would come, with leaves and dying plants to clean up and compost. Winter. Snip, snip. He would cut up the branches brought down by the storms, make sure that the pond's drain stayed open so that it didn't overflow and ruin the paths.

The pile of smooth, shiny shoots grew around his feet, and the light began to fade. He could feel the house growing beyond the hill, rising from the yawning pit of the burned-out foundation. He moved on to the next tree. It would take him the rest of the day to finish the job. In the dusk, he would climb the hill, and before he went out to his spot to watch evening give way to night, he would take a look at the house. It would be there, its many windows full of warm yellow light because Mr. Wright would be entertaining. The gates would be open, and the lawn would be neatly mowed by Sutherlin, the daytime yard man. And after it was dark, he would go back to his room, and he would put the sheets back on his bed.

They wouldn't smell like her anymore.

Her. For a moment he couldn't remember her name. "Carey," he cried. "Carey!"

Like an incantation, those syllables conjured it all—her shadowed eyes as she told him about her art and her doubts, the touch of her hands on his skin, the rhythm of her breathing as she slept against him in the narrow bed. The anguish in her eyes as she had said *I love you* down by the main gate. "I love you," he whispered. And flung the shears down.

They bounced and disappeared into the pile of cut shoots. He shouldn't leave them there, they would rust if it rained tonight, and he'd need them to head back the grapes in the arbor at the edge of the orchard. . . . Lin broke into a run. The unpruned branches slashed accusingly at his face and he ducked, but didn't slow down. He ran past the pond—leaves were going to clog the drain, he should stop and clear it—and down the path that led to the side gate. The rusty bars mocked him and the shrubs on the far side barred his way.

Panting, he wrenched the gate open, ignoring its shriek of protest. The branches clawed at his eyes as he forced his way through them. Arms shielding his face, he burst out onto the sidewalk.

And stopped.

The sun had gone down. Cars sped past on the street, and a man in bright loose clothes strolled toward him with a small black dog on a leash. Beyond the rusty iron fence, tangled shrubbery and overgrown trees blocked his view of the estate. They shouldn't look that bad, Lin thought in confusion. He had pruned them last month. Fear seized him—that

the garden was the same way. Overgrown. Ruined. He
started to push his way back through the bushes, but
then the dog began to yap. Straining against its leash,
it fixed its eyes on Lin.

"Stop it, Jock." The man sounded irritated. "There's
nothing there." And he walked past Lin without a
glance.

Lin began to tremble. He reached out, touched the
iron fence. He could feel it, but it was a diminished
sensation, as if he wore gloves, thick cotton ones.
Trash skittered along the curb, but he didn't feel the
wind. He looked back at the rank tangle of branches
that blocked the side gate, and hesitated.

She had said that her gallery was only a couple of
blocks from the estate. The streetlight came on and he
jumped, then began to walk briskly along the sidewalk.

Dead. Could you die and not *remember*? The streets
looked strange—clothes, sleek rounded cars—he didn't
remember it like this. Nobody looked at him, although
a cat arched her back and hissed at him. He came to
the corner, looked down a cross street that was filled
with neon signs glowing in the dusk. The estate was
behind him. He could feel it tugging at him. He began
to walk slowly down the lighted street, past stores selling food, or books, or clothes. He was leaving it behind,
and with every step he took, he was . . . fading. He
could barely feel the sidewalk beneath his feet, and a
stocky woman with a shaved scalp walked right
through him. Lin reeled against the side of a building.
Go back, he thought dizzily. Before it was too late.
Before he simply . . . vanished.

He pushed himself away from the wall, looked
through the plate-glass window. Epyx Gallery. The
words were formed in purple neon, and more neon
glowed in twisted shapes that turned slowly. A shimmering fog hung above a round black pedestal, and

Carey's face stared moodily at him from the center of it. *Carey Androcles, Holoturist.* The words were written beneath her image in flowing, three-dimensional script.

Lin tried to push the door open, but it didn't move. There was an instant of resistance, and then he fell through the closed door and onto the polished wood floor. The gallery was a long narrow space, with stark white walls hung with paintings, and hangings woven from what looked like scrap paper. Huge neon sculptures stood here and there, and stairs led up to a loft. A man walked through Lin, opened the door, and went out into the street. Shivering, Lin got unsteadily to his feet. He could see the floor through his flesh now. Go *back*, a part of his mind shrieked at him. The garden needs you.

Yes, the garden needed him. And Lin remembered it suddenly—not dying, but . . . before. He laughed bitterly, and a woman behind a desk looked up frowning. Lin began to run through the long narrow room. What if she wasn't here? It hadn't occured to him that she would be anywhere else. He couldn't feel the floor, couldn't feel the rail as he stumbled up the stairs. A stage stood in the center of the dimly lighted loft, as big as a small room. On the stage was . . . the outcrop. Gasping for breath, Lin stared at it. There was the pine, and the violet blooming in the crevice. Carey sat cross-legged at the foot of the tree, her face buried in her hands. She didn't raise her head as he walked across the floor.

The hair stood up on the back of his neck as Lin stepped up onto the stage. He smelled moist earth, resin, and a hint of old wool, like a muffler forgotten in a closet. He felt the gentle spring breeze, and saw the first lights of the city in the distance.

A terrible loneliness closed his throat. And he started to turn away, because she couldn't see him, would never know that he had come here, had seen this. Would never know . . .

Carey looked up, although he hadn't made a sound. "Lin?" Her eyes widened and she rose slowly. "You're here? You're really *here*?"

"I promised." It came out a whisper, and he made no move to touch her. "You were right about me," he said, and closed his eyes. "Only I was a ghost even before I . . . died. It's not any different now . . . than then." He looked into her shadowed eyes, full of terrible loss. "I'm not real outside the garden. I never was." He looked with wonder at his solid flesh. He could feel the pine needles beneath his feet. "But I'm . . . real here," he said softly. "You're *that* good." He wanted to touch her, was afraid that she would flinch away from him. "I just wanted you to know that . . . I love you." He touched the pine, realized that it was an image only, as unreal as he had been on the city street.

"Where are you going?" she asked breathlessly. "Back to the estate?"

He shook his head. He would walk on down the street, resisting the garden's tug until he faded completely, blew away on the wind. Somebody else would have to finish pruning the apple trees. Because he didn't want to be alone anymore. "Good-bye, Carey."

"Lin, wait." She blocked his path, and her arms went around him, firm on his back. "You're talking about dying . . . only you're a ghost, so you can't *die*. . . ." She laughed brokenly, her cheek pressed against his. "I realized it—as I was working on this— why I can touch you, why you can touch me. Because *I'm* a ghost, too, even if I haven't died yet. And this stage is *my* garden. Out on the street, I'm no more real than you are. And I don't care if you're alive or dead, as long as you're there in your garden. Because I love you. And yes, I guess I'm crazy, and I don't care about that either. Lin, please don't go away!" She took his a with stories set in such locales, including "Black Coral," "Fire Zone Emerald," "Surrender," e Border," "The End of Life as We Know It," "A er's Tale"—and the exotic and fascinating story that , in which a man deep in the steaming jungle nters Unearthly Love in one of its most terrifying , and learns that the line between the hunter and unted is sometimes hard to define. . . .

face between her palms, her eyes full of the shadows that lay beneath the pine. "Please?" she whispered.

He kissed her slowly, reveling in the warmth of her lips, the taste of her, the soft curve of her breasts beneath his palms. "I'll stay there as long as you want me to," he said. She was crying, and he wiped the tears from her cheeks.

"I'm going to get old," she whispered.

"It doesn't matter." He kissed her again. And they didn't talk, because there was nothing and everything to say, and they had lots of time in which to say it.

After a while, he would let the garden tug him back through the terrifying streets, because he needed to finish the pruning, and she would go work in her studio.

But she would come to share the evening with him. She had promised. They would sit on the rock together, and watch the dusk fade into night, and she would tell him about the project she was working on and the gallery offer she had gotten, and he would tell her about the new shoots on the elderberry and the ducklings that the old mallard had hatched.

And maybe one day, she would stay forever.

THE JAGUAR H

Lucius Shepard

Lucius Shepard was one of the most
influential new writers of the 1980s, ri
stature only by William Gibson, Connie W
Stanley Robinson, and his popularity ha
right into the 1990s as well. Shepard won
Campbell Award in 1985 as the year's
Writer, and no year since has gone by
name adorning the final ballot for one maj
another, and often for several. In 1987,
Nebula Award for his landmark novella
1988, he picked up a World Fantasy Aw
monumental short-story collection *The Ja*
following it in 1992 with a second Wo
Award for his second collection, *The Ends*
and in 1993 he won the Hugo Award for
"Barnacle Bill the Spacer." His novels inc
Eyes, the best-selling *Life During Wa*
Kalimantan. His most recent book is the
Golden. He's currently at work on a mainstr
Family Values. Born in Lynchburg, Virgini
lives in Seattle, Washington.

Stories set in authentically described Tl
milieus are a specialty of Shepard's, and as
has become strongly identified with Central

Ameri
"R&R,
"On tl
Travel
follow
encou
forms
the h

The Jaguar Hunter

It was his wife's debt to Onofrio Esteves, the appliance dealer, that brought Esteban Caax to town for the first time in almost a year. By nature he was a man who enjoyed the sweetness of the countryside above all else; the placid measures of a farmer's day invigorated him, and he took great pleasure in nights spent joking and telling stories around a fire, or lying beside his wife, Encarnación. Puerto Morada, with its fruit company imperatives and sullen dogs and cantinas that blared American music, was a place he avoided like the plague: indeed, from his home atop the mountain whose slopes formed the northernmost enclosure of Bahía Onda, the rusted tin roofs ringing the bay resembled a dried crust of blood such as might appear upon the lips of a dying man.

On this particular morning, however, he had no choice but to visit the town. Encarnación had—without his knowledge—purchased a battery-operated television set on credit from Onofrio, and he was threatening to seize Esteban's three milk cows in lieu of the eight hundred *lempira* that was owed; he refused to accept the return of the television, but had sent word that he was willing to discuss an alternate method of payment. Should Esteban lose the cows, his income would drop below a subsistence level and he would be forced to take up his old occupation, an occupation far more onerous than farming.

As he walked down the mountain, past huts of
thatch and brushwood poles identical to his own, following a trail that wound through sun-browned thickets
lorded over by banana trees, he was not thinking of
Onofrio but of Encarnación. It was in her nature to be
frivolous, and he had known this when he had married
her; yet the television was emblematic of the differences
that had developed between them since their children
had reached maturity. She had begun to put on sophisti-
cated airs, to laugh at Esteban's country ways, and she
had become the doyenne of a group of older women,
mostly widows, all of whom aspired to sophistication.
Each night they would huddle around the television and
strive to outdo one another in making sagacious com-
ments about the American detective shows they
watched; and each night Esteban would sit outside the
hut and gloomily ponder the state of his marriage. He
believed Encarnación's association with the widows was
her manner of telling him that she looked forward to
adopting the black skirt and shawl, that—having served
his purpose as a father—he was now an impediment to
her. Though she was only forty-one, younger by three
years than Esteban, she was withdrawing from the life of
the senses; they rarely made love anymore, and he was
certain that this partially embodied her resentment of the
fact that the years had been kind to him. He had the look
of one of the Old Patuca—tall, with chiseled features and
wide-set eyes; his coppery skin was relatively unlined
and his hair jet black. Encarnación's hair was streaked
with gray, and the clean beauty of her limbs had dissolved beneath layers of fat. He had not expected her to
remain beautiful, and he had tried to assure her that
he loved the woman she was and not merely the girl
she had been. But that woman was dying, infected by the
same disease that had infected Puerto Morada, and
perhaps his love for her was dying, too.

The dusty street on which the appliance store was

situated ran in back of the movie theater and the
Hotel Circo del Mar, and from the inland side of the
street Esteban could see the bell towers of Santa María
del Onda rising above the hotel roof like the horns of
a great stone snail. As a young man, obeying his
mother's wish that he become a priest, he had spent
three years cloistered beneath those towers, preparing
for the seminary under the tutelage of old Father
Gonsalvo. It was the part of his life he most regretted,
because the academic disciplines he had mastered
seemed to have stranded him between the world of
the Indian and that of contemporary society; in his
heart he held to his father's teachings—the principles
of magic, the history of the tribe, the lore of nature—
and yet he could never escape the feeling that such
wisdom was either superstitious or simply unimportant. The shadows of the towers lay upon his soul as
surely as they did upon the cobbled square in front of
the church, and the sight of them caused him to pick
up his pace and lower his eyes.

Farther along the street was the Cantina Atómica,
a gathering place for the well-to-do youth of the town,
and across from it was the appliance store, a one-story
building of yellow stucco with corrugated metal doors
that were lowered at night. Its facade was decorated by
a mural that supposedly represented the merchandise
within: sparkling refrigerators and televisions and washing machines, all given the impression of enormity by
the tiny men and women painted below them, their
hands upflung in awe. The actual merchandise was
much less imposing, consisting mainly of radios and
used kitchen equipment. Few people in Puerto Morada
could afford more, and those who could generally
bought elsewhere. The majority of Onofrio's clientele
were poor, hard-pressed to meet his schedule of payments, and to a large degree his wealth derived from
selling repossessed appliances over and over.

Raimundo Esteves, a pale young man with puffy cheeks and heavily lidded eyes and a petulant mouth, was leaning against the counter when Esteban entered; Raimundo smirked and let out a piercing whistle, and a few seconds later his father emerged from the back room: a huge slug of a man, even paler than Raimundo. Filaments of gray hair were slicked down across his mottled scalp, and his belly stretched the front of a starched *guayabera*. He beamed and extended a hand.

"How good to see you," he said. "Raimundo! Bring us coffee and two chairs."

Much as he disliked Onofrio, Esteban was in no position to be uncivil: he accepted the handshake. Raimundo spilled coffee in the saucers and clattered the chairs and glowered, angry at being forced to serve an Indian.

"Why will you not let me return the television?" asked Esteban after taking a seat; and then, unable to bite back the words, he added, "Is it no longer your policy to swindle my people?"

Onofrio sighed, as if it were exhausting to explain things to a fool such as Esteban. "I do not swindle your people. I go beyond the letter of the contracts in allowing them to make returns rather than pursuing matters through the courts. In your case, however, I have devised a way whereby you can keep the television without any further payments and yet settle the account. Is this a swindle?"

It was pointless to argue with a man whose logic was as facile and self-serving as Onofrio's. "Tell me what you want," said Esteban.

Onofrio wetted his lips, which were the color of raw sausage. "I want you to kill the jaguar of Barrio Carolina."

"I no longer hunt," said Esteban.

"The Indian is afraid," said Raimundo, moving up behind Onofrio's shoulder. "I told you."

Onofrio waved him away and said to Esteban, "That is unreasonable. If I take the cows, you will once again be hunting jaguars. But if you do this, you will have to hunt only one jaguar."

"One that has killed eight hunters." Esteban set down his coffee cup and stood. "It is no ordinary jaguar."

Raimundo laughed disparagingly, and Esteban skewered him with a stare.

"Ah!" said Onofrio, smiling a flatterer's smile. "But none of the eight used your method."

"Your pardon, Don Onofrio," said Esteban with mock formality. "I have other business to attend."

"I will pay you five hundred *lempira* in addition to erasing the debt," said Onofrio.

"Why?" asked Esteban. "Forgive me, but I cannot believe it is due to a concern for the public welfare."

Onofrio's fat throat pulsed, his face darkened.

"Never mind," said Esteban. "It is not enough."

"Very well. A thousand." Onofrio's casual manner could not conceal the anxiety in his voice.

Intrigued, curious to learn the extent of Onofrio's anxiety, Esteban plucked a figure from the air. "Ten thousand," he said. "And in advance."

"Ridiculous! I could hire ten hunters for this much! Twenty!"

Esteban shrugged. "But none with my method."

For a moment Onofrio sat with his hands enlaced, twisting them, as if struggling with some pious conception. "All right," he said, the words squeezed out of him. "Ten thousand!"

The reason for Onofrio's interest in Barrio Carolina suddenly dawned on Esteban, and he understood that the profits involved would make his fee seem pitifully small. But he was possessed by the thought of what ten thousand *lempira* could mean: a herd of cows, a small truck to haul produce, or—and as he thought it, he realized this was the happiest possibility—the little

stucco house in Barrio Clarín that Encarnación had set
her heart on. Perhaps owning it would soften her
toward him. He noticed Raimundo staring at him, his
expression a knowing smirk; and even Onofrio, though
still outraged by the fee, was beginning to show signs of
satisfaction, adjusting the fit of his *guayabera*, slicking
down his already-slicked-down hair. Esteban felt
debased by their capacity to buy him, and to preserve a
last shred of dignity, he turned and walked to the door.

"I will consider it," he tossed back over his shoulder. "And I will give you my answer in the morning."

Murder Squad of New York, starring a bald American
actor, was the featured attraction on Encarnación's
television that night, and the widows sat cross-legged
on the floor, filling the hut so completely that the
charcoal stove and the sleeping hammock had been
moved outside in order to provide good viewing
angles for the latecomers. To Esteban, standing in the
doorway, it seemed his home had been invaded by a
covey of large black birds with cowled heads, who
were receiving evil instruction from the core of a flickering gray jewel. Reluctantly, he pushed between
them and made his way to the shelves mounted on
the wall behind the set; he reached up to the top shelf
and pulled down a long bundle wrapped in oil-stained
newspapers. Out of the corner of his eye, he saw
Encarnación watching him, her lips thinned, curved
in a smile, and that cicatrix of a smile branded its mark
on Esteban's heart. She knew what he was about, and
she was delighted! Not in the least worried! Perhaps
she had known of Onofrio's plan to kill the jaguar,
perhaps she had schemed with Onofrio to entrap him.
Infuriated, he barged through the widows, setting
them to gabbling, and walked out into his banana
grove and sat on a stone amidst it. The night was

cloudy, and only a handful of stars showed between the tattered dark shapes of the leaves; the wind sent the leaves slithering together, and he heard one of his cows snorting and smelled the ripe odor of the corral. It was as if the solidity of his life had been reduced to this isolated perspective, and he bitterly felt the isolation. Though he would admit to fault in the marriage, he could think of nothing he had done that could have bred Encarnación's hateful smile.

After a while, he unwrapped the bundle of newspapers and drew out a thin-bladed machete of the sort used to chop banana stalks, but which he used to kill jaguars. Just holding it renewed h s confidence and gave him a feeling of strength. It had been four years since he had hunted, yet he knew he had not lost the skill. Once he had been proclaimed the greatest hunter in the province of Nueva Esperanza, as had his father before him, and he had not retired from hunting because of age or infirmity, but because the jaguars were beautiful, and their beauty had begun to outweigh the reasons he had for killing them. He had no better reason to kill the jaguar of Barrio Carolina. It menaced no one other than those who hunted it, who sought to invade its territory, and its death would profit only a dishonorable man and a shrewish wife, and would spread the contamination of Puerto Morada. And besides, it was a black jaguar.

"Black jaguars," his father had told him, "are creatures of the moon. They have other forms and magical purposes with which we must not interfere. Never hunt them!"

His father had not said that the black jaguars lived on the moon, simply that they utilized its power; but as a child, Esteban had dreamed about a moon of ivory forests and silver meadows through which the jaguars flowed as swiftly as black water; and when he had told his father of the dreams, his father had said that such dreams were representations of a truth, and that sooner or later he would discover the truth underlying them. Esteban had never stopped believing in the dreams, not even in face of the rocky, airless place depicted by the science programs on Encarnación's television: that moon, its mystery explained, was merely a less enlightening kind of dream, a statement of fact that reduced reality to the knowable.

But as he thought this, Esteban suddenly realized that killing the jaguar might be the solution to his problems, that by going against his father's teaching, that by killing his dreams, his Indian conception of the world, he might be able to find accord with his wife's; he had been standing halfway between the two conceptions for too long, and it was time for him to choose. And there was no real choice. It was this world he inhabited, not that of the jaguars; if it took the death of a magical creature to permit him to embrace as joys the television and trips to the movies and a stucco house in Barrio Clarín, well, he had faith in this method. He swung the machete, slicing the dark air, and laughed. Encarnación's frivolousness, his skill at hunting, Onofrio's greed, the jaguar, the television . . . all these things were neatly woven together like the elements of a spell, one whose products would be a denial of magic and a furthering of the unmagical doctrines that had corrupted Puerto Morada. He laughed again, but a second later he chided himself: it was exactly this sort of thinking he was preparing to root out.

Esteban waked Encarnación early the next morning and forced her to accompany him to the appliance store. His machete swung by his side in a leather sheath, and he carried a burlap sack containing food and the herbs he would need for the hunt. Encarnación trotted along beside him, silent, her face hidden by a shawl. When they reached the store, Esteban had Onofrio stamp the bill PAID IN FULL, then he handed the bill and the money to Encarnación.

"If I kill the jaguar or if it kills me," he said harshly, "this will be yours. Should I fail to return within a week, you may assume that I will never return."

She retreated a step, her face registering alarm, as if she had seen him in new light and understood the consequences of her actions; but she made no move to stop him as he walked out the door.

Across the street, Raimundo Esteves was leaning against the wall of the Cantina Atómica, talking to two girls wearing jeans and frilly blouses; the girls were fluttering their hands and dancing to the music that issued from the cantina, and to Esteban they seemed more alien than the creature he was to hunt. Raimundo spotted him and whispered to the girls; they peeked over their shoulders and laughed. Already angry at Encarnación, Esteban was washed over by a cold fury. He crossed the street to them, rested his hand on the hilt of the machete, and stared at Raimundo; he had never before noticed how soft he was, how empty of presence. A crop of pimples straggled along his jaw, the flesh beneath his eyes was pocked by tiny indentations like those made by a silversmith's hammer, and, unequal to the stare, his eyes darted back and forth between the two girls.

Esteban's anger dissolved into revulsion. "I am Esteban Caax," he said. "I have built my own house, tilled my soil, and brought four children into the world. This day I am going to hunt the jaguar of Barrio Carolina in order to make you and your father even fatter than you are." He ran his gaze up and down Raimundo's body, and, letting his voice fill with disgust, he asked, "Who are you?"

Raimundo's puffy face cinched in a knot of hatred, but he offered no response. The girls tittered and skipped through the door of the cantina; Esteban

could hear them describing the incident, laughter, and
he continued to stare at Raimundo. Several other girls
poked their heads out the door, giggling and whispering. After a moment Esteban spun on his heel and
walked away. Behind him there was a chorus of unre-
strained laughter, and a girl's voice called mockingly,
"Raimundo! Who are you?" Other voices joined in,
and it soon became a chant.

Barrio Carolina was not truly a barrio of Puerto
Morada; it lay beyond Punta Manabique, the south-
ernmost enclosure of the bay, and was fronted by a
palm hammock and the loveliest stretch of beach in all
the province, a curving slice of white sand giving way
to jade-green shallows. Forty years before, it had been
the headquarters of the fruit company's experimental
farm, a project of such vast scope that a small town
had been built on the site: rows of white frame houses
with shingle roofs and screen porches, the kind you
might see in a magazine illustration of rural America.
The company had touted the project as being the key-
stone of the country's future and had promised to
develop high-yield crops that would banish starvation;
but in 1947 a cholera epidemic had ravaged the coast
and the town had been abandoned. By the time the
cholera scare had died down, the company had become
well entrenched in national politics and no longer
needed to maintain a benevolent image; the project
had been dropped and the property abandoned
until—in the same year that Esteban had retired from
hunting—developers had bought it, planning to build
a major resort. It was then the jaguar had appeared.
Though it had not killed any of the workmen, it had
terrorized them to the point that they had refused to
begin the job. Hunters had been sent, and these the
jaguar *had* killed. The last party of hunters had been

equipped with automatic rifles, all manner of technological aids; but the jaguar had picked them off one by
one, and this project, too, had been abandoned.
Rumor had it that the land had recently been resold
(now Esteban knew to whom), and that the idea of a
resort was once more under consideration.

The walk from Puerto Morada was hot and tiring,
and upon arrival Esteban sat beneath a palm and ate a
lunch of cold banana fritters. Combers as white as
toothpaste broke on the shore, and there was no
human litter, just dead fronds and driftwood and
coconuts. All but four of the houses had been swallowed by the jungle, and only sections of those four
remained visible, embedded like moldering gates in a
blackish green wall of vegetation. Even under the
bright sunlight, they were haunted-looking: their
screens ripped, boards weathered gray, vines cascading
over their facades. A mango tree had sprouted from
one of the porches, and wild parrots were eating its
fruit. He had not visited the barrio since childhood: the
ruins had frightened him then, but now he found
them appealing, testifying to the dominion of natural
law. It distressed him that he would help transform it
all into a place where the parrots would be chained to
perches and the jaguars would be designs on table-
cloths, a place of swimming pools and tourists sipping
from coconut shells. Nonetheless, after he had finished
lunch, he set out to explore the jungle and soon discovered a trail used by the jaguar: a narrow path that
wound between the vine-matted shells of the houses
for about a half mile and ended at the Río Dulce. The
river was a murkier green than the sea, curving away
through the jungle walls; the jaguar's tracks were
everywhere along the bank, especially thick upon a
tussocky rise some five or six feet above the water. This
baffled Esteban. The jaguar could not drink from the
rise, and it certainly would not sleep there. He puzzled

over it awhile, but eventually shrugged it off, returned to the beach, and, because he planned to keep watch that night, took a nap beneath the palms.

Some hours later, around midafternoon, he was startled from his nap by a voice hailing him. A tall, slim, copper-skinned woman was walking toward him, wearing a dress of dark green—almost the exact color of the jungle walls—that exposed the swell of her breasts. As she drew near, he saw that though her features had a Patucan cast, they were of a lapidary fineness uncommon to the tribe; it was as if they had been refined into a lovely mask: cheeks planed into subtle hollows, lips sculpted full, stylized feathers of ebony inlaid for eyebrows, eyes of jet and white onyx, and all this given a human gloss. A sheen of sweat covered her breasts, and a single curl of black hair lay over her collarbone, so artful-seeming it appeared to have been placed there by design. She knelt beside him, gazing at him impassively, and Esteban was flustered by her heated air of sensuality. The sea breeze bore her scent to him, a sweet musk that reminded him of mangoes left ripening in the sun.

"My name is Esteban Caax," he said, painfully aware of his own sweaty odor.

"I have heard of you," she said. "The jaguar hunter. Have you come to kill the jaguar of the barrio?"

"Yes," he said, and felt shame at admitting it.

She picked up a handful of sand and watched it sift through her fingers.

"What is your name?" he asked.

"If we become friends, I will tell you my name," she said. "Why must you kill the jaguar?"

He told her about the television set, and then, to his surprise, he found himself describing his problems with Encarnación, explaining how he intended to adapt to her ways. These were not proper subjects to discuss with a stranger, yet he was lured to intimacy;

he thought he sensed an affinity between them, and that prompted him to portray his marriage as more dismal than it was, for though he had never once been unfaithful to Encarnación, he would have welcomed the chance to do so now.

"This is a black jaguar," she said. "Surely you know they are not ordinary animals, that they have purposes with which we must not interfere?"

Esteban was startled to hear his father's words from her mouth, but he dismissed it as coincidence and replied, "Perhaps. But they are not mine."

"Truly, they are," she said. "You have simply chosen to ignore them." She scooped up another handful of sand. "How will you do it? You have no gun. Only a machete."

"I have this as well," he said, and from his sack he pulled out a small parcel of herbs and handed it to her.

She opened it and sniffed the contents. "Herbs? Ah! You plan to drug the jaguar."

"Not the jaguar. Myself." He took back the parcel. "The herbs slow the heart and give the body a semblance of death. They induce a trance, but one that can be thrown off at a moment's notice. After I chew them, I will lie down in a place that the jaguar must pass on its nightly hunt. It will think I am dead, but it will not feed unless it is sure that the spirit has left the flesh, and to determine this, it will sit on the body so it can feel the spirit rise up. As soon as it starts to settle, I will throw off the trance and stab it between the ribs. If my hand is steady, it will die instantly."

"And if your hand is unsteady?"

"I have killed nearly fifty jaguars," he said. "I no longer fear unsteadiness. The method comes down through my family from the Old Patuca, and it has never failed, to my knowledge."

"But a black jaguar . . ."

"Black or spotted, it makes no difference. Jaguars

are creatures of instinct, and one is like another when it comes to feeding."

"Well," she said, "I cannot wish you luck, but neither do I wish you ill." She came to her feet, brushing the sand from her dress.

He wanted to ask her to stay but pride prevented him, and she laughed as if she knew his mind.

"Perhaps we will talk again, Esteban," she said. "It would be a pity if we did not, for more lies between us than we have spoken of this day."

She walked swiftly down the beach, becoming a diminutive black figure that was rippled away by the heat haze.

That evening, needing a place from which to keep watch, Esteban pried open the screen door of one of the houses facing the beach and went onto the porch. Chameleons skittered into the corners, and an iguana slithered off a rusted lawn chair sheathed in spiderweb and vanished through a gap in the floor. The interior of the house was dark and forbidding, except for the bathroom, the roof of which was missing, webbed over by vines that admitted a gray-green infusion of twilight. The cracked toilet was full of rainwater and dead insects. Uneasy, Esteban returned to the porch, cleaned the lawn chair, and sat.

Out on the horizon the sea and sky were blending in a haze of silver and gray; the wind had died, and the palms were as still as sculpture; a string of pelicans flying low above the waves seemed to be spelling a sentence of cryptic black syllables. But the eerie beauty of the scene was lost on him. He could not stop thinking of the woman. The memory of her hips rolling beneath the fabric of her dress as she walked away was repeated over and over in his thoughts, and whenever he tried to turn his attention to the matter at hand, the memory became more compelling. He imagined her naked, the play of muscles rippling her haunches, and this so inflamed him that he started to pace, unmindful of the fact that the creaking boards were signaling his presence. He could not understand her effect upon him. Perhaps, he thought, it was her defense of the jaguar, her calling to mind of all he was putting behind him . . . and then a realization settled over him like an icy shroud.

It was commonly held among the Patuca that a man about to suffer a solitary and unexpected death would be visited by an envoy of death, who—standing in for family and friends—would prepare him to face the event; and Esteban was now very sure that the woman had been such an envoy, that her allure had been specifically designed to attract his soul to its imminent fate. He sat back down in the lawn chair, numb with the realization. Her knowledge of his father's words, the odd flavor of her conversation, her intimation that more lay between them: it all accorded perfectly with the traditional wisdom. The moon rose three-quarters full, silvering the sands of the barrio, and still he sat there, rooted to the spot by his fear of death.

He had been watching the jaguar for several seconds before he registered its presence. It seemed at first that a scrap of night sky had fallen onto the sand and was being blown by a fitful breeze; but soon he saw that it was the jaguar, that it was inching along as if stalking some prey. Then it leaped high into the air, twisting and turning, and began to race up and down the beach: a ribbon of black water flowing across the silver sands. He had never before seen a jaguar at play, and this alone was cause for wonder; but most of all, he wondered at the fact that here were his childhood dreams come to life. He might have been peering out onto a silvery meadow of the moon, spying on one of its magical creatures. His fear was eroded by the sight, and like a child he pressed his nose to the screen, trying not to blink, anxious that he might miss a single moment.

At length the jaguar left off its play and came prowling up the beach toward the jungle. By the set of its ears and the purposeful sway of its walk, Esteban recognized that it was hunting. It stopped beneath a palm about twenty feet from the house, lifted its head, and tested the air. Moonlight frayed down through the fronds, applying liquid gleams to its haunches; its eyes, glinting yellow-green, were like peepholes into a lurid dimension of fire. The jaguar's beauty was heart-stopping—the embodiment of a flawless principle—and Esteban, contrasting this beauty with the pallid ugliness of his employer, with the ugly principle that had led to his hiring, doubted that he could ever bring himself to kill it.

All the following day he debated the question. He had hoped the woman would return, because he had rejected the idea that she was death's envoy—that perception, he thought, must have been induced by the mysterious atmosphere of the barrio—and he felt that if she was to argue the jaguar's cause again, he would let himself be persuaded. But she did not put in an appearance, and as he sat upon the beach, watching the evening sun decline through strata of dusky orange and lavender clouds, casting wild glitters over the sea, he understood once more that he had no choice. Whether or not the jaguar was beautiful, whether or not the woman had been on a supernatural errand, he must treat these things as if they had no substance. The point of the hunt had been to deny mysteries of this sort, and he had lost sight of it under the influence of old dreams.

He waited until moonrise to take the herbs, and then lay down beneath the palm tree where the jaguar had paused the previous night. Lizards whispered past in the grasses, sand fleas hopped onto his face: he hardly

felt them, sinking deeper into the languor of the herbs.
The fronds overhead showed an ashen green in the
moonlight, lifting, rustling; and the stars between their
feathered edges flickered crazily as if the breeze were
fanning their flames. He became immersed in the landscape, savoring the smells of brine and rotting foliage
that were blowing across the beach, drifting with them;
but when he heard the pad of the jaguar's step, he came
alert. Through narrowed eyes he saw it sitting a dozen
feet away, a bulky shadow craning its neck toward him,
investigating his scent. After a moment it began to circle
him, each circle a bit tighter than the one before, and
whenever it passed out of view he had to repress a
trickle of fear. Then, as it passed close on the seaward
side, he caught a whiff of its odor.

A sweet, musky odor that reminded him of mangoes left ripening in the sun.

Fear welled up in him, and he tried to banish it, to
tell himself that the odor could not possibly be what
he thought. The jaguar snarled, a razor stroke of
sound that slit the peaceful mesh of wind and surf,
and realizing it had scented his fear, he sprang to his
feet, waving his machete. In a whirl of vision he saw
the jaguar leap back, then he shouted at it, waved the
machete again, and sprinted for the house where he
had kept watch. He slipped through the door and went
staggering into the front room. There was a crash
behind him, and turning, he had a glimpse of a huge
black shape struggling to extricate itself from a moon-
lit tangle of vines and ripped screen. He darted into the
bathroom, sat with his back against the toilet bowl,
and braced the door shut with his feet.

The sound of the jaguar's struggles subsided, and
for a moment he thought it had given up. Sweat left
cold trails down his sides, his heart pounded. He held
his breath, listening, and it seemed the whole world
was holding its breath as well. The noises of wind and

surf and insects were a faint seething; moonlight shed
a sickly white radiance through the enlaced vines overhead, and a chameleon was frozen among peels of
wallpaper beside the door. He let out a sigh and wiped
the sweat from his eyes. He swallowed.

Then the top panel of the door exploded, shattered by a black paw. Splinters of rotten wood flew
into his face, and he screamed. The sleek wedge of the
jaguar's head thrust through the hole, roaring. A gateway of gleaming fangs guarding a plush red throat.
Half-paralyzed, Esteban jabbed weakly with the machete.
The jaguar withdrew, reached in with its paw, and
clawed at his leg. More by accident than design, he
managed to slice the jaguar, and the paw, too, was
withdrawn. He heard it rumbling in the front room,
and then, seconds later, a heavy thump against the
wall behind him. The jaguar's head appeared above
the edge of the wall; it was hanging by its forepaws,
trying to gain a perch from which to leap down into
the room. Esteban scrambled to his feet and slashed
wildly, severing vines. The jaguar fell back, yowling.
For a while it prowled along the wall, fuming to itself.
Finally there was silence.

When sunlight began to filter through the vines,
Esteban walked out of the house and headed down the
beach to Puerto Morada. He went with his head lowered, desolate, thinking of the grim future that awaited
him after he returned the money to Onofrio: a life of
trying to please an increasingly shrewish Encarnación,
of killing lesser jaguars for much less money. He was so
mired in depression that he did not notice the woman
until she called to him. She was leaning against a palm
about thirty feet away, wearing a filmy white dress
through which he could see the dark jut of her nipples.
He drew his machete and backed off a pace.

"Why do you fear me, Esteban?" she called, walking toward him.

"You tricked me into revealing my method and tried to kill me," he said. "Is that not reason for fear?"

"I did not know you or your method in that form. I knew only that you were hunting me. But now the hunt has ended, and we can be as man and woman."

He kept his machete at point. "What are you?" he asked.

She smiled. "My name is Miranda. I am Patuca."

"Patucas do not have black fur and fangs."

"I am of the Old Patuca," she said. "We have this power."

"Keep away!" He lifted the machete as if to strike, and she stopped just beyond his reach.

"You can kill me if that is your wish, Esteban." She spread her arms, and her breasts thrust forward against the fabric of her dress. "You are stronger than I, now. But listen to me first."

He did not lower the machete, but his fear and anger were being overridden by a sweeter emotion.

"Long ago," she said, "there was a great healer who foresaw that one day the Patuca would lose their place in the world, and so, with the help of the gods, he opened a door into another world where the tribe could flourish. But many of the tribe were afraid and would not follow him. Since then, the door has been left open for those who would come after." She waved at the ruined houses. "Barrio Carolina is the site of the door, and the jaguar is its guardian. But soon the fevers of this world will sweep over the barrio, and the door will close forever. For though our hunt has ended, there is no end to hunters or to greed." She came a step nearer. "If you listen to the sounding of your heart, you will know this is the truth."

He half believed her, yet he also believed her words masked a more poignant truth, one that fitted inside the other the way his machete fitted into its sheath.

"What is it?" she asked. "What troubles you?"

"I think you have come to prepare me for death," he said, "and that your door leads only to death."

"Then why do you not run from me?" She pointed toward Puerto Morada. "That is death, Esteban. The cries of the gulls are death, and when the hearts of lovers stop at the moment of greatest pleasure, that, too, is death. This world is no more than a thin covering of life drawn over a foundation of death, like a scum of algae upon a rock. Perhaps you are right, perhaps my world lies beyond death. The two ideas are not opposed. But if I am death to you, Esteban, then it is death you love."

He turned his eyes to the sea, not wanting her to see his face. "I do not love you," he said.

"Love awaits us," she said. "And someday you will join me in my world."

He looked back to her, ready with a denial, but was shocked to silence. Her dress had fallen to the sand, and she was smiling. The litheness and purity of the jaguar were reflected in every line of her body; her secret hair was so absolute a black that it seemed an absence in her flesh. She moved close, pushing aside the machete. The tips of her breasts brushed against him, warm through the coarse cloth of his shirt; her hands cupped his face, and he was drowning in her heated scent, weakened by both fear and desire.

"We are of one soul, you and I," she said. "One blood and one truth. You cannot reject me."

Days passed, though Esteban was unclear as to how many. Night and day were unimportant incidences of his relationship with Miranda, serving only to color their lovemaking with a spectral or a sunny mood; and each time they made love, it was as if a thousand new colors were being added to his senses. He had never been so content. Sometimes, gazing at the haunted facades of the barrio, he believed that they might well conceal shadowy avenues leading to another world; however, whenever Miranda tried to convince him to leave with her, he refused: he could not overcome his fear and would never admit—even to himself—that he loved her. He attempted to fix his thoughts on Encarnación, hoping this would undermine his fixation with Miranda and free him to return to Puerto Morada; but he found that he could not picture his wife except as a black bird hunched before a flickering gray jewel. Miranda, however, seemed equally unreal at times. Once as they sat on the bank of the Río Dulce, watching the reflection of the moon—almost full— floating upon the water, she pointed to it and said, "My world is that near, Esteban. That touchable. You may think the moon above is real and this is only a reflection, but the thing most real, that most illustrates the real, is the surface that permits the illusion of reflection. Passing through this surface is what you fear, and yet it is so insubstantial, you would scarcely notice the passage."

"You sound like the old priest who taught me philosophy," said Esteban. "His world—his heaven—was also philosophy. Is that what your world is? The idea of a place? Or are there birds and jungles and rivers?"

Her expression was in partial eclipse, half-moonlit, half-shadowed, and her voice revealed nothing of her mood. "No more than there are here," she said.

"What does that mean?" he said angrily. "Why will you not give me a clear answer?"

"If I were to describe my world, you would simply think me a clever liar." She rested her head on his shoulder. "Sooner or later you will understand. We did not find each other merely to have the pain of being parted."

In that moment her beauty—like her words—

seemed a kind of evasion, obscuring a dark and frightening beauty beneath; and yet he knew that she was right, that no proof of hers could persuade him contrary to his fear.

One afternoon, an afternoon of such brightness that it was impossible to look at the sea without squinting, they swam out to a sandbar that showed as a thin curving island of white against the green water. Esteban floundered and splashed, but Miranda swam as if born to the element; she darted beneath him, tickling him, pulling at his feet, eeling away before he could catch her. They walked along the sand, turning over starfish with their toes, collecting whelks to boil for their dinner, and then Esteban spotted a dark stain hundreds of yards wide that was moving below the water beyond the bar: a great school of king mackerel.

"It is too bad we have no boat," he said. "Mackerel would taste better than whelks."

"We need no boat," she said. "I will show you an old way of catching fish."

She traced a complicated design in the sand, and when she had done, she led him into the shallows and had him stand facing her a few feet away.

"Look down at the water between us," she said. "Do not look up, and keep perfectly still until I tell you."

She began to sing with a faltering rhythm, a rhythm that put him in mind of the ragged breezes of the season. Most of the words were unfamiliar, but others he recognized as Patuca. After a minute he experienced a wave of dizziness, as if his legs had grown long and spindly, and he was now looking down from a great height, breathing rarefied air. Then a tiny dark stain materialized below the expanse of water between him and Miranda. He remembered his grandfather's stories of the Old Patuca, how—with the help of the gods—they had been able to shrink the world, to bring enemies close and cross vast distances in a matter of moments. But the gods were dead, their powers gone from the world. He wanted to glance back to shore and see if he and Miranda had become coppery giants taller than the palms.

"Now," she said, breaking off her song, "you must put your hand into the water on the seaward side of the school and gently wiggle your fingers. Very gently! Be sure not to disturb the surface."

But when Esteban made to do as he was told, he slipped and caused a splash. Miranda cried out. Looking up, he saw a wall of jade-green water bearing down on them, its face thickly studded with the fleeting dark shapes of the mackerel. Before he could move, the wave swept over the sandbar and carried him under, dragging him along the bottom and finally casting him onto shore. The beach was littered with flopping mackerel; Miranda lay in the shallows, laughing at him. Esteban laughed, too, but only to cover up his rekindled fear of this woman who drew upon the powers of dead gods. He had no wish to hear her explanation; he was certain she would tell him that the gods lived on in her world, and this would only confuse him further.

Later that day as Esteban was cleaning the fish, while Miranda was off picking bananas to cook with them—the sweet little ones that grew along the river-bank—a Land Rover came jouncing up the beach from Puerto Morada, an orange fire of the setting sun dancing on its windshield. It pulled up beside him, and Onofrio climbed out the passenger side. A hectic flush dappled his cheeks, and he was dabbing his sweaty brow with a handkerchief. Raimundo climbed out the driver's side and leaned against the door, staring hatefully at Esteban.

"Nine days and not a word," said Onofrio gruffly. "We thought you were dead. How goes the hunt?"

Esteban set down the fish he had been scaling and

stood. "I have failed," he said. "I will give you back the money."

Raimundo chuckled—a dull, cluttered sound—and Onofrio grunted with amusement. "Impossible," he said. "Encarnación has spent the money on a house in Barrio Clarín. You must kill the jaguar."

"I cannot," said Esteban. "I will repay you somehow."

"The Indian has lost his nerve, Father." Raimundo spat in the sand. "Let me and my friends hunt the jaguar."

The idea of Raimundo and his loutish friends thrashing through the jungle was so ludicrous that Esteban could not restrain a laugh.

"Be careful, Indian!" Raimundo banged the flat of his hand on the roof of the car.

"It is you who should be careful," said Esteban. "Most likely the jaguar will be hunting you." Esteban picked up his machete. "And whoever hunts this jaguar will answer to me as well."

Raimundo reached for something in the driver's seat and walked around in front of the hood. In his hand was a silvered automatic. "I await your answer," he said.

"Put that away!" Onofrio's tone was that of a man addressing a child whose menace was inconsequential, but the intent surfacing in Raimundo's face was not childish. A tic marred the plump curve of his cheek, the ligature of his neck was cabled, and his lips were drawn back in a joyless grin. It was, thought Esteban—strangely fascinated by the transformation—like watching a demon dissolve its false shape: the true lean features melting up from the illusion of the soft.

"This son of a whore insulted me in front of Julia!" Raimundo's gun hand was shaking.

"Your personal differences can wait," said Onofrio.

"This is a business matter." He held out his hand. "Give me the gun."

"If he is not going to kill the jaguar, what use is he?" said Raimundo.

"Perhaps we can convince him to change his mind." Onofrio beamed at Esteban. "What do you say? Shall I let my son collect his debt of honor, or will you fulfill our contract?"

"Father!" complained Raimundo; his eyes flicked sideways. "He . . ."

Esteban broke for the jungle. The gun roared, a white-hot claw swiped at his side, and he went flying. For an instant he did not know where he was; but then, one by one, his impressions began to sort themselves. He was lying on his injured side, and it was throbbing fiercely. Sand crusted his mouth and eyelids. He was curled up around his machete, which was still clutched in his hand. Voices above him, sand fleas hopping on his face. He resisted the urge to brush them off and lay without moving. The throb of his wound and his hatred had the same red force behind them.

". . . carry him to the river," Raimundo was saying, his voice atremble with excitement. "Everyone will think the jaguar killed him!"

"Fool!" said Onofrio. "He might have killed the jaguar, and you could have had a sweeter revenge. His wife . . ."

"This was sweet enough," said Raimundo.

A shadow fell over Esteban, and he held his breath. He needed no herbs to deceive this pale, flabby jaguar who was bending to him, turning him onto his back.

"Watch out!" cried Onofrio.

Esteban let himself be turned and lashed out with the machete. His contempt for Onofrio and Encarnación, as well as his hatred of Raimundo, was involved in the blow, and the blade lodged deep in Raimundo's side, grating on bone. Raimundo shrieked and would have fallen, but the blade helped to keep him upright; his hands fluttered around the machete as if he wanted to adjust it to a more comfortable position, and his eyes were wide with disbelief. A shudder vibrated the hilt of the machete—it seemed sensual, the spasm of a spent passion—and Raimundo sank to his knees. Blood spilled from his mouth, adding tragic lines to the corners of his lips. He pitched forward, not falling flat but remaining kneeling, his face pressed into the sand: the attitude of an Arab at prayer.

Esteban wrenched the machete free, fearful of an attack by Onofrio, but the appliance dealer was squirming into the Land Rover. The engine caught, the wheels spun, and the car lurched off, turning through the edge of the surf and heading for Puerto Morada. An orange dazzle flared on the rear window, as if the spirit who had lured it to the barrio was now harrying it away.

Unsteadily, Esteban got to his feet. He peeled his shirt back from the bullet wound. There was a lot of blood, but it was only a crease. He avoided looking at Raimundo and walked down to the water and stood gazing out at the waves; his thoughts rolled in with them, less thoughts than tidal sweeps of emotion.

It was twilight by the time Miranda returned, her arms full of bananas and wild figs. She had not heard the shot. He told her what had happened as she dressed his wounds with a poultice of herbs and banana leaves. "It will mend," she said of the wound. "But this"—she gestured at Raimundo—"this will not. You must come with me, Esteban. The soldiers will kill you."

"No," he said. "They will come, but they are Patuca . . . except for the captain, who is a drunkard, a shell of a man. I doubt he will even be notified. They will listen to my story, and we will reach an accommodation. No matter what lies Onofrio tells, his word will not stand against theirs."

"And then?"

"I may have to go to jail for a while, or I may have to leave the province. But I will not be killed."

She sat for a minute without speaking, the whites of her eyes glowing in the half-light. Finally she stood and walked off along the beach.

"Where are you going?" he called.

She turned back. "You speak so casually of losing me. . . . " she began.

"It is not casual!"

"No!" She laughed bitterly. "I suppose not. You are so afraid of life, you call it death and would prefer jail or exile to having it! That is hardly casual." She stared at him, her expression a cipher at that distance. "I will not lose you, Esteban," she said. She walked away again, and this time when he called she did not turn.

Twilight deepened to dusk, a slow fill of shadow graying the world into negative, and Esteban felt himself graying along with it, his thoughts reduced to echoing the dull wash of the receding tide. The dusk lingered, and he had the idea that night would never fall, that the act of violence had driven a nail through the substance of his irresolute life, pinned him forever to this ashen moment and deserted shore. As a child he had been terrified by the possibility of such magical isolations, but now the prospect seemed a consolation for Miranda's absence, a remembrance of her magic. Despite her parting words, he did not think she would be back—there had been sadness and finality in her voice—and this roused in him feelings of both relief and desolation, feelings that set him to pacing up and down the tidal margin of the shore.

The full moon rose, the sands of the barrio burned silver, and shortly thereafter four soldiers came in a jeep from Puerto Morada. They were gnomish copper-skinned men, and their uniforms were the dark blue of the night sky, bearing no device or decoration. Though they were not close friends, he knew them each by name: Sebastian, Amador, Carlito, and Ramón. In their headlights Raimundo's corpse—startlingly pale, the blood on his face dried into intricate whorls—looked like an exotic creature cast up by the sea, and their inspection of it smacked more of curiosity than of a search for evidence. Amador unearthed Raimundo's gun, sighted along it toward the jungle, and asked Ramón how much he thought it was worth.

"Perhaps Onofrio will give you a good price," said Ramón, and the others laughed.

They built a fire of driftwood and coconut shells, and sat around it while Esteban told his story; he did not mention either Miranda or her relation to the jaguar, because these men—estranged from the tribe by their government service—had grown conservative in their judgments, and he did not want them to consider him irrational. They listened without comment; the firelight burnished their skins to reddish gold and glinted on their rifle barrels.

"Onofrio will take his charge to the capital if we do nothing," said Amador after Esteban had finished.

"He may in any case," said Carlito. "And then it will go hard with Esteban."

"And," said Sebastian, "if an agent is sent to Puerto Morada and sees how things are with Captain Portales, they will surely replace him and it will go hard with us."

They stared into the flames, mulling over the problem, and Esteban chose the moment to ask Amador, who lived near him on the mountain, if he had seen Encarnación.

"She will be amazed to learn you are alive," said Amador. "I saw her yesterday in the dressmaker's shop. She was admiring the fit of a new black skirt in the mirror."

It was as if a black swath of Encarnación's skirt had folded around Esteban's thoughts. He lowered his head and carved lines in the sand with the point of his machete.

"I have it," said Ramón. "A boycott!"

The others expressed confusion.

"If we do not buy from Onofrio, who will?" said Ramón. "He will lose his business. Threatened with this, he will not dare involve the government. He will allow Esteban to plead self-defense."

"But Raimundo was his only son," said Amador. "It may be that grief will count more than greed in this instance."

Again they fell silent. It mattered little to Esteban what was decided. He was coming to understand that without Miranda, his future held nothing but uninteresting choices; he turned his gaze to the sky and noticed that the stars and the fire were flickering with the same rhythm, and he imagined each of them ringed by a group of gnomish copper-skinned men, debating the question of his fate.

"Aha!" said Carlito. "I know what to do. We will occupy Barrio Carolina—the entire company—and *we* will kill the jaguar. Onofrio's greed cannot withstand this temptation."

"That you must not do," said Esteban.

"But why?" asked Amador. "We may not kill the jaguar, but with so many men we will certainly drive it away."

Before Esteban could answer, the jaguar roared. It was prowling down the beach toward the fire, like a black flame itself shifting over the glowing sand. Its ears were laid back, and silver drops of moonlight

gleamed in its eyes. Amador grabbed his rifle, came to
one knee, and fired: the bullet sprayed sand a dozen
feet to the left of the jaguar.

"Wait!" cried Esteban, pushing him down.

But the rest had begun to fire, and the jaguar was
hit. It leaped high as it had that first night while playing, but this time it landed in a heap, snarling, snap-
ping at its shoulder; it regained its feet and limped
toward the jungle, favoring its right foreleg. Excited by
their success, the soldiers ran a few paces after it and
stopped to fire again. Carlito dropped to one knee,
taking careful aim.

"No!" shouted Esteban, and as he hurled his
machete at Carlito, desperate to prevent further harm to
Miranda, he recognized the trap that had been sprung
and the consequences he would face.

The blade sliced across Carlito's thigh, knocking him onto his side. He screamed, and Amador,
seeing what had happened, fired wildly at Esteban
and called to the others. Esteban ran toward the
jungle, making for the jaguar's path. A fusillade of
shots rang out behind him, bullets whipped past
his ears. Each time his feet slipped in the soft sand,
the moonstruck facades of the barrio appeared to
lurch sideways as if trying to block his way. And
then, as he reached the verge of the jungle, he was
hit.

The bullet seemed to throw him forward, to
increase his speed, but somehow he managed to keep
his feet. He careened along the path, arms waving,
breath shrieking in his throat. Palmetto fronds swatted
his face, vines tangled his legs. He felt no pain, only a
peculiar numbness that pulsed low in his back; he pictured the wound opening and closing like the mouth
of an anemone. The soldiers were shouting his name.
They would follow, but cautiously, afraid of the jaguar,
and he thought he might be able to cross the river

before they could catch up. But when he came to the river, he found the jaguar waiting.

It was crouched on the tussocky rise, its neck craned over the water, and below, half a dozen feet from the bank, floated the reflection of the full moon, huge and silvery, an unblemished circle of light. Blood glistened scarlet on the jaguar's shoulder, like a fresh rose pinned in place, and this made it look even more an embodiment of principle: the shape a god might choose, that some universal constant might assume. It gazed calmly at Esteban, growled low in its throat, and dove into the river, cleaving and shattering the moon's reflection, vanishing beneath the surface. The ripples subsided, the image of the moon re-formed. And there, silhouetted against it, Esteban saw the figure of a woman swimming, each stroke causing her to grow smaller and smaller until she seemed no more than a character incised upon a silver plate. It was not only Miranda he saw, but all mystery and beauty receding from him, and he realized how blind he had been not to perceive the truth sheathed inside the truth of death that had been sheathed inside her truth of another world. It was clear to him now. It sang to him from his wound, every syllable a heartbeat. It was written by the dying ripples, it swayed in the banana leaves, it sighed on the wind. It was everywhere, and he had always known it: if you deny mystery—even in the guise of death—then you deny life and you will walk like a ghost through your days, never knowing the secrets of the extremes. The deep sorrows, the absolute joys.

He drew a breath of the rank jungle air, and with it drew a breath of a world no longer his, of the girl Encarnación, of friends and children and country nights . . . all his lost sweetness. His chest tightened as with the onset of tears, but the sensation quickly abated, and he understood that the sweetness of the past had been subsumed by a scent of mangoes, that nine magical days—a magical number of days, the number it takes to sing the soul to rest—lay between him and tears. Freed of those associations, he felt as if he were undergoing a subtle refinement of form, a winnowing, and he remembered having felt much the same on the day when he had run out the door of Santa María del Onda, putting behind him its dark geometries and cobwebbed catechisms and generations of swallows that had never flown beyond the walls, casting off his acolyte's robe and racing across the square toward the mountain and Encarnación: it had been she who had lured him then, just as his mother had lured him to the church and as Miranda was luring him now, and he laughed at seeing how easily these three women had diverted the flow of his life, how like other men he was in this.

The strange bloom of painlessness in his back was sending out tendrils into his arms and legs, and the cries of the soldiers had grown louder. Miranda was a tiny speck shrinking against a silver immensity. For a moment he hesitated, experiencing a resurgence of fear; then Miranda's face materialized in his mind's eye, and all the emotion he had suppressed for nine days poured through him, washing away the fear. It was a silvery, flawless emotion, and he was giddy with it, light with it; it was like thunder and fire fused into one element and boiling up inside him, and he was overwhelmed by a need to express it, to mold it into a form that would reflect its power and purity. But he was no singer, no poet. There was but a single mode of expression open to him. Hoping he was not too late, that Miranda's door had not shut forever, Esteban dove into the river, cleaving the image of the full moon; and—his eyes still closed from the shock of the splash—with the last of his mortal strength, he swam hard down after her.

SHE'S NOT THERE
Pat Cadigan

Pat Cadigan was born in Schenectady, New York, and now lives in Overland Park, Kansas. She made her first professional sale in 1980, and has subsequently come to be regarded as one of the best new SF writers. She was the coeditor of *Shayol*, perhaps the best of the semi-prozines of the late 1970s; it was honored with a World Fantasy Award in the "Special Achievement, Non-Professional" category in 1981. She has also served as chairman of the Nebula Award jury and as a World Fantasy Award judge. Her first novel, *Mindplayers*, was released in 1987 to excellent critical response, and her second novel, *Synners*, released in 1991, won the prestigious Arthur C. Clarke Award as the year's best science fiction novel. Her third novel, *Fools*, came out in 1992, and she is currently at work on a fourth, tentatively entitled *Parasites*. Her story "Pretty Boy Crossover" has recently appeared on several critics' lists as among the best science fiction stories of the 1980s, her story "Angel" was a finalist for the Hugo Award, the Nebula Award, *and* the World Fantasy Award (one of the few stories ever to earn that rather unusual distinction), and her collection *Patterns* has been hailed as one of the landmark collections of the decade. Her most recent book is a major new collection, *Dirty Work*.

In the passionate and disturbing story that follows, she asks the question, Is there anything in this life that you'd give up *everything* for? And suggests that you'd better be *very* careful how you *answer* it. . . .

She's Not There

There was once such a thing as a single, as in music, as in rock 'n' roll, as in hear it on a radio with a speaker that made it sound like listening to music over the telephone. Didn't matter—if the speaker was small, the music was big. *Big.* What made it big could reach out through that fuzzy-muzzy speaker and change the world, change the universe. At least change your life.

Don't you remember how music changed your life? Of course not, why am I even asking? You *couldn't* remember, even though you were there.

How would you know, why would you care. . . ?

That's not how you remember the line, I know. But that's how it was originally sung. Not by a group of young guys who managed to chart one more near-miss before passing into nostalgia, but by a young woman who committed suicide the day after it hit number one, cementing her place in the pantheon of rock music deities for all time and sending a good part of the civilized world into a mourning that eclipsed the deaths of Buddy Holly, Elvis, and John Lennon combined.

You've never heard of her.

It was a dirty little town. I mean that literally. Grimy little industrial town, blot on the New England landscape. There are those who even now will tell you that it was and is a pretty town, but they probably lived up on the west side or out on Summer Street. I lived where the dirt settled.

Kathy didn't. The Beaver would have been at home in her neighborhood. In mine, we'd have mugged him for his lunch money, and then made him pay protection so we wouldn't do it again. And then we'd have done it again anyway, just to see the look on his face. *That's right, kid, there ain't no justice in* this *world.*

You think that's bad—punching out a harmless, mediocre little kid like the Beav? Well, it was. But the Beav got over it. He had a nice home to run to, June kissed his boo-boos, Ward taught him a few boxing moves, and he never walked through our turf again anyway.

And just for the record, *I* never laid a glove on him. I wasn't even there that day. I was in my room, studying. Because there were three things I knew better than anything:

1. There's no justice.
2. There's no Santa Claus.
3. I was getting *out.*

Kathy was the first one who ever believed me. Believed *in* me. We were little girls in Catholic school; navy-blue jumper dresses over white blouses and sky-blue bow ties, with kneesocks and saddle shoes, marching two by two into school in the morning. People would say, *Bet you hate it, all that Catholic school stuff, all that regimentation, all that praying, those uniforms.* Yeah, sure, all of it, except the uniforms. I secretly loved the uniforms even while I pretended to hate them. When you had a flock of kids in identical uniforms, you couldn't tell who was from Summer Street and who was from that patch of blight just two blocks down from the church. You couldn't tell unless you already knew. Kathy knew; she was from Summer Street. She didn't care.

She was always solemn, one of those skinny, paper-white girls you figure will grow up to be a professional neurotic. Because she was so brilliant. *Brilliant.* One of the Smart Kids in the class.

I was Smart, too, but they made me fight for it. So I fought like I was mugging the Beaver, taking everything he owned. Because it was supposed to be useless for me—my kind didn't go to college, dirt didn't get *out. They* said.

The music told me different. Listen, you think a fuzzy-muzzy transistor radio is a silly thing to hang on to? It was the music, really; when there was no radio, I played it in my head. Anything on that list of Things They Can't Take Away From You, what you know and what you hear in your head, that's what I hung on to. Maybe you've got something better. If you do, don't go walking through my old neighborhood with it.

Then I heard Kathy sing, and I knew what *she* was hanging on to.

I hit the eighth grade the year that Kennedy hit the White House. A Catholic makes president—that must mean there's a God, right? Well, there was something; maybe it was a pony. My face was breaking out; my *breasts* were breaking out, God help me. And Kathy was getting thinner.

She was the only one doing *that* that *I* could see. I keep thinking it got cold early in the fall of 1960, but nobody else remembers it that way. No one else remembers it being especially cold or hot or anything else. An unremarkable year except for the election of the first Catholic president in history, which was supposed to mean something good to all us women in uniform, good little Catholic girls and the nuns who taught us.

Every autumn, that's what I think of—those weeks leading up to the election and after, the air growing cold, the last of the leaves falling off the trees, and, in spite of everything, in spite of where I was, what I was, and how it was then, I feel that same happy-sad feeling that comes with remembering really good things you don't have anymore. But then, I guess that about sums it all up, doesn't it?

By the time we were all saying a rosary in class every day to thank Holy Mary for interceding with her Son to make Kennedy president, I had already heard Kathy sing. One afternoon over at her house, up in her room, she'd suddenly jumped up off the bed in the middle of some forgettable conversation, put a record on her record player, and then just stood in the middle of the room and *sang*. It was some folk song I'd never heard before, but if she'd been singing "Mary Had a Little Lamb" it would have been something I'd never heard before. She didn't just have a voice, she had a voice, a *voice*. *The Voice*. Two seconds and I'd forgotten what a strange thing it was for her to do, just get up and perform. I was just so glad she'd done it for me, that *I* could hear it. And after she finished, I'd been going to make some kind of weak joke about getting her to sing at my wedding to some movie star or other, except that when she was through, I couldn't say a word. I remember feeling like the sound of my voice would profane the quiet left after hers. I remember that it *was* quiet, too, very quiet, because there was no one else in the house that day.

That didn't happen often, that there would be no one home at Kathy's. Her mother was a licensed practical nurse who worked at a convalescent home mostly and sometimes filled in at Tri-County General Hospital, usually around the holidays when the combination of vacations and sick leave would leave them shorthanded. Her father was an electrician or something, and I figured he made his own hours, because there wasn't any pattern to when he was home and when he wasn't. Kathy's older sister, Sarah, was in high school, a place that was as mysterious to me as Timbuktu or Cleveland. The younger sister, Barbara, wasn't home either—good thing for her, because Kathy was always chasing her out, telling her to go find something to do and some friend to do it with. I didn't really understand that, because the kid never bothered her. She was okay, the kid; I'd have let her stay and even hang around us, but Kathy wouldn't hear of it. One time I asked her why.

"Because I can't miss her if she won't go away," she snapped. It should have been funny, but Kathy really wasn't much for humor. There's only one joke she ever told me, so long ago, two lifetimes ago, but I still remember it. Because it was not the sort of joke I'd have expected her to tell me and I didn't get it at the time. It went like this:

Kathy: *Do you know how to use the word "pagoda" in a sentence?*
Me: *There's a pagoda in Japan?*
Kathy: *My father said, "Kathy, go to your room" and I said, "Pagoda hell."*

I'd get it now. A lot of people would. But in 1960, at the beginning of the first American Catholic administration, nobody got it.

"Does anybody else know you can sing?" It took me two days to get up the nerve to ask her that question because I had the feeling she was pretty sensitive about her singing. Now that I had, it sounded so damned vapid.

Kathy only twisted her shoulders in an awkward shrug. "Anyone like who? Sister Mary Aloysius? Mrs. What's-Her-Name, the choir director? Dick Clark? My father?"

She looked away. We were standing just inside the doors of the public library, protected from the raw pre-Christmas wind (though not the damp, which was creeping up my ankles from my toes), watching the bus stop for our respective buses home. I took the Putnam Park Via Water Street; Kathy rode the less frequent Lunenburg Via John Bell Hwy. It was getting dark fast, earlier every day. I'd always hated the darkening descent to the Christmas season. Even though the days started getting longer just before Christmas Day, it never felt that way to me. I found winter depressing; so did Kathy, as far as I could tell.

"Did you ever think of—you know, doing something with your, um, music?"

"You mean, singing in front of people?" She turned to look at me, and I thought she'd be irritated with me—she'd sounded irritated—but the expression on her face was more frightened than anything else. "How? Where? And for who?"

"The Glee Club? Or the choir?" Her eyes might have been boring two holes through me. "The Shangri-Las?"

That made her smile, but it was a small one, sad and fleeting. "I don't want them to know."

I waited for her to say something else, to say she thought that kind of thing was a big waste of time, that she didn't want to sing moldy old show tunes and hymns, but she just kept staring at me, chewing on the inside of her lower lip. Waiting, I realized, for reassurance from me.

"Well, for heaven's sake, Kath, who's going to tell them? Not me, you can bet the farm on that. I'm sick of how the Shangri-Las never take my advice anyway."

She started to smile again at that but she forced herself not to. "Okay. That's the way I want it."

"Well, okay," I said.

And then her bus came, for once ahead of mine, and I watched her bustle out and join the small group waiting in front of the bus door. She almost looked over her shoulder at me, except the scarf on her head was tucked into her coat collar and she couldn't quite manage it.

It wasn't actually my business—I mean, I was curious, and in those days, you tended to feel like you deserved a full explanation for any weirdness that might crop up in a friend. Usually, you'd get it. But I never did. I'd ask her from time to time, broaching the subject carefully. Most times, she just ignored any questions—everything was too personal. Or she wouldn't even hear me. Frustration? I'll tell the world.

I also wanted to tell the world about Kathy's voice. Well, I wanted to tell somebody. Someone important, someone who would count, who could do something, give her the reward she deserved for having such a talent. I wanted somebody to put a smile on her pale face; I wanted that so bad I could taste it.

Actually, I wanted it to be *me* so bad I could taste it. That's how it is when you want to rescue someone, rush into whatever bad shit is going on in their lives and be the big hero. Of course, you want to do that in your own way, because it's someone else you're rescuing but it's yourself that you're gratifying.

I thought about that one so much afterwards that I don't have to think about it anymore. It's in me the way oxygen's in the atmosphere.

Anyway, I discovered that there *was* someone who could put a smile on her face. He went to the boys' branch of the school, which was a block away from the girls' building. They kept us separated and penned up, so that by the time we went off to any of the coed high schools, the hormones were virtually audible.

Eddie Gibbs was the name on Kathy's smile. I could see why. He was cute but nice, too, not stuck-up like a lot of the more popular boys. We all got to see each other briefly during the daily lunch hour—our school let us out for lunch in those days—but for much longer and more substantially every Friday evening, when most of us would go to Miss Fran's School of Ballroom Dancing where, to our wicked, sinful delight, the girls and boys could even *touch* each other.

Miss Fran's was a rite of puberty. Not to enroll was tantamount to checking the yes box for *Have you ever been hospitalized for mental illness?* on an employment application; you were marked permanently as odd, and nobody wanted that. So everyone signed up and went fox-trotting and box-waltzing and cha-cha-ing on Friday nights, even the oddest kids, the class outcasts and misfits, future doctors and future ex-cons, even me. Everyone, except Kathy.

Now, somehow, all those years of hanging out with me hadn't done anything to diminish her stature among our classmates, or with our teachers. She was Kathy, after all, Kathy who lived on Summer Street, and I guess they all figured that someday she'd out-grow her silly attachment to me. Sometimes one of the popular girls would take it into her head that she should Talk To Kathy About Her Friend. I guessed they were afraid that someday they'd look out the front window of their sorority house and see me following Kathy up the walk to the pledge party. Kathy would tell me about it sometimes, and one girl actually did say she would be pledging her mother's sorority in college, and Kathy could, too, but I couldn't. Can't tell you how crushed I was.

Anyway, what her association with me couldn't

do, her absence from Miss Fran's did. It was more than odd, it was shocking and unnatural, and it wasn't because of me. Suddenly, they were Talking To Me About Kathy.

I don't know what I would have told them if I'd known the truth. What I could say, in all honesty, was that I didn't know. I didn't know why she wasn't there, I really didn't. I asked her a couple of times, but she would just shake her head and look miserable. She was all pulled into herself, closed off; even her posture was like that, she was walking around with her chest all caved in. She looked thinner than ever, too. Everybody was talking, but to give them credit (something I don't do too easily), all the talk was still pretty kind. Maybe she was sick, maybe someone she knew was sick, maybe her parents were fighting. That last could have meant anything from chronic arguing to having the police at your house every Saturday night, telling your father to sober the hell up (and your mother to shut the hell up).

Kathy wouldn't say, but she stopped inviting me over, and she stopped coming over to my place. I thought maybe she was mad at me, maybe one of those future sorority sisters had told her I'd cut her up, trying to break up our friendship. All I finally got out of her was that she was being punished. I didn't ask her what for. Having to tell all in confession was humiliating enough; nobody wanted to have to tell anything sensitive to someone who *wasn't* bound by the secrecy of the confessional.

I'd have let it go even with Kathy getting sadder and thinner all the time, except that Eddie Gibbs came to me about her.

I didn't realize it was about her at first. I thought Eddie had a crush on *me*. It wasn't so impossible. Ron

Robillard had had a crush on me for a while early in the school year, and he was the most popular boy. Of course, he hated having a crush on me, and I always had to be careful to stay out of his way at Miss Fran's because he'd stomp on my foot or pinch my arm or whisper something mean. It made me glad he wasn't in love with me for real.

Eddie was different, though. Eddie was kind, a real nice guy. Where Ron was your basic crew-cut blond all-American athlete and wife-beater-in-training, Eddie was slender and dark. My mother saw him once and said he was Mediterranean. He was a Smart Kid, too, and it only took a tiny little bit of extra attention from him to hook me, choosing me to dance with at Miss Fran's, even sitting in the same pew at church one Sunday. And as we walked out together after Mass was over, he asked me why Kathy didn't come to Miss Fran's.

I felt pretty dumb, but that lasted all of about a minute. Well, of *course*, Kathy. Why not Kathy? I couldn't even be jealous about it, not really. I didn't fit into that scheme, but Kathy did.

Still, I felt pretty good that Eddie Gibbs had come to me, rather than one of the accepted girls. To me, it meant that I had his respect if not his heart, and knowing that gave me a bigger charge than him having a crush on me ever could have. That was why I did what I did.

Actually, I didn't do so much in the beginning. I promised Eddie three things: one, I would find out why she didn't go to Miss Fran's (well, I would *try*); two, I would show him how to get to her house. And then three, I would talk to her about him, find out if she liked him, too. Then they could officially be *going out*. This didn't mean they were going anywhere together, just that they were boyfriend and girlfriend. Thirteen used to be too young to date.

The easiest thing was, of course, showing him where Kathy lived. The Summer Street address didn't even make him blink. He managed to contrive all kinds of excuses to pass by it. Sometimes he'd even ask me to go with him and I would. I thought maybe if Kathy's family saw me with Eddie, they'd think he was my boyfriend instead of hers, and she wouldn't get into trouble.

I'm not sure what put that thought in my head, that Kathy's family would object to her having a boyfriend. And hell, Eddie wasn't her boyfriend, not formally. I wasn't sure she even knew his name. Maybe it was just that they wouldn't let her go to Miss Fran's. Everybody knows a few kids with families like that, who over-protect them so much that they can't wait to go to college and go nuts. Except I was pretty sure that Kathy wouldn't, unless her folks stayed unreasonable after she got to high school.

But the summer before high school, her father caught us, and she almost didn't get there at all.

Saying her father caught us makes it sound a lot more than it was, and yet, that doesn't begin to tell it. A whole lot of people saw it; nobody saw it. All that showed on that sunny afternoon in early July was Eddie and I on the sidewalk in front of Kathy's house, and Kathy sitting on the porch. Kathy's father came out, looked at us, and then looked at her; she got up from her chair and went inside and we walked away.

But that's not what happened.

What happened was, Eddie had talked me into walking over the Fifth Street bridge and down Hayward to Summer so he could check out Kathy's, maybe see her outside and get a chance to talk to her.

At that point, I couldn't tell if Eddie really had it that bad for her, or whether he was dying of curiosity as to how any girl could be so resistant to his good looks and hot status. *I* wasn't resisting him—even though he never made like he was interested in me in that way, even though I knew he wouldn't have bothered even making friends with me if I hadn't been a way to get next to Kathy, I went along with whatever he wanted. God knows, in this life the only reason anyone ever bothers with anyone else is for purposes of usefulness. In this life, or any other.

So there we were, Eddie and I, walking along like we really were good buddies, even talking about this and that. Eddie had this surprisingly high political awareness—he was the only kid I knew who could actually discuss HUAC and Senator Joseph McCarthy. Well, the only kid besides Kathy, of course. Kathy seemed to know about a lot of things.

The front of Kathy's house was visible from the corner of Summer and Hayward, and we could see her on the porch as soon as we crossed the intersection. Eddie started to walk faster, and some impulse made me tug on his shirt and tell him to slow down. "You don't want to stampede her, do you?" I said, only half-joking.

He looked puzzled; why would any girl object to the sight of the great Eddie Gibbs coming toward her as fast as possible? Well, maybe that's not fair, but it's not totally unfair, either. In any case, Eddie slowed up, and we finally got to the middle of the block where Kathy's house was without him exploding with frustration or hormones.

I made Eddie stand there on the sidewalk until I could get Kathy's attention. I was thinking we had to do this fast, say hello, get her to come with us, and be gone before someone else in the family saw the three of us together.

Looking back on it, I think that she must have

seen us all along and she was trying to ignore us into going away. But discouraging Eddie Gibbs wasn't that easy. I felt envious; I couldn't imagine that any handsome guy was ever going to chase *me* so persistently, and I couldn't figure out why Kathy wasn't thrilled, or at least flattered.

She sat there for a long time paging through the Sears catalog, of all things, and not looking up. The neighbors on either side of her were out in their gardens and doing some lawn work and they'd noticed us. Not in any big way, they just waved at me and I waved back. Eddie went from baffled to annoyed. "Kathy?" he asked.

It wasn't that his voice was so loud as that it just carried well, through all those outdoor sounds to the porch. Kathy finally looked up, and my first thought on seeing her face was, *Who died?*

That moment became one of those mental snapshots you can never lose, no matter how much changes afterwards. I could see that the white posts were going to need painting before the summer was out, that some of the boards were a little bit warped, that someone had put out some geraniums to be planted. There was a transistor radio sitting on a small wicker table to Kathy's right. She was wearing what I thought of as a school blouse, with a softly rounded collar, a silver crucifix, and one of her good skirts. I wondered if she were going somewhere.

Then I realized it wasn't sadness on Kathy's face but rage. The last thing she could have wished for was to have someone like Eddie Gibbs standing in front of her house, looking at her. I thought I saw her make a move to get up, and I don't know whether she meant to come down the walk to us or go inside to get away from us, because before she could do anything at all, her father came out onto the porch.

He wasn't a big man, Kathy's father, neither

exceptionally ugly nor handsome nor anything else. My impression was that I could stare at him all day and forget what he looked like as soon as I turned away. He gazed at me and Eddie as if he suspected we'd come to steal the silver. After some unmeasurable span of time, he turned to Kathy.

Pagoda hell. It might as well have been painted on her forehead. This was bad, I thought; this was really, really bad, whatever was going on between them. But even that wasn't so remarkable. Lots of people our age were at war with one or both parents; it was the way things went. I kept thinking that was all it was, one of those generation gap problems, as, in response to some cue I hadn't caught, Kathy got up without a word and went into the house.

Eddie and I looked at each other. An airplane droned overhead, and when I looked back to Kathy's house, the porch was empty. I turned back to Eddie and shrugged. "I don't know."

"Me, either," Eddie replied, and we went back the way we had come. I was sort of hoping that Eddie would ask me to be his girlfriend, since Kathy's rejection had been unmistakable, but Eddie seemed to be lost in thought. Probably needed some time, I decided as our paths diverged at the corner of Hayward and Fifth.

Two days later, I called Kathy, thinking I'd sound her out about Eddie—was she interested or not? His interest in her had lasted longer than the usual crush, and I wasn't sure whether to be worried by Eddie's attention span or just impressed.

The line was busy, and still busy when I tried again a half hour later. After three hours, I gave up. Maybe someone had knocked the phone off the hook.

The phone was still beeping busy the following morning, so I figured I'd just walk over and see what the problem was. Without Eddie, this time; considering the expression on Kathy's father's face, I didn't think I should bring anyone with me. No, scratch that—any *boy*. Some parents got overly nervous. I wouldn't have thought Kathy's would be, but there was no telling, really; I just didn't know them very well.

This time, Kathy's mother was sitting on the porch, with the newspaper and a big glass of pink lemonade. Not an uncommon sight in July, but there was something weird about it. Kathy's mother looked like she was posing for a picture. Or just posing—I kept thinking that the lemonade and the paper were props, but that didn't make any sense.

Maybe some of what I was feeling showed on my face; Kathy's mother got this defensive look, as if she expected me to challenge her right to do this, sit on her own porch with a cold drink. Or maybe she was just worried that I'd ask her for a sip, or even my own glass. Neither of Kathy's parents had ever been in danger of winning a medal for hospitality.

I was kind of annoyed, so I just walked right up onto the porch and said, "Hi, Kathy home?"

She stared straight ahead, newspaper in one hand, lemonade in the other. "No."

"Oh." I waited for a few moments. "Will she be back soon?"

Now the woman shrugged. Lemonade sloshed over the rim of the glass and spotted her white pants.

"Okay, then, when would be a good time for me to call her?"

She didn't say anything for the longest time. I'd been going to wait her out, and then decided I was tired of her game, whatever it was. No wonder Kathy was so strange, I thought as I stumped down the porch steps. Next to her parents, she was positively normal.

"Kathy's in the hospital."

I turned around to see Barbara standing just inside

the screen door. Her mother gave her a really furious look, but Barbara ignored her, hugging herself. Barbara was built much more solidly, not thin like Kathy.

"She's in the hospital with blood poisoning," Barbara said. "She's going to be all right, but she can't have any visitors. Because of *germs*."

That was the last straw for her mother, I guess. She got up in a big hurry, and Barbara fled. Her mother yanked open the screen door with such force that it flew all the way back, banging against the front of the house. I waited, thinking I'd hear some yelling and find out what Kathy's mother was so upset about, but there wasn't a sound. Yelling would have been embarrassing, but the silence was downright weird. I went home and phoned Eddie. I figured he should know.

As it turned out, Eddie's older sister was a nurse in training at the hospital, so he could find out more than I could. I made him promise to tell me when he did, and he kept assuring me that he would, don't worry.

Guys lie. All guys, young and old, boyfriends, fathers, brothers, all of them. They lie and lie and lie. Either that or they don't pay any attention to what they're saying while they say it. He found out. He even sneaked in and saw her. And after that he wouldn't even speak to me.

Kathy had to be an invalid for the rest of the summer, or so her mother the nurse said. She got hold of a wheelchair—maybe borrowed it from the convalescent home. Kathy sat in it on the porch for the last part of July and all of August, listening to the radio. She couldn't go anywhere or spend much time with anyone. I only went over when her house would be at its emptiest. And even so, she wouldn't say much. Not just about how she happened to end up in the hospital, but about anything. Trying to hold a conversation with her was impossible.

I was pretty mad at Kathy's mother, and also at Eddie Gibbs for being such a fair-weather boyfriend. I didn't know what his problem was, except he obviously wasn't interested in Kathy anymore. Maybe some cheerleader with big breasts had given him a tumble, I thought. Guys were a lot more trouble than they were worth.

Toward the end of August, Kathy seemed to be getting a lot better, but she was still in that damned wheelchair. "Why does your mother insist on keeping you in that thing?" I asked her finally. "You can walk, can't you?"

She shook her head.

"You can't walk?" I couldn't believe it.

"No, it's not my mother. My father makes me stay in the chair."

"Well, that's ridiculous," I said. "How are you supposed to stay healthy—"

"My father doesn't want me to put any excess strain on my heart before school starts." She turned up the radio, which was supposed to end the conversation.

"But that doesn't make any sense," I said, raising my voice to talk over Elvis. "Your mother's a nurse, she could tell him—"

"No, she can't," Kathy said. "She can't, and we can't. Nobody can tell him anything."

After that, she didn't want to talk about anything anymore, but I was getting tired of that and all her neurotic shit. Her and her mother and her weirdo father—by far, the only sensible one seemed to be Barbara, and I was starting to wonder about her.

"I think this year you ought to do something with *your* singing," I told her abruptly, reaching over to turn Elvis down. "Get involved with the Glee Club and the choir. They'll probably make you a soloist. Looks good on your transcript when you apply to college."

"Oh, I plan to do something with my singing," she said, giving me this sideways look.

"What?" I asked her.

"You'll see."

"Come on, Kathy, *what*."

"You'll *see*." Suddenly she smiled. "You will." She turned up the radio again and was happy for all of fifteen seconds. Her father materialized on the porch like a magic trick. He snapped off the radio, then picked it up, yanked the batteries out of the compartment in the bottom, and put them in his pocket.

"Trash," he said, glaring at Kathy. "You know what kind of people listen to that trash, don't you?" His gaze moved to me. "Don't you, Katherine? Answer me."

She ducked her head and I thought I heard her whisper, *Yes, Daddy.*

"People like *her*." He jerked his thumb toward the sidewalk. "Hit the road, trash. I don't want you near my daughters, any of them. The next time one of those horny young apes you go around with gets a yen for some, you take him to the whores you live with. Do I make myself clear to you?"

It all came out in such a quiet, calm voice, I wasn't sure that I'd actually heard what I heard. And then Kathy whispered, *Go.* Please. *Get out of here.*

I was so shocked, that was just what I did. Maybe her father had blown some kind of gasket in his brain, I thought. I'd have to ask Kathy when I saw her at school, even though she would probably be embarrassed to death over it. Because she lived on Summer Street; in my neighborhood, I'd have just figured him for yet another guy who got mean when he got drunk.

Actually, it was the last time I saw Kathy for years. The week before school started, she ran away. Without the wheelchair.

*   *   *

High school was hell anyway, but without Kathy, it was even more rotten. I was so mad at her for leaving me to face it alone, after we'd stuck together for so long. At the same time, I couldn't blame her. What wasn't boring was incomprehensible or embarrassing. I fell into my radio and stayed there.

Not the local stations, which were all easy listening or country-western or yak-yak-yak, but the ones from Boston and Worcester, where everything seemed to be faster, happier, better. I loved to sit alone and listen after school. In Worcester, the kids called in requests every afternoon, and it sounded like they all knew each other. I daydreamed about getting out, finding my way to some place like that. Maybe that was what Kathy had done, gone off to find some better place to be, where her parents couldn't keep her in a wheel-chair, and as soon as she was sure it really was a bet-ter place, she'd let me know. Somehow, she'd send me a message to come join her without giving it away to her parents or anyone else.

I hung on to that for a while, even though I knew it was a complete fantasy. But as long as it *was* a com-plete fantasy, I pulled out all the stops and imagined that her message would come in the music. Like we were spies or secret agents in hostile country, trying to get home.

So fourteen and fifteen is a little old to be playing Spy. It was better than playing with Eddie Gibbs. He'd gone on to become high school aristocracy, and, as near as I could tell, he'd forgotten all about Kathy and me. I gave him a dirty look every time I saw him; he would stare right through me, like he didn't see me at all.

Yeah, well, like I should have expected more out of a fourteen-year-old guy.

*   *   *

I spent my junior year sleeping with Jasper Townshend.
It was the next best thing to getting *out*.

Every night of the week, I could drift off to sleep
at the sound of Jasper's low, velvety voice urging me
to believe in the power of my own dreams. It didn't
bother me that he said this to *everyone* who slept with
him. I didn't expect a whole lot of Jasper; all I wanted
to do was forget this world for seven or eight hours,
and Jasper knew exactly how to help me do that.

Being so good at what he did, he became a very
popular guy, number one in the overnight time slot.
All the other radio stations might as well have been off
the air. It wasn't just that he had the best voice in the
business, or a lot of great things to say. It was that he
really knew how to program the music, and when to
shut up.

You could tell the music meant a lot to him. I
think it meant as much to him as it did to me. With
Kathy gone, it meant more to me than it ever had.
Sometimes I'd even forget that my little fantasy wasn't
real, and I'd listen for Kathy's voice, the song she
would sing to let me know she'd found someplace
safe.

I guess if you listen hard enough for something,
you'll finally hear it.

The first time I heard it was in a dream, literally. I was
back in Kathy's room and she was singing for me, but
it wasn't the folk song I remembered but something
slow called "In My Room." I seemed to remember
some surfer-types singing it and it had sounded pretty
lame. But Kathy had stolen it and made it into some
kind of hymn to privacy. And why not a hymn? All us
good little Catholic girls sang hymns best.

The song ended and I was captivated all over again. I didn't want anything to break the silence that fell after that last pure note, I wanted to listen to it echo in my mind, but Kathy's father suddenly barged in without knocking. I thought he was going to tell me I was trash and throw me out. Instead, he started singing, too.

Shock woke me up. But Kathy's father was still singing, and I realized I was hearing the radio. I could feel my emotions going up and down, like a flock of seagulls riding on waves. I mean, I was *really* glad Kathy's father wasn't singing *or* throwing me out, but I was really sorry the Kathy version of "In My Room" wasn't available.

Then I found out I was wrong, and I didn't know *how* I felt.

I wish you still knew what happened after that—it would make all of this so simple. But I've resigned myself to the fact that no one remembers The Voice except me.

That was what they called her—*Billboard, Variety, Hit Parade,* Dick-for-chrissakes-Clark. George Martin, too; he'd been trying to get some British group with funny haircuts to smooth out their sound, get respectable. When he heard The Voice, he dropped them and hopped a jet for America. He tracked her down in L.A. and spent three months wooing her with promises of all kinds.

I could have told him she'd have been a tough nut to crack. I giggled whenever I thought of some high-powered music promoter or manager or whatever they were coming to me for advice on how to reach The Voice. I'd have told them just not to bother. The Voice couldn't be bought, wasn't for sale.

I didn't really expect her to think of me, either. She'd run away from all of it years ago, me included.

I didn't know *why* it included me; I didn't want to know, either. I was afraid I'd find out that her father had finally brainwashed her into believing I was the trash he said I was. Instead, I went on pretending that she was sending me messages in the music, messages of encouragement. I hung on to the music and hung on to her.

And what the hell—the miracle came to pass, and I got my ticket *out*. It was labeled *Full Scholarship, State University*. One way only, and that was all right with me.

That was the time that I was really tempted to try to get in touch with her, to show her that I'd done it after all, the way she had always believed I would. I thought maybe she really might want me to get in touch with her now. She may have been The Voice to the world, but I was the one who had heard The Voice first. Before she had sung for anyone else, she had sung for *me*.

I wish you all remembered her world tour. I was at the State University then, majoring in parties and becoming radicalized, when I found out she was going to play that blot on the New England escutcheon we had both escaped. I'd go see her in both places, I decided. I was still going back to see my mother once in a while; I could make an extra trip for Kathy.

Eddie Gibbs was long gone, as far as I knew. He'd joined the army right after graduation and been shipped off to somewhere in southeast Asia. Too bad, I thought, he'd never get a chance to see what he'd missed.

So I went. She was as thin as ever, maybe even a little thinner. Her hair had grown out long, down past her shoulders. Sometimes, when she moved her head in a certain way, it reminded me of a nun's veil; I wondered how she was living and with who, if anyone.

I wondered through her rendition of "Tobacco Road," and then was startled to hear my name mentioned.

"This next song I also stole, from four good kids who could probably have a hit single with it, and maybe they will. But not till I'm done with it. This is for my friend who always said she was getting *out*. I hope she got out."

A wave of laughter swept through the audience—I swear, she could have stood up there and castigated everyone and they would all still have loved her. She waited a beat and then launched into "I'm Not There."

> No one told you about me
> The way I cried . . .
> Nobody told you about me
> How many people cried . . .
> . . . don't bother trying to find me
> I'm not there . . .

Very spooky song, and not in a good way. If there was such a thing as being allergic to a song, I was allergic to that one. I couldn't stand to listen to it, watching her move back and forth across the stage, looking carefully at all the upturned faces.

I knew she was searching for *me*, and, suddenly, I didn't want her to find me. During the break, I pushed through all the people milling around and got outside none too soon. My stomach had been turning over and over. Much to the disapproval of some of the well-muscled group in T-shirts that proclaimed *Security* front and back, I puked into a garbage can just outside the hall and then went back to my mother's. I figured that would be the end of it, but I was wrong. Again.

*   *   *

"It took a while to find you," she said on the telephone. Her speaking voice, as well as The Voice, sounded just the way I remembered, full and textured.

"What do you want?" I asked her. "I mean, you seem to have everything."

"I'd give it all up just to get some peace of mind." I thought that was a pretty weird thing to say. I couldn't think of how to respond to her. "There aren't any easy answers," she added, as if she had read my mind. "I'm just letting you know how I feel."

I switched the receiver to my other ear. "And how *do* you feel?"

"Did you stay long enough to hear "I'm Not There?" she asked suddenly. "That's the song I stole. That's what they call it when you take a song some-one else wrote and change it to fit your own prefer-ence. Did you like it?"

"It was strange," I said.

"But did you *like* it?" There was such an urgent note in her voice, I felt I had to be completely honest.

"No."

She gave a short laugh. "No. You wouldn't. Because you *are* there, aren't you?"

"Yeah. I'm here." I paused. "You're the one who left."

"No," she said patiently, "I wasn't there to begin with. I was never there. Because no one told you about me."

"Don't," I said.

"Don't what—tell you?"

"You're not telling me anything, you're just spook-ing me. I was hanging on because you were supposed to be there to hang on with me. You believed—"

"No, *you* believed," she said snappishly.

"And *you* let me."

There was a long pause. "Yes," she said at last. "I suppose I did." She paused again. "Is there anything—

has there ever been anything—that you'd give it all up for?"

I laughed. "What have *I* ever had to give up?"

"Everything."

I laughed some more. "'Everything.' Jesus, Kathy, I think you're getting *your* 'everything' confused with *my* 'everything.' In case you hadn't noticed, you've got a hell of a lot more in your 'everything' than I do in mine."

"It wasn't always that way," she said gravely. I squirmed a little because I had just been thinking something along the same lines.

"No, but it sure is now, isn't it?" I sighed. "What did you call for, Kathy? And how did you know to call me here?"

"I was hoping I'd find you."

"You were hoping I'd still be living here?"

"No. That you'd come back here for the concert."

I was annoyed with myself for being so predictable. "Okay. So *why* did you call?"

"I wanted to ask you if you thought there was anything in this life that you'd give up everything for?"

I sighed. "Don't tell me—you're top of the charts and suddenly you think you have a calling to become a nun."

"No."

"Then what?"

"Answer the question."

"I can't," I said, annoyed. "It's *your* question, not mine. I don't know what you're talking about."

Another one of those pauses. I couldn't even hear her breathe. "You're right. I can't ask you a question I'm supposed to answer. So let me ask you this: Do you think you could ever forgive me?"

I hadn't expected that one at all. "For what? For leaving me to get it all figured out on my own? Build my own life?"

"Among . . . other things," she said, a bit hesitant.

"Yeah, sure. What the hell. Forgiveness is one of the cornerstones of the Church we grew up in. And you can take the girl out of the Church, but you can't take the Church out of the girl, right?"

Kathy didn't laugh. "Oh, you'd be surprised what you can do if you want to badly enough."

"I would?"

"You will." Dead line. It was the last thing she ever said to me. In *that* life.

"I'm Not There" took off like an epidemic. It was really like that. People got infected with it. I didn't understand it, it was the world's biggest downer, and yet it seemed like you couldn't put on a radio without hearing it five times an hour. The world tour kept adding shows and dates, and it looked like she planned to spend the rest of her life touring and singing "I'm Not There." Rock groups were fighting each other to open for her, and she couldn't walk down a street in any city or town without getting mobbed.

Still, the news about her was either very sparse or very controlled. What interviews she gave were enigmatic at best, and made her sound like a weirdo at worst. Which I guess she was, thanks to her parents.

I thought about them a lot, wondered if they were touched by Kathy's good fortune. The house always looked the same on my visits back to Blight City, and there was never anything about her parents or her hometown in the news about her. As if she had x-ed it all out of her life and reinvented herself. She wouldn't have been the first.

Ultimately, I couldn't blame her. Some impulse made me drop into the chapel on campus and light a candle for both Kathy and me. *Peace between us,* I thought. Or maybe prayed is a better word for it. I hoped that when she called again—if she ever did—we'd be friends.

My clock radio woke me the next morning with the news of her suicide.

There was the usual controversy, lots of editorials about how fame, success, and money couldn't buy happiness. Crowds holding vigils outside the concert hall where she was to have performed that night, prayer services, tributes by various of the rock aristocracy.

I spent that day in a state of shock. Without thinking about it, I threw some clothes and books in a bag, went down to the bus station, and bought a ticket home. I was too much of a zombie to cope with anything more demanding than a bus. I couldn't even register the passage of time—I got on the bus, then I got off the bus. Then I walked one step after another through a darkness until I saw the lights in the windows and I knew I was at the house.

Kathy's mother answered the door. She only looked at me and then turned away, disappearing into the kitchen. Barbara and Sarah were sitting on the couch in the living room. All these years and it was the same couch. Sarah looked as if someone had been threatening her with a beating; she was all but cowering while Barbara sat holding both her hands. Barbara was bigger than she'd been the last time I'd seen her, not fat, just husky, like an athlete.

Barbara and I gazed at each other for a long moment. Then she flicked a glance at the staircase leading to the second floor. I nodded and went up.

Her father was in her room, sitting on her bed with his hands on his knees. "What do *you* want?" he said.

The room was just as it had been back when she had sung for me, a thousand years ago in this empty house. I went over to her desk and put on her radio.

" . . . vigil in London at the Odeon, as well as in

cities across America," a disc jockey was saying
solemnly. "At a candlelight service in Manhattan,
protest singer Bob Dylan performed a new song he
called 'Sad-Eyed Lady of the Lowlands,' which he says
he wrote specifically for—"

Kathy's father was at the desk so quickly I
flinched. He snapped the radio off. "*Lady,*" he sneered.
"She was no *lady*. She was just another teenaged
whore with hot pants. Like *you*. She took off because
what she was getting here wasn't enough for her, she
had to have them by the dozens—"

I backed away from him, looking around for something to defend myself with, in case he got violent.

"I knew *you* would start bringing them around
here for her. I know your kind, I *know*."

Even if there had been anything vaguely like a
weapon handy, I don't think I'd have known how to
use it. I felt as if I were shrinking in the face of this creature passing for human. I turned and ran for the door.

He caught the back of my collar just as I put my
hand on the doorknob. The neck of my shirt pressed
into my windpipe, choking me, but I managed to get
the door open. He was trying to reel me in, but I
clamped both hands on either side of the doorway,
braced myself, and opened my mouth to scream.

Kathy was standing in the hallway, near the top of
the stairs. The sight startled me so much, I froze.
Fortunately, Kathy's father saw her too, and stopped
struggling with me as well.

"*You!*" he growled at her, and shoved me aside. I
fell to the floor and scrambled up again quickly,
watching him advance on Kathy. She didn't yell or
scream or try to run away—she just stood there and
let him come at her.

For a few moments, his body hid her completely,
and I screamed as hard and as loud as I could, as if I
were trying to stun him with sound. "*Stop!*"

Kathy's father turned on me, letting her go. She sagged against the banister and I saw that it wasn't Kathy as I had last seen her, but Kathy at fourteen. "Lesbo!" he snarled at me. "Is that it, you're teaching her your dirty little girlie tricks, is that it, lesbo?"

Panic was like an electric shock. I couldn't make myself do anything except point at Kathy, fourteen-year-old Kathy on the stairs, watching her father and me with the strangest expression of calm detachment. Was she really there, was she—?

His hand went completely around my bicep, because suddenly I was only fourteen myself. He dragged me toward the stairs as if I weighed nothing. I tried to pull away and I thought my arm would tear out of the socket. He was cursing and ranting about dirty little girls and pulling me to the head of the stairs. I clung to the banister just next to where Kathy was standing and looked up at her. She seemed about to say something, but then I felt my feet become entangled with her father's legs. There wasn't even time to yell *Ouch*—we were on our way down the stairs together the quick way.

I was pretty sure we hit every step, separately and together. At each impact, I could hear a collection of different noises, some of it music, some of it just voices, and sometimes just *her* voice. *The* Voice.

No one told you about me
Though they all knew . . .

Sometime later, I had stopped falling down the stairs, but a big hole must have opened up in the floor because I was still falling, but through empty space, unimpeded even by the vision of Kathy leaning over me and explaining, " . . . *my eyes are clear and bright, but I'm not there.*"

And she wasn't, and neither was I.

*   *   *

I woke up here, where you all believe I've been waking up every day for ten of the last thirty years. I'm not disoriented, I can remember what you remember of this world. But I also remember *that* world. I know there's no going back to the way things were.

The funny thing is, if she'd asked me, if Kathy had *just asked me,* I might have done it for her anyway. Except I'd have tried a lot harder to fix it so that we could both come out with something better for each of us.

If she had told me, back then, I would have helped her. I wouldn't have just looked the other way, I'd have believed her. After all, she believed in *me*.

But for some reason, she couldn't believe in herself, I guess. Which was why she needed me. She didn't believe she could get *out*, you see. She didn't believe there would ever be an escape for her, so she took *mine*. My escape, and my belief. And it worked.

It took some big sacrifices on her part, though. She couldn't just *take*, she had to give up something in return. That was the suicide after the day "I'm Not There" hit number one, the sacrifice she had to offer to get my faith for her own.

She gave up The Voice, too. Maybe someone else wouldn't have, but then, someone else didn't have to endure her father's weight on top of her in her own room, crushing her spirit. But she had to give up *all* of The Voice. That was the big price, the biggest price of all, really.

So it turned out that I was *there* that afternoon when we were both fourteen, and her father came home to find that she had disobeyed his rules about no visitors, and I went tumbling down the stairs with him. You see that sort of thing in the movies and it never occurs to you that it's the sort of thing you can break your back doing. Of course, it could have been worse—Kathy's father might have lived.

The parish was very good to me and my mother, but even a church collection plate isn't a bottomless well. My mother's insurance should keep me in this place for maybe another five years. After that—well, I don't know. Maybe I'll be getting *out.* You know? That's a joke, you can laugh.

I keep hoping that Kathy will suddenly reappear, come back from wherever she went—someone told me she became a nurse, but out of state somewhere. I keep hoping she'll come back and thank me. I keep hoping, and hoping, and hoping. I don't believe I'll ever be getting out of this chair, but I've been trying to make myself believe that Kathy's coming back.

I can *see* her, too. I can see just how she'll look, and suddenly I'll get this feeling that if I turn around real quick—

But of course, she's still not there.

THE AFFAIR

Robert Silverberg

Robert Silverberg is one of the most famous SF writers of modern times, with dozens of novels, anthologies, and collections to his credit. Silverberg has won five Nebula Awards and four Hugo Awards. His novels include *Dying Inside, Lord Valentine's Castle, The Book of Skulls, Downward to the Earth, Tower of Glass, The World Inside, Born with the Dead, Shadrack in the Furnace, Tom O' Bedlam, Star of Gypsies,* and *At Winter's End.* His collections include *Unfamiliar Territory, Capricorn Games, Majipoor Chronicles, The Best of Robert Silverberg, At the Conglomeroid Cocktail Party,* and *Beyond the Safe Zone.* His most recent books are two novel-length expansions of famous Isaac Asimov stories, *Nightfall* and *The Ugly Little Boy,* the solo novels *The Face of the Waters* and *Hot Sky at Midnight,* and a massive retrospective collection *The Collected Stories of Robert Silverberg, Volume One: Secret Sharers.* For many years he edited the prestigious anthology series *New Dimensions,* and recently, along with his wife, writer Karen Haber, took over the editing of the *Universe* anthology series. He lives in Oakland, California.

Absence makes the heart grow fonder? Well . . . perhaps. But in the sly and elegant story that follows, Silverberg portrays an unearthly love affair for which absence is an absolute *necessity.* . . .

The Affair

He found her by accident, the way it usually happens, after he had more or less given up searching. For years, he had been sending out impulses like messages in bottles; random waves of telepathic energy; *hello, hello, hello,* one forlorn SOS after another from the desert isle of the soul on which he was a castaway. Occasionally, messages came back; but all they amounted to was lunacy, strident nonsense, static, spiritual noise, gabble up and down the mind band. There were, he knew, a good many like him out there—a boy in Topeka, an old woman in Buenos Aires, another one in Fort Lauderdale, someone of indeterminate sex in Manitoba and plenty of others, each alone, each lonely. He fell into short-lived contact with them, because they were, after all, people of his special kind. But they tended to be cranky, warped, weird, often simply crazy, all of them deformed by their bizarre gift, and they could not give him what he wanted, which was communion, harmony, the marriage of true minds. Then one Thursday afternoon, when he was absentmindedly broadcasting his identity wave—not in any way purposefully trolling the seas of perception but only humming, so to speak—he felt a sudden startling *click* as of perfectly machined parts locking into place. Out of the grayness in his mind an unmistakably warm, eager image blossomed, a dazzling giant yellow flower unfolding on the limb of a gnarled, spiny cactus, and the image translated itself instantly into *Hi, there. Where've you been all my life?*

He hesitated to send an answering signal, because he knew that he had found what he was looking for and he was aware of how much of a threat that was to the fabric of the life he had constructed for himself. He was thirty-seven years old, stable, settled. He had a wife who tried her best to be wonderful for him, never knowing quite what it was that she lacked but seeking to compensate for it anyway, and two small, pleasing children, who had not inherited his abnormality, and a comfortable house in the hills east of San Francisco and a comfortable job as an analyst for one of the big brokerage houses. It was not the life he had imagined in his old romantic fantasies, but it was not a bad life, either, and it was *his* life, familiar and in its way rewarding; and he knew he was about to rip an irreparable hole in it. So he hesitated. And then he transmitted an image as vivid as the one he had received: a solitary white gull soaring in enormous sweeps over the broad blue breast of the Pacific.

The reply came at once: the same gull, joined by a second one that swooped out of a cloudless sky and flew tirelessly at its side. He knew that if he responded to that, there could be no turning back; but that was all right. With uncharacteristic recklessness, he switched to the verbal mode.

—OK. Who are you?

—Laurel Hammett. I'm in Phoenix. I read you clearly. This is better than the telephone.

—Cheaper, too. Chris Maitland. San Francisco.

—That's far enough away, I guess.

He didn't understand, then, what she meant by that. But he let the point pass.

—You're the first one I've found who sends images, Laurel.

—I found one once, eight years ago, in Boston.
But he was crazy. Most of us are crazy, Chris.
—I'm not crazy.
—Oh, I know! Oh, God, I know!

So that was the beginning. He got very little work done
that afternoon. He was supposed to be preparing a
report on oil-royalty trusts, and after fifteen minutes of
zinging interchanges with her, he actually did beg off;
she broke contact with a dazzling series of visuals,
many of them cryptic, snowflakes and geometrical dia-
grams and fields of blazing red poppies. Depletion per-
centages and windfall-profits tax recapture were
impossible to deal with while those brilliant pictures
burned in his mind. Although he had promised not to
reach toward her again until tomorrow—judicious self-
denial, she observed, is the fuel of love—he finally did
send out a flicker of abashed energy and drew from her
a mingling of irritation and delight. For five minutes,
they told each other it was best to go slow, to let it
develop gradually, and again they vowed to keep mental silence until the next day. But when he was crossing the Bay Bridge a couple of hours later, heading for
home, she tickled him suddenly with a quick flash of
her presence and gave him a wondrous view of the
Arizona sunset, harsh chocolate brown hills under a
purple-and-gold sky. That evening, he felt shamefully
and transparently adulterous, as if he had come home
flushed and rumpled, with lipstick on his shirt. He pretended to be edgy and wearied by some fictitious
episode of office politics and helped himself to two
drinks before dinner and was more than usually curious about the details of his wife's day—the little suburban crises, the small challenges, the tiny triumphs.
Jan was playful, amiable, almost kittenish. That told
him she had not seen through him to the betrayal

within, however blatant it seemed to him. She was no actress; there was nothing devious about her.

The transformation of their marriage that had taken place that afternoon saddened him, yet not deeply, because it was an inevitable one. He and Jan were not really of the same species. He had loved her as well and as honestly as was possible for him, but what he had really wanted was someone of his kind, with whom he could join mind and soul as well as body, and it was only because he had not been able to find her that he had settled for Jan. And now he had found her. Where that would lead, and what it meant for Jan and him, he had no idea yet. Possibly he would be able to go on sharing with her the part of his life that they were able to share, while secretly he got from the other woman those things that Jan had never been able to give him; possibly. When they went to bed, he turned to her with abrupt, passionate ferocity, as he had not for a long time, but even so, he could not help wondering what Laurel was doing now, in her bed a thousand miles to the east, and with whom.

During the morning commute, Laurel came to him with stunning images of desert landscapes, eroded geological strata, mysterious dark mesas, distant flame-colored sandstone walls. He sent her Pacific surf, cypresses bending to the wind, tide pools swarming with anemones and red starfish. Then, timidly, he sent her a kiss and had one from her in return; and then, as he was crossing the toll plaza of the bridge, she shifted to words.

—What do you do?

—Securities analyst. I read reports and make forecasts.

—Sounds terribly dull. Is it?

—If it is, I don't let myself notice. It's okay work. What about you?

—I'm a potter. I'm a very good one. You'd like my stuff.

—Where can I see it?

—There's a gallery in Santa Fe. And one in Tucson. And, of course, Phoenix. But you mustn't come to Phoenix.

—Are you married?

There was a pause.

—Yes. But that isn't why you mustn't come here.

—I'm married, too.

—I thought you were. You feel like a married sort of man.

—Oh? I do?

—That isn't an insult. You have a very stable vibe, do you know what I mean?

—I think so. Do you have children?

—No. Do you?

—Two. Little girls. How long have you been married, Laurel?

—Six years.

—Nine.

—We must be about the same age.

—I'm thirty-seven.

—I'm thirty-four.

—Close enough. Do you want to know my sign?

—Not really.

She laughed and sent him a complex, awesome image: the entire wheel of the zodiac, which flowered into the shape of the Aztec calendar stone, which became the glowing rose window of a Gothic cathedral. An undercurrent of warmth and love and amusement rode with it. Then she was gone, leaving him on the bridge in a silence so sharp it rang like iron.

He did not reach toward her but drove on into the city in a mellow haze, wondering what she looked like. Her mental "voice" sounded to him like that of a tall, clear-eyed, straight-backed woman with long brown hair, but he knew better than to put much faith in that; he had played the same game with people's telephone voices and he had always been wrong. For all he knew, Laurel was squat and greasy. He doubted that; he saw no way that she could be ugly. But why, then, was she so determined not to have him come to Phoenix? Perhaps she was an invalid; perhaps she was painfully shy; perhaps she feared the intrusion of any sort of reality into their long-distance romance.

At lunchtime, he tuned himself to her wavelength and sent her an image of the first page of the report he had written last week on Exxon. She replied with a glimpse of a tall, olive-hued porcelain jar of a form both elegant and sturdy. Her work in exchange for his; he liked that. Everything was going to be perfect.

A week later, he went out to Salt Lake City for a couple of days to do some field research on a mining company headquartered there. He took an early-morning flight, had lunch with three earnest young Mormon executives overflowing with joy at the bounty of God as manifested by the mineral wealth of the Overthrust Belt in Wyoming, spent the afternoon leafing through geologists' survey sheets, and had dinner alone at his hotel. Afterward, he put in his obligatory call to Jan, worked up his notes of the day's conferences, and watched TV for an hour, hoping it would make him drowsy. Maitland didn't mind these business trips, but he slept badly when he slept alone, and any sort of time-zone change, even a trifling one like this, disrupted his internal clock. He was still wide-awake when he got into bed about eleven.

He thought of Laurel. He felt very near to her, out here in this spacious, mountain-ringed city with the wide, bland streets. Probably Salt Lake City was not significantly closer to Phoenix than San Francisco was, but he regarded both Utah and Arizona as the true wild West, while his own suburban and manicured part of California, paradoxically, did not seem western to him at all. Somewhere due south of here, just on the far side of all these cliffs and canyons, was the unknown woman he loved.

As though on cue, she was in his mind:

—Lonely?

—You bet.

—I've been thinking of you all day. Poor Chris, sitting around with those businessmen, talking all that depletion gibberish.

—I'm a businessman, too.

—You're different. You're a businessman outside and a freak inside.

—Don't say that.

—It's what we are, Chris. Face it. Flukes, anomalies, sports, changelings—

—Please stop, Laurel. Please.

—I'm sorry.

A silence. He thought she was gone, taking flight at his rebuke. But then:

—Are you *very* lonely?

—Very. Dull, empty city; dull, empty bed.

—*You're* in it.

—But you aren't.

—Is that what you want? Right now?

—I wish we could, Laurel.

—Let's try this.

He felt a sudden astounding intensifying of her mental signal, as if she had leaped the hundreds of miles and lay curled against him here. There was a sense of physical proximity, of warmth, even the light perfume of her skin, and into his mind swept an image so acutely clear that it eclipsed for him the drab realities of his room: the shore of a tropical ocean, fine pink sand, gentle pale green water, a dense line of heavy-crowned palms.

—Go on, Chris. Into the water.

He waded into the calm wavelets until the delicate sandy bottom was far below his dangling feet and he floated effortlessly in an all-encompassing warmth, in an amniotic bath of placid, soothing fluid. Placid but not motionless, for he felt, as he drifted, tiny convulsive quivers about him, an electric oceanic caress, pulsations of the water against his bare skin, intimate, tender, searching. He began to tingle. As he moved farther out from shore, so far now that the land was gone and the world was all warm water to the horizon, the pressure of those rhythmic pulsations became more forceful, deeply pleasurable: The ocean was a giant hand lightly squeezing him. He trembled and made soft sighing sounds that grew steadily more vehement and closed his eyes and let ecstasy overwhelm him in the ocean's benignly insistent grip. Then he grunted and his heart thumped and his body went rigid and then lax, and moments later he sat up, blinking, astonished, eerily tranquil.

—I didn't think anything like that was possible.

—For us, anything's possible. Even sex across seven hundred miles. I wasn't sure it would work, but I guess it did, didn't it? Did you like it?

—Do you need an answer, Laurel?

—I feel so happy.

—How did you do it? What was the trick?

—No trick. Just the usual trick, Chris, a little more intense than usual. I hated the idea that you were all alone, horny, unable to sleep.

—It was absolutely marvelous.

—And now we're lovers. Even though we've never met.

—No. Not altogether lovers, not yet. Let me try to do it to you, Laurel. It's only fair.

—Later, okay? Not now.

—I want to.

—It takes a lot of energy. You ought to get some sleep, and I can wait. Just lie there and glow and don't worry about me. You can try it with me another time.

—An hour? Two hours?

—Whenever you want. But not now. Rest now. Enjoy. Good night, love.

—Good night, Laurel.

He was alone. He lay staring up into the darkness, stunned. He had been unfaithful to Jan three times before, not bad for nine years, and always the same innocuous pattern: a business trip far from home, a couple of solitary nights, then an official dinner with some woman executive, too many drinks, the usual half-serious banter turning serious, a blurry one-night stand, remorse in the morning, and never any follow-up. Meaningless, fragmentary stuff. But this—this long-distance event with a woman he had never even seen—seemed infinitely more explosive. For he had the power and Jan did not and Laurel did; and Jan's mind was closed to his and his to hers, and they could only stagger around blindly trying to find each other, while he and Laurel could unite at will in a communion whose richness was unknown to ordinary humans. He wondered if he could go on living with Jan at all now. He felt no less love for her than before, and powerful ties of affection and sharing held him to her; but yet—even so—

In guilt and confusion, Maitland drifted off into sleep. It was still dark when he woke—3:13 A.M., said the clock on the dresser—and he felt different guilt, different confusion, for it was of Laurel now that he thought. He had taken pleasure from her, and then he had collapsed into postorgasmic stupor. Never mind that she had told him to do just that. He felt, and always had, a peculiarly puritanical obligation to give pleasure for pleasure, and unpaid debts were troublesome to him. Taking a deep breath, he sent strands of consciousness through the night toward the south, over the fire-hued mountains of central Utah, over the silent splendor of the Grand Canyon, down past the palm trees into torrid Phoenix, and touched Laurel's warm, sleepy mind.

—Hnhh.

—It's me. I want to, now.

—All right. Yes.

The image she had chosen was a warm sea, the great mother, the all-encompassing womb. He, reaching unhesitatingly for a male equivalent, sent her a vision of himself coming forth on a hot, dry summer day into a quiet landscape of grassy hills as round as tawny breasts. Cradled in his arms he held her gleaming porcelain jar, the one she had shown him. He bent, tipping it, pouring forth from it an enormous snake, long and powerful but not in any way frightening, that flowed like a dark rivulet across the land, seeking her, finding, gliding up across her thighs, her belly. Too obvious? Too coarsely phallic? He wavered for a moment but only a moment, for he heard her moan and whimper, and she reached with her mind for the serpent as it seemed he was withdrawing it; he drove back his qualms and gave her all the energy at his command, seizing the initiative as he sensed her complete surrender. Her signal shivered and lost focus. Her breathing grew ragged and hoarse, and then into his mind came a quick, surprising sound, a strange, low growling that terminated in a swift, sharp gasp.

—Oh, love. Oh. Oh. Thank you.

—It wasn't scary?

—Scare me like that as often as you want, Chris.

He smiled across the darkness of the miles. All was well. A fair exchange: symbol for symbol, metaphor for metaphor, delight for delight.

—Sleep well, Laurel.

—You too, love. Mmm.

*   *   *

This time, Jan knew that something had happened while he was away. He saw it on her face, which meant that she saw it on his; but she voiced no suspicions, and when they made love the first night of his return, it was as good as ever. Was it possible, he wondered, to be bigamous, to take part with Laurel in a literally superhuman oneness while remaining Jan's devoted husband and companion? He would, at any rate, try. Laurel had shared his soul as no one ever had and Jan never could, yet she was a phantom, faceless, remote, scarcely real; and Jan, cut off from him as most humans are from all others, nevertheless was his wife, his partner, his bedmate, the mother of his children. He would try.

So he took the office gossip home to her as always and went out with her twice a week to the restaurants they loved and sat beside her at night watching cassettes of operas and movies and Shakespeare, and on weekends they did their weekend things, boating on the bay and tennis and picnics in the park and dinner with their friends, and everything was fine. Everything was very fine. And yet he managed to do the other thing, too, as often as he could. Just as he had successfully hidden from Jan the enigmatic secret mechanism within his mind that he did not dare reveal to anyone not of his sort, so, too, now did he hide the second marriage, rich and strange, that that mechanism had brought him.

His lovemaking with Laurel had to be furtive, of course, a thing of stolen moments. She could hardly draw him into that warm, voluptuous ocean while he lay beside Jan. But there were the business trips—he was careful not to increase their frequency, which would have been suspicious, but she came to him every night while he was away—and there was the occasional Saturday afternoon when he lay drowsing in the sun of the garden and found that whispering transparent surf beckoning to him, and once she enlivened a lunchtime for him on a working day. He roused the snake within his soul as often as he dared; and nearly always she accepted it, though there were times when she told him no, not now, the moment was wrong. They had elaborate signals to indicate a clear coast. And for the ordinary conversation of the day, there were no limits; they popped into each other's consciousness a thousand times a day, quick, flickering interchanges, a joke, a bit of news, a job triumphantly accomplished, an image of beauty too potent to withhold. As he was crossing the bridge, entering his office, reaching for the telephone, unfolding a napkin—suddenly, there she was, often for the briefest flare of contact, a tag touch and gone. He loved that. He loved her. It was a marriage.

He snooped in Mountain Bell directories at the library and found her telephone number, which he hardly needed, and her address, which at least confirmed that she really did exist in tangible, actual Phoenix. He manufactured a trip to Albuquerque to appraise the earnings prospects of a small electronics company and slipped off up the freeway to Santa Fe to visit the gallery that showed her pottery: eight or ten superb pieces, sleek, wondrously skilled. He bought one of the smaller ones. "You don't have any information about the artist, do you?" he asked the proprietor, trying to be casual, heart pounding, hoping to be shown a photograph.

The proprietor thought there might be a press release in the files and rummaged for it. "She lives down Phoenix way," she said. "Comes up here once or twice a year with her new work. I think it's museum quality, don't you?" But she could not find the press release. When Laurel flashed into his mind that night back in Albuquerque, he did not tell her he owned one of her jars or that he had been researching her. But he wondered desperately what she looked like. He played with the idea of visiting Phoenix and somehow getting to meet her without telling her who he was. So long as he kept his mind sheathed, she would never know, he thought. But it seemed sneaky and treacherous; and it might be dangerous, too. She had told him often enough not to come to her city.

In the fourth month of their relationship, he could no longer control his curiosity. She sent him a view of her studio, amazingly neat, the clay, the wheels, the kiln, the little bowls of pigment and glaze all fastidiously in their proper places.

—You left one thing out, Laurel.

—What's that?

—The potter herself. You didn't show me her.

—Oh, Chris.

—What's the matter? Aren't you ever curious about what I look like? We've been all over each other's minds and bodies for months and I still don't have any idea what you look like. That's absurd.

—It's so much more abstract and pure this way.

—Wonderful. Abstract love! I want to see you.

—I have to confess. I want to see you, too.

—Here, then. Now.

He sent her, before she could demur, a mental snapshot of his face, trying not to retouch and enhance it. The nose a trifle too long, the cleft chin absurdly Hollywood, the dark hair thinning a bit at the part line. Not a perfect face but good enough, pleasant, honest, nothing to apologize for, he thought. It brought silence.

—Well? Am I remotely what you expected?

—Exactly, Chris. Steady-looking, strong, decent—
no surprise at all. I like your face. I'm very pleased.

—Your turn.

—You'll promise not to be disappointed?

—Stop being silly.

—All right.

She flared in his mind, not just her face but all of
her, long-legged, broad-shouldered, a woman of physical presence and strength, with straightforward open
features, wide-set brown eyes, a good smile, a blunt
nose, conspicuous cheekbones. She was not far from
the woman he had imagined, and one aspect, the
dark, thick, straight hair falling past her shoulders,
was amazingly as he had thought.

—You're beautiful.

—No, not really. But I'm okay.

—Are you an Indian?

—I must have sent you a good picture, then. I'm
half. My mother was Navaho.

—You learned your pottery from her?

—No, dopey. Navahos make rugs. Pueblos make
pottery. I learned mine in New York, Greenwich
Village. I studied with Hideki Shinoda.

—Doesn't sound Pueblo.

—Isn't. Little Japanese man with marvelous hands.

—I'm glad we did this, Laurel.

—So am I.

But seeing her in the eye of his mind, while gratifying one curiosity, had only intensified another. He
wanted to meet her. He wanted to touch her. He
wanted to hold her.

Snake. Ocean. They were practiced lovers now, a year
of constant mental communion behind them. She
came to him as a starfish, thousands of tiny suction-
cup feet and a startling devouring mouth, and at

another time as a moist, voluptuous mass of warm, smooth white clay and as a whirlpool and as a great, coy, lighthearted amoeba; and he manifested himself to her as a flash flood roaring down a red-rock canyon and as a glistening vine coiling through a tropic night and as a spaceship plunging in eternal free fall between worlds. All of these were effective, for they needed only to touch each other with their minds to bring pleasure; and each new access of ingenuity brought an abstract pleasure of its own. But even so, they tended often to revert to the original modes, snake and ocean, ocean and snake, the way one might return to a familiar and modest hotel where one had spent a joyous weekend at the beginning of an affair, and somehow it was always best that way.

Their skill at pleasuring each other struck them both as extraordinary. They liked to tell each other that the kind of lovemaking they had invented and of which they were perhaps the sole practitioners in the history of humanity was infinitely superior to the old-fashioned type, which was so blatant, so obvious, so coarse, so messy. Even so, even as he said things like that, he knew he was lying. He wanted her skin against his skin, her breath on his breath.

She was no longer so coy about her life outside their relationship. Maitland knew now that her husband was an artist from Chicago, not very successful, a little envious of her career. She showed him some of his work, unremarkable abstract-expressionist stuff. Maitland was jealous of the fact that this man—Tim, his name was—shared her bed and enjoyed her proximity, but he realized that he had no jealousy of the marriage itself. It was all right that she was married. Maitland had no wish to live with her. He wanted to go on living with Jan, to play tennis with her and go to restaurants with her and even to make love with her; what he wanted from Laurel was just what he was getting from her, that cool, amused, intelligent voice in his mind, and now and then the strange ecstasy that her playful spirit was able to kindle in his loins across such great distances. That much was true. Yet also he wanted to be her lover in the old, blatant, obvious, coarse, messy way, at least once, once at least. Because he knew it was a perilous subject, he stayed away from it as long as he could, but at last it broke into the open one night in Seattle, late, after the snake had returned to its jar and the lapping waves had retreated and he lay sweaty and alone in his hotel-room bed.

—When are we finally going to meet?

—Please, Chris.

—I think it's time to discuss it. You told me a couple of times, early on, that I must never come to Phoenix. Okay. But couldn't we get together somewhere else? Tucson, San Diego, the Grand Canyon?

—It isn't the place that matters.

—What is it, then?

—Being close. Being too close.

—I don't understand. We're so close already.

—I mean physically close. Not emotionally, not even sexually. I just mean that if we came within close range of each other, we'd do bad things to each other.

—That's crazy, Laurel.

—Have you ever been close to another telepath? As close as ten feet, say?

—I don't think so.

—You'd know it if you had. When you and I talk long-distance, it's just like talking on the phone, right, plus pictures? We tell each other only what we want to tell each other, and nothing else gets through. It's not like that close up.

—Oh?

—There's a kind of radiation, an aura. We broadcast all sorts of stuff automatically. All that foul, stink-

ing, nasty cesspool stuff that's at the bottom of everybody's mind, the crazy prehistoric garbage that's in us.
It comes swarming out like a shriek.

—How do you know that?

—I've experienced it.

—Oh. Boston, years ago?

—Yes. Yes. I told you, I did this once before.

—But he was crazy, you said.

—In a way. But the craziness isn't what brought
the other stuff up. I felt it once another time, too, and
she wasn't crazy. It's unavoidable.

—I want to see you.

—Don't you think I want to see you, too, Chris?
But we can't risk it. Suppose we met and the garbage
got out and we hated each other ever afterward?

—We could control it.

—Maybe. Maybe not.

—Or else we could make allowances for it. Bring
ourselves to understand that this stuff, whatever it is
that you say is there, is normal, just the gunk of the
mind, nothing personal, nothing that we ought to
take seriously.

—I'm scared. Let's not try.

He let the issue drop. When it came up again, four
months later, it was Laurel who revived it. She had
been thinking about his idea of controlling the sinister
emanation, throttling it back, shielding each other.
Possibly it could be done. The temptation to meet him
in the flesh, she said, was overwhelming. Perhaps
they could get together and suppress all telepathic
contact, meet just like ordinary humans having a little
illicit rendezvous, keep their minds rigidly walled off
and that way at last consummate the intimacy that
had joined their souls for a year and a half.

—I'd love to, Laurel.

—But promise me this. Swear it to me. When we
do get together, if we can't hold back the bad stuff, if

we feel it coming out, that we go away from each other instantly. That we don't negotiate, we don't try to work it out, we don't look for angles—we just split, fast, if either of us says we have to. Swear?

—I swear.

He flew to Denver and spent a fidgety hour and a half having cocktails in the lounge at the Brown Palace Hotel. Her flight from Phoenix was supposed to have landed only half an hour after his, and he wondered if she had backed out at the last minute. He got up to call the airport when he saw her come in, unmistakably her, taller than he expected, a big, handsome woman in black jeans and a sheepskin wrap. There were flecks of melting snow in her hair.

He sensed an aura.

It wasn't loathsome, it wasn't hideous, but it was there, a kind of dull, whining, grinding thing, as of improperly oiled machinery in use three blocks away. Even as he detected it, he felt it diminish until it was barely perceptible. He struggled to rein in whatever output he might be giving off himself.

She saw him and came straight toward him, smiling nervously, cheeks rigid, eyes worried.

"Chris."

He took her hand in his. "You're cold, Laurel."

"It's snowing. That's why I'm late. I haven't seen snow in years."

"Can I get you a drink?"

"No. Yes. Yes, please. Scotch on the rocks."

"Are you picking up anything bad?"

"No," she said. "Not really. There was just a little twinge when I walked in—a kind of squeak in my mind."

"I felt it, too. But then it faded."

"I'm fighting to keep it damped down. I want this to work."

"So do I. We mustn't use the power at all today."

"We don't need to. The old snake can have the day off. Are you scared?"

"A little."

"Me, too." She gulped her drink. "Oh, Chris."

"Is it hard work, keeping the power damped down?"

"Yes. It really is."

"For me, too. But we have to."

"Yes," she said. "Do you have a room yet?"

He nodded.

"Let's go upstairs, then."

Like any unfaithful husband having his first rendezvous with a new lover, he walked stiffly and somberly through the lobby, convinced that everyone was staring at them. That was ridiculous, he knew; they were more truly married, in their way, than anybody else in Denver. But yet—but yet—

They were silent in the elevator. As they approached their floor, the aura of her burst forth again, briefly, a fast, sour vibration in his bones, and then it was gone altogether, shut off as though by a switch. He worked at holding his down, too. She smiled at him. He winked. "To the left," he said. They went into the room. Heavy snowflakes splashed against the window; the wide bed was turned down. She was trembling. "Come on," he said. "I love you. You know that. Everything's all right."

They kissed and undressed. Her body was lean, athletic, with small, high breasts, a flat belly, a dark appendectomy scar. He drew her toward the bed. It seemed strange, almost perverse, to be doing things in this antiquated fleshly way, no snake, no ocean, no meeting of the minds. He was afraid for a moment that in the excitement of their coupling, they would lose control of their mental barriers and let their inner selves come flooding out, fierce, intense, a contact too powerful to handle at such short range. But there was no loss of control. He kept the power locked behind the walls of his skull; she did the same; there were only the tiniest leakages of current. But there was no excitement, either, in their lovemaking. He ran his hands over her breasts and trapped her nipples between his fingers and gently parted her thighs with his knee and pressed himself against her as though he had not been with a woman in a year, but the excitement seemed to be all in his head, not in his nerve endings. Even when she ran her lips down his chest and belly and teased him for a moment and then took him fiercely and suddenly into her mouth, it was the *idea* that they were finally doing this, rather than what they were actually doing, that resonated within him. They sighed a little and moaned a little and finally he slipped into her, admiring the tightness of her and the rhythms of her hips and all that, but nevertheless, it was as though this had happened between them a thousand times before: He moved, she moved, they did all the standard things and traveled along to the standard result. Not enough was real between them; that was the trouble. He knew her better than he had ever known anyone, yet in some ways he knew her not at all, and that was what had spoiled things. That and holding so much in check. He wished he could look into her mind now. But that was forbidden and probably unwise, too; he guessed that she was annoyed with him for having insisted on this foolish and fore-doomed meeting, that she held him responsible for having spoiled things between them, and he did not want to see those thoughts in her mind.

When it was over, they whispered to each other and stroked each other and gave each other little nibbling kisses, and he pretended it had been marvelous, but his real impulse was to pull away and light a cigarette and stare out the window at the snow, and he wasn't even a smoker. It was simply the way he felt. It had been only a mechanical thing, only a hotel-room screw, not remotely anything like snake and ocean: a joining of flesh of the sort that a pair of rabbits might have accomplished, or a pair of apes, without content, without fire, without joy. He and she knew an ever so much better way of doing it.

He took care to hide his disappointment.

"I'm so glad I came here, Chris," she said, smiling, kissing him, taking care to hide her disappointment, too, he guessed. He knew that if he entered her mind, he would find it bleak and ashen. But, of course, he could not do that. "I wish I could stay the night," she said. "My plane's at nine. We could have dinner downstairs, though."

"Is it a terrible strain, keeping the power back?"

"It isn't easy."

"No. It isn't."

"I'm so glad we did this, Chris."

"Are you?"

"Yes. Yes. Of course."

They had an early dinner. The snow had stopped by the time he saw her to her cab. So: You fly up to Denver for a couple of hours of lust and steak, you fly back home, and that's that. He had a brandy in the lounge and went to his room. For a long while, he lay staring at the ceiling, sure that she would come to him with the ocean and make amends for the unsatisfactory thing they had done that afternoon. She did not. He wondered if he ought to send her the snake as she dozed on her plane and did not want to. He felt timid about any sort of contact with her now. It had all been a terrible mistake, he knew. Not because of that emanation from the dirty depths of the psyche that she had so feared but only because it had been so anticlimactic, so meaningless. He waited for a sending from her, some bright little flash out of Arizona. She must surely be home now. Nothing came. He went on waiting, not daring to reach toward her, and finally he fell asleep.

*   *   *

Jan said nothing to him about the Denver trip. He was moody and strange, but she let him be. When the silence out of Phoenix continued into the next day and the next, he grew even more grim and skulked about wrapped in black isolation. Gradually, it occurred to him that he was not going to hear from Laurel again, that they had broken something in that hotel room in Denver and that it was irreparable, and, oddly, the knowledge of that gave him some ease: If he did not expect to hear from her, he did not have to lament her silence. A week, two, three, and nothing. So it was over. That hollow little grunting hour had ruined it.

Somehow he picked up the rhythms of his life: work, home, wife, kids, friends, tennis, dinner. He did an extensive analysis of southwestern electric utilities that brought him a commendation from on high, and he felt only a mild twinge of anguish while doing his discussion of the prospects for Arizona Public Service as reflected in the municipal growth of the city of Phoenix. He missed the little tickle in his mind immensely, but he was encapsulating it, containing it, and after a fashion, he was healing.

One day a month and a half later, he found himself idly scanning the mind-noise band again, as he had not done for a long while, just to see who else was out there. He picked up the loony babble out of Fort Lauderdale and the epicene static from Manitoba, and then he encountered someone new, a bright, clear signal as intense as Laurel's, and for a dazzled instant a sudden fantasy of a new relationship blossomed in him, but then he heard the nonsense syllables, the slow, firm, strong-willed stream of gibberish. There were no replacements for Laurel.

Two months later, in Chicago, where he had been

sent to do a survey of natural-gas companies, he began talking to a youngish woman at the Art Institute, and by easy stages some chatter about Monet and Sisley turned into a dinner invitation and a night in his hotel room. That was all right. Certainly, it was simpler and easier and less depressing than Denver. But it was a bore, it was empty and foolish, and he regretted it deeply by breakfast time, even while he was taking down her number and promising to call the next time he was in the Midwest. Maitland saw the post-Laurel pattern of his life closing about him now: the Christmas bonus, the trip to Hawaii with Jan, braces for the kids, the new house five years from now, the occasional quickie romance in far-off hotel rooms. That was all right. That was the original bargain he had made, long ago, entering adult life: not much ecstasy, not much grief.

On the long flight home that day, he thought without rancor or distress about his year and a half with Laurel and told himself that the important thing was not that it had ended but that it had happened at all. He felt peaceful and accepting and was almost tempted to reach out to Laurel to thank her for her love and wish her well. But he was afraid—afraid that if he touched her mind in any way, she would pull away, timid, fearful of contact in the wake of that inexplicably sundering day in Denver. She was close by now, he knew, for the captain had just told them that they were passing over the Grand Canyon. Maitland did not lean to the window, as everyone else was doing, to look down. He sat back, eyes closed, tired, calm.

And felt warmth, heard the lapping of surf, saw in the center of his mind the vast ocean in which Laurel had so many times engulfed him. Really? Was it happening? He let himself slide into it. A little flustered, he hid himself behind a facade of newspapers, the *Chicago Tribune*, *The Wall Street Journal*. His face grew flushed. His breathing became rougher. Ah. Ah. It was happening, yes, she had reached to him, she had made the gesture at last. Tears of gratitude and relief came to him, and he let her sweep him off to a sharp and pounding fulfillment five miles above Arizona.

—Hello, Chris.

—Laurel.

—Did you mind? I felt you near me and I couldn't hold back anymore. I know you don't want to hear from me, but—

—What gave you that idea?

—I thought—it seemed to me—

—No. I thought you were the one who wanted to break it up.

—I? I missed you so much, Chris. But I was sure you'd pull away.

—So was I, about you.

—Silly.

—Laurel. Laurel. I'm so glad you took the chance, then.

—So am I. Let me have the snake, Chris.

—Yes. Yes.

He stepped out into the tawny sunbaked hills with the heavy porcelain jar and tipped it and let the snake glide toward her. It was all right after all. They had made mistakes, but they were the mistakes of too much love, and they had survived them. It was going to be all right: snake and ocean, ocean and snake, now and always.

HARD DRIVE

Nancy Kress

The wedding vows tell us that marriages last "until death do us part," but, as the following razor-edged shocker demonstrates, sometimes death just isn't *enough*. . . .

Born in Buffalo, New York, Nancy Kress now lives in Brockport, New York. She began selling her elegant and incisive stories in the mid-seventies, and has since become a frequent contributor to *Asimov's Science Fiction, The Magazine of Fantasy and Science Fiction, Omni,* and elsewhere. Her books include the novels *The Prince of Morning Bells, The Golden Grove, The White Pipes, An Alien Light,* and *Brain Rose,* and the collection *Trinity and Other Stories.* Her most recent books are the novel version of her Hugo- and Nebula-winning story, *Beggars in Spain,* a sequel, *Beggars and Choosers,* and a new collection, *The Aliens of Earth.* She has also won a Nebula Award for her story "Out of All Them Bright Stars."

Hard Drive

After the funeral, I went back with Maia to her apartment, even though she said she didn't want any company. "No, don't bother, Cal," she said as my brother's coffin was lowered into the ground. The funeral director gently cupped his hand under her elbow to turn her away. "I'll be fine alone."

I gazed down at her, small and shivering in her black coat and veiled hat, and said, "Robert wouldn't have wanted you to be alone." I took her other arm. She didn't protest, of course. Not at something Robert wanted.

I could smell her perfume, something light and old-fashioned, as I helped her into the limo. Reluctantly, the funeral director relinquished her elbow. She sat quiet beside me, her hands folded on her lap. Behind her black veil, her pale skin gleamed, ghostly, in the half-light. Was she crying? I couldn't tell.

"Maia," I said gently, "Robert went easily—short illness, no pain. The way he wanted to die."

She said, in a surprisingly strong voice, "Robert didn't want to die at *all*. Ever." She put up her veil. She wasn't crying. "Robert was furious about dying."

"Well," I said inanely. Furious. Of course, he would have been. Robert always got furious when he couldn't control something, and death certainly qualified. I groped for something else to comfort Maia.

"He had a long and productive life, Maia."

No response. But did her face look a little less set, less despairing?

"Not that seventy-two is all that old, of course," I said. Maia was twenty-nine. "But Robert had a genuinely full life. Think of his fame, his books, his honors, all those psychologists begging him to come and speak, everywhere. A full life."

I heard my own clichés. Maia looked out the limousine window.

"And you, too, of course," I added, unable to stop. "Since his marriage to you he was so happy, you gave him such a—"

"Do you know why Robert married me?" Maia demanded, and it *was* a demand. She had turned from the window and was staring directly at me from those gold-bronze eyes. "Do you, Cal?"

I hesitated. Of course I knew why Robert had married her. Everybody knew. Robert told them.

Maia radiated sex. It wasn't just the perfect pale skin, the glossy black hair braided into a chignon so heavy it tilted her head backward, the astonishing golden eyes. It wasn't even her tiny, lush body, balanced perversely between adult curves and the delicate bones of a child. It was Maia herself. Something that rose from her pores, her hair follicles, like a fine mist that drenched you before you even knew it was raining.

She said, "Sex doesn't matter that much to you, Cal, does it? At all." And now it was my turn to look away, out the window. But I didn't wince. I was proud of that.

We didn't speak again until we were inside the apartment. Flowers everywhere, vases and baskets and urns of them. The smell hung heavy in the quiet air. Robert's dog, a huge German shepherd named Helmutt, nuzzled her hand.

"I have to walk him soon, poor animal," Maia said. "Christ, let's go into the study. At least there aren't any flowers there."

There weren't, but Robert's latest book lay on his desk, half lying across his computer keyboard. *Confronting Ourselves: The Real Truth About Sex and Power.* It had been a best-seller. The dust jacket was the same gold-bronze as Maia's eyes.

"Martini?" Maia said, and didn't wait for my answer. "I'm sorry this room is so dusty. Robert would never let the cleaning woman touch anything in here."

Helmutt, shut outside the study door, whimpered and scratched. Maia handed me a drink. She tossed her veiled hat on a marble table and sat beside me on the sofa. "To Robert. Wherever he is."

"To Robert." I sipped from my glass; she drank down half of hers.

"Cal, listen—I'm sorry about that crack I made in the car. About you not being interested in sex. It was . . . uncalled for."

"Why? It's true." It was *not* true. But it was my only cover.

Maia's eyes widened. "Really? But I always assumed . . . *we* always assumed . . ."

Not accurate, but she didn't know it. Robert had never assumed. He'd known the truth.

"No, Maia, there's no young man hidden away in my life somewhere. Nor is there one, or many, women unsuitable for introducing to you and Robert."

"But you must need—" She stopped, and sipped her drink. I didn't answer. Of course Maia thought I must need. People judge others by themselves, and Maia needed all the time. You only had to watch her watch Robert to know that. And I had watched. For all three years she was the fifth Mrs. Carson-Jones I had watched. But I also remembered what Maia had been once, before she married my brother.

"I'm sorry," Maia said again. "I'm just getting in deeper, aren't I? It's just that you're twenty years younger than Robert, and yet when you looked at me, I never even picked up any vibrations that . . . not that it'd have to be *me* that you . . . oh, God, Maia, shut the fuck up! I'm sorry!"

She got up and wandered distractedly around the room, touching things, not shutting up.

"It's just that, without Robert, I don't know what I'm going to do. How I'm going to *be*." She picked up a Fabergé egg, put it down again. "Robert always made all the decisions, always was the one who . . . but it isn't even *that* . . . I can't just . . ." She poured a glass of water at the side table, left it there. "Even in bed, we . . . but I can't let any of that determine whether . . . God, Maia, get a grip!" She picked up Robert's book.

I said soothingly, "I know, Maia. I know how you'll miss him. I know how much you loved him."

She stared at me. "'Love'? You thought I *loved* Robert?"

Now it was my turn to stare: at her scornful tone, at the barely leashed strain in her tiny body, at the book in her hand. Something wild leaped in my chest. And, behind her, Robert's computer came on.

"Hello, Maia," it said. "This is my ghost."

Robert's voice. His face, on the screen. Maia glanced, startled, from the book in her hand to the keyboard where it had rested. *Confronting Ourselves: The Real Truth About Sex and Power.*

"I know you miss me, my darling. And the ghost that I am now obviously can't be everything to you that we once were to each other. But the important thing is that you're not alone, Maia. I'm still *here*. Don't be afraid, my darling—I know how terrified you are of being alone, of being abandoned—but you're *not* alone. I'm still here for you."

Maia, golden eyes huge, gazed at the screen. Robert: tanned, fit, dressed in one of his Armani blazers and an open-necked shirt. He looked out at Maia with possessive fondness.

"You can talk to me, darling. I'm not just a CD video. We can *talk* to each other. Go ahead, Maia."

She whispered, "Why are you doing this?"

The computer light for the hard drive went on. Voice activated? Robert's image said, in his own voice, "Because I can't bear to leave you. Or have you left so alone." As he spoke, Robert looked down, retrieving a pack of cigarettes from somewhere below screen level. It made it hard to see if his lip movements matched his actual words.

Maia said, "You're not a ghost. You're a *program!*"

Robert lit the cigarette, put it in his mouth, looked pensively off to one side, as if considering what Maia had said. It all hid the verbal synchronization, or lack of it.

"Well, of course I am, darling. I'm not claiming the supernatural here. I'm just doing the best I can to see that you're not *alone*, that you are taken care of, that you get everything you need. *Everything*. Maia, have you been rereading my book, as you promised? Ten pages every night?"

"Yes," she whispered.

"Then last night you read *this*, didn't you: 'The erotic impulse is far more than merely the need for sex. It's the underlying buoyancy that drives delight in all things, the wonder and sensuality that well up in us when we stand in spring sunshine, or smell a thunderstorm, or suddenly feel, in all its dark mystery, our own heart beating in our chest, linking us with the self we were as unabashedly physical babies and the self we will become at the hour that heart ceases to beat. Eroticism drives all of this. As it drives us—when we let it—to the deepest expression of our true selves,

which the erotic impulse both uncovers and glorifies.'
Did you read that last night, Maia?"

"Yes, Robert," she said, and she was no longer
whispering. The stunned look had left her beautiful
face. It showed now what it had shown for the last
four years: the intense watching, watching, watching.
The look of the disciple watching the master, careful
not to miss that vital moment when the master let slip
the secret that *must* be there. The one piece of wisdom
that would make everything suddenly clear. On the
computer screen, Robert smoked his cigarette, and
dabbed at his face with a silk handkerchief, and
moved slightly into shadow, his lip syncs blurred.

And then the screen flickered, cigarette and
handkerchief disappeared, and his words matched lip
motions perfectly. A different digital sequence, I
guessed. Maia, from the look on her face, was beyond
noticing.

Robert said, "I love you so much, darling. You are
the first woman in my life who is so much more than
she seems on the surface. There's so much *to* you—
layers and layers." He smiled. "My little onion.
Multilayered and pungent. Do you miss me?"

"Oh, God, *yes.*"

"I miss you, too. More than I can say. But words
aren't what's most important, are they? We always
knew that. Words don't really express what's deepest
in human beings. . . ."

His voice had changed. He stared out at her from
the screen with an intensity, a sheer animal force, I
had never personally witnessed in my brother. But, of
course, I'd known it must be there. Measured by his
success, his power, what he *was.* And what I was *not.*

And Maia stared back at him with an answering
intensity in those golden eyes.

Then the computer did something: blinked—no,
that's not the right word. The hard drive lit up and the

image of Robert thrust itself off the screen and into the air, a three-dimensional hologram that stopped just short of Maia's body.

"Maia, darling—take off your blouse. For me. Unbutton the top button . . . the next . . ."

"I think," Maia said thickly to me, "you'd better go."

"Maia, that isn't Robert, it's a—"

"Please!" She fingered the top button on her blouse. Inches away, the translucent Robert leaned forward, and his hands moved to his shirt.

I left. Helmutt wagged his tail forlornly as I passed through the living room, but I ignored him. I went to my club, and I drank until everything was a blur, and not even that blotted out the jealous pictures in my brain.

It was almost a month before I went near her again. For the first two weeks, I stayed at work at the bank all day, at the club bar all evening, and awake too much of the night. After that, I spent my time in the library, reading about Eliza programs, voice activation, CD-ROM capabilities, the new technologies being developed by private cable-TV channels, holographic attributes of the 786 computers. It was slow going. My mind doesn't move easily in these areas. But I kept at it, not trying to learn how these things were done, but only what *could* be done.

Then I read my brother's book.

When Maia opened her apartment door, my chest tightened. She looked terrible. How could anyone so tiny lose that much weight that fast? Her skin, always pale, had a pasty look. She wore jeans and a man's shirt with the third button missing. Through the gap, I glimpsed red lace. Her long hair hung greasily around her face, and her feet were bare. I tried not to picture what she'd been doing when I had leaned, over and over, on the bell.

"Cal, hello. I wasn't expecting . . ."

"I know, I should have called. But I was on this side of town and suddenly realized I'd been neglecting you, so I thought I'd stop by. Here, Maia, I know you like these."

She took the Godiva chocolates without interest. "Thanks, Cal, that's so sweet of you. But I'm afraid I'm in the middle of something, so maybe another time would be—"

I'd practiced in front of the mirror. "Maia, I'm sorry to interrupt, really. But the truth is, I'm in some trouble at the bank, and I need to talk to someone who can understand. *Please.*"

"But I don't know anything about banking . . . oh, God, Cal, don't *cry*! What is it, what's wrong? Come in!"

Robert had never been capable of appreciating what a kind person his sexual serf actually was.

She led me toward his study. I grabbed her arm. "Maia, can we sit in the living room?"

"You wouldn't want to," she said, and took my hand to lead me through it. I almost gagged. Helmutt lay listlessly on the Louis Quatorze sofa, and the air reeked with his shit, overlaid with sickeningly powerful deodorant sprays. Maia must not have walked him for two weeks, must not have left the apartment at all, must have just given up on everything except . . .

"The cleaning woman quit," Maia said. "I'm sorry, I can't seem to . . . watch where you step. Come in here."

The study didn't stink. The door was thick and well fitted, and the window was open slightly. Seven stories below, traffic hummed. Blankets and a pillow draped the sofa. A few dishes, most crusted with untouched food, rested on the Chippendale table beside mounds of frilly lingerie. A peach teddy, a sheer black peignoir, pairs of crotchless panties, something in white leather . . . I looked away.

Maia seemed oblivious. She poured two drinks. "Now, tell me what's wrong. It must be bad, for you to . . . did you lose your job at the bank? But you have your trust fund, don't you? Is it . . . oh, God, did you break some banking law? Are the cops after you?"

"Yes," I lied. "The SEC. Securities and Exchange Commission."

"What did you *do*?"

"I tried to control something I had no business trying to control. Something it's illegal to try to control."

"I don't understand," Maia said.

Of course she didn't. I counted on that. Carefully I laid out for her my fabricated story: insider trading, stock churning, just trying to control transactions for the good of my clients, who trusted me to act in their best interests. Maia listened intently. I finished by saying, "I could go to jail. Maia . . . I'm frightened."

I had her total attention. "Do you have a lawyer?"

"Yes. In fact, I'm supposed to see him this afternoon. But I can't without . . . I just don't believe there's any hope. Not in this situation. The paper trail is too clear."

"There's always hope."

I seized her hand. "Do you really believe that?"

"Of course I do. Things can always change."

"But I . . . maybe it would just be better to give up and not fight it."

"No, you can't do that. I mean . . . *jail.* No. You can't just give up!"

"But, Maia, darling . . . *you* have."

She stared at me. I didn't push it. Not yet. "Will you come with me to see my lawyer?"

She dropped my hand. "I can't."

"Please? I need you."

"I can't just leave Ro—"

"I *need* you, Maia!"

She chewed on her bottom lip. "All right. If you need me . . . all right."

"Go get dressed," I said. "I'll wait here."

She glanced at the dark monitor screen, at the closed study door, behind which Helmutt whimpered softly. "Okay. I won't be long."

But long enough. My fingers itched to get at the computer.

She just opened the door, slipped through, then stuck her head back into the room. Her face floated, disembodied, in her long black hair. "There's scotch and water and some nice brandy. Oh, and Cal—"

The computer came on.

"Cal," Robert's image said coldly. "How nice to see you."

Maia came slowly back into the room.

"But even better, little brother, if you leave. I'm afraid I know what you've been up to."

I tried to remember if Maia had spoken my name aloud before. I couldn't remember. She stared at Robert's image, her eyes huge and yet somehow dead, like piles of soft gold ash.

"I know you think you're only trying to help Maia," Robert's image said, "but not by lying to her. Lies never help anything. You should know that, Cal."

Maia's hand had gone to her own throat. Between the slim fingers, a pulse beat hard.

"Maia," I said, "he doesn't know. He *can't* know what I've been doing. Don't you see, he set this all up before he died in order to go on controlling you, because the bastard can't bear to give up controlling you even when he's *dead*—"

But that was a misstep. Maia said, "Control is an illusion. Cal, you should read—listen: 'Only when we give up—completely, with the deepest possible surrender—*all* delusions that we can control our sexual response, do we really begin to feel its actuality, its power to transform us by connection to a universe deeper and more real than we can imagine. Eroticism means surrender, and surrender means we gain ourselves.' It's *true*, Cal—I've felt it. Why, all the great thinkers from Jesus to Buddha to—"

"I recognize chapter six of Robert's book," I said harshly. "But, Maia—surrender to *what*? Just a few minutes ago you told me to not surrender to the SEC without a fight!"

"That's not the same as—"

"It is! It *is*! Oh, Maia, don't you see? Even before Robert's death, you were so completely captured by him that you lost yourself! And sex was the way he did it, that awful power that—no, forget that. But Maia, dear, don't you remember what you were when you first met Robert? *I* remember! When was the last time you painted a picture, or visited your sister, or went skiing, or any of the other things you used to love to do? When was the last time you were *Maia*?"

I reached out my hand for her. Robert's image had been silent, watching us. I guessed that somehow I'd avoided all the key words that would trigger its next programmed sequence. What were they? How long could I continue avoiding them? I had to get Maia out of the room.

She resisted my pulling her toward me. "Cal, I don't think—"

"But you *do*! God, Maia, you *can*! Even the day of his funeral, you sat here on that sofa and said, 'Love? You thought I *loved* Robert?' In just that tone. Remember that?"

"'Love,'" Robert's computer image said. "Ah, yes. That's the heart of this, isn't it, Cal? You've been in love with Maia yourself for years. I knew it, even if she didn't. A pale, washed-out, antiseptic love. Hardly worth the name. Without any elemental force behind it, any appreciation of the Dionysian surge to self-power, the erotic force someone like Maia is capable of . . . but love nonetheless, right? You're in love with my wife, and you can't stand either of us because of your pathetic jealousy."

Maia gazed at the computer screen, then at me. Her red mouth quirked. She leaned toward me and quite deliberately unfastened the next button of her shirt. Her full breasts above the lacy red bra rose and fell. She reached out one slim, dirty-nailed hand and lightly stroked my crotch.

And laughed delightedly.

I stepped backward. Robert's image said, "Am I right, Cal?" And Maia shook her head at me, the beautiful greasy hair dancing around her shoulders.

"Cal, Cal . . . That was unworthy of you. Why, you're not in trouble with the SEC at all, are you?"

"I am, yes. I—"

"It was just lies. Robert was right." She shook her head at me, smiling. "You see, then? He's *always* right. And I'm lucky to have this much of him even after death."

"*Maia*—"

"Oh, you don't know, Cal! You just don't *know*. But maybe you can learn. Read Robert's book, find yourself a woman in touch with her own elemental power—there are still some around—and practice surrender. To yourself. Maybe it's not too late for you." She was still smiling at me, as at a child, or a slow college student who just doesn't get it.

I stood completely still for maybe half a minute. The Robert-image was saying something, but I didn't hear it. I looked slowly around the filthy study, at the filthy smiling woman in front of me. I picked up the poker from the fireplace and brought it down hard on the monitor.

Maia screamed and lunged at me. I held her off easily with my left hand—she was so tiny. With my right, I smashed at the keyboard, CPU, even the speakers, over and over. Sparks flew. Briefly. I dropped the poker.

"I'll kill you!" Maia screamed, in her elemental power. "You son of a bitch, you *murdered* him!"

"He's already dead, Maia," I said coldly, and with great clarity. I suddenly felt better than I ever had in my life. "He's been dead for three weeks. And now you're free of him."

"I'll sue you! I'll call the police! I'll—"

"Go ahead," I said, still coldly. God, I felt good. "I'll wait till they get here."

"Get out! Get out, I never want to see you again, I *hate* you!"

"You won't," I said, and I could feel the power flowing into me, thrilling along my nerves and spine. "And do you know why? Because underneath your sick obsession with Robert and his even sicker one with controlling you through sex—underneath that, you're a basically sensible person. And a sound one. And a good one. With him gone, you'll come to realize that—"

She pounded on me with her small fists and sobbed. I didn't mind. I had done it.

We were both free of him.

I had won.

The erotic power, the fundamental Dionysian energy, is only fully available to us through the fundamental acts: love and war. An opponent as much as an orgasm makes the energy flow. . . . Chapter eight.

"Get out! Get out!" Maia sobbed.

"For now," I said tenderly, and opened the study door. No use to make her take any more this afternoon. There was time. The smell of dog shit hit my nose, and Helmutt tried to stagger toward me. I picked

my way across the living room and down the hall. I'd
reached the apartment door and opened it when Maia
came racing after me.

"Bastard! Prick! Asshole! Get *out*!"

"Aren't those supposed to be terms of endearment
in Robert's sexually open philosophy?" I jeered tenderly—God, I felt good—and she shoved me out the
door and theatrically fastened the chain. I kept my
foot in the door.

"Good-bye, darling. I'm right about this, you'll
see. I'll call you later. And I'm sending over cleaning
and dog-walking services."

"Don't you ever—"

"Hello, Maia," Robert's voice said.

We both froze. I peered over her, over the chain,
into the living room. The big wall-screen TV had
turned itself on. Robert's face, looking stern, towered
five feet high. "Maia, you didn't mean for that to happen, did you? I can't believe you did."

"*No!* No, I didn't!" Maia cried, and shoved me the
rest of the way out the door. I heard the bolts slide
into place, a New York triple-locked steel door. It shut
out all sound, and I stood on the other side and heard
nothing more.

I couldn't have her committed.

My lawyer said so, gazing at me across his desk
and choosing his words carefully. I wasn't sure why he
used the tone he did when he told me that. I hadn't
described any of my own behavior, nor let him see
what I really felt for Maia. I was in control.

But on thinking it over, I didn't want to have her
committed anyway. That wasn't the way to do it. I'd
underestimated how deeply Robert had warped her,
how strong his perverse hold on her was. I'd have to
approach the problem from another direction.

I couldn't believe how angry I'd been after the funeral, how despairing. Drinking to forget Maia—what a stupid idea! There was no forgetting Maia, and no need to. Anger and despair were ineffectual, soul-blunting. What was needed was decisive action. I was going to win.

The key was Helmutt. Lying listlessly on the sofa, staggering when he walked toward me, his nose warm in the palm of my hand.

I made an anonymous call to the Humane Society, and then sat in my car across the street from her apartment. The next day the ASPCA van pulled up.

I followed the two uniformed men inside and loitered at the end of the hall.

Maia never answered the bell.

One of the men took out a small electronic device of some sort and applied it to the steel door. The other rang the bell again. The first man studied the device's screen.

"Okay," he said. "It's a large dog, and the barking is in the pain range, or at least almost. Definitely in the nonnormal range. Get the warrant."

I was there in the hallway when they returned with a cop who looked like she had better things to do.

"This better be good," she snarled. The two uniformed humane men didn't bother to answer. Neither did Maia. The cop went through her routines and finally blasted the lock with her laser torch. Mayor Jenson is famous for his love of animals.

The smell made her retch.

It didn't affect the animal lovers. They moved purposefully through the apartment, and I followed them. "I'm her brother-in-law," I said to the cop. "I made the initial call. She's mentally ill."

The cop muttered something I didn't catch.

Robert's study was empty. I picked my way over the dog shit to the bedroom.

Maia sat up on the bed, blinking and clutching the blanket around her. She was dressed in a white nightgown that made her look about fifteen. Her long black hair still hadn't been washed. The bedroom TV turned on as soon as the cop said, "Ma'am, are you Maia Carson-Jones? I have a warrant here for your arrest on two counts of suspected animal abuse and—"

"'Abuse' is a term that means different things to unenlightened people than to the enlightened," Robert's image said.

The cop stared. In the other room I could hear the ASPCA men crooning at Helmutt.

"For instance, is it 'abuse' to force a child into the pain of a vaccination? Of course not, if it will protect him from disease. Is it 'abuse' to force a student to reach past what he thinks he can do, staying up all night to complete reading and writing assignments, if it teaches him that he can extend his range to master more than he ever thought he could? Is it abuse to force you, my sweet child and student, to do things you initially resist, if it helps you to discover and extend your capacity for pleasure and joyful surrender?"

The cop said, "Turn off the TV."

Maia said, in a strangled voice, "I can't. Cal . . ."

Robert said, "Cal? What are you doing in my wife's bedroom?"

The cop, mouth open, looked from me to the TV. She looked back at me, at Maia, at the TV. She put her hand on her gun.

I said gently, "What is it, Maia?"

"Helmutt . . . Helmutt's sick . . ."

"I know. I knew it. The animal people will take him to the vet."

She said, "How did you know?" The cop said, "What do you mean you can't turn it off?" Robert said in his tone of absolute command, "Maia. Get these people out of my bedroom."

I put a hand on Maia's shoulder. The strap of her nightgown was lacy and thin. A thrill ran through me, a whiplash of pure hot adrenaline.

Robert thrust out of the TV, a full-length hologram standing beside the bed. In a different tone he said, "Maia, darling . . ."

She put her hands over her ears, her eyes wild. "Turn him off! Helmutt's dying! He won't eat, he just lies there—*He* doesn't let me talk to him about it, he doesn't let me talk about anything but *sex*, he doesn't . . . oh, God, Robert, I'm sorry!"

"Sorry only means something if it's followed by action," Robert said. "Genuine contrition is empowering, my darling, it aids surrender. . . . "

The cop said evenly, "Unplug that thing. Now."

"You can't unplug it," Maia said hopelessly. "The plug is inside the wall or something, with all the rest of the electronics. Cal, destroy *this* one, too, please . . . *poor Helmutt* . . . and do you know the worst of it? I don't really *care* if the poor dog is dying. That's what makes me as bad as *he* is, doesn't it, Cal? . . . Destroy us both . . ."

"No," I said. "Only *him*. To set you free, Maia. Listen to me. You're not yourself, or you wouldn't have let that happen to poor Helmutt. Just listen to me, my poor darling . . ."

I had her now. I *had* her.

She looked at the screen. From the other room, a man called, "All right. We're taking the dog." The cop shook her head in disgust, handed Maia the warrant, and left the room. The apartment door closed behind the three of them.

Robert was talking, leaning forward, a compelling light in his eyes. I gave Maia the gun in my jacket. I put it in her hand, folded my fingers around hers, and aimed.

Maia gave a last sob, as if the sound were torn out of her thin bones. Then she squeezed the trigger.

The wall screen exploded in a shower of plastic and sparks. I laughed. It was like a thunderstorm breaking, a flash flood roaring along an unsuspecting canyon in all its elemental power. Maia dropped the gun, buried her face in her hands, and cried.

I climbed into the bed beside her and held her while she sobbed. Her body was damp and soft beneath the thin silk. She cried and cried.

"There sweetheart, there there, it's over now . . ." Her breasts pushed against my chest.

I held her, lying full-length on the bed, until she stopped crying.

"There, Maia, there . . . oh, you've been through so much . . ."

"Cal, don't," she said, and I had the sense to stop. It was the hardest thing I've ever done. But the power was on me still, and there was time. There was all kinds of time.

When I left her, she lay exhausted and drained of tears. Softly I closed the bedroom door, hoping she'd sleep.

I made phone calls from Robert's study. There wasn't anything I couldn't do, couldn't arrange. The cleaning service said they'd be over within an hour, if it really was a triple-fee emergency. My lawyer said there probably wouldn't be any problem defending Maia on the animal-abuse charges: new widow, temporarily under great stress. Lutece gave me a reservation for eight o'clock. *Without erotic power at the unseen, unbidden, sometimes dark core of all action, there is no action. Our sterilized, cheerful, emasculated society does not want to admit this, and so we remain ineffective and miserable. But not all of us.* Chapter three.

I hung up the phone and stretched deeply, luxuriously, feeling my muscles pull and relax, pull and relax.

"Very good, Cal," said Robert's voice behind me.

A section of the wall had rolled back, revealing a

small wall screen covered by what looked like bullet-proof glass. Robert's face smiled out at me. A blue silk scarf was knotted at his throat.

"Is Maia standing there with you? Maia? . . . No. Just as well. We'll get to her in a minute."

He smiled at something off-screen to his left. Involuntarily, I glanced to my right.

"You think, Cal, that you're free of me, don't you? Both of you. Cal, Cal. Don't you think I know you better than *that*, after a lifetime of observing you? I know you better than you know yourself. You are what you are—and that's not what I am."

I took a step toward the screen.

"No, don't come any closer," Robert said, smiling. He folded his arms across his chest. "Just listen to me. You can't escape. You aren't smart enough, strong enough, confident enough. Most of all, you're not *me*. You don't understand people, not even Maia. Especially not Maia. How could I not know my influence would wear off when I'm not actually here in the flesh? Of course I knew. I knew she'd become a little restless, and I'd hold her for a while through sex, and you'd make your eventual move. Are you listening, Cal? I knew you'd destroy the initial hardware. I knew she'd help you. I planned it. I'm *still in control*."

"No, you son of a bitch, you're not!"

He smiled. "False defiance. Give up, Cal. You can't win. Not against *me*."

I said, "In a right triangle, the square of the hypotenuse is equal to the sum of the squares of the other two sides."

He said, "Erotic triangles are as old as history. But the intelligence and electronics to manipulate them—that's new."

I said, "I lost *my* . . . *uh* . . . umbrella."

He said, "Maia is mine. And always will be."

I flipped his image the finger and turned to go.

And he said, "Just because you can miscue the Eliza program doesn't mean you're free."

Slowly I turned back to his smiling image—and realized I had nothing to say. Nothing that the motion sensors, ghost programming, voice activators, and all the rest of it wouldn't interpret. But—I didn't *need* to say anything. I had Maia.

"Wrong, Robert," I said. "Stuff it up your tantric control."

If he made any response behind me, I didn't see or hear it.

On the way back through the shit-filled living room, I planned. I'd take Maia to a hotel; she wasn't ready yet for my place. Rent a two-bedroom suite. See some shows: comedies and musicals. Good restaurants. The Picasso exhibit. Remind her of the world beyond Robert. And then, eventually . . .

No ghost in a machine could match living flesh. *Maia's* flesh, creamy and smooth, naked . . . No. Not naked. Dressed in the lingerie she'd bought for my brother. Who was irretrievably dead.

As soon as I opened her bedroom door, I heard it. A soft murmuring, silence, murmuring. She was in the bathroom, the door ajar. I shoved through so fast the door sprang into the wall, ricocheted back, smacked me in the arm.

It was a small portable television, the cable connections disappearing into the wall. Robert's face smiled tenderly at her, murmuring, murmuring. Maia, kneeling on the bath mat, looked up guiltily.

"Oh, Cal, there you are . . . we were wrong, dear. I'm sorry. So wrong . . . You see, he *knew* I would do it. Destroy the computer. He understands me so well, and to be understood like that by another person, to be actually *seen* . . . I'm sorry. You'd better go."

"Maia! Don't *you* see? He's still controlling you!"

She stood. "No, you're wrong. I chose to destroy

the ghost, and I choose to go back to him. But not forever. Just a little while longer. It can't be too long,
don't you see? Robert is dead. But for a little while
longer . . . I'll know when it's time to go, won't I,
Robert?"

"You'll know when it's time to go, darling," my
brother's image said. "Trust your own erotic instincts."

Maia said to me, "I'll call you, Cal."

I choked out, "I won't be there when you call, Maia!
I won't! Damn it, I'm not a thing you can just . . . just
set aside until you're good and ready, and done fucking a ghost!"

She said, "Get out."

"You can't just . . . damn it . . ."

"Get out, Cal."

"Yes, Cal, leave," Robert said, and smiled beyond
her, over her shoulder. At me.

"Maia . . . Maia, I didn't mean it . . . I didn't . . .
oh, God, listen, I will call you soon, I will, please let
me, Maia . . ."

"Suit yourself," she said coldly. "But now—*get out.*"

I went, cursing myself. I'd almost blown it. I'd
almost let him goad me into losing. But Maia was kind
under her sickness, and her kindness would let me
back in. I could still win.

Outside the building, I suddenly felt weak, and
leaned for a minute against the brick facade before hailing a taxi. But it was only a temporary dizziness. I
would not let it be more than that. Robert was not
going to beat me. Nothing he did would keep me away
permanently, would end the battle for Maia . . . he
wanted me gone.

Or—*did* he?

*"Are you listening, Cal? I knew you'd destroy the initial
hardware. I knew she'd help you. I planned it. I'm still in
control."*

Was it possible my brother *wanted* me to keep on

fighting for Maia? But, then, the way to escape his control
would be to give up. . . .

*The erotic power, the fundamental Dionysian energy, is
only fully available to us through the fundamental acts: love
and war. An opponent as much as an orgasm makes the
energy flow . . .*

But . . . what if he was actually fighting me so I
would *really* give up, so that he could have Maia to
himself even from beyond the grave? Then the way to
escape his control would be to . . .

Or *did* he . . . ?

The dizziness was stronger now. I put my head in
my hands and leaned against the brick building in the
warm spring sunshine. I could smell the dank newly
opened earth, and around me in the close darkness
rose the ghostly holographic images, smiling and
tanned, looking at me, but saying nothing.

Relationships

Robert Sampson

The late Robert Sampson was a veteran pulp-era author who had sold to *Planet Stories* and *Weird Tales*, and who, in recent years, retired from NASA's Marshall Space Flight Center and began to revitalize his career with a number of sales to some of the top short-fiction markets in both the science fiction and mystery fields. In mystery, he won the Edgar Award for the best mystery story of 1986. In the science fiction genre, his stories appeared in *Full Spectrum*, *Strange Plasma*, *Asimov's Science Fiction*, and elsewhere. His most recent book was *Dangerous Horizons*, a study of famous series characters of the pulp magazine era. He lived for many years in Huntsville, Alabama, and died in 1993 at the age of 65.

Here he gives us a mysterious and evocative story about the persistence of love.

Relationships

A few days after his forty-eighth birthday, Hadley Jackson learned that he could materialize the women from his past. Only think a little at an angle and there they sat, sassy as life, talking as if time were nothing. As if their lives had continued to touch his. The ability to call them upset him considerably. Not fearfully though; he never felt fear.

To that time, he had been spending ever larger chunks of the evening burrowed in his apartment. He lived with two cats, Gloria and Bill. He had developed the habit of reading aloud to them: selections from news magazines, the poems of Emily Dickinson. The cats were unconcerned by his choices. Reading aloud gave him the feeling that his life still retained both direction and a trace of high white fire.

One Monday he thought of Mildred Campbell. At one time he had cared a good deal for her. They had never reached what, in the contemporary tongue, was called a relationship. Between them, something essential had been omitted. She didn't, or couldn't, return his feelings. Eventually they allowed each other to drift away amid a sort of wan regret.

All of a sudden, there she sat in a chair by his table. She wore a blue dress of some slinky material and dark hose and dark blue heels. The tip of her left shoe vibrated against the carpet, as it did when she wanted to go home and was about to tell him so.

He knew at once that she was not real. Apparently she did, too. It did not seem to bother her.

"This won't do you any good," she said. Her voice, quick and pleasant as ever, was tinted with dark impatience. Sooner or later that emotion marred all their meetings.

"I was just thinking about you."

"Well, I'm far away. To tell the truth, I haven't thought about you for years."

"You never did. Not much," he said.

She laughed at that, and a cat stuck its head through her left shoulder and looked out at him. It made him feel a little sick, then irritated, since it established so clearly that Mildred was some kind of cloud.

"Let's not bother with this," she said. "I liked you for about ten minutes once. But, Lord God, you can't stretch ten minutes forever."

"I liked you longer than that."

"Don't kid yourself," she said. And was gone. The cat still looked at him. It jumped down and slipped under the table.

He touched the chair she had sat in and sniffed the air. No trace of her fragrance remained. It occurred to him that if Mildred came, others might follow. So he sat down again and thought of Ruth. He couldn't angle his thoughts properly; the correct mind-set eluded him. Later he wandered slowly around the block, smelling night leaves, wondering if it were possible to leave Creative Chemicals and set up a consulting business.

The following night, he thought of Ruth again. This time she appeared promptly. She wore a long white formal-looking dress with gold at ears and neck. Her hair was paler blond than he had remembered. She was a little tight; that, too, was familiar. Sprawling back on the davenport, she grinned at him and crossed her ankles.

"Old friends meet again." Her lips were bright red. Only something was wrong with her eyes. A whitish film covered them.

"Twenty-odd years," he said. "Pretty long between visits. Where you living now?"

"I'm dead," she replied. "Years and years ago."

"I'm sorry. I thought about you a lot. But I didn't know where you'd moved to."

"That's the way of it," she said. "You get separated and the space between just keeps getting bigger. You never know where a person gets to or what they do when they get there."

He was shocked at her eyes and could think of nothing to say. Her voice was low and amused. As she turned her head, gold flashed.

"Just because I'm dead, there's nothing wrong with me. I mean, I'm not about to tear out your throat or any dumb thing like that."

"What's it like being dead?"

"I don't know. It isn't anything you can describe. You hear all this foolishness . . ."

Her fingers minutely adjusted her skirt. "I guess I better go," she said. "The damn whiskey's dying in me."

As she rose, he said with sudden regret: "I'm sorry you died."

"It was quick. I remember that."

After she was gone, he sat silently, thinking. A cat nudged his dangling hand. Her eyes had been very terrible. He realized that he had forgotten to ask where she had lived or how her life had been. Shame leaped in him. Or perhaps guilt. The emotion tasted metallic, gray, the taste of nails.

She had recognized him, he thought. After all these years.

He slept in his chair. When he woke, it was still dark outside but the light was on and the cats had crowded between his leg and the chair arm.

*   *   *

The following evening, his daughter, Janet, called from Phoenix. Her voice was enthusiastic, warm, and slipped over certain subjects quickly, as if a question from him would drop them both through a fragile crust. The combination of effusiveness and reticence annoyed him.

"I'm fine," she told him. "Everybody's fine."

"I mean, how are you, really?"

"Just fine, Dad." Her voice took on a note of remote querulousness. His ex-wife, Helen, Janet's mother, another man's wife, had banged up her car on the way to a class in stained glass. Helen wanted to know, Janet said, if he'd like a suncatcher for his window— a glass cactus or sleeping Mexican. He refused. Helen constantly offered him small gifts through his daughter, never directly talking with him. The effect was of receiving messages relayed from another planet. Perhaps, he thought, it's Janet trying to keep us in touch. A cat rubbed its neck against his calf.

"Good-bye," she said. The telephone droned hollowly against his ear.

Later he drove slowly across town to the theater at the mall. Bright clouds streaked the sky like strips of stained glass, rose and green, whitish-gray.

In the theater, the lights faded down, and an endless succession of commercial messages shouted across the screen. No one in them was older than twenty-five.

As the sales messages jittered past, Hadley thought suddenly of Rosemary Chalson. Years ago, they had met accidentally at a showing of *South Pacific*. For nearly the entire picture, he agonized whether to take her hand. As he finally decided to reach out, laughter stirred through the audience. Rosemary clapped both hands under her chin and leaned back, laughing, exposing her gums. This he found disagreeable. Before he decided what to do about her hand, the film ended.

Thinking of her now, and the long tortures of adolescence, he glanced right. Rosemary sat in the next seat, a tub of popcorn in her lap. As ferocious youth bounced across the screen, she lifted a single kernel to her lips.

He blurted: "It's been years . . ."

He saw the startled white flicker in her eyes. Her body angled infinitesimally from him.

Immediately he saw that she was not Rosemary. Dull horror ran through him. He blurted: "Excuse me. Excuse me."

Rising, he struggled past a succession of knees to the aisle. People stared irritably past him, intent on the yelling screen.

Outside the theater, he felt the icy crawl of his back. She looked exactly like Rosemary, he thought. The error frightened him. His mind felt full of dangerous potential, like a cocked gun.

He drove from the mall, passing beneath apricot lights mounted on high silver poles. The street angled through rows of beige apartments. Nothing moved. The smooth dark sky was unmarred by star or moon. In the hollow street, in the dull light, the apartments seemed images painted on air. Behind them hung featureless nothing, waiting to be shaped.

Some basic similarity existed, he thought, between the street and his laboratory where, for the past week, the complex process of installing a computer system was under way. Behind ranks of cabinets and boxes dangled a wilderness of black cords. The tip of each glittered silver, waiting for connection.

In his life, he thought, there had been too much disconnection. Too many dangling cords. Only past connections remained. He seemed hardly linked to the present.

The woman beside him bent to adjust her seat. When she straightened, he recognized Helen Wycott— Wrycott. He was sharply disturbed. He had not seen her since college. Nor had he thought of her since.

Now they come without being called, he thought.

She eyed him disdainfully. "You always acted too good for everybody."

"I didn't feel that way," he said.

"That's not what it looked like."

They turned into a dark street with dark houses behind strips of yard. Mailboxes shone dully along the curb. He could think of no reason why she came. Over the years, she had put on much weight, and her remembered features floated within a cruel expanse of cheek.

He said: "You always were so clever and quick. I never knew what to say to you."

"You spent too much time thinking about yourself."

"That isn't true," he said, trying to remember.

"It's true, all right. You do it now."

They rode in silence for several blocks. She looked steadily at him, shaking her head.

"You better give this up," she told him. "There's more to life than people you used to know."

"Listen," he said, "I didn't call you here."

"I want off here," she said.

He stopped the car. When he opened her door, she was gone. Night air smelled moistly cool and his hands trembled faintly. Aggravation, he thought.

On going back over their conversation, it struck him that he had, however slightly, won an advantage over her. He drove home briskly, humming to himself and tapping time to himself on the steering wheel. Objectively, of course, he was showing all the signs of dementia. He considered the possible collapse of his mind cheerfully. Perhaps he had now entered a mania phase. How interesting that the symptoms of his detachment from reality expressed themselves as women. That seemed distantly amusing.

When he opened the door of the apartment, the cats ran toward him uttering sharp cries of greeting. Above their noise he heard the light flutter of feminine voices.

In the living room, two women smiled at him. One was Ruth, this evening wearing neatly tailored black with pearls. She lolled effusively on the davenport, clearly having had a great deal to drink. The other woman, wearing a ragged blue cardigan and jeans, sat primly in a straight chair, knees together. He did not recognize her.

Ruth waved breezily at him. "You come sit right down here. We've been deciding what to do with you."

The other woman said: "I bet you don't remember me."

When she smiled, sweetness suffused her bony face. A former friend of his ex-wife. He recalled the smile. Nothing else.

"I remember," he said tentatively.

"Virginia Cox," she said. "Virginia Ames now. I have four grandchildren now."

"That's nice," he said. Ruth tittered. Her fingers floated over his hand, and she leaned toward him.

"It's just been ages," Virginia said. "I thought you were so handsome. Of course, you were married, so I didn't tell you that."

"It's different now," Ruth said.

"Same as it always was," Virginia said. "Just more open."

Ruth slumped back, laughing loudly. "She's right, Hadley. More open."

"I suppose so," he said, still unable to look at her eyes.

"We're shocking him," Virginia said.

"That's a man," Ruth said. She patted his knee, her bright-tipped fingers vanishing and reappearing in the material of his trousers. "Weren't you in love with me once, Hadley?"

He looked from the floor to the amused faces of the women. "I guess once I was."

"He guesses," Ruth purred. "He doesn't know. He guesses."

"Well, the point is, you can't hang in the past forever," Virginia said. The quick smile illuminated her face.

"The past was fun," Ruth added.

"But it's gone now, you know," Virginia said. "You can't keep raking it up. So Ruth and I, we've decided to help you out."

She stood up, not looking at all like a grandmother. "What a pretty cat. What's his name?"

"Bill," he said.

As he glanced toward the cat, Virginia was gone.

"Wait a minute," he cried, turning quickly to Ruth.

"That's all we wanted to tell you," she said.

Her figure wavered and her arms and body slipped sideways, separating from her shoulders and head. She said, "Don't think for a minute we weren't here. Mania, my foot."

"I wanted to say . . ."

"You're sweet," she said. "Can you be home at five tomorrow night?"

Her figure came to pieces, flowing across the room in translucent strands. It was after ten o'clock. Dropping onto the davenport, he ground his face against the flowered cushions.

At five the following evening, the doorbell rang once, briefly. As if it had been touched in embarrassment, as a duty, and once was going to be all. When he opened the door, Bill attempted to dart out and had to be captured and held. Facing him in the doorway was a tall, lean-faced woman with heavy dark hair. She smiled tentatively at him and dropped her eyes, which were dark gray. Embarrassment rose in waves from her. In a low voice, she asked:

"Are you Mr. Jackson? Hadley Jackson?"

"Yes, ma'am."

"Did you know Ruth Payne once?"

"Ruth? Oh, yes."

Her lips thinned and she looked so uneasy, he felt a pulse of sympathy.

"This probably sounds awful funny," she said, not looking at him. "She wanted me—she kept telling me to see you."

"I see," he said.

She looked directly at him then and their eyes touched. As she examined him some of the tension left her. She seemed intelligent and wary.

"You know about Ruth?" she asked.

"She died."

"Yes, she died."

He thought that she would say more but she did not.

After a moment, he said, "Reconnection," not loudly.

Faint color touched her face; she looked away.

He said swiftly before she could recover herself and flee: "I was just going down the street for a cup of coffee. Would you like one?"

She regarded the air between them as if it were imprinted with complex instructions. "Yes. I think so. That would be nice."

"I'll just get my coat. Come in."

Still holding the cat, he stepped aside. Head lifted, smiling faintly, she entered his apartment for the first time.

WALTZING ON A DANCER'S GRAVE

Kristine Kathryn Rusch

New writer Kristine Kathryn Rusch, one of the fastest-rising and most prolific young authors on the scene today, has had a very busy few years. She was the editor of *Pulphouse* in its original incarnation as a quarterly anthology series, and won a World Fantasy Award along with publisher Dean Wesley Smith (to whom she was recently married) for her work on it. In 1991, she stepped down as editor of the *Pulphouse* anthology series to become the new editor of *The Magazine of Fantasy and Science Fiction*, taking over from longtime editor Edward Ferman, and last year won a Best Editor Hugo for her work on *it*. As a writer, she won the John W. Campbell Award, and she is also a frequent contributor to *Amazing, Aboriginal SF, Full Spectrum, Asimov's Science Fiction,* and others. Her first novel was *The White Mists of Power,* and she has sold more than ten other novels. Her most recent books are a novel, *Facade,* and, coedited with Edward L. Ferman, the anthology *The Best from Fantasy & Science Fiction: A 45th Anniversary Anthology.* She lives in Eugene, Oregon.

In the compelling story that follows, she puts her characters, both living and dead, through an intricate pavane of love, memory, hate, betrayal, and the kind of obsession to which death is no obstacle. . . .

Waltzing on a Dancer's Grave

i

Greta held the railing tightly and peered over the edge.
Twenty years ago, he had fallen from here, fallen, fallen,
spiraling slowly until he landed five stories below with a
thud that echoed through the yard. She had clutched
her hands together, squeezing them, trying to erase the
feel of his silk shirt against her palms, thinking that for
someone as graceful as Karl, falling should have seemed
like flying.

At least he hadn't screamed.

"Greta!"

She jumped, her breath caught in her throat.
Timothy pulled open the glass doors and crossed the
balcony.

"You shouldn't be out here," he said. "You'll catch
your death." Then he flushed in the deep, almost pur-
plish way that seemed exclusive to redheads. "I mean
that—"

"I know what you mean," Greta said. She ran her
hands over the goosebumps on her bare shoulders.
"It's cold out here."

He put his arm around her back, warming her as
he led her inside. The mansion still had a musty, unused
air. Half of the company stretched out in the sunken
living room. Long, graceful bodies reclined on the

white sofas. Too many bare feet, with their corns, bunions, and bandages, rested on footstools. She always saw the bodies first. Her dancers were less human and more instruments to her.

Timothy closed the glass door. Sebastian glanced up from his place in the corner, his arm around the new brunette. Amanda Thigopolos. He was trying to get Greta's attention by playing at jealousy. She concentrated instead on the brunette. The girl was perhaps eighteen, just out of high school, and could dance as if she had been born in toe shoes. Amanda was fine. Thigopolos had to go—too long and too Greek. She could shorten it when she had her own name on the program. Thigopolos would be fine as long as she was part of the *corps de ballet*.

"I assume you're all settled," Greta said. The company turned to her as a unit. Faces—white, black, and brown, circles under most eyes and skin gray with pain—stared at her. Pain was part of being a dancer. She had learned that from Karl. *Ballet is impossible*, he would say. *Pain is a small price for doing the impossible*. She ignored the evidence of the dancers' exhaustion and overwork, and glared at them. "This isn't Sunday. I didn't say we would have the day off. Class in two hours."

They groaned. Dale sewed a knot on his shoe, bit the thread, and gave the needle back to Katrina. Lisa rubbed her feet. Sebastian frowned at Greta. She ignored him. "Well?" she said. They stood, stretched, and left the room in a jumbled line caught at the door, looking like a company on the first day of rehearsal season instead of one that had been together nearly six months. She sighed and pushed back the scarf covering her graying black hair. No. The hair was silvering, not graying. She was growing old elegantly, as Karl predicted she would.

Karl. He filled the room. She could almost catch the scent of his cologne, rich and overpowering, like Karl himself. Sometimes she thought she saw him out of the corner of her eye. Six feet tall and too thin, his leg muscles nearly bulging out of his jeans, his hair silver, and his brown eyes blazing. She remembered those eyes mostly in anger, never in repose. Anger, and that deep fierce hunger he seemed to have for her, the hunger she had once thought would consume her.

"Sorry you came?"

Timothy. She had forgotten about him. He stood next to her, as he always had, protecting her and backing her, the silent partner who liked to remain silent.

"It's the fiftieth anniversary of the company," she said. "It's only fitting that we do the anniversary performance here."

The words were by rote. She had said them ever since she had decided to return to Grayson Place. Usually the answer satisfied Timothy, but this time, he touched her arm. "I was asking about you, Greta."

She nodded. She remembered calling Timothy on the phone by the fireplace, her hands shaking so that she could barely dial. *Karl's dead*, she had said. *Did you call the police?* Timothy asked. *I want you to*, she said. Always there, always beside her, from the trial to the fight to save the company and onward, always caring about her and never asking for himself.

"I think that if we are going to keep the place, we'll have to redecorate." She reached across the table beside her and touched the rounded lampbase. Its garish brown-and-orange glass was the height of sixties tastelessness. "It feels as if time has stopped here."

"Maybe it has," Timothy said, and in his eyes she saw Karl, falling, falling, reaching out to her as he spun, his shirt fluttering in the wind, his gaze on her, strong as Karl himself, pulling part of her with him.

She shivered. That had been twenty years ago. She ran her hands along her upper arms. The goosebumps were still there. Timothy put his arms around her, but she ducked out of his grasp.

"Class in two hours," she said, smiling slightly. "And I want to eat."

ii

Timothy watched her leave. Greta still moved like a young girl. Up close, though, her body gave her away. Her skin was wrinkling, softly, adding an elegance to her features, but the elegance was one of age. She was old for a dancer, especially one who still practiced the art, but she was strong.

Greta was strong.

Timothy turned toward the balcony. Even now, he could feel the chill from that night. It had been cold when Karl died. Near freezing, although it was spring. When Timothy arrived, he found Greta, her hands shaking, still hovering near the phone. He had walked through the open glass doors, past the plastic patio furniture with its fringed umbrellas, past the deck chairs, Karl's portable record player, and the small television set where they had watched the *Wizard of Oz* because Karl loved watching Ray Bolger dance. The concrete structure seemed almost a mile long and Timothy walked it inch by agonizing inch, knowing that when he reached the wrought-iron railing, he would have to look down.

The railing still seemed to vibrate, but the trembling was caused by the cold and his own fear. Timothy touched the iron gently.

The imitation gaslight on the courtyard four and a half stories below illuminated Karl's mangled, twisted body. Karl, who had never made an ungraceful motion in his life, looked like a young boy who had tried his first *tour en l'air*, tripped, fallen, and refused to try again. Timothy wanted to whisper, "Get up, Karl, it's all right," but he knew that Karl would never get up and everything would not be all right. Karl had died, and, in the living room, Greta washed her hands together like Lady Macbeth.

Timothy shivered. He'd tried to argue with Greta when she wanted to return to Grayson Place, but she wouldn't listen. She wanted to do the anniversary event, wanted to do it here, and nothing he could say would change her mind.

She hadn't been back to Grayson Place since the night Karl died. Even though she had inherited the mansion with Karl's estate, she had let Timothy take care of it. He rented it out to friends and dancers, keeping it in constant use, but he hadn't returned either. Not since the night he had decided to lie for her, the night before he first spoke to Greta's attorney, two weeks after Karl died and almost a year before Timothy actually testified at the murder trial.

"Mr. Masson?"

The brunette, the new one, the one Sebastian was dallying with, stood at the door. Timothy frowned, but couldn't recall her name.

"My room is cold," she said.

The whole place is cold, Timothy thought, but said, "The thermostat is on the baseboard heaters. You'll have to turn it up."

"It's up all the way and the heaters are warm." She shrugged. "But the room itself is freezing."

Timothy sighed inwardly. More and more, managing this company meant playing nursemaid. If he were a little more trusting, he would hire someone to do this part of the job, the road work, and the day-by-day scheduling. He smiled. Trusting had nothing to do with it. He couldn't leave Greta.

"Where's your room?" he asked.

"Third floor, last one on the left."

Greta's old room. Timothy didn't know why his heart started knocking at his rib cage. He followed the girl up the stairs, remaining one step behind her. Her long hair smelled of floral shampoo and he could see the muscles that had already developed into hardened lumps along her legs and arms.

The third floor was filled with light conversation, some laughter. A few doors were open, dance bags sprawled in the hall, leotards hanging over doorknobs.

As he passed one room, he heard a woman gasp. The door swung closed before he could look. He hadn't really wanted to look anyway. He had seen it all before—twenty-five years of before.

"Hey, Amanda's doing the casting couch school of dance," someone called from a half-open doorway.

The girl in front of him blushed a little, but kept walking. Timothy admired that. She had guts. She. Amanda. Timothy repeated the name in his head so that he would remember. Amanda. Amanda the Greek, the one whose last name Greta hated.

"Right here," the girl said. She stood to the side of the door in the last room, the one under the eaves.

Timothy stepped inside. The room was cold. Ice cold. Or perhaps the chill from the living room had returned. He hadn't been in this room in over twenty years. Not since the night (*he and Greta had made love in the big double bed under the slanting ceiling. He had scraped his back against the drywall and hadn't cared because he was with Greta. Everything was fine with Greta*) Karl had called Greta from the room. Timothy didn't know until the next morning that she had gone to Karl's bed, although he should have guessed, should have known. Karl, the great dancer who had become an even greater choreographer. Greta used to breathe his name when she spoke it: *Karl says . . . Karl wants . . . Karl believes . . .*

"I'm being silly, right?" the girl asked.

Timothy spun, half expecting to see Greta at the door. Amanda looked like Greta—tall, slim with long, dark hair. But there the resemblance ended. Greta hadn't looked that young, that innocent, for twenty years. "No," he said. "There's a definite draft. We'll have to move you to another part of the wing."

"That's okay," Amanda said. "I kind of like the room and it's only for a couple of days. I don't mind staying here."

I mind, Timothy thought. He crouched, touching the baseboard heaters. They were hot and the air coming through the outduct was warm. The chill seemed to be something that the heat couldn't dissipate, like an iceberg with its own refrigerator unit. "The heat's on. I could call someone—"

"No." The girl shrugged. "I'm not going to be in here much anyway. All I need is a few extra blankets."

"All right." Timothy left the room. The hallway felt like a sauna. Tension rippled off his back. He had been wrong coming to Grayson. There were as many memories here for him as there were for Greta. Perhaps more. "I'll see to it that the house staff brings up some blankets."

If the house staff was fully together. Timothy sighed. He had too much work to do. He wouldn't even get to watch class. Sometimes he wished that he hadn't stopped dancing. The pain and the constant physical exhaustion seemed easier to deal with than the myriad of tiny details that commanded his attention all day.

He walked down the hall, wondering how badly it would hurt the anniversary performance if he simply flew home.

iii

Greta felt as if she were twenty years old as she walked these stairs. They hadn't changed much. The white carpet had been pressed by too many feet, its nap matted and turned downward. The wooden railing had a newly polished feel. If she closed her eyes, she could imagine Karl waiting for her in the practice room.

She used to love to be near him, couldn't wait to touch him. The scent of his cologne used to send shivers down her back. But that had been in the early days, the first days. He continued to demand things of her, twist her to fit his shape, and she realized that nothing she ever did would be right for Karl.

Bend, Greta, arch—no, no, no, with finesse. Goddammit, girl, you could be a real dancer if you used that body of yours. Now, bend. No, like this . . .

It had grown worse after she had become his prima ballerina, the star of his company, and had moved in with him here at Grayson. Sometimes he would get her up in the middle of the night to try a new movement or run through a variation that had come to him in a dream. She had been always tired, aching, dancing with a constant pain in her left ankle, but that hadn't been the worst of it. The worst of it had been the choreography.

She took a deep breath to ease the tension from herself and then rounded the corner. The dance wing of Grayson Place had been hidden back in the trees. When Karl built Grayson, he had been afraid that rival choreographers would send spies, that dance critics would try to see his works before the premiere. So the dance wing had no windows. Pines and overgrowth protected the outside. No one could get to the auditorium and practice rooms without coming through the center of the mansion.

This wing had stayed closed after Karl died, but someone had cleaned it, polished it. Greta could remember when the white walls held dozens of sweaty fingerprints and long black slashes from brushes with dirty dance bags. Down here, she felt at home.

She walked into the practice room. Dancers were already parading in front of the mirror on the far wall. Mike, the rehearsal pianist, played random chords, checking to see if the piano was tuned. The floor glistened. Several dancers warmed up along the barre. Some stretched along the floor, while still others sat on the sides, sewing shoes and wrapping ankles. The room smelled of sweat and medicated lotion.

Greta didn't announce her presence. She went up behind Amanda and held the girl's waist to straighten her. No wonder Sebastian flirted with her. Her skin was smooth and supple, and she moved easily. Greta grabbed Amanda's right arm and bent it above the girl's head. "Your movements have to be softer," Greta said.

Sebastian was watching her. She couldn't read his dark eyes. She was growing tired of him. She was growing tired of all the young men. She hadn't had a lover older than twenty-four in nearly two decades. It was time to stop hiding behind their responsive skin and quicksilver moods, time to take a real risk in a relationship again.

She knew that Timothy was waiting for that.

"As usual," she said. "*Battement tendu.*"

Mike began the *battement tendu* music. Dancers slid into fifth position, feet touching and the heel of the right foot in front of the left toe. Then they extended one leg, moving the toe forward until it touched the floor directly in front of the body. Greta watched, seeing the differences in movement, the variations in style. The dancers slid their left foot back and then to the side, slid the foot back and behind. The movements seemed to take only a fraction of a second, but Greta saw each one.

"Sebastian," she said. "You're sloppy. Head up."

He didn't look at her, but continued watching the mirror as she instructed them through *battement tendu jeté*. Small thuds echoed as feet slapped against the floor.

Greta walked over to Sebastian, and kicked his left foot into place. "Don't look down," she said. He frowned.

They moved to the *battement frappé, battement fondu, rond de jambe*. The smell of sweat grew. Greta watched them, adjusted an arm here, a leg there. Finally she clapped her hands and the music stopped.

"Sebastian only. *Grand battement*," she said. The dancers near Sebastian moved away. Under Greta's command, he brought his foot forward into a high extension. "Stay," she said.

He held the position, leg at a hundred-and-thirty-degree angle in front of him. His entire body started to tremble and his mouth opened into a small "o."

"Go on," Greta said. He moved down into a deep *plié* with one leg, the other in front. "Stay." She stopped beside him. "Messy, Sebastian. Your line isn't clean."

"What are you doing?" he whispered. Sweat rolled down the bridge of his nose and dropped to the floor. His body was still trembling.

She didn't answer. "Finish," she said. He slipped his legs back into fifth position. Then he stood, bent over, and clutched the back of his knees, stretching and taking deep breaths. Greta put her hand on his back. She could feel the ridges of his spine beneath her palms. "You're breathing too hard. Your posture's bad and you look as if you are thinking about your feet. You're lazy, Sebastian."

"Why are you singling me out?" he whispered. "What are you doing, Greta?"

A thread of anger traced its way through her stomach. If she hadn't slept with him, he would never have asked the question. She was Madame, the head of the company, and no one was supposed to question her.

"I am conducting class." She clapped her hands. "Whole group."

The dancers returned to the barre. She started

again: *battement tendu, tendu jeté, frappé, fondu, rond de jambe*. But she wasn't watching the dancers. In her mind, she could see Karl moving among the dancers, yanking an arm out, extending a leg. One of the dancers exclaimed as if in pain, but Greta kept them moving.

"How much longer you want to repeat this pattern?" Mike asked. His voice had an edge to it, as if he had asked the question more than once.

Greta's heart was pounding. She didn't want to stay in the practice room any longer. If she did, the ghost of Karl's memory would have her out there, moving through her paces like she had moved Sebastian. Like she had moved Sebastian. Singling out one dancer had been Karl's trick. Karl had always done that to her as his way of proving that she was not his favorite.

Her stomach twisted and for a moment, she thought she was going to be sick. She clapped her hands and the dancers stopped. "Lead class, Katrina," Greta said and walked out of the room.

iv

Sebastian stood under the shower, letting the hot water caress his tired muscles, soothe his aching legs. He opened his mouth and listened to the droplets tap against his throat. The water tasted slightly of rust, but he didn't care. He frowned, remembering the odd note of command in Greta's voice. *Stay . . . Go on . . . Stay . . .*

A bar of soap hit him in the back and skated across the tile. Sebastian spit the water out of his mouth and turned. Dale hung a fluffy blue towel he had stolen from the Hyatt on the peg beside his shower. "Get this," he said. "A shower room in a house."

"This isn't a house," Sebastian said. His back muscles twitched where the soap had hit him. "It's a goddamn fortress."

"No shit. Not even the American Ballet Theater has facilities this good."

"The American Ballet Theater didn't have several hundred million dollars *and* Karl Grayson." Sebastian picked the soap off the floor, rubbed the bar between his hands until it lathered and then began scrubbing his chest.

"I wonder why we don't use this place more."

Sebastian's hands had moved to his belly. The last three nights before they had come to Grayson, Greta had screamed *Nooooo!* in her sleep and then had said, a few minutes later, in a very flat voice, *Karl is dead, Timothy.* Her entire body would shake and when Sebastian tried to ease her into wakefulness, she would scream again. "Grayson died here," he said.

"So? Someone afraid it's haunted?" Dale ducked his head under the nozzle, spraying water in several directions.

Maybe for Greta it is, Sebastian thought, but said nothing. He finished soaping his legs, then moved to his feet. He had a new pain, almost like a bruise, between the first and second toes of his right foot.

"Madame was sure a bitch today, wasn't she?" Dale shook the water from his hair. "You gonna share that soap?"

Sebastian stood up. He tossed the bar as hard as he could, hitting Dale in the stomach. The soap bounced off and skittered away, as it had after it hit him. "I don't think Greta likes it here."

"Greta, Greta, Greta," Dale mimicked as he went for the soap. "I don't think she's too happy with you either."

"Yeah." Sebastian frowned. Greta's voice seeped back up to him. *Stay . . . . Go on . . . Finish . . .*

"I think maybe you should keep your hands off

that little girl for a couple of days and maybe Madame will let you dance like the rest of us."

"Yeah," Sebastian said, but he wasn't really listening. Amanda wasn't the problem. Greta didn't get jealous, not in the normal way. She knew that no one compared with her, knew that Sebastian needed a little adulation too.

She only got angry when his dalliances became disrespectful and this one wasn't even close yet. No. Something else was bothering her. Something she hadn't told him about.

Sebastian shut off the shower. He wrapped a towel around his waist, sloshed across the tile, and tiptoed onto the icy concrete floor lining the dressing room. He would ignore Amanda tonight and he would talk with Greta. Maybe then he would know what was really going on.

V

Greta looked at the long, polished wood table in the dining room. Four white tapered candles flickered along its length. Twenty places, set with bone china, ran along the sides. One place had been set at the head. Greta stared at it. Her place now. She was head of this company. She sat in Karl's chair.

She had never really realized it before. She had been sitting in Karl's chair since the trial and since Timothy had found an attorney good enough to settle the estate. But she had never before let herself think about what sitting in Karl's place actually meant.

Bowls and empty wineglasses sat on the serving board behind the table. The dark red curtains were closed, blocking the view of the lake. Karl would have left the curtains open to watch the moonlight reflected on the waters.

She shook her head. That was wrong. He used to do that when they were alone. When the company was in residence here, the curtains remained closed so that no one would be distracted from Karl's petty games and speeches.

The smell of roast beef dominated the food scents coming from the kitchen. Greta's mouth watered. As she aged, she let herself eat things like red meat again, but she knew most of the company wouldn't touch the stuff.

Dancers were vegetarians, usually, trying to keep the calories down so that the body remained thin. She was thin and almost always cold—especially here, in this place. Thin, but strong. The muscles in her arms and legs were as powerful as they had been when she was twenty-four. When Karl had died.

Laughter echoed in the hallway. Greta started and turned away from the empty table. She didn't want to be down here when the company arrived. She wanted to make an entrance, to command their attention. That too was like Karl, but she couldn't care. Many things she would do here would remind her of Karl. They had to. She had gotten her start in Karl's company. He had been her first choreographer and the head of her first dance troupe. She had been in others, during and after the trial, but none were as well run as Karl's. She had adopted many of his techniques in her own. It was no wonder that here, in his home, she would remember that.

She went into the kitchen. A man dressed in a white chef's uniform placed broccoli florets on a bed of rice. A woman opened the long oven and pulled out the beef. On the other oven, over to the side, another woman set stuffed mushroom caps on a serving plate.

Once before, Greta had come through the kitchen to escape the dining room. Only that night, she had been escaping Karl and Timothy arguing over her.

Timothy had been young then, and very hotheaded.
The perfect male dancer, Karl used to say, tempera-
mental, passionate, and very precise. It had been her
relationship with Karl that had driven Timothy from
the dance. And it had been Karl's death that brought
Timothy back into that world.

She pushed open the other door and went up the
back stairs to her room. Timothy had placed her in the
guest bedroom suite, thoughtfully keeping her away
from Karl's old room. She checked her appearance in
the mirror.

Her skin was too pale and the shadows beneath her
eyes were too deep. The long burgundy shirtdress that
she wore open over her black silk camisole gave her
additional height. The matching burgundy pants creased
over the arch of her foot. If no one looked at her face,
she appeared important, expensive, and powerful.

Then why was it that she felt like a trapped little
girl again? The mansion brought back all of her help-
lessness, all of her rage. She clenched her fists together.
Her fingertips were cold.

A sharp rap on the door startled her and she
nearly cried out. She whirled around, staring at the
door's mahogany surface.

"Greta?"

It was Sebastian.

"Can we talk?"

She glanced at the gold watch on her left wrist.
"Dinner is in less than fifteen minutes, Sebastian."

"I know. This won't take long."

She sighed and pulled the door open. He looked
wonderful. Sebastian, the company's star, in a black
satin tuxedo that lengthened his shoulders and tapered
his already thin hips into nearly nothing. She felt a
heat on her cheeks as she stood away from the door.
"Come on in."

He bent over to kiss her, and she turned her head

so that his lips brushed her cheek. "You're stunning," he said.

"Thank you." She pulled away from him and walked to the table near the window. She put her hands on the leather armchair, indicating where he should sit. He ignored her.

"What happened this afternoon?" he asked.

The male animal in its youth. So proprietary. He let her lead him in the dance, but once the doors were closed, he seemed to think he was in charge. "You mean because I worked you harder in class than you've been worked in a long time? You're the headline star, the one who supposedly draws the crowds. If you can't dance at command, then the entire company is in trouble."

Sebastian ran a hand through his dark brown hair, leaving it slightly messy, making him look rakish and even more handsome than before. "It's not that," he said. "It's a lot of things. You don't seem like yourself."

So he had noticed that. He was more observant than she gave him credit for. She turned her back on him and looked out the window. Tall pine trees swished softly in the wind. She had been paying so much attention to the mansion itself that she had hardly noticed what was going on outside it.

"You don't know what *myself* is, little boy," she said and heard Karl in the words. He had been standing in the dining room, his hands tucked in the pockets of his jeans. *You don't understand me at all, Greta,* he'd said. *And why should you? To you, I am Oz, The Great and Terrible, and I am afraid that when you pull back that curtain and see that I am, in truth, a little old man without magic powers, but with the wisdom brought by age and experience, you will walk away, not realizing that wisdom is infinitely more valuable than illusion.*

"I know you well enough to know that you're on edge and upset."

She snorted and leaned on the chair she had been

holding. Upset didn't describe how she was feeling. She hadn't been in the place since Karl died—Timothy had taken care of all of the arrangements—and she was feeling frightened. "I don't like it here."

"Then why did we come back?"

"To do the anniversary performance." She looked down at her short, stubby fingernails. Even the burgundy nail polish couldn't hide the fact that, at forty-four, she still bit her nails.

Sebastian put a finger under her chin and lifted her face to his. He smelled faintly of cologne. "What's the real reason, Greta?"

She could see the brown flecks in his irises, the way his lashes turned upwards, and the tiny creases near the lids which narrowed his eyes and made his concern obvious.

The real reason. What was the real reason that she had returned to Grayson Place? The anniversary performance could have been held in New York. They would have had a less exclusive crowd, but a larger one. Something Karl had said. Something, the night before he died—

She shrugged to shake the memory away. "I don't really know," she said and to her surprise, tears lined her eyes. Sebastian slipped her in his arms. His body felt firm against hers, the satin warm against her skin.

"Stay with me tonight," she whispered. The words came from the little girl, the one who seemed a part of this place, the girl who was afraid to be alone.

Sebastian kissed the crown of her head. "I'll be here," he said.

vi

Amanda's mouth watered. The food smelled wonderful—roast beef, gravy, cheese-covered vegetables, and fresh bread. She hadn't eaten well since she had quit her waitressing job to join the company. An apple and scrambled eggs often served for all three meals. Dancers were supposed to be slim, but not anorexic. She watched the caterers carry the appetizers through the swinging doors. Amanda wondered how much she could eat without making herself sick.

Someone touched her shoulder. Amanda looked up. Katrina smiled at her. "Nice dress."

Amanda blushed. It wasn't a nice dress. Madame had insisted on formal attire for dinner, and all Amanda owned was her prom dress. She felt silly in a clingy, strapless gown that had seemed elegant in her high school gymnasium a year ago, but now seemed out of place and childish. Katrina, the petite principal dancer who had been with the company for six years, wore a bone ivory blouse over black silk pants. "You look beautiful," Amanda said.

Katrina handed Amanda a fluted glass filled with wine. "The secret to looking beautiful," Katrina whispered, "is to be comfortable. Everyone looks ridiculous in evening clothes. Look at Dale."

Amanda glanced across the room. Dale stood near the window, deep in conversation with Lisa. He constantly ran his finger around the neck of his shirt as if it were too tight, and when he leaned forward, she could see the cummerbund bunch around his narrow waist. She glanced back at Katrina, who smiled. "The imperfections are always there," Katrina said. "The secret is to pretend that no one will notice them. You really do look lovely."

She touched Amanda's arm and then walked away. Amanda took a deep breath. She looked lovely. Katrina's words gave her a sense of power.

Timothy took an appetizer off one of the trays as a signal that the food was available for consumption. Several other dancers picked items off the trays.

Amanda walked over to the countertop. Stuffed mushroom caps, vegetables and dip, crackers and a dozen varieties of cheese—there was enough food here to last her for an entire week. She set down her wine, grabbed a napkin, and filled it. Her stomach rumbled.

"I love these things. I can always tell who starves themselves for art."

Amanda nearly dropped the napkin, but Timothy placed a hand beneath hers. "Careful," he said. "You can't let all that food go to waste."

His palm was warm and his eyes understanding. She smiled to hide the blush that was returning to her cheeks. "Thanks," she said.

"Is your room still so cold?"

She nodded. The goosebumps were just now beginning to recede. She had felt, as she slipped into her gown, as if she were changing clothes on a ski slope.

"I think maybe we should move you, then."

"No." The word escaped before she had a chance to think about it. Despite the chill, she liked the room. It reminded her of her bedroom back home, with the slanting ceilings and a view of the pines.

Timothy shrugged. "All right," he said.

She put a mushroom cap in her mouth. Her stomach grumbled appreciatively. The cap had been stuffed with spinach, cream cheese, onions, and various spices, the mushroom itself sauteed in garlic and butter. Food had never tasted so good.

Then Timothy stiffened beside her. She followed his gaze.

Sebastian stood in the doorway, his arm protectively around Greta. Madame wore her hair in a topknot, strands framing her face, making her look younger and more vulnerable. Sebastian was watching her, and even from across the room, Amanda could see the love, admiration, and concern on his face.

She swallowed the mushroom cap. It felt like a lump in her throat. Suddenly she became conscious of the dress, her ragged haircut, and her inexpertly applied makeup. She started inching her way to the kitchen, but Timothy grabbed her elbow.

"Stay here," he said softly.

She looked up at him and saw her feelings reflected in his eyes. Only the feelings were deeper, older. She felt something flutter in her stomach, a sense of kinship, perhaps, and then she looked away.

Amanda watched as Sebastian led Madame through the room. What was there to love about that woman? She was beautiful, yes. Her thinness made her eyes wider and gave her a power that seemed to belong only to eastern European women. She moved with a grace and strength that all dancers had. But beneath that exquisite surface, Madame was cold. She had never said a kind word to Amanda in six months with the company, and the way she had treated Sebastian in class had bordered on nasty. When Amanda had gotten the job with the company, her roommates had warned her about Madame, saying that she was the cruelest choreographer in the business. She demanded perfection. But her company attracted crowds because she usually achieved it.

Madame made her way through the room, stopping to talk with an occasional dancer. Her movements seemed less fluid than usual, more brittle, and Sebastian's expression reflected a concern that Amanda had never seen. She shouldn't be feeling so out of place and jealous. She had known from the first that his main affection was for Madame. But Amanda had thought that the affection would die when he turned his attention to someone more reasonable. Once he had gotten to know her.

Being a professional dancer didn't stop childish daydreams. She took a deep breath. Timothy squeezed her arm. She nodded, as if to tell him that she would stay.

Madame took her place at the head of the table. Sebastian sat at her right. The rest of the company brought their drinks and picked seats. Timothy kept his hold on Amanda's elbow. He led her to the chair beside his, to the left of Madame.

Sebastian nodded at her. His eyes held no apology. It was as if he didn't see her. Perhaps he never had. Amanda's stomach tightened. The servers placed a large plate of roast beef in the center of the table, two gravy bowls, potatoes, but the food had lost its appeal. She could feel Timothy watching her.

He leaned over, placed his hand on her bare back in a gesture of familiarity. "You have to eat," he whispered. "You have to smile and you have to enjoy yourself."

The words were kind and she knew their basic truth. If she had problems with Madame, Amanda would have to leave. A thousand dancers lived in New York, but the company had only one Madame.

Timothy took his hand from Amanda's back. Shivers ran up and down her spine. He handed her the platter of roast beef. The china was warm. She took two slices and passed the platter on.

"It's cold," Madame said.

Amanda looked at the other woman. Deep circles ran under Madame's eyes and, up close, her face seemed drawn and pale.

"I'll see if they can turn up the heat." Timothy put his napkin on the table.

Madame covered his hand with her own. "I don't think this has anything to do with the heat, Timothy."

Something seemed to pass between them, some knowledge that Amanda didn't catch. Timothy nodded. He grabbed a spoon and loaded his plate with broccoli and rice. Then he picked up Amanda's plate and did the same.

She turned her attention to the meal as, all around her, the room grew colder.

vii

Karl sat on the balcony railings, one ankle resting on his knee, his hands on his thighs. He was talking to her, but Greta couldn't hear him. A chill, light breeze fluttered through her hair. Her ankle ached and her muscles were sore. She was exhausted, physically and mentally. Tired of fighting. Tired of Karl.

Behind him, the tall silhouettes of the pine trees were blue in the darkness. Through the trees, she could see the moon shimmering against the surface of the lake. Then she realized that it wasn't the moon. It was the northern lights.

Karl was still talking, gesturing now. She still couldn't hear him. She didn't feel like a twenty-four-year-old woman. She felt fifty and defeated, her life over before it had begun, trapped here in this place, under this sky, these stars, with this man.

"Karl," she said, her voice low, husky, seductive.

He stopped talking and watched her. She stepped forward, hitting the heels of her hands against his chest, hitting him with such force that he fell over the rail, clutching for her and missing. She thought, in a second of clarity, that if he had grabbed the railing, he wouldn't have fallen. But she had applied the right pressure to the right place and he fell, spinning, his shirt fluttering, his hands reaching for her, until he landed against the flagstones of the patio with a crack that echoed through the yard. She grabbed the railing and leaned over. His body was twisted, unnaturally even for a dancer, and a dark stain was seeping across the pavement.

For a minute, she thought he was fooling, waiting

until she ran across the pavement to grab her wrist and wrench it behind her back, to hurt her as much as she had hurt him. But he didn't move. He didn't call to her. He was dead.

The realization brought her—freedom. Freedom. She had to call Timothy.

Suddenly he was there beside her, holding her in the darkness. Not Timothy, but Sebastian. How did Sebastian get in her room? And then she remembered letting him in because the mansion frightened her.

"You were talking about northern lights and calling for Timothy," he said. "Everything okay?"

She swept her hair out of her face. The hair fell to the center of her back, wrapping her in warmth. The soft, shining smoothness of it had seemed like her only comfort with Karl. "Nightmare," she said.

"You've been having them a lot since we decided to come back here."

"We didn't decide," she said. "*I* did."

And then she knew what was wrong. Karl had said to her in the dark, his lean body against hers, his hands caressing the insides of her thighs, *What I want most is to come back here in twenty years, at the fiftieth anniversary of the company—*

Thirty-fifth for you, Greta had said.

He shrugged, waving it away. *We'll have a gala here, at Grayson, showcasing the best of the company. You'll be a choreographer then, Greta. . . .*

If I live that long, she thought.

. . . And we will make a small fortune on memories.

He had been talking about that when she pushed him. The thought of another twenty years with Karl, under his thumb, losing the best of herself to his wishes—

She shivered. Sebastian drew the blanket up. "Must have been some nightmare," he said.

She nodded, remembering Karl, the feel of his

hands on her skin. "You ever have those dreams that start out scary and you turn them into something freer, more pleasant, and then they start to get scary again, only worse—?"

Her voice shook. She wasn't sure if she was talking about her dream or her life. Sebastian still held her, but his grip had loosened. "Should we leave?" he asked.

She laughed, but the laugh sounded forced. "Because of nightmares? Don't be silly."

He eased her back down on the pillow, running his hand through her hair as if she were the child, and she clung to him, thinking about what she would have to do to cancel the fiftieth-anniversary gala. The ads were done, the promotion campaign had run for nearly two years. They were in the final stages. She couldn't pull the company away now without losing a fortune.

"We'll stay," she whispered against Sebastian's broad, furred chest. But, as she drifted off to sleep, she thought she heard Karl, laughing.

viii

Timothy sat on the bed, his hands clasped tightly together and shoved between his thighs for warmth. He waited for Amanda to return from the bathroom. He wasn't supposed to be sitting on her bed. He was supposed to be investigating the room, seeing if he could find the source of the draft. But the room seemed warmer to him than it had before, and he wondered if perhaps the heaters had merely needed time to function properly. This entire wing had been closed off until a month ago. They should have expected more troubles than one room with poorly operating baseboard heaters.

He heard a movement in the hall and his heart started pounding again. He felt foolish, waiting here for a girl who could have been his daughter. It would be so easy to say that he had found nothing and leave her, pretending that the reason he had used to walk her to her room hadn't even existed. Easy, if it weren't for that expression she had worn when Greta entered the dining room with Sebastian. He knew that expression intimately; it was etched into the grooves of his face. Only he had let it eat at him, become part of him, as the betrayals were repeated over and over again. He wouldn't let that happen to this little girl.

Amanda. If he truly cared about her, he would use her name. Timothy stood up and tugged on the crease in his satin pants. He should go before he did more damage. He knew what it was like to be on the wrong end of a relationship. Amanda didn't need two men to teach her the same lesson.

Her door opened and he saw Greta there, the young Greta, the one he had fallen in love with. "Find anything?" she asked.

The voice was all Amanda, but it didn't entirely destroy the illusion. He saw two women, a ghostly one—the remembered one—superimposed on the real one.

"No," he said. He took her hand and brought her inside, closing the door behind her. Then he wrapped his arms around her, letting the light floral scent of her fill him. Her arms caressed his back, pulling him closer. He could feel the need in her grasp.

The room seemed warm, almost too warm, as he bent down to kiss her. Her hands found his hair, holding him, as their kissing grew more passionate. He slipped his fingers into her gown, unhooking the back, and it fell off her into a pile on the floor. She managed to unbutton him, free him, and he lifted her, her dark hair flowing over his arms, onto the bed.

He felt young again, a dancer again, strong and in love. As he entered her, his back scraped against the drywall, but the pain seemed worth it, worth this moment, Greta writhing beneath him, loving him as he loved her. Finally the pressure grew too much, the love too much, and he poured himself inside her, calling her name over and over, collapsing, sticky body against sticky body, his back aching and raw.

Something warm trickled against his ear. He pushed up onto his elbows. The girl's face looked back at him, mascara ringing her eyes and leaving black streaks down her cheeks.

"Jesus," he said. "Amanda." And his heart went out to her. He had made it worse. She had lost to Greta twice in one day. The chill returned, almost as if it left Amanda's body and seeped into the air around them.

"I'm sorry." Timothy buried his face into the hollow of her shoulder. Her skin was damp, but whether with tears or perspiration, he couldn't tell. "I'm so very sorry."

ix

Greta wrapped the velour robe tightly around herself. She grabbed her hair, shook it a little, and let it cascade down her back. Sebastian grunted, sighed, and rolled over. She glanced at the bed. He had a fist pressed against his cheek. He looked like an exhausted child who had fallen asleep in the middle of a ballet. Poor boy. She had kept him awake half of the night.

The dreams were getting worse. She had thought that she had put them past her after the trial, but since she decided to return to Grayson, Karl had reentered her mind.

She opened the bedroom door and stepped into

the hallway. It was dark, the thick grainy darkness that allowed her to see vague shapes. The carpet scratched her bare feet.

She had left her youth in this place. Karl wasn't the only thing that had died in the fall from the balcony. All of Greta's dreams had died with him. Funny that she had gone on to achieve them anyway. Here she was, a major choreographer, head of her own dance company, wealthy beyond what she had anticipated, and she felt empty.

Light filtered through the balcony doors, reflecting off the living room's white furniture. A too-full moon? Or the northern lights? She crossed the room, stubbing her toe against a table leg and wincing with pain. When she reached the balcony doors, she touched the glass. It was cold.

This was the center of the mansion to her, the place she could not get out of her mind. At the trial, the experts had presented life in this room as verbally abusive, and her response as that of a classic victim pushed too far. All she remembered was the rage, the blind pure hatred. When Karl mentioned the anniversary performance again, she realized that he would never let her go, never let her be free to dance for anyone else. He would continue to borrow her choreographic suggestions and never let her work on her own. Forever, she would be his plaything, his woman, Karl's Greta, something he had molded in his Svengali-like wisdom.

Her feet were cold.

She was standing on the concrete balcony, looking over the edge. She had been acquitted of the crime. The best defense attorney in New York had planted a reasonable doubt in the jury's mind—there was no real proof that Greta had killed Karl—that, and Timothy's willingness to lie for her, to say he was with her the entire time. She had been acquitted, everywhere but in her own mind.

And in this place.

The hair on the back of her neck prickled. Someone was on the balcony with her. She turned and saw something white and see-through shimmering near the patio table. Goosebumps rippled up her arm. The shimmering shape had a vaguely human form.

"Karl?" she whispered. Her entire body was one large heartbeat. Her hands were shaking and she felt vulnerable pressed up against the railing. Would he get his revenge by killing her?

The shape gained solidity. Hands, splayed and flat, stretched out to her. Greta stifled a scream and moved away from the edge, tripping and nearly falling forward. Arms grew from the hands' wrists, slender, muscular arms. The hands grabbed at Greta, but slipped through her, dousing her in cold mist. She shivered, backed away, then remembered the railing. She would not trip and fall to her death. If she did that, she would be trapped here, with Karl, forever. But Karl couldn't grab her. Karl had no strength.

She circled around, away from the hands, until her back pressed against the glass. She groped for the metal door handle and yanked on it. The door stuck for a moment. The hands came for her, dripping mist, dripping cold. Greta tugged. The door slid open and she fell through it onto the thick carpet.

The hands hovered in the darkness. Greta was breathing heavily. She swallowed, then whispered, "I'm sorry, Karl. Really. If there had been some other way—"

"Karl forgives you." The voice was husky, female. "But *I* don't."

Greta stood up. Her legs were shaking as if she were about to perform. She grabbed the balcony door and swung it shut with a bang.

The hands faded. Greta turned and ran out of the living room, her robe flying behind her. The room was

safe. Her room was safe. Sebastian was there and he
would awaken her, comfort her, make her forget.

She so needed to forget.

X

Sebastian's eyes felt rough and gritty. His entire body
ached. At least Greta was sleeping now. She had come
back to bed ice-cold, shivering, and terrified. She
wouldn't tell him what had scared her—perhaps that
loud bang that had shaken him from sleep—and it took
him the better part of an hour to calm her down. Then
he slipped into a fitful doze, waking as sunlight spilled
into the bedroom.

Food, some in trays hovering over Sterno, had
been laid out across the table, and used plates were
stacked on the buffet. It looked as if most of the company was already awake. They were probably walking
or in the practice room stretching. The only person left
in the dining room was Timothy. Sebastian grabbed a
plate and heaped it with scrambled eggs, sausages, and
fruit. He poured himself some orange juice and sat
down next to Timothy.

Timothy looked old this morning. His hair was
tousled and lines creased his face. He didn't look up to
acknowledge Sebastian, but continued staring into his
coffee.

"Greta hardly slept at all last night," Sebastian
said.

Timothy looked up. His eyes focused on Sebastian
for the first time, and Sebastian realized that the man
hadn't even known he was there. "What?" Timothy
asked.

"I said Greta hardly slept last night. Nightmares.
And they seem to be getting worse. I think she was
sleepwalking."

"Wonderful." Timothy got up, grabbed the silver coffeepot, and poured more coffee in his cup.

"I don't think she should stay here."

Timothy sat back down. "I don't think any of us should." He shrugged. "But we're committed."

"Can't we at least get Greta out of here? This place isn't very healthy for her." Sebastian's hands were trembling. He had never been this direct with Timothy before.

"It's never been healthy for her. No reason it should change now."

Sebastian swallowed, feeling the frustration build. "I don't think she should stay here, Timothy."

"If the company stays, she stays. You know that."

"Then let's cancel the performance."

Timothy smiled, but the smile was wan. "We've spent too much time and too much money on this performance. We couldn't cancel it if we wanted to. It'll all be over tomorrow. I think we can all make it until then." He took a final sip of his coffee and stood up. Sebastian watched the other man leave. Timothy had never been that curt with him before. Perhaps it was the mention of Greta's night. It was clear even to the half-observant how Timothy felt about Greta.

Sebastian sighed and picked up his fork. Water from his eggs had congealed on the side of his plate. He pushed the plate away, grabbed an orange from the fruit basket, and headed for the practice room.

<u>xi</u>

Greta awoke to the feeling of hands around her throat. She touched her neck, but found nothing. Then she reached for Sebastian. He too was gone.

She sat up, her heart racing. It was a dream, nothing but a dream. But she knew it wasn't. As she dressed, she noted a loose flap of skin on the toe she had stubbed. Her velour robe was streaked with dirt. She had been on the balcony during the night—and something had been there with her.

She tied her hair up in a kerchief and glanced at the clock. She was running late. Class in fifteen minutes. She decided not to eat—eating would simply get in the way. She would go down and warm up with her dancers. Exercise would remove the crawlies from her skin. And the memory of that voice.

Karl forgives you.

I don't.

She had heard that voice before, but she couldn't place it. It had sounded half-familiar, like the speaking voice of a famous singer. She took a deep breath to calm herself. It was daylight. Ghosts didn't emerge in the daylight. And the performance was tomorrow. She could last that long.

But as she walked down the stairs to the rehearsal wing, she wondered. It felt as if something were stalking her, following her. Twice she stopped on the stairs only to hear a stair creak behind her. She turned, but saw nothing.

An overactive imagination, she told herself. *If it wasn't the ghost of Karl, who could it be?* She was safe as long as she remembered that the thing which tracked her was intangible, trying to get her to make her own mistakes so that she would die.

Most of the company was already in the practice room. Greta stretched and then took a place at the barre. Her legs hurt—she hadn't been working out as she usually did—but she forced herself to work anyway, putting herself through paces that she hadn't done in years. The woman's face gazing back at her from the mirror was too old, and then she remembered. This was what she used to do when she had had too much of Karl, or when the trial got too rough. She would bend and twist her body beyond human

measure and let her mind dwell on the physical
aches instead of the mental and emotional pain.

Timothy used to accuse her of willing the emotions away.

A flash in the mirror caught her eye. Something
white, not quite solid. She whirled, nearly lost her balance, and had to grip the thick wooden barre for support. Nothing. Nothing but dancers staring at themselves
in the mirror, stretching their bodies as she had
stretched hers. Sebastian wasn't even here, so no
white Danskins appeared in the room.

Greta took a deep breath. She was tired and too
tense. She always got this way at the end of the season. Add to that the stresses of the mansion and its
memories, and it was no wonder she was spooked.

Spooked. She tucked herself into a *plié*, feeling the
muscles in her legs tremble. She had killed Karl here,
pushed him with all of her strength off the balcony. A
woman should not be haunting her. The ghost in this
place should have been Karl.

A cold hand touched her shoulder. Greta whirled.
No one stood behind her.

"Are you all right, Madame?" Dale asked.

Greta nodded, feeling slightly foolish. "Are you
cold?"

Dale smiled and wiped at his flushed face. "God, no.
I think we could probably turn off the heat in this room."

She turned back and gripped the barre tightly,
doing another *plié* and going down until her thighs
were horizontal. She was the only one who felt the
cold, the only one who saw the ghost. She had to handle this one all by herself.

xii

Amanda stood in the door of the practice room, watching Greta. The old woman moved with a perfection that

Amanda's young body could not hope to achieve. Amanda rubbed her hands against her leotard. She was cold. She had been cold ever since she awakened, alone, Timothy gone. Timothy, with his cries of "Greta!" in what Amanda had hoped would be a moment of mutual comfort. Greta. Madame. The bitch.

Amanda dropped her dance bag beside all the others, taking in the familiar scents of sweat, leather, and lotion. She stretched, then rubbed powder on the inside of her shoes and took her place at the barre.

Madame whirled, her face pinched and frightened. She appeared to be looking for something, something she had seen. Amanda felt something touch her, cold hands running down her spine. For a minute she had the impression of a man falling, falling, spinning, his hands reaching out, and then she got dizzy as she followed him, clinging to him because he wouldn't let her go.

"You okay?" Katrina held her shoulders. Amanda blinked at the other dancer, still feeling off balance.

"I got dizzy for a minute."

"Sit down." Katrina led her to the side of the room. "You haven't been eating well, have you?"

Amanda started to deny it, but Katrina put up her hand. "I saw the way you ate last night. You can't cut out food. You need your strength for the dance."

Amanda nodded. Food wasn't what she needed. She needed to go somewhere warm. The cold had settled in the pit of her belly like a little iceberg fetus. She frowned, remembering the rush of chill air past her ears and the feeling of falling. "I'll be all right," she said.

"Okay." Katrina got up and walked to the barre. Amanda hugged herself and closed her eyes. She was lying on the flagstones, covered with blood—a man's blood. She looked up and saw herself leaning over the balcony. Then she reached up a hand and realized that it was etched in mist, that she had no substance.

Something was inside her. Those weren't her memories. That was Madame leaning over the balcony—a young Madame, looking vulnerable and frightened. "Get out," Amanda whispered, but the thing's icy fingers gripped her even tighter and she stood up, even though she didn't want to.

xiii

It was in the room. Greta couldn't ignore it any longer. She turned and looked at the dancers, keeping an eye on the mirror. She hadn't seen any more white flashes, no hands appearing mysteriously out of the air. If she stayed here, she *would* see that. It would reveal itself to her and she would look foolish in front of her dancers. She couldn't risk that.

If she left the practice room, it would follow. She adjusted her kerchief, stepped away from the barre and crossed the polished floor into the hallway.

Amanda followed.

Amanda. That little slip of a girl. Greta glanced over her shoulder. The girl's eyes held something strange. Fear? The girl glanced at her and for a moment, Greta thought she was seeing herself. No. She was simply looking at a leggy, dark-haired teenager. All new dancers had that frightened expression, especially around their choreographer.

Greta hurried out into the hall, Amanda forgotten. The living room would be the place to go. No one would be there now. She hurried up the stairs. The bones in her ankles felt brittle, especially the left ankle, where she had had the old injury. She remembered this feeling in the pit of her stomach from those last days with Karl—a feeling of heaviness, oppression, coupled with the knowledge that if something didn't change, she would crack.

Sebastian nearly crashed into her as she rounded the top stair. He caught her arms. "Greta, are you okay?"

"Fine," she snapped. She didn't have time for Sebastian and his concerns. She was going to settle this. She could feel the shape at her heels, like a bad dream, hovering, threatening to reveal things that should remain secret. Greta opened the door to the living room.

Timothy sat in the overstuffed chair, staring at the silent phone. He glanced up at her, his eyes sunken and haunted. She couldn't stay here either. Timothy would try to handle it for her, and he couldn't. This was one that she had to handle herself.

Greta pulled open the balcony door, feeling cool air wash over her. Fear rose in her stomach, but she pushed it away. She thought she had ended things here once. She would try again. The ghosts lived on the balcony, not in the mansion. The memories centered around this concrete overhang with its molded iron railing.

She stepped onto the concrete, past the patio furniture, feeling the breeze whip at her kerchief. Behind her, the patio door closed. Amanda stood there, looking young, powerful, and angry.

"Leave me alone," Greta said.

"Like you left me all these years?"

The voice was not Amanda's. It was the voice Greta had heard the night before, in the darkness. A gauzy film completely obscured Amanda. Greta squinted, recognized the shape.

She should have recognized it. She had seen it enough in the mirror years back, dancing across from her, mimicking her moves. The dancer. The prima ballerina. The girl Karl had loved, used, and misused. The one who had approached Karl and hit him with the heels of her hand.

"You killed him," the voice said. "Then you *left* me

here with him. And the only way I can get rid of him is to give him *you*."

Amanda seemed diminished. Greta reached for her, and stopped when she felt coldness around the girl's body.

"Who are you?" Greta asked.

"So long that you don't even remember." There was pain in the voice. Amanda came closer.

Greta did not move.

"Let me show you," the voice said. Amanda touched Greta's arm. The chill slipped into her, filling her. Pain flooded in with the chill. Physical pain first, from the years of stretching an underdeveloped body into the dance. Then dreams of being a prima ballerina, adored by the crowd, by people, by those close to her. And then Karl, taking those dreams, shattering them, image by image. *You could be a dancer if you use that body of yours,* he had said at the height of her career. She had the adulation, but she couldn't enjoy it. She was talented, loved, but imperfect. Karl kept stretching her and stretching her until she thought that she would break, she *knew* that she would break, and she hit him with both hands and sent him flying—

The balcony door opened with a snap. Greta backed away. She didn't want Timothy and Sebastian to see her like this. Sebastian stopped at the doorway, but Timothy kept coming. Timothy, who had loved the girl, would recognize the girl who had possessed Amanda.

Suddenly the cold left Greta, separated from her, and she felt hands slap against her chest, Amanda's hands, chill hands. Greta's balance shifted, and she knew that she was going to fall. She grabbed for Amanda's wrists, but the cold was too thick. Greta's fingers slid off Amanda's skin. The iron railing dug into Greta's thighs and she fell, spinning, turning. Timothy leaned over the railing and she reached up to him—*Timothy!*—he had always saved her, always, but then there was nothing, nothing but flagstones, sharp, all-encompassing pain (*the last dance move, the final impossible twist*) and Karl's hands on her, lifting her.

Everything will be all right, he said, his voice kind and sad.

She looked up, saw herself—the other part of herself, the part made up of dreams and hopes, the part she used to think was the best part of herself—as mist engulfing Amanda. And as she watched, the mist disappeared.

Karl ran his hand along her hair. *Silver,* he said. *Just like I told you.* He put his arm around her. She looked down and saw her body twisted and bleeding on the flagstones. *You don't need it,* Karl said. *You will dance so much better without it. Come. There is much work for us to do.*

Work. With Karl. *Timothy!* she cried, but he turned away and she knew that he couldn't hear her, that he would never hear her or save her again.

You are mine, Greta, Karl said. He led her back inside, toward the auditorium. As they went though the open door, she thought she heard laughter, female laughter, following them.

xiv

The rusted iron cut into the palm of his hand. Timothy leaned over the railing. Greta lay there in a final, obscene curl, her body at last failing her. He sighed, having seen it before, from the same balcony, knowing that she, too, was dead. Only this time, it didn't come as a shock. Somehow he had always known that Greta would die, perhaps because she had never seemed completely alive—not since Karl's death.

Timothy turned. Sebastian stood against the glass doors, his eyes wide. Amanda clutched the railing, swaying. Her face was white, her features jutting out prominently against hollow cheekbones. He wondered how he'd ever thought that she looked like Greta. Amanda looked like herself.

Timothy closed his eyes, again seeing the young Greta push her older self off the balcony. Amanda was simply a tool, nothing more.

"Did you see it?" Timothy asked. He opened his eyes.

"Amanda pushed her," Sebastian whispered.

"No!" Amanda cried. Her voice was shaking. Timothy put a hand on hers. Her skin was damp, chill, as if she had been buried in snow.

"Madame fell," Timothy said. The second lie was easier than the first, perhaps because this time, it was not really a lie. "Greta slipped and fell."

Sebastian locked eyes with him for a moment, then looked away in tacit agreement.

Timothy took a deep breath. Time to go to the phone, to tell the police about another body at Grayson. And when that was over, he would have decisions to make, about the company, about the performance (*it wouldn't be an anniversary performance. It would be a memorial*), about the publicity. Funny that he didn't feel tired. Or sad. Or even empty.

He felt free.

IN THE AIR
Maureen F. McHugh

You may think that *you* had trouble getting your relatives to approve of your choice of a mate—well, as the
wry and funny story that follows demonstrates, it could
have been *much* worse. At least your disapproving relatives were probably *alive*. . . .

Born in Ohio, Maureen F. McHugh spent some
years living in Shijiazhuang in the People's Republic of
China, an experience that has been one of the major
shaping forces on her fiction to date. Upon returning
to the United States, she made her first sale in 1989,
and has since made a powerful impression on the SF
world of the early 1990s with a relatively small body
of work, becoming a frequent contributor to *Asimov's
Science Fiction*, as well as selling to *The Magazine of
Fantasy and Science Fiction*, *Alternate Warriors*, *Aladdin*,
and other markets. In 1992, she published one of the
year's most widely acclaimed and talked-about first
novels, *China Mountain Zhang*, which received the
prestigious Tiptree Memorial Award. Her most recent
book is a new novel, *Half the Day Is Night*. She lives
with her family (including a dog named Smith, who is
suspiciously like a certain character in this story) in
Twinsburg, Ohio.

In the Air

I join a dog club. I take along Smith, my seven-month-old Golden Retriever, because, of course, if you are going to join a dog club, it should be because you want to train your dog. Smith can already slap her butt on the floor when she hears the rattle of the dog biscuit box. Smith will even sometimes sit when told to, even if no puppy cookie is in evidence. But Smith doesn't heel and doesn't stay.

This doesn't strike me as a major problem. Smith is housebroken, which is what really matters. And if she jumps on people when they come to the door, well, the only person who's come recently was UPS delivering my videotape on "Decorating with Sheets," and if I've become the kind of person who lives in the suburbs and has a golden retriever and orders videotapes called "Decorating with Sheets," then life is already too surreal to worry about whether or not Smith can heel and stay.

"I'm thinking about sponge painting," I say, to the air, to Michael, who is practically air anyway.

Michael nods. Even though I'm not looking at him, I can tell that he nods; we're twins, and I know these things about Michael.

"Imagine it, *sponge* painting. Wallpaper." My back window opens on trees and sometimes cows, and I'm looking out of it instead of at Michael. "Next will be fabric painting and decoupage."

"There's no rule that says that just because you live in the suburbs you *have* to be vapid," Michael says, oh so softly, softly enough that his voice might not even be there.

Michael is wearing a plaid shirt and a white T-shirt and boots. I realize that the shirt looks like one of Joe's. Which is probably on purpose, although, with Michael, I don't know if "purpose" is exactly the right description. (Does grass have "purpose" when it grows? Do cats have "purpose" when they hunt?)

Joe is still in Brooklyn and I'm here in Ohio, and I haven't seen Joe since he moved in with Keith five years ago, and I'm not a fag hag anymore, I'm a suburban matron. I don't even miss Joe or all that sexual tension—his for guys, mine for him.

I think about those abortive attempts at sex with Joe, and I'm embarrassed for both Joe and myself yet again.

"I'm middle-aged," I say.

Michael says nothing. He doesn't say that thirty-six is hardly middle-aged. He doesn't say that just because I've put on ten pounds and now weigh 140, that doesn't mean that I've become suddenly soft and frowsy and invisible.

I don't know why weighing 140 pounds means I'm middle-aged, but it does. It is a magic number. A matronly number. More important than wishing young people would get their hair out of their eyes and more important than thinking Green Day sounds banal and that MTV is too sexist. If I could lose ten pounds, then maybe I could put off middle age for a while. But the thought of dieting, of thinking of food *all the time*, seems like too much to contemplate.

"You need to get out of this place," Michael says. "You need to meet people."

So I join a dog club to stave off middle age.

*   *   *

The dog club meets at an armory. There are obedience classes and then a meeting. There are eleven people in the obedience class: eight women and three men. There are two golden retrievers, a Labrador retriever, a cocker spaniel, a Doberman, a boxer, two poodles, and three dogs that may be mutts for all I know. The cocker spaniel and one of the mutty-looking dogs are complete and total spazzes, which makes me feel better about Smith. Smith is a noodlehead, straining at the end of her leash until she strangles in her ecstasy of meeting other people and other dogs, but the cocker spaniel snaps at whoever comes near and the one mutty-looking dog is so oblivious to its owner that it might as well be deaf.

I get far away from both the cocker spaniel and the mutty-looking dog when they line up, and the Labrador retriever ends up behind us. A very large lady in stonewashed jeans is in front of us. The lady has a tiny pink poodle—it is really white, but it's so white that its skin shows through its fur and makes it look pink. It has a pink collar.

"It's probably named 'Angel' or 'Sweetie,'" the man with the Labrador says, *sotto voce*.

The pink poodle barely comes to the middle of the woman's calf. It doesn't have a clue what it is supposed to do, and the giant woman is quite uncomfortable.

"Jerk on the collar," the teacher says. The giant woman gives a tentative jerk that the pink poodle doesn't really notice. The pink poodle dances around on its tiny feet, looking up. Poodles have old faces, like midgets.

"No," the teacher says to the giant woman, "you have to be firm. He has to know what you want."

"Sit, Armand!" says the giant woman, and jerks, and the little poodle bounces up off its tiny poodle toes and flies up to about the woman's thigh. The giant woman goes to her knees, stricken, and comforts Armand, who doesn't seem particularly concerned. Armand's tongue is pink, too.

At least Smith weighs sixty pounds and is not likely to fly at the end of her lead like a tetherball.

The teacher finally gets the pink poodle to sit.

We are next. I reach into my pocket and say, "Sit." Smith, who knows what the hand in the pocket means, plops her butt obediently on the mat on the concrete armory floor.

"Is it okay if I give her a cookie?" I ask.

"No," the teacher says, "she'll learn to respond to you out of love."

"Good girl!" I say, full of enthusiasm, and Smith smiles with her eyes on my pocket. Smith does love me, but she'd really like a cookie and I've implicitly promised one, so it is rotten not to give it to her, but at least Smith has sat on command. The teacher is pleased and moves on.

I could sneak the dog biscuit to Smith, but there is nothing subtle in the way Smith eats a dog biscuit. Ah well, sometimes even dogs have to have their expectations dashed. I kneel down and ruffle Smith's ears and whisper that the world is not fair, but Smith doesn't care about philosophy and wants into my pocket.

Behind us, the teacher is working with the man and the black Labrador. "Cruise," says the man, "sit!" The black Lab jumps excitedly at the teacher. Cruise is so black he shines like a wet seal under the flourescent light.

"Cruise!" says the man, exasperated. Cruise's tongue appears to be about a foot long, and he wants desperately to lick the teacher.

"It's okay," the teacher says. He pets Cruise for a minute and then steps back.

"Sit!" says the man. Cruise wavers, looking up, intelligence perhaps creeping into that walnut-sized brain, as Michael would say. "Sit!" Cruise drops his butt to the ground.

"Good boy!" says the man, relieved. And Cruise

lunges for the teacher, tail whipping, excited to death, all sloppy tongue and paws the size of dinner dishes. "Cruise!" says the man, bracing himself and grimacing; the shock of the Lab going to the end of the lead is almost enough to jerk him off his feet. The teacher goes on to the next student, and the man yanks at the leash. Cruise doesn't care. I know all about being yanked off my feet—Smith could happily strangle herself on her choke chain, apparently unconcerned that no oxygen is getting in. Michael always says it's because her brain is so small that it doesn't require a lot of oxygen.

The guy is obviously embarrassed. Cruise hadn't been that bad. "He's a happy fellow, isn't he?" I say. Cruise smiles at me with his long tongue and tries to leap on me.

"At least his toenails aren't pink," the man says, grimly hauling on the dog.

The man's name is Larry, and Cruise was named by his thirteen-year-old daughter, who is in love with Tom Cruise and the vampire movie, *Interview with a Vampire*. Larry isn't wearing a wedding ring. "I see her every other weekend," he says. "She lives with her mother." He smiles in a self-deprecating way. "Her mother lets her see R-rated movies. I live with Cruise here."

"Cruise is a good name for him," I say, not thinking about the vampire movie, which I haven't seen, but of the movies with the fighter jets and the race cars. Tom Cruise has a kind of boyishness that fits black Labradors.

Larry is okay. An ally in this class. One, because he is wicked in the right way, about things like poodles with pink toenails. Two, because Smith is better-behaved than Cruise. I'm not sure I could have liked Larry if he'd had a perfect dog, which is petty, but there it is.

"Maybe we could get together this weekend to practice," Larry says.

"Okay," I say.

"I'm living in an apartment," Larry says. "Do you have a place where we could practice?"

"We could practice on my driveway," I say before I even think it through. "Edify the neighbors." Entertain Michael, too.

Michael is there when I get home. "Were you waiting for us?" It's hard to tell if Michael waits for people or not.

"How was the first day of kindergarten?" he asks. He isn't dressed like Joe. This time he's dressed like Tony, khaki pants and loafers and cool, artsy black shirt. Married Tony.

"Why the costumed history of my romantic disasters?" I ask.

Michael doesn't answer.

Smith runs to him, tail waving in ecstasy. Smith always appears to have just met someone she loves who she hasn't seen for months. Sometimes, I can get her to go nuts by going outside, ringing the doorbell, and coming back in. But Smith does love Michael, even when she can't touch him. She dances around him, leaping and jumping.

"You really should be dressed like Sharon," I say. Sharon was Tony's wife, and she haunted our affair much more than Michael ever did. I don't know what Sharon dressed like; I never met her. I only knew her through what Tony said. Tony said she went to a manicurist. "Class was okay," I say. I look in the fridge for a can of diet. "I met someone. A guy, named Larry, with a black Labrador named Cruise. We're going to practice together this weekend."

I look over the fridge door to see Michael's reaction, but Michael is gone.

Smith leaps onto the couch and sniffs. Did Michael leave a scent, an ectoplasmic remnant?

I suspect that Michael is pissed about Larry.

"He's divorced," I say to the still and empty air. "He has a thirteen-year-old daughter. I'm not interested in anybody with a kid."

The air stirs, which sometimes means Michael, and sometimes just means a draft.

"I'm not crazy," I say, meaning that I wouldn't be interested in someone with a thirteen-year-old girl.

There is no reaction.

Sometimes, at night, when I put the dog in the crate and go upstairs, Smith barks. Smith won't sleep with me; she's always slept in the crate, and if I bring her up to sleep in bed with me, she sits at the door and whines. But she's like a little kid, and sometimes she isn't ready to go to bed at bedtime.

Smith barks, and then there's the sound of something thumping against metal. The sound is Smith wagging her tail and hitting the crate. A muted ching, ching, ching. A greeting wag. A happy wag. Michael is with the dog. I don't ever hear anything else, not the crate opening, not Michael saying anything. Is he inside the crate with Smith?

Smith isn't the only one that Michael visits at night. Not every night, not even most nights, but enough. I never see anything. He just sits on the bed, or I feel his knees behind mine, my back is to his chest, warming me. I go to sleep with his arm around me. He used to steal my covers when I was little. He was all elbows when we were kids. He was gone for years and years, from about twelve to sometime in college. But came back then, sliding in with me while Laurie, my roommate the education major, slept unaware in the other bed. He is always my age. A ghost that grows older as I do. A ghost that was never legally alive.

My stillborn twin.

*   *   *

Larry drives an old Accord, and Cruise sits in the passenger seat next to him, pink tongue lolling. Cruise flings himself across the gearshift and across Larry's lap, and Larry can't open the door for a moment while he struggles with the dog, but finally they are both on the driveway.

Smith is wiggling, alternately crouching and leaping at the end of her lead. Cruise lunges against his lead. "Hi!" Larry calls, and he lets Cruise drag him up the walk to the house, and the two dogs meet nose to nose, then head to tail, and then start to tear madly around, tangling their leads.

I'm smiling, grinning, even though the two dogs are being such a pain and Larry is calling Cruise a "dumbshit." "Dumbshit" is said with such well-worn practice and deep affection that I know that Cruise thinks it's his name.

"Come in," I say.

"Are you sure you want me to?" Larry asks.

There's nothing two dogs are going to do to my house that one dog hasn't already done. So he comes into my empty house. There is no furniture in the living room or the dining room, just Smith's crate. There's a couch and two chairs in the family room, but I don't have any end tables, just a lettuce crate, a real one, taken from behind a grocery store. Real crates don't quite have the panache of the ones that people buy for furniture. There aren't any pictures on the walls.

"When I pulled up I thought this neighborhood didn't look anything like I'd expect you to live in," Larry says.

"I haven't lived here long," I say. I practically apologize. "I just bought this place." I feel compelled to explain that my mother died and left her house that I sold so I could buy this place, but I don't want to tell him that because he will feel compelled to offer me sympathy, and my mother's death was awful and I don't want sympathy right now, I want to train dogs.

We train on the driveway, parading up and down and saying "SIT!" a lot. Larry is nervous, jerking Cruise roughly to get his attention. Not that this seems to bother Cruise, who sits on one hip, tongue lolling, looking around. Smith is in a flaky mood, more interested in chewing on the leash than listening.

"You can put bitter apple on that leash to stop her from chewing it," Larry says.

"I don't know, I mean, does it really *matter* if she chews it?" Is it bad? Are dogs not supposed to chew leashes? Smith always chews her leash.

"I guess not," Larry says. This seems to make him obscurely happy. "I read some dogs actually like bitter apple anyway."

"I spray it in the garbage can," I say.

"That's a good idea," Larry says—

Michael comes around the house, and Smith and Cruise both leap up and bound toward him.

It's hard not to look at Michael. But since no one else can see him, I try not to when anyone else is around.

"Shit," Larry is saying. "Cruise! You dumbshit! Cruise!"

Go away, I think. Michael, don't play games, go away.

Smith crouches, ears back, tail wagging, wheezing at the end of her leash. She is so sweet on Michael. Michael stops, watching the kids down the street. Cruise barks, but Michael doesn't seem to notice. I'm trying to watch him out of the corner of my eye.

"What is it?" Larry asks. "What are they after?"

"I don't know," I lie.

Larry lets Cruise drag him toward Michael, but Michael won't stay, of course. Cruise bounds around, barking, barking. Smith wants to look around the side of the house, but when she doesn't see Michael there, she decides instead to go to Larry. I realize too late, and Smith crosses leashes and Cruise comes back to see what's going on, and every time I try to get around Larry to untangle Smith, Smith and Cruise follow.

It should be funny, but it isn't because I'm upset about Michael. "Smith!" I keep yelling. "Smith, you damn dog!"

"Hold still," Larry is saying. "Wait, let me—no, go *that* way—"

He is too busy trying to get me to do it his way to see what I'm after, and I find myself thinking about how typical he is while at the same time trying not to be angry. We're both entirely too polite when the dogs are finally untangled and Cruise is sitting on one hip, tongue lolling, watching the kids across the street, and Smith is belly to the driveway, trying to cool off.

I get the dogs some water and bring Larry a glass of iced tea, and we sit on the porch and contemplate the day.

"Caitlin's mother told me that her husband is probably going to be transferred to San Diego," Larry says.

It takes me a moment to remember that Caitlin is Larry's daughter. "Oh no," I say, "they can't do that, can they?"

"We'll have to renegotiate the visitation schedule. Maybe have her stay with me in the summer or something." Larry is looking at Cruise.

I don't know what to say.

"I think they've had enough of a break," Larry says. "Come on, you sluggard, let's whip you into shape."

Cruise levers himself up, and we go back to the driveway. Smith isn't at all interested in heeling.

Michael comes back around the house.

The dogs erupt.

"Damn it," Larry says. "Cruise!" and yanks the strain-

ing dog into a sitting position and smacks his back with
the flat of his hand.

Startled, Cruise cringes.

For the first time this afternoon, Michael looks
over at Cruise on his back, paws in the air, submissive,
and then at me.

He's not cruel, I want to say. *You're* cruel, you're
causing this!

I refuse to acknowledge Michael's presence. In the
morning, Smith is rattling in her crate. I hear her before
I get downstairs. Smith has her ball in her mouth and is
growling delightedly. Dancing with her paws. Raugh-
raugh-row-ru. Let me out. Let me out and play.
Michael must be there, because Smith insists on believing that Michael can let her out. Maybe he does at
night, how would I know? At the bottom of the stairs I
can see only Smith and the crate. Smith looks over and
sees me and happily switches her attention. Raugh-
raugh-row-ru. No one else is there.

After I drink my coffee and go upstairs, he is
reflected in my bathroom mirror as I brush my teeth,
but I stoically brush without so much as flicking my
eye in his direction. He leans against the doorframe,
silent and apologetic. He shoves his hands in the pockets of his jeans. At least he's not dressed like some old
boyfriend. Is his hairline receding? But I avoid the
temptation to really look. Perhaps it's been receding
all along and I just hadn't noticed, the way you don't
notice the gradual change of something familiar. The
way you don't notice things getting dusty until there
they are, covered in dust.

I rap my brush against the sink, all efficiency and
business. When I turn around, he's not there. I undress
and take my shower. I'm used to showering with
Michael around. I don't think he watches.

When I get out of the shower, the mirror is all steamed, and in the steam is written, "Without you I am not."

I turn on the fan and open the window, and the words dry up and leave no trace. If I had written it, after it was dry you could see the smear of my fingers, but when Michael does it, it just dries away.

I turn the fan off before I go to work.

Larry calls me at work. He's called me twice before, once to get directions to my house and another time just to chat. He *is* interested in me, which I sort of like and sort of don't. I'm not really attracted to him, so in the end this will probably end up being more trouble than it's worth. He misrepresented himself. He said he wasn't interested in dating, that he just wanted to spend a little time getting himself back on his feet, concentrating on his job. "I don't want to rebound," he said. I had the image of him leaping up after a basketball, which, since Larry is tall, is not so strange.

Larry wants to know if we could meet for dinner. "I'd ask you for lunch," he said, "but I'm all the way downtown. I don't want to ask you on a date," he says and then stops. "I mean, it's not that I think you're not attractive or anything, but I really have the feeling that we're getting to be friends, you know? And I don't have very many friends. I mean, it's not that I don't have *friends*, I'm not saying that. I really *do* have friends. I don't know why I said that. But I don't want to jeopardize our friendship, you know?"

"Why don't we go dutch," I say. "I like the idea of friendship and I'm not looking for a relationship either."

He sighs on the other end of the phone, relieved. He is having trouble with his daughter, Caitlin, the thirteen-year-old, he says. "I don't know anything about thirteen-year-old girls," he says.

"It's a pretty horrible age," I say, sympathetic.

He laughs. "So there's hope she'll grow out of it?"

"Well," I say, "if her only problem is that she's thirteen, then she's in pretty good shape."

After work, I drive home to let Smith out of the crate. Out into the backyard, let the dog pee, throw a stick a couple of times, and then back into the crate. Smith isn't happy after having been in the crate all day.

I don't want to go back and meet Larry. I have this feeling, this antipathy, before parties, before most social events. If I just go, it will be fine. Most of the time, once I get there I have a much better time than I expected. It seems like so much trouble to sit and listen to a man I hardly know sit and talk about his daughter.

The air stirs, warms. Smith looks up, ears forward, nose working. The tip of Smith's tail switches. I could stay home. I could stay home with Michael and Smith. It would be easy.

I grab my jacket and run.

Applebee's is crowded, and we have to stand and wait for a table. "We should have gotten here earlier," Larry says.

"The price of dependents," I say, and then realize that since Larry is worried about his daughter, calling our dogs dependents may suggest that I think they're as important as Caitlin. But Larry grins.

Larry is wearing a suit, which makes him look very different. His dog clothes change him, make him accessible and a little silly, the way men's casual clothes do. He isn't silly at all in a gray suit. He makes me uncomfortable, but interested somehow.

I expect him to start talking about Caitlin, his daughter. I am braced for him to do so, but instead he starts talking about his job. He runs the graphics and design department for a stationery company. He used to be an artist, but, he says, he sold out for the promise of a mortgage and a family. "Not really such a bad idea," he explains. "I really don't have the right temperament for a fine artist. I hate to be by myself. You know, working in my studio, nothing but me and the muse. My muse doesn't carry on much of a conversation, I guess."

He likes his job, something that comes through even his talk of too-short deadlines. He likes working with the young designers, he likes their music and their strange haircuts.

He is really much more interesting than I expected. We never actually do get around to talking about Caitlin.

I'm a little sorry when he doesn't kiss me before I get into my car. I hope he is, too.

Michael is in the air, but that is all. I don't know if that is good or not. I'll have to pick. Michael has never made me pick before. It isn't fair that he is going to make me pick, because I've only gone out with this man for dinner and that was only just as friends. Why is he doing this? What if I pick Larry and it doesn't work out?

"Puppy," I whisper to Smith, looking for comfort. Smith holds my fingers in her mouth, not biting, not really. Smith is happy, lying there on the couch, holding on to my fingers.

In the kitchen, something hits the floor and shatters. Smith starts. The plate I ate dinner on is broken on the floor. My glass slides off the counter, shatters on the hardwood.

"Michael," I say.

The refrigerator door opens and a jar of mustard slides out and hits the floor but does not break. It rolls toward the cabinet.

He has never done anything like this.

"Michael," I whisper. "Stop it."

Nothing else happens.

Smith cowers behind my legs. "It's okay, baby," I say. I sit on the floor and she runs to me and stands on my lap, sixty pounds of dog.

"You scared the *dog*," I say accusingly to the air. Michael likes Smith. At least, I think that Michael likes Smith.

If Michael starts doing things like this, what will I do? I can't leave Michael; it isn't some building he haunts, it's *me*. Anywhere I go to live, Michael will come *with* me.

Imagine life without Michael.

I cannot, I cannot.

"You used me." That's what it says in the steam on the mirror the next morning.

I don't know what it means, so I pretend not to see it.

I open my closet and look at my clothes. I can't wear my city clothes anymore, I'm too fat. My gypsy skirts and silk shirts. All I can wear are the things I have bought since then. My wardrobe of suburbia, my fat-assed jeans and sweatshirts.

"Are you warning me?" I ask the air. "What's so different about Larry?"

The indifferent air doesn't answer.

Choose. Choose the living or the dead. Put like that, it should be easy.

I have to do something. I call Larry, half expecting that when I pick up the phone, the contents of my desk will go flying across the room, or the file cabinets will open and spill tongues of manila. But nothing happens.

Larry sounds as if I woke him up. Eight-thirty on

a Saturday morning, maybe *he* was asleep, but Smith won't let me sleep that late.

"I was just wondering if you wanted to bring Cruise over and do some practice," I say.

"Sure," he says. "Yeah. What time is it?"

"Maybe you can come over in a while and leave Cruise here and we'll go get breakfast. Unless you've eaten." Although I know he hasn't eaten.

"Okay," he says.

"He's coming," I tell the room after I hang up the phone.

There's no response. I don't expect one.

I let Smith out in the backyard. I turn on the television and flip through the channels, turn off the television. I start to put dishes in the dishwasher and decide to make tea first, and then while tea is brewing, I go upstairs and make my bed and forget about the tea. The house is empty.

Where does Michael *go* when he isn't here?

It is forever before Larry calls back and says he's awake now, that he's on his way, should we eat at Bob Evans?

Does the room air stir as his car pulls up, or am I only anticipating?

"You want a cup of coffee before you go?" I ask, standing on my front step.

"Sure," says Larry. He's wearing khaki shorts, and briefly I think of Tony, but Tony always wanted to look like he was on his way to a Soho gallery opening and Larry looks like a department manager. What is different about Larry? Why does Michael suddenly want me to choose?

Cruise leaps exuberantly into the foyer. Larry looks tired. From work? From getting up in the morning? What do I know about this man?

The air stirs. Smith barks, and Cruise whirls in ecstasy. I look for Michael, but I don't see anything.

"Cruise!" Larry says. "Jesus, why does he always do this?"

"No," I say, "it's okay."

I can't see Michael. Has there ever been a time when Smith could see Michael and I couldn't? There've been times Michael left just as I got there, but never a time Smith could see him and I couldn't.

I feel sick.

Cruise bounds and rears to put his paws on Michael's chest or shoulders or something—and falls through. The dog's astonishment would be comic if I weren't so frightened. Smith barks, tail happy and delighted.

Larry watches without comprehension.

Cruise tries again, then tries to shove his nose in Michael's hand.

Larry goes over to see what's going on, walks into the space where Cruise is trying to get to Michael. Are Michael and Larry occupying the same space? The idea makes me feel ill, Michael within Larry, Larry within Michael.

I cover my mouth with my hand, but I can't think of anything to say. For a moment, I feel so angry at Larry. Bumbling, unwitting man in my house! Outsider! But Larry is on one knee, trying to calm Cruise.

"Hey, hey, hey," Larry is saying, letting Cruise lick his face and dance and just be the big, black animal that he is. Larry likes Cruise. Of course Larry likes Cruise, but somehow every time I see Larry, he's worried about whether or not Cruise is behaving.

Smith flops down, tongue out. Is Michael gone? And if he's gone, is he ever coming back?

Michael. Michael. Don't leave me!

Something thuds upstairs, and for a second I think it's a body. Something big and heavy. Suicide! But Michael doesn't really *have* a body. I run upstairs and find my bookcase pushed over.

So he's not gone.

I don't mind that he's angry, as long as he's not *gone*.

Larry comes upstairs slowly. "What happened?"

"The bookcase fell over," I say.

There's no earthly reason for the bookcase to have fallen over, and yet, there it is. As we stand there, looking at it, my tall, four-drawer filing cabinet tips slowly and majestically forward, drawers sliding open, papers just beginning to spill when it completely over-balances and falls.

"Oh, my God," says Larry.

"It's a ghost," I say. "It's the ghost of my brother. We're having an argument about you."

Larry looks at me, frowning.

"I'm really sorry," I say lamely. "Michael, stop it, you'll scare the dogs." And then to Larry again, "He likes dogs. At least, I think he does."

"Is this a *joke*?" Larry asks. He looks at the wall and then at the four-drawer. Probably wondering if this is some sort of bizarre humor. Like I'm David Copperfield or Penn and Teller or something, and this is what I do to all my prospective boyfriends.

Michael is standing in the middle of the room, chest heaving from exertion. "Don't ignore me," he says to me.

Larry is standing gape-mouthed.

"Do you *see* him?" I ask.

"What," Larry says, "what's going on?" He *does* see him! No one has *ever* seen Michael before!

"Larry," I say, "this is my brother, Michael. Michael, this is Larry."

I feel light-headed. Looking at Larry, I don't know if he'll leave or if he'll stay. I don't know what *either* of them is going to do. But I don't care. I am oddly, in fact, deliriously, happy.

NORTH OF
DIDDY-WAH-DIDDY

Michael Swanwick

Michael Swanwick made his debut in 1980 and has
gone on to become one of the most popular and
respected of all that decade's new writers. He has several times been a finalist for the Nebula Award, as well
as for the World Fantasy Award and for the John W.
Campbell Award, and has won the Theodore Sturgeon
Award and the *Asimov's* Readers Award poll. In 1991,
his novel *Stations of the Tide* won him a Nebula Award
as well. His other books include his first novel, *In The
Drift*, published in 1985, a novella-length book,
Griffin's Egg, and 1987's popular novel *Vacuum Flowers*.
His critically acclaimed short fiction has been assem-
bled in *Gravity's Angels* and in a collection of his col-
laborative short work with other writers, *Slow Dancing
Through Time*. His most recent book is a new novel, *The
Iron Dragon's Daughter*, which was a finalist for the
World Fantasy Award and the Arthur C. Clarke Award.
Swanwick lives in Philadelphia with his wife,
Marianne Porter, and their son Sean.

In the wild, headlong, and vivid adventure that

follows, he demonstrates that some kinds of ties can't be broken even by death, and that some kinds of love are strong enough to stick with you no matter *where* you go—even if you go all the way to Hell . . . or *beyond*.

North of Diddy-Wah-Diddy

The train to Hell don't stop in New Jersey. It pulls out of Grand Central Station at midnight, moving slow at first but steadily picking up speed as it passes under the Bay, and by the time we hit the refineries, it's cannonballing. We don't stop for nothing. We don't stop for nobody. And if you step in our way expecting Old Goatfoot to apply the brakes, well, pardon me for saying it, but you're going to get exactly what's coming to you.

We don't stop and we don't slow down once that gleaming black-and-silver locomotive leaves the station. Not till we get to where we're going. Once we're rolling, there's no second chances. And no exceptions neither.

So that night the train *did* stop, I knew straight off that we were in for some serious trouble.

We were barreling through the Pine Barrens, shedding smoke and sulfur and sparks, when I heard the air brakes squeal. The train commenced to losing velocity. I was just about to open the snack bar, but right off I heard that sound, I flipped around the CLOSED sign, grabbed my cap, and skittered off to see what the matter was.

The damned were slumped in their seats. Some of them stared straight ahead of themselves at nothing in particular. Others peered listlessly out the windows or else at their own gray reflections in the glass. Our passengers are always a little subdued in the early stages of the trip.

"Oh, porter!" one of the damned called to me. She was a skinny little white woman with a worried-looking kind of pinched-in face. "Would it be all right for me to open the window just a crack, so I could get some air?"

I smiled gently into those big pleading eyes of hers and said, "Why, bless you, honey, you can do whatever you want. What difference could it possibly make now?"

She flinched back like I'd hit her.

But I reached over and took the window clips and slid it down two inches. "Don't go no further, I'm afraid. Some of the lost souls might take it into their heads to try and . . . you know?" I lowered my voice in a confidential manner.

Timidly, she nodded.

I got a pillow out of the overhead and fluffed it up for her. "Now you just let me slide this behind your head. There! Isn't that better? You relax now, and in a couple minutes the kitchen will be open. When I come back, I'll give you a menu. Got a nice selection of sandwiches and beverages. You rest up and have a comfy ride."

All the while I was talking, I was just about dying inside of curiosity. Through the window behind the old lady, I could see that we'd stopped in a small clearing in the pines. We were miles from the nearest town. The only light here was what came from the moon and the greenish spill from the windows of the train itself. There were maybe half a dozen dim figures out there. I could see them hoist up a long crate of some kind. Somebody—and who else could it be but Billy Bones?—leaned out from the caboose with a lantern and waved them forward.

The damned stared out the windows with disinterest. Most likely they thought we were picking up more passengers. Only the crew knew different.

Still, I take pride in my work. I fussed over that little lady, and by the time I left her she was actually smiling. It was only a tense little smile, but it was a smile still.

People can fool themselves into believing anything.

Soon as I got myself clear, I made straight for the baggage car. I had got me a real bad feeling about what was going on, and I intended to pry a few answers out of Billy Bones. But I didn't get beyond the door. When I tried to slide it back, it wouldn't budge. I seized it with both hands and applied some muscle. Nothing.

It was locked from inside.

I banged on the door. "Mr. *Bones*!"

A silence, and then the peephole slide moved aside. A cadaverous slice of Billy Bones's face appeared. Flesh so tight it didn't hide the skull. Eyes as bright and glittery as a rat's. "What is it?"

"Don't you give me that what-is-it bullshit—why did we stop?" The pines made a dark, jagged line against the sky. I could smell them. If I wanted, I could step down off the train and walk into them. "Just what kind of unholy cargo have you taken on?"

Billy Bones looked me straight in the eye. "We ain't taken on no cargo."

"Now don't get me started," I said. "You open up and—"

He slammed that little slide door right in my face.

I blinked. "Well!" I said. "You may think you've had the last word, Mr. Billy Bones, but you have *not*, I assure you that!"

But I didn't feel nowhere near so brash as I made out. Billy Bones was a natural-born hustler down to his fingertips, the kind of man that could break you a quarter and short-change you a dollar in the process. Ain't nobody never outbluffed him. Ain't nobody never got nothing out of him that he didn't want to give. In my experience, what he didn't wish to say, I wasn't about to hear.

So back I strode, up the train, looking for Sugar. My old stomach-ulcer was starting to act up.

"Diddy-Wah-DIDDY!" Sugar bawled. He strolled briskly through the car, clacking his ticket punch. "Diddy-Wah-Diddy, Ginny Gall, WEST Hell, Hell, and BeluthaHATCHie! Have your tickets ready."

I gave him the high sign. But a portly gent in a pinstripe suit laid hold of his sleeve and launched into a long complaint about his ticket, so I had to hold back and wait. Sugar listened patiently to the man for a time, then leaned over him like a purple storm cloud. The man cringed away. He's big, is Sugar, and every ounce of him is pure intimidation.

"I tell you what, sir," he said in a low and menacing way. "Why don't you take a spoon and jab it in your eye? Stir it around good. See how clean you can scrape out the socket." He punched the ticket. "I guarantee you that a week from now, you gone look back upon the experience with nostalgia."

The man turned gray, and for an instant I thought he was going to rise up out of his seat. But Sugar smiled in a way that bulged up every muscle in his face and neck, and the man subsided. Sugar stuck the ticket stub in the seat clip. Then, shaking his head, he came and joined me between cars.

His bulk filled what space there was pretty good. "Make it brief, Malcolm. I got things to do."

"You know anything 'bout why we stopped?" Those dim people were trudging away into the pines. None

of them looked back, not even once. They just dissolved into the shadows. "I saw Billy Bones take on a
crate, and when I asked him about it, he clammed
right up."

Sugar stared at me with those boogeyman eyes of
his. In all the three-four years he'd been on the train,
I don't recall ever seeing him blink. "You ain't seen
nothing," he said.

I put my hands on my hips. "Now, don't *you* start in
on me! I was a porter on this train back when your
mama was sucking tittie."

Sugar seemed to swell up then, a great black
mountain with two pinpricks of hellfire dancing in his
eyes. "You watch what you say about my mother."

The hairs on the back of my neck prickled. But I
didn't back down. "Just what you intending to do?" I
shook my finger in his face. "You know the regs. If
you so much as touch me, you're off the train. And
they don't let you out in Manhattan, neither!"

"Can't say I much care." He put those enormous
hands on my shoulders. His voice was small and
dreamy. "After this run, I don't much care whether I
keep this job or not."

All the while he spoke, those hands kept knead-
ing my shoulders. He laid one huge thumb alongside
my face and shoved my head to the side. I didn't much
doubt he could crush my bones and snap my spine, if
he wanted to. He was that strong. And I could see that
he'd enjoy it.

"I ain't said nothing!" I was terrified. "I ain't said
nothing about your mama!"

Sugar considered this for a long time, that sleepy
little smile floating on his face. At last he said, "See
that you don't."

And he turned away.

I exhaled. I can't say I knew Sugar at all well. He
was a recent addition to the crew; the conductor

before him took to visiting the juke joints and gambling dens of Ginny Gall during stopovers and lost his precariously held spiritual balance. But if ever anyone was meant to be a badman, it was Sugar. He was born just naturally brimming-over with anger. They say when the midwife slapped his bottom, the rage in his voice and the look on his face were so awful that straightaway she threw him down on the floor. He was born with a strangler's hands and a murderer's eyes. The rest of him, the size and bulk of him, just grew so's to have a package big enough and mean enough to contain all the temper there inside.

And they also say that when the midwife lifted up her foot to crush Sugar to death, his mama rose up off of the bed and thrashed her within an inch of her life. She was one of those tiny little women too, but her love for her baby was that strong. She threw that midwife right out of the room and down the stairs, broken bones and all. Then she picked up Sugar and put him to her breast and cooed at him and sang to him until he fell asleep. That's the kind of blood flowed in Sugar's veins, the kind of stuff he was made from.

There was a sudden lurch and the train started to move again. Whatever was going down, it was too late to stop it now.

With Billy Bones and Sugar refusing to talk to me, there wasn't any chance none of the girls would either. They were all three union, and Billy was their shop steward. Me, I was union too, but in a different shop.

The only remaining possible source of information was Old Goatfoot. I headed back for the concession stand to fetch a bottle of rye. I had it in a paper bag under one arm and was passing through the sleeper cars when a door slid open and a long slim hand crooked a red-nailed finger.

I stepped into the compartment. A ginger-colored woman closed the door and slid between me and it. For an instant we just stood there looking at each other. At last she said, "Porter."

"Yes'm?"

She smiled in a sly kind of way. "I want to show you something." She unbuttoned her blouse, thrusting her chest forward. She was wearing one of those black lacy kinds of bras that squeeze the breasts together and up. It was something to behold.

"If you'll excuse me, ma'am," I said uncomfortably. "I have to get back to work."

"I got work for you right here," she said, grabbing at me. I reached for the doorknob, but she was tugging at my jacket, trying to get it open. I grabbed her by the wrists, afraid of losing a button.

"Please, ma'am." I was just about dying of embarrassment.

"Don't you please ma'am *me*, boy! You know I got what you want and we both know I ain't got long to use it." She was rubbing herself against me and at the same time trying to shove my head down into her bosom. Somehow her brassiere had come undone and her breasts were slapping me in the face. It was awful. I was thrashing around, struggling to get free, and she was all over me.

Then I managed to slip out of her grip and straight-arm her so that she fell on her back onto the bunk. For a second she lay there, looking rumpled and expectant.

I used that second to open the door and step out into the hall. Keeping a wary eye on the woman, I began to tug my uniform back into place.

When she realized I wasn't going to stay, her face twisted, and she spat out a nasty word.

"Cocksucker!"

It hurt. I'm not saying it didn't. But she was under a lot of pressure, and it wouldn't have been professional for me to let my feelings show. So I simply said, "Yes'm. That's so. But I'm sure there are plenty of men on board this train who would be extremely interested in what you got to offer. The dining room opens soon. You might take a stroll up that way and see what sort of gents are available."

I slipped away.

Back when I died, men like me called ourselves "queers." That's how long ago it was. And back then, if you were queer and had the misfortune to die, you were automatically damned. It was a mortal sin just *being* one of us, never mind that you didn't have any say in the matter. The Stonewall Riots changed all that. After them, if you'd lived a good life you qualified for the Other Place. There's still a lot of bitterness in certain circles of Hell over this, but what are you going to do? The Man in charge don't take complaints.

It was my misfortune to die several decades too early. I was beat to death in Athens, Georgia. A couple of cops caught me in the backseat of a late-model Rambler necking with a white boy name of Danny. I don't guess they actually meant to kill me. They just forgot to stop in time. That sort of thing went on a lot back then.

First thing I died, I was taken to this little room with two bored-looking angels. One of them sat hunched over a desk, scribbling on a whole heap of papers. "What's this one?" he asked without looking up.

The second angel was lounging against a filing cabinet. He had a kindly sort of face, very tired looking, like he'd seen the worst humanity had to offer and knew he was going to keep on seeing it until the last trump. It was a genuine kindness, too, because out of all the things he could've called me, he said, "A kid with bad luck."

The first angel glanced up and said, "Oh." Then went back to his work.

"Have a seat, son," the kindly angel said. "This will take a while."

I obeyed. "What's going to become of me?" I asked.

"You're fucked," the first angel muttered.

I looked to the other.

He colored a little. "That's it," he said. "There just plain flat-out ain't no way you're going to beat this rap. You're a faggot, and faggots go to Hell." He kind of coughed into his hand then and said, "I'll tell you what, though. It's not official yet, but I happen to know that the two yahoos who rousted you are going to be passing through this office soon. Moonshining incident."

He pulled open a file drawer and took out a big fat folder overflowing with papers. "These are the Schedule-C damnations in here. Boiling maggots, rains of molten lead, the whole lot. You look through them, pick out a couple of juicy ones. I'll see that your buddies get them."

"Nossir," I said. "I'd rather not."

"Eh?" He pushed his specs down his nose and peered over them at me. "What's that?"

"If it's all the same to you, I don't want to do nothing to them."

"Why, they're just two bull-neck crackers! Rednecks! White-trash peckerwoods!" He pointed the file at me. "They beat you to death for the *fun* of it!"

"I don't suppose they were exactly good men," I said. "I reckon the world will be better off without them. But I don't bear them any malice. Maybe I can't find it in me to wish them well, and maybe I wasn't what you'd call a regular churchgoer. But I know that we're supposed to *forgive* our trespassers, to whatever degree our natures allow. And, well, I'd appreciate it if you didn't do any of those things to them."

The second angel was staring at me in disbelief, and his expression wasn't at all kindly anymore. The first angel had stopped scribbling and was gawking at me too.

"Shit!" he said.

Three days they spent bickering over me.

I presented something of a political problem for those who decide these matters, because, of course, they couldn't just let me go Upstairs. It would have created a precedent.

The upshot of it was that I got a new job. They gave me a brass-button uniform and two weeks' training, and told me to keep out of trouble. And so far, I had.

Only now, I was beginning to think my lucky streak was over.

Old Goatfoot looked over his shoulder with a snarl when I entered the cab of the locomotive. Of all the crew, only he had never been human. He was a devil from the git-go, or maybe an angel once, if you believe Mr. Milton. I pulled the bag off of the bottle of rye and let the wind whip it away, and his expression changed. He wrapped a clawed hand around the bottle and took a swig that made a good quarter of its contents disappear.

He let out this great rumbling sigh then, part howl and part belch, like no sound that had ever known a human throat. I shuddered, but it was just his way of showing satisfaction. In a burnt-out cinder of a voice, Old Goatfoot said, "Trouble's brewing."

"That so?" I said cautiously.

"Always is." He stared out across the wastelands. A band of centaurs, each one taller than a ten-story building, struggled through waist-high muck in the distance. Nasty stuff it was—smelled worse than the Fresh Kill landfill over to New Jersey. "*This* time, though." He shook his head and said, "Ain't never seen nothing like it. All the buggers of Hell are out."

He passed me back the bottle.

I passed my hand over the mouth, still hot from his lips, and took a gingerly little sip. Just to be companionable. "How come?"

He shrugged. "Dunno. They're looking for something, but fuck if I can make out *what*."

Just then, a leather-winged monster larger than a storm cloud lifted over the horizon. With a roar and a flapping sound like canvas in the wind, it was upon us. The creature was so huge that it covered half the sky, and it left a stench behind that I knew would linger for hours, even at the speeds we were going. "That's one ugly brute," I remarked.

Old Goatfoot laughed scornfully and knocked back another third of the bottle. "You worried about a little thing like *that*?" He leaned his head out the window, closed one nostril with a finger, and shot a stream of snot into the night. "Shitfire, boy, I've seen *Archangels* flying over us tonight!"

Now I was genuinely frightened. Because I had no doubt that whatever the powers that be were *looking* for, it was somewhere on our train. And this last meant that all of Heaven and Hell were arrayed against us. Now, you might think that Hell was worry enough for anybody, but consider this—they *lost*. Forget what folks say. The other side are *mean* mothers, and don't let nobody tell you different.

Old Goatfoot finished off the bottle and ate the glass. Then, keeping one hand on the throttle all the while, he unbuttoned his breeches, hauled out his ugly old thing, and began pissing into the firebox. There were two firemen standing barefoot in the burning coals, shoveling like madmen. They dropped their shovels and scrambled to catch as much of the spray as they could, clambering all over each other in their anxiousness for a respite, however partial, however brief, from their suffering. They were black as carbon, and little blue flames burned in their hair. Old Goatfoot's piss sizzled and steamed where it hit the coals.

Damned souls though they were, I found it a distressing sight.

"Y'all have to excuse me," I said uneasily. "They'll be opening the casino round about now. I got work to do."

Old Goatfoot farted. "Eat shit and die," he said genially.

Back in the casino car, Billy Bones had set up his wheel, and folks that even on an *ordinary* day gambled like there was no tomorrow were pulling out all the stops. They were whooping and laughing, talking that big talk, and slapping down paper money by the fistful. Nobody cared that it was a crooked game. It was their last chance to show a little style.

Billy Bones was in his element, his skull-face grinning with avarice. He spun the wheel with one hand and rested the other on the haunch of a honey in smoke gray stockings and a skirt so short you could see all the way to Cincinnati. She had one hand on Billy's shoulder and a martini and a clove cigarette both in the other, and you could see she was game for anything he might happen to have in mind. But so far as Billy was concerned, she was just a prop, a flash bit of glamor to help keep the money rolling in.

LaBelle, Afreya, and Sally breezed by with their trays of cigarettes, heroin, and hors d'oeuvres. They were all good girls, and how they got here was—well, I guess we all *know* how good girls get in trouble. They fall for the wrong man. They wore white gloves, and their uniforms were tight-cut but austere, for they none of them were exactly eager to be confused with the damned. Sally gave me a bit of a smile, sympathetic but guarded.

We had some good musicians died for this trip, and they were putting in some hot licks. Maybe they sensed that with the caliber of competition Down Below, they were going to be a long time between gigs. But they sure were cooking.

Everybody was having a high old time.

This was the jolly part of the trip, and normally I enjoyed it. Not today.

Sugar stood by the rear door, surrounded by a bevy of the finest honeys imaginable. This was nothing new. It was always a sight how they flocked to him on the southbound platform at Grand Central Station, elegantly dressed women rolling their eyes and wriggling their behinds something outrageous. Sooner or later one would ask, "You ever seen . . . him?" and then, when he squinted at her like he couldn't quite make out what she was getting at, "You know— Lucifer? The Devil."

At which point Sugar would say, "*Seen* him? Why, just this last run, I had a private audience with His Satanic Majesty. Sugar, he says to me, You been talking mighty big of late, I guess it's time to remind you who's boss."

"What did you say?" They would all hold their breaths and bend close.

"I said, Drop your pants and bend over, motherfucker. *I'm* driving now!"

They'd shriek then, scandalized and delighted. And when Sugar opened his arms, two of the honeys would slide in under them neat as you please.

Business was brisk at the bar. I tried not to let my thoughts show, but I must've made a bad job of it, for I was just thrusting one of those little paper umbrellas into a frozen daiquiri when a hand closed upon my shoulder.

I whirled around, right into the most knowing smile I'd ever seen. It was a smart-dressed lady, all in red. She had on a bowler hat and she smoked a cigar. Her skirt went all the way to the ground, but there was a slit up one side, and you could see the silver derringer stuck into her garter.

"You look worried," she said. "I wouldn't think the crew had much of anything to worry about."

"We're human, ma'am. Subject to the thousand natural shocks the flesh is heir to." I sighed. "And I will confess that if I weren't obliged to be here behind the bar—well. What's your pleasure?"

For a long moment she studied me.

"You interest me," she said at last, and vanished into the crowd.

Not much later she was back, steering a shy little porcelain doll of a girl by the elbow. "Missy can tend bar," she said. She slipped one hand between the girl's legs and the other behind her shoulder blades and hoisted her clear over the bar. It was an astonishing display of strength, and she did it with no special emphasis, as if it were the most natural thing in the world. "She's had more than sufficient experience."

"Now hold on," I said. "I can't just—"

"Missy doesn't mind. Do you, little sweet?"

The girl, wide-eyed, shook her head no.

"Wait for me here." The lady leaned down and kissed her full on the mouth—full, and deep too. Nobody paid any mind. The festivities had reached that rowdy stage. "You come with me."

I didn't have much choice but to follow.

Her name, she said, was Jackie. And, when I'd introduced myself, "I'm going to help you, Malcolm."

"Why?"

"I have observed," she said, "that other people are

often willing to accept whatever events may chance to happen to them, rather than take an active part in their unfolding. That's not me." She glanced scornfully back at the casino car. "I'm no gambler. All my pleasure lies in direct action. Tell me your problem. Make it interesting."

When I'd told my story, Jackie took the cigar out of her mouth and stared at it thoughtfully. "Your friend's attention is currently given over entirely to the pursuit of money. Can't you just go back to the baggage car now and look?"

I shook my head. "Not with Sugar standing by the rear door."

We were in the space between the casino and the next car forward, with the rails flashing by underneath and the cars twisting and rattling about us. Jackie put a hand on the bottommost rung of the access ladder and said, "Then we'll go over the roof."

"Now, just a minute!"

"No delays." She frowned down at her skirt. "As soon as I can arrange a change of clothing."

Up the sleeper car she strode, opening doors, glancing within, slamming them shut again. Fifth one she tried, there was a skinny man in nothing but a white shirt working away on top of his ladylove. He looked up angrily. "Hey! What the fuck do you—"

Jackie pressed her derringer against his forehead and nodded toward a neatly folded bundle of clothing. "May I?"

The man froze. He couldn't die here, but that didn't mean he'd relish a bullet through his skull. "They're yours."

"You're a gent." Jackie scooped up the bundle. Just before closing the door, she paused and smiled down at the terrified face of the woman underneath her victim.

"Pray," she said, "continue."

In the hallway, she whipped off her skirt, stepped into the slacks, and zipped them up before I had the chance to look away. The jacket she tossed aside. She buttoned the vest over her blouse and tentatively tried on one of the man's wing tips. "They fit!"

I went up the rungs first. The wind was rushing over the top of the train something fierce. Gingerly, I began crawling across the roof of the casino car. I was scared out of my wits and making no fast progress, when I felt a tap on my shoulder. I looked back.

My heart about failed me. Jackie was standing straight up, oblivious to the furious rattling speed of the train. She reached down and hauled me to my feet. "Let's dance!" she shouted into my ear.

"What?" I shouted back, disbelieving. The wind buffeted us wildly. It whipped off Jackie's bowler hat and sent it tumbling away. She laughed.

"*Dance!* You've heard of dancing, haven't you?"

Without waiting for a reply, she seized me by the waist and whirled me around, and we were dancing. She led and I followed, fearful that the least misstep would tumble us from the train and land us broken and lost in the marshes of Styx. It was the single most frightening and exhilarating experience of my entire existence, more so even than my first time with that traveling man out by the gravel quarry at the edge of town.

I was so frightened by now that it no longer mattered. I danced, hesitantly at first, and then with abandon. Jackie spun me dizzily around and around. The wind snatched sparks from her cigar and spangled the night with stars. Madness filled me and I danced, I danced, I danced.

At last Jackie released me. She looked flushed and satisfied. "That's better. No more crawling, Malcolm.

You and I aren't made for it. Like as not, all our striv-
ings will come to nothing in the end; we must celebrate our triumph *now,* while yet we can." And somehow
I knew precisely how she felt and agreed with it too.

Then she glanced off to the side. The dark wastelands were zipping past. A ghastly kind of corpse-fire
was crawling over the muck and filth to either side of
the tracks. "A person might jump off here with no
more damage than a broken arm, maybe a couple of
ribs. We can't be more than—what?—two hundred
fifty, three hundred miles south of New Jersey? It
would not be difficult for a determined and spirited
individual to follow the tracks back and escape."

"Nobody escapes," I said. "Please don't think of it."

A flicker of sadness passed over her face then, and
she said, "No, of course not." Then, brisk again, "Come.
We have work to do. Quickly. If anybody heard us
stomping about up here, they'll know what we're up to."

We came down between cars at the front of the baggage car. There was a tool closet there I had the key to,
and inside it a pry bar. I had just busted open the padlock when LaBelle suddenly slammed through the
door from the front of the train, wild-eyed and sweaty.

"Malcolm," she said breathlessly, "don't!"

From somewhere about her person—don't ask me
where—Jackie produced a wicked-looking knife. "Do
not try to stop us," she said softly.

"You don't understand," LaBelle cried. "There's a
Hound on board!"

I heard it coming then.

The Hounds of Hell aren't like the earthly sort:
They're bigger than the biggest mastiffs and they bear
a considerable resemblance to rats. Their smell is
loathsome beyond description and their disposition
even worse.

LaBelle shrieked and shrank aside as the Hound came bounding down the aisle.

With something between a howl and a scream, it was upon us.

"Go!" Jackie shoved me through the doorway. "I'll handle this. You do your part now."

She slammed the door shut.

Silence wrapped itself about me. It was ghastly. For all I could hear, the Hound didn't even exist.

I flicked on the electric, and, in its swaying light, took a look around. All the usual baggage: cases of fine French wines and satin sheets for the Lords of Hell, crates of shovels and rubber hip boots and balky manual typewriters for the rest. But to the rear of the car there was one thing more.

A coffin.

It was a long, slow walk to the coffin. I thought of all the folks I'd known who'd died and gone where I'd never see them again. I thought of all those things it might contain. It seemed to me then like Pandora's box, filled with nameless dread and the forbidden powers of Old Night. There was nothing I wanted to do less than to open it.

I took a deep breath and jammed the edge of the pry bar into the coffin. Nails screamed, and I flung the top back.

The woman inside opened her eyes.

I stood frozen with horror. She had a wrinkled little face, brown as a nut, and you could tell just by looking at it that she'd led a hard life. There was that firmness about the corners of her mouth, that unblinking quality about the eyes. She was a scrawny thing, all bones and no flesh, and her arms were crossed over her flat chest. Light played about her face and lit up the coffin around her head. I looked at her and I was just flat-out afraid of what was going to happen to Sugar and to me and to all of us when word of this got out.

"Well, young man?" she said in a peppery sort of way. "Aren't you going to help me up?"

"Ma'am?" I gaped for an instant before gathering myself together. "Oh! Yes, ma'am. Right away, ma'am." I offered her my hand and helped her sit up. The little shimmer of light followed her head up. Oh, sweet Heaven, I thought. She's one of the Saved!

I opened the door from the baggage compartment reluctantly, fearful of the Hound that must surely wait just outside. Still, what other choice did I have?

There was Jackie, spattered from head to foot with shit and gore, and her clothes all in tatters. She stood with her legs braced, a cocky smile on her face, and the butt-end of her cigar still clenched in her teeth. LaBelle crouched by her feet—she shakily stood up when I emerged—staring at something in the distant marshes. Away off behind us, a howl of pain and rage like nothing I'd ever heard before dwindled to nothing.

The Hound was nowhere to be seen.

First thing the old woman said then was, "Young lady. Do you think it seemly to be walking about dressed as a man?"

Jackie took the cigar butt out of her mouth.

"Get rid of that filthy thing, too."

For an instant, I thought there was going to be trouble. But then Jackie laughed and flung the cigar out into the night. It was still lit, and I could see by the way the old lady frowned that she'd noticed that too.

I offered her my arm again, and we made our way slowly up the train.

She was Sugar's mother. I never had any doubt about that. As we walked up the train, she questioned LaBelle and me about her son, whether he was well, was he behaving himself, did he have a special lady-

friend yet, and what exactly did he have in mind for
her and him?

LaBelle was all in a lather to tell us how Sugar had
arranged things. He'd kept in regular touch with the
folks back home. So he'd been informed how his
mother had spent her life just waiting and praying for
the fullness of time so that she could die and get to see
her baby boy again. Nobody'd had the heart to tell her
about his new job. Sugar and his relations figured that
since Divine Providence wasn't going to bring them
together again, it was up to him.

"He got it all worked out. He saved all his money,"
LaBelle said, "enough to set himself up in a little place
on the outskirts of Ginny Gall. You'll like it there," she
assured the old lady. "People say it's not half bad. It's
where the folks in Hell go for a big Saturday night."

The old lady said nothing. Something about the
way her jaw clenched, though, gave me an uneasy
feeling.

The casino car fell silent when we entered.

"*Mama!*" Sugar cried. He ran to her side and hugged
her. They were both crying, and so were the girls.
Even Billy-B had a strange kind of twisted smile on his
face.

Mrs. Selma Green took a long, slow look around
the car and its inhabitants. She did not look content.
"Sugar, what are you doing in such raffish company?
What bad thing have you done to bring you to such a
pass? I thought I'd watched over you better than that."

Sugar drew himself up proudly. "I never did a
cruel or evil thing in all my life, Mama. You know
that. I never did nothing you'd've disapproved of." His
eyes swept the room disdainfully, and to the damned
and the crew alike he said, "Not because I much cared,
one way or the other. But because I knew what *you*

expected of me, Mama. There was bad company, at times, tried to mislead me. Wicked women urged wicked things upon me. But never was a man big enough or a woman sweet enough to make me go against your teachings."

Personally, I believed it. A man like Sugar—what need had he of violence? People just naturally made room for him. And those who wouldn't . . . well, that was only self-defense, wasn't it?

But his mother did not look convinced. "What, then, are you doing *here*?" And there is absolutely no way I could do justice to the scorn with which she said that last word.

Sugar looked abashed. "I dunno," he mumbled. "They just didn't like my looks, I guess."

"The *truth*, boy!"

"I, uh, kind of mouthed-off to the Recording Angel, Mama. That's how I wound up here." He grew angry at the memory; you could see it still rankled. "You oughta be grateful we're letting a roughneck like you squeak by, he said. Don't bend no rules for *me*, I told him. I'd expect a little more gratitude than you're showing, he says. Ain't grateful to man nor angel, says I, for something I earned on my own right. Oh, that angel was mad enough to spit nails! He wanted me to bow and truckle to him. But I got my pride. I told him I wouldn't play nigger for nobody. And I guess that's what brought me here."

"We don't use that word," Mrs. Green said smartly. Her son looked puzzled. "The N-word."

"No, Mama," he said, all contrite.

"That's better. You're a good boy, Sugar, only sometimes you forget yourself." She allowed herself a small, austere smile. "You've got yourself in another fix, and I guess it's up to *me* to see you right again."

She yanked the emergency brake cord.

With a scream of brakes that could be heard all

the way to Diddy-Wah-Diddy, the train ground toward a halt. In the blackness of the night, I heard monstrous things struggling toward us through the shit and filth of the marshes of Styx. I heard the sound of dangerous wings.

"Oh, Mama!" Sugar wailed. "What have you done?"

"Deceit don't cure nothing. We're going to have it all out, and bring everything into the open," she said. "Stand up straight."

So there it was.

The trial was held up front in the locomotive, with two Judges towering over the engine, and the damned crowded into the front cars, climbing up on each other's shoulders and passing every word back so those in the rear could follow. To one side of the engine crouched Bagamothezth, Lord of Maggots. Two long, sagging pink paps hung limply down over his hairy belly, and living filth dropped continually from his mouth. A rank wind blew off of his foul body. To look upon his squirmily tentacled eyelids and idiot gaze was to court despair.

The other judge was an Archangel. He shone whiter than house paint and brighter than an incandescent bulb, and to look upon him . . . Well. You know that awful feeling you get when you look through a telescope at some little fuzzy bit of light that's maybe not even visible to the naked eye? Only there it *is*, resolved into a million billion stars, cold and clear and distinct, and you and the Earth and everything you've ever known or thought about just dwindles down to insignificance? That's what the Archangel was like, only infinitely worse.

I found myself staring at first one Judge and then the other, back and forth, repulsed by the one, repelled by the majesty of the other, but unable to look away.

They were neither of them something you could turn your back on.

Bagamothezth spoke in a voice shockingly sweet, even cloying. "We have no claim upon the sanctified Mrs. Selma Green. I presume that you are declaring an immediate writ of sainthood upon her?"

The Archangel nodded. And with that, the old lady was wrapped in blazing light and shot up into the night, dwindling like a falling star in reverse. For a second, you could see her shouting and gesturing, and then she was gone.

"Sugar Green," Bagamothezth said. "How do you plead?"

Sugar stood up before the Judges, leaning forward a little as if into a great wind. His jaw was set and his eyes blazed. He wasn't about to give in an inch. "I just wanted to be with my—"

Bagamothezth clucked his tongue warningly.

"I just—"

"*Silence!*" the Archangel roared; his voice shook the train and rattled the tracks. My innards felt scrambled. Him and Sugar locked eyes. For a minute they stood thus, longer than I would've believed any individual could've stood up to such a being. At last, Sugar slowly, angrily, bowed his head and stared down at the ground.

"How do you plead?"

"Guilty, I guess," he mumbled. "I only—"

"William Meredith Bones," the Archangel said. "How do you plead?"

Billy-B squared his shoulders and spoke up more briskly than I would've expected him to. "All my life," he said, "I have followed the dollar. It has been my North Star. It has proved comprehensible to me in ways that men and women were not. It has fetched me here where human company would have brought me to a worse place. To the best of my lights, I have remained true to it." He spread his arms. "Sugar offered me money to smuggle his mother on board. What was I to do? I couldn't turn him down. Not and be true to my principles. I had no choice."

"How much," asked the Archangel in a dangerously quiet voice, "were you paid?"

Billy Bones lifted his jaw defiantly. "Forty-five dollars."

Those of us who knew Billy roared. We couldn't help it. We whooped and hollered with laughter until tears ran down our cheeks. The thought of Billy inconveniencing himself for so paltry a sum was flat-out ludicrous. He blushed angrily.

"So you did not do it for the money," said Bagamothezth.

"No," he muttered, "I guess not."

One by one, LaBelle, Afreya, and Sally were called upon to testify and acknowledge their guilt. Then I was called forward.

"Malcolm Reynolds," the Archangel said. "Your fellows have attested that, out of regard for your spiritual welfare, they did not involve you in this plot. Do you nevertheless wish to share their judgment?"

Something inside of me snapped. "No, no!" I cried. I couldn't help noticing the disgusted expression that twisted up Billy Bones's lips and the pitying looks that the girls threw my way, but I didn't care. I'd been through a lot, and whatever strength I had in me was used up. Then too, I had seen what goes on in Diddy-Wah-Diddy and points south, and I wanted no part of any of it. "It was all them—I had nothing to do with any of it! I swear if I'd known, I would've turned them all in before I would've let this happen!"

The Judges looked at one another. Then one of them—and for the life of me, I can't remember which—cleared his throat and passed judgment.

*   *   *

We got a new crew now. Only me and Goatfoot are left over from the old outfit. The train goes on. The Judges ruled that Sugar's love for his mother, and the fact that he was willing to voluntarily undergo damnation in order to be with her, was enough to justify his transfer to a better place, where his mama could keep an eye on him. LaBelle and Afreya and Sally, and Billy Bones too, were deemed to have destroyed the perfect balance of their souls that kept them shackled to the railroad. They were promoted Upstairs as well.

Me, I'd cooked my own goose. They accepted my plea of noninvolvement, and here I remained. The girls were pretty broken up about it, and to tell the truth, so was I, for a time. But there it was. Once these things've been decided, there ain't no court of appeal.

I could've done without Billy-B's smirk when they handed him his halo and wings, like he'd out-smarted all the world one more time. But it was a pure and simple treat to see LaBelle, Afreya, and Sally transformed. They were good girls. They deserved the best.

With all the fuss, we were all the way to the end of the line in Beluthahatchie before anybody noticed that Jackie had taken advantage of the train being stopped for the trial to slip over the side. She believed, apparently, that it would be possible to backtrack through 380 miles of black-water marshes, evade the myriad creatures that dwell therein, the *least* of which is enough to freeze the marrow in your bones, cross the Acheron trestle bridge, which is half a mile high and has no place to hide when the trains cross over, and so pass undetected back to New Jersey.

It made me sad to think on it.

And that's all there is to tell. Except for one last thing.

I got a postcard, just the other day, from Chicago. It was kind of battered and worn like it'd been kicking around in the mails a long time. No return address. Just a picture of a Bar-B-Q hut which, however, I don't expect would be any too difficult for a determined individual to locate. And the message:

> If one boundary is so ill-protected, then how difficult can the *other* be? I have a scheme going that should reap great profit with only moderate risk. Interested?
>
> J.
>
> P.S. Bring your uniform.

So it seems I'm going to Heaven. And why not? I've surely seen my share of Hell.

NUNC DIMITTIS

Tanith Lee

Of course, no anthology of stories about Unearthly
Love would be complete without a story about that
most stylish, erotic, and darkly elegant of all unearthly
lovers, the vampire—and here we bring you what
may be one of the best vampire stories ever written,
and certainly one of the most eccentric: the lush, erot-
ically charged, and somberly lyrical story of a servant
devoted to the point of death . . . and beyond.

Tanith Lee is one of the best-known and most pro-
lific of modern fantasists, with well over a dozen books
to her credit, including (among many others) *The Birth
Grave, Drinking Sapphire Wine, Don't Bite the Sun, Night's
Master, The Storm Lord, Sung in Shadow, Volkhavaar,
Anackire, Night Sorceries*, and the collections *Tamastara,
The Gorgon*, and *Dreams of Dark and Light*. Her short
story "Elle Est Trois (La Mort)" won a World Fantasy
Award in 1984, and her brilliant collection of retold
folktales, *Red as Blood*, was also a finalist that year in the
Best Collection category. Her most recent books are
the collection *Nightshades* and a novel, *The Blood of Roses*.

Nunc Dimittis

The Vampire was old, and no longer beautiful. In common with all living things, she had aged, though very slowly, like the tall trees in the park. Slender and gaunt and leafless, they stood out there, beyond the long windows, rain-dashed in the gray morning. While she sat in her high-backed chair in that corner of the room where the curtains of thick yellow lace and the wine-colored blinds kept every drop of daylight out. In the glimmer of the ornate oil lamp, she had been reading. The lamp came from a Russian palace. The book had once graced the library of a corrupt pope named, in his temporal existence, Roderigo Borgia. Now the Vampire's dry hands had fallen upon the page. She sat in her black lace dress that was 180 years of age, far younger than she herself, and looked at the old man, streaked by the shine of distant windows.

"You say you are tired, Vassu. I know how it is. To be so tired, and unable to rest. It is a terrible thing."

"But, Princess," said the old man quietly, "it is more than this. I am dying."

The Vampire stirred a little. The pale leaves of her hands rustled on the page. She stared, with an almost childlike wonder.

"Dying? Can this be? You are sure?"

The old man, very clean and neat in his dark clothing, nodded humbly.

"Yes, Princess."

"Oh, Vassu," she said, "are you glad?"

He seemed a little embarrassed. Finally he said:

"Forgive me, Princess, but I am very glad. Yes, very glad."

"I understand."

"Only," he said, "I am troubled for your sake."

"No, no," said the Vampire, with the fragile perfect courtesy of her class and kind. "No, it must not concern you. You have been a good servant. Far better than I might ever have hoped for. I am thankful, Vassu, for all your care of me. I shall miss you. But you have earned," she hesitated, then said, "You have more than earned your peace."

"But you," he said.

"I shall do very well. My requirements are small, now. The days when I was a huntress are gone, and the nights. Do you remember, Vassu?"

"I remember, Princess."

"When I was so hungry, and so relentless. And so lovely. My white face in a thousand ballroom mirrors. My silk slippers stained with dew. And my lovers waking in the cold morning, where I had left them. But now, I do not sleep, I am seldom hungry. I never lust. I never love. These are the comforts of old age. There is only one comfort that is denied to me. And who knows. One day, I too . . ." She smiled at him. Her teeth were beautiful, but almost even now, the exquisite points of the canines quite worn away. "Leave me when you must," she said. "I shall mourn you. I shall envy you. But I ask nothing more, my good and noble friend."

The old man bowed his head.

"I have," he said, "a few days, a handful of nights. There is something I wish to try to do in this time. I will try to find one who may take my place."

The Vampire stared at him again, now astonished.

"But Vassu, my irreplaceable help—it is no longer possible."

"Yes. If I am swift."

"The world is not as it was," she said, with a grave and dreadful wisdom.

He lifted his head. More gravely, he answered:

"The world is as it has always been, Princess. Only our perceptions of it have grown more acute. Our knowledge less bearable."

She nodded.

"Yes, this must be so. How could the world have changed so terribly? It must be we who have changed."

He trimmed the lamp before he left her.

Outside, the rain dripped steadily from the trees.

The city, in the rain, was not unlike a forest. But the old man, who had been in many forests and many cities, had no special feeling for it. His feelings, his senses, were primed to other things.

Nevertheless, he was conscious of his bizarre and anachronistic effect, like that of a figure in some surrealist painting, walking the streets in clothes of a bygone era, aware he did not blend with his surroundings, nor render them homage of any kind. Yet even when, as sometimes happened, a gang of children or youths jeered and called after him the foul names he was familiar with in twenty languages, he neither cringed nor cared. He had no concern for such things. He had been so many places, seen so many sights; cities which burned or fell in ruin, the young who grew old, as he had, and who died, as now, at last, he too would die. This thought of death soothed him, comforted him, and brought with it a great sadness, a strange jealousy. He did not want to leave her. Of course he did not. The idea of her vulnerability in this harsh world, not new in its cruelty but ancient, though freshly recognized—it horrified him. This was the sadness. And the jealousy . . . that, because he must try to find another to take his place. And that other would come to be for her, as he had been.

The memories rose and sank in his brain like waking dreams all the time he moved about the streets. As he climbed the steps of museums and underpasses, he remembered other steps in other lands, of marble and fine stone. And looking out from high balconies, the city reduced to a map, he recollected the towers of cathedrals, the starswept points of mountains. And then at last, as if turning over the pages of a book backwards, he reached the beginning.

There she stood, between two tall white graves, the chateau grounds behind her, everything silvered in the dusk before the dawn. She wore a ball dress, and a long white cloak. And even then, her hair was dressed in the fashion of a century ago; dark hair, like black flowers.

He had known for a year before that he would serve her. The moment he had heard them talk of her in the town. They were not afraid of her, but in awe. She did not prey upon her own people, as some of her line had done.

When he could get up, he went to her. He had kneeled, and stammered something; he was only sixteen, and she not much older. But she had simply looked at him quietly and said: "I know. You are welcome." The words had been in a language they seldom spoke together now. Yet always, when he recalled that meeting, she said them in that tongue, and with the same gentle inflection.

All about, in the small café where he had paused to sit and drink coffee, vague shapes came and went. Of no interest to him, no use to her. Throughout the morning, there had been nothing to alert him. He would know. He would know, as he had known it of himself.

He rose, and left the café, and the waking dream walked with him. A lean black car slid by, and he recaptured a carriage carving through white snow—

A step brushed the pavement, perhaps twenty feet behind him. The old man did not hesitate. He stepped on, and into an alleyway that ran between the high buildings. The steps followed him; he could not hear them all, only one in seven, or eight. A little wire of tension began to draw taut within him, but he gave no sign. Water trickled along the brickwork beside him, and the noise of the city was lost.

Abruptly, a hand was on the back of his neck, a capable hand, warm and sure, not harming him yet, almost the touch of a lover.

"That's right, old man. Keep still. I'm not going to hurt you, not if you do what I say."

He stood, the warm and vital hand on his neck, and waited.

"All right," said the voice, which was masculine and young and with some other elusive quality to it. "Now let me have your wallet."

The old man spoke in a faltering tone, very foreign, very fearful. "I have—no wallet."

The hand changed its nature, gripped him, bit.

"Don't lie. I can hurt you. I don't want to, but I can. Give me whatever money you have."

"Yes," he faltered, "yes—yes—"

And slipped from the sure and merciless grip like water, spinning, gripping in turn, flinging away—there was a whirl of movement.

The old man's attacker slammed against the wet gray wall and rolled down it. He lay on the rainy debris of the alley floor, and stared up, too surprised to look surprised.

This had happened many times before. Several

had supposed the old man an easy mark, but he had all the steely power of what he was. Even now, even dying, he was terrible in his strength. And yet, though it had happened often, now it was different. The tension had not gone away.

Swiftly, deliberately, the old man studied the young one.

Something struck home instantly. Even sprawled, the adversary was peculiarly graceful, the grace of enormous physical coordination. The touch of the hand, also, impervious and certain—there was strength here, too. And now the eyes. Yes, the eyes were steady, intelligent, and with a curious lambency, an innocence—

"Get up," the old man said. He had waited upon an aristocrat. He had become one himself, and sounded it. "Up. I will not hit you again."

The young man grinned, aware of the irony. The humor flitted through his eyes. In the dull light of the alley, they were the color of leopards—not the eyes of leopards, but their *pelts*.

"Yes, and you could, couldn't you, granddad."

"My name," said the old man, "is Vasyelu Gorin. I am the father to none, and my nonexistent sons and daughters have no children. And you?"

"My name," said the young man, "is Snake."

The old man nodded. He did not really care about names, either.

"Get up, Snake. You attempted to rob me, because you are, having no work and no wish for work. I will buy you food, now."

The young man continued to lie, as if at ease, on the ground.

"Why?"

"Because I want something from you."

"What? You're right. I'll do almost anything, if you pay me enough. So you can tell me."

The old man looked at the young man called Snake,

and knew that all he said was a fact. Knew that here was one who had stolen and whored, and stolen again when the slack bodies slept, both male and female, exhausted by the sexual vampirism he had practiced on them, drawing their misguided souls out through their pores as later he would draw the notes from purse and pocket. Yes, a vampire. Maybe a murderer, too. Very probably a murderer.

"If you will do anything," said the old man, "I need not tell you beforehand. You will do it anyway."

"Almost anything, is what I said."

"Advise me then," said Vasyelu Gorin, the servant of the Vampire, "what you will not do. I shall then refrain from asking it of you."

The young man laughed. In one fluid movement he came to his feet. When the old man walked on, he followed.

Testing him, the old man took Snake to an expensive restaurant, far up on the white hills of the city, where the glass geography nearly scratched the sky. Ignoring the mud on his dilapidated leather jacket, Snake became a flawless image of decorum, became what is always ultimately respected, one who does not care. The old man, who also did not care, appreciated this act, but knew it was nothing more. Snake had learned how to be a prince. But he was a gigolo with a closet full of skins to put on. Now and then the speckled leopard eyes, searching, wary, would give him away.

After the good food and the excellent wine, the cognac, the cigarettes taken from the silver box— Snake had stolen three, but, stylishly overt, had left them sticking like porcupine quills from his breast pocket—they went out again into the rain.

The dark was gathering, and Snake solicitously took the old man's arm. Vasyelu Gorin dislodged him, offended by the cheapness of the gesture after the acceptable one with the cigarettes.

"Don't you like me anymore?" said Snake. "I can go now, if you want. But you might pay for my wasted time."

"Stop that," said Vasyelu Gorin. "Come along."

Smiling, Snake came with him. They walked, between the glowing pyramids of stores, through shadowy tunnels, over the wet paving. When the thoroughfares folded away and the meadows of the great gardens began, Snake grew tense. The landscape was less familiar to him, obviously. This part of the forest was unknown.

Trees hung down from the air to the sides of the road.

"I could kill you here," said Snake. "Take your money, and run."

"You could try," said the old man, but he was becoming weary. He was no longer certain, and yet, he was sufficiently certain that his jealousy had assumed a tinge of hatred. If the young man were stupid enough to set on him, how simple it would be to break the columnar neck, like pale amber, between his fleshless hands. But then, she would know. She would know he had found for her, and destroyed the finding. And she would be generous, and he would leave her, aware he had failed her, too.

When the huge gates appeared, Snake made no comment. He seemed, by then, to anticipate them. The old man went into the park, moving quickly now, in order to outdistance his own feelings. Snake loped at his side.

Three windows were alight, high in the house. Her windows. And as they came to the stair that led up, under its skeins of ivy, into the porch, her pencil-thin shadow passed over the lights above, like smoke, or a ghost.

"I thought you lived alone," said Snake. "I thought you were lonely."

The old man did not answer anymore. He went up the stair and opened the door. Snake came in behind him, and stood quite still, until Vasyelu Gorin had found the lamp in the niche by the door, and lit it. Unnatural stained glass flared in the door panels, and the window-niches either side, owls and lotuses and far-off temples, scrolled and luminous, oddly aloof.

Vasyelu began to walk toward the inner stair.

"Just a minute," said Snake. Vasyelu halted, saying nothing. "I'd just like to know," said Snake, "how many of your friends are here, and just what your friends are figuring to do, and how I fit into their plans."

The old man sighed.

"There is one woman in the room above. I am taking you to see her. She is a Princess. Her name is Darejan Draculas." He began to ascend the stair.

Left in the dark, the visitor said softly:

"What?"

"You think you have heard the name. You are correct. But it is another branch."

He heard only the first step as it touched the carpeted stair. With a bound the creature was upon him, the lamp was lifted from his hand. Snake danced behind it, glittering and unreal.

"Dracula," he said.

"Draculas. Another branch."

"A Vampire."

"Do you believe in such things?" said the old man. "You should, living as you do, preying as you do."

"I never," said Snake, "pray."

"Prey," said the old man. "Prey upon. You cannot even speak your own language. Give me the lamp, or shall I take it? The stair is steep. You may be damaged, this time. Which will not be good for any of your trades."

Snake made a little bow, and returned the lamp.

They continued up the carpeted hill of stair, and reached a landing and so a passage, and so her door.

The appurtenances of the house, even glimpsed in the erratic fleeting of the lamp, were very gracious. The old man was used to them, but Snake, perhaps, took note. Then again, like the size and importance of the park gates, the young thief might well have anticipated such elegance.

And there was no neglect, no dust, no air of decay, or, more tritely, of the grave. Women arrived regularly from the city to clean, under Vasyelu Gorin's stern command; flowers were even arranged in the salon for those occasions when the Princess came downstairs. Which was rarely, now. How tired she had grown. Not aged, but bored by life. The old man sighed again, and knocked upon her door.

Her response was given softly. Vasyelu Gorin saw, from the tail of his eye, the young man's reaction, his ears almost pricked, like a cat's.

"Wait here," Vasyelu said, and went into the room, shutting the door, leaving the other outside it in the dark.

The windows that had shone bright outside were black within. The candles burned, red and white as carnations.

The Vampire was seated before her little harpsichord. She had probably been playing it, its song so quiet it was seldom audible beyond her door. Long ago, nonetheless, he would have heard it. Long ago—

"Princess," he said, "I have brought someone with me."

He had not been sure what she would do, or say, confronted by the actuality. She might even remonstrate, grow angry, though he had not often seen her angry. But he saw now she had guessed, in some tangible way, that he would not return alone, and she had been preparing herself. As she rose to her feet, he beheld the red satin dress, the jeweled silver crucifix at her throat, the trickle of silver from her ears. On the thin hands, the great rings throbbed their sable colors. Her hair, which had never lost its blackness, abbreviated at her shoulders and waved in a fashion of only twenty years before, framed the starved bones of her face with a savage luxuriance. She was magnificent. Gaunt, elderly, her beauty lost, her heart dulled, yet— magnificent, wondrous.

He stared at her humbly, ready to weep because, for the half of one half moment, he had doubted.

"Yes," she said. She gave him the briefest smile, like a swift caress. "Then I will see him, Vassu."

Snake was seated cross-legged a short distance along the passage. He had discovered, in the dark, a slender Chinese vase of the *yang ts'ai* palette, and held it between his hands, his chin resting on the brim.

"Shall I break this?" he asked.

Vasyelu ignored the remark. He indicated the opened door.

"You may go in now."

"May I? How excited you're making me."

Snake flowed upright. Still holding the vase, he went through into the Vampire's apartment. The old man came into the room after him, placing his black-garbed body, like a shadow, by the door, which he left now standing wide. The old man watched Snake.

Circling slightly, perhaps unconsciously, he had approached a third of the chamber's length toward the woman. Seeing him from the back, Vasyelu Gorin was able to observe all the play of tautening muscles along the spine, like those of something readying itself to spring, or to escape. Yet, not seeing the face, the eyes, was unsatisfactory. The old man shifted his position, edged shadowlike along the room's perimeter, until he had gained a better vantage.

"Good evening," the Vampire said to Snake. "Would you care to put down the vase? Or, if you prefer, smash it. Indecision can be distressing."

"Perhaps I'd prefer to keep the vase."

"Oh, then do so, by all means. But I suggest you allow Vasyelu to wrap it up for you, before you go. Or someone may rob you on the street."

Snake pivoted, lightly, like a dancer, and put the vase on a side table. Turning again, he smiled at her.

"There are so many valuable things here. What shall I take? What about the silver cross you're wearing?"

The Vampire also smiled.

"An heirloom. I am rather fond of it. I do not recommend you should try to take that."

Snake's eyes enlarged. He was naive, amazed.

"But I thought, if I did what you wanted, if I made you happy—I could have whatever I liked. Wasn't that the bargain?"

"And how would you propose to make me happy?"

Snake went close to her; he prowled about her, very slowly. Disgusted, fascinated, the old man watched him. Snake stood behind her, leaning against her, his breath stirring the filaments of her hair. He slipped his left hand along her shoulder, sliding from the red satin to the dry uncolored skin of her throat. Vasyelu remembered the touch of the hand, electric, and so sensitive, the fingers of an artist or a surgeon.

The Vampire never changed. She said:

"No. You will not make me happy, my child."

"Oh," Snake said into her ear. "You can't be certain. If you like, if you really like, I'll let you drink my blood."

The Vampire laughed. It was frightening. Something dormant yet intensely powerful seemed to come alive in her as she did so, like flame from a finished coal. The sound, the appalling life, shook the young man

away from her. And for an instant, the old man saw
fear in the leopard yellow eyes, a fear as intrinsic to
the being of Snake as to cause fear was intrinsic to the
being of the Vampire.

And, still blazing with her power, she turned on
him.

"What do you think I am?" she said, "some senile
hag greedy to rub her scaly flesh against your smoothness; some hag you can, being yourself without sanity
or fastidiousness, corrupt with the phantoms, the left-
overs of pleasure, and then murder, tearing the gems
from her fingers with your teeth? Or I am a perverted
hag, wanting to lick up your youth with your juices.
Am I that? Come now," she said, her fire lowering
itself, crackling with its amusement, with everything
she held in check, her voice a long, long pin, skewer-
ing what she spoke to against the farther wall. "Come
now. How can I be such a fiend, and wear the crucifix
on my breast? My ancient, withered, fallen, empty
breast. Come now. What's in a name?"

As the pin of her voice came out of him, the
young man pushed himself away from the wall. For
an instant there was an air of panic about him. He was
accustomed to the characteristics of the world. Old
men creeping through rainy alleys could not strike
mighty blows with their iron hands. Women were
moths that burnt, but did not burn, tones of tinsel and
pleading, not razor blades.

Snake shuddered all over. And then his panic went
away. Instinctively, he told something from the aura
of the room itself. Living as he did, generally he had
come to trust his instincts.

He slunk back to the woman, not close, this time,
no nearer than two yards.

"Your man over there," he said, "he took me to a
fancy restaurant. He got me drunk. I say things when
I'm drunk I shouldn't say. You see? I'm a lout. I

shouldn't be here in your nice house. I don't know how to talk to people like you. To a lady. You see? But I haven't any money. None. Ask him. I explained it all. I'll do anything for money. And the way I talk. Some of them like it. You see? It makes me sound dangerous. They like that. But it's just an act." Fawning on her, bending on her the groundless glory of his eyes, he had also retreated, was almost at the door.

The Vampire made no move. Like a marvelous waxwork she dominated the room, red and white and black, and the old man was only a shadow in a corner.

Snake darted about and bolted. In the blind lightlessness, he skimmed the passage, leaped out in space upon the stairs, touched, leaped, touched, reached the open area beyond. Some glint of starshine revealed the stained-glass panes in the door. As it crashed open, he knew quite well that he had been let go. Then it slammed behind him and he pelted through ivy and down the outer steps, and across the hollow plain of tall wet trees.

So much, infallibly, his instincts had told him. Strangely, even as he came out of the gates upon the vacant road, and raced toward the heart of the city, they did not tell him he was free.

"Do you recollect," said the Vampire, "you asked me, at the very beginning, about the crucifix."

"I do recollect, Princess. It seemed odd to me, then. I did not understand, of course."

"And you," she said. "How would you have it, after—" She waited. She said, "After you leave me."

He rejoiced that his death would cause her a momentary pain. He could not help that, now. He had seen the fire wake in her, flash and scald in her, as it had not done for half a century, ignited by the presence of the thief, the gigolo, the parasite.

"He," said the old man, "is young and strong, and can dig some pit for me."

"And no ceremony?" She had overlooked his petulance, of course, and her tact made him ashamed.

"Just to lie quiet will be enough," he said, "but thank you, Princess, for your care. I do not suppose it will matter. Either there is nothing, or there is something so different I shall be astonished by it."

"Ah, my friend. Then you do not imagine yourself damned?"

"No," he said. "No, no." And all at once there was passion in his voice, one last fire of his own to offer her. "In the life you gave me, I was blessed."

She closed her eyes, and Vasyelu Gorin perceived he had wounded her with his love. And, no longer peevishly, but in the way of a lover, he was glad.

Next day, a little before three in the afternoon, Snake returned.

A wind was blowing, and seemed to have blown him to the door in a scurry of old brown leaves. His hair was also blown, and bright, his face wind-slapped to a ridiculous freshness. His eyes, however, were heavy, encircled, dulled. The eyes showed, as did nothing else about him, that he had spent the night, the forenoon, engaged in his second line of commerce. They might have drawn thick curtains and blown out the lights, but that would not have helped him. The senses of Snake were doubly acute in the dark, and he could see in the dark, like a lynx.

"Yes?" said the old man, looking at him blankly, as if at a tradesman.

"Yes," said Snake, and came by him into the house.

Vasyelu did not stop him. Of course not. He allowed the young man, and all his blown gleamingness and his wretched roué eyes to stroll across to the doors of the salon, and walk through. Vasyelu followed.

The blinds, a somber ivory color, were down, and the lamps had been lit; on a polished table hothouse flowers foamed from a jade bowl. A second door stood open on the small library, the soft glow of the lamps trembling over gold-worked spines, up and up, a torrent of static, priceless books.

Snake went into and around the library, and came out.

"I didn't take anything."

"Can you even read?" snapped Vasyelu Gorin, remembering when he could not, a woodcutter's fifth son, an oaf and a sot, drinking his way or sleeping his way through a life without windows or vistas, a mere blackness of error and unrecognized boredom. Long ago. In that little town cobbled together under the forest. And the chateau with its starry lights, the carriages on the road, shining, the dark trees either side. And bowing in answer to a question, lifting a silver comfit box from a pocket as easily as he had lifted a coin the day before. . . .

Snake sat down, leaning back relaxedly in the chair. He was not relaxed, the old man knew. What was he telling himself? That there was money here, eccentricity to be battened upon. That he could take her, the old woman, one way or another. There were always excuses that one could make to oneself.

When the Vampire entered the room, Snake, practiced, a gigolo, came to his feet. And the Vampire was amused by him, gently now. She wore a bone white frock that had been sent from Paris last year. She had never worn it before. Pinned at the neck was a black velvet rose with a single drop of dew shivering on a single petal: a pearl that had come from the crown jewels of a czar. Her tact, her peerless tact. *Naturally*, the pearl was saying, *this is why you have come back. Naturally. There is nothing to fear.*

Vasyelu Gorin left them. He returned later with the decanters and glasses. The cold supper had been laid out by people from the city who handled such things, paté and lobster and chicken, lemon slices cut like flowers, orange slices like suns, tomatoes that were anemones, and oceans of green lettuce, and cold, glittering ice. He decanted the wines. He arranged the silver coffee service, the boxes of different cigarettes. The winter night had settled by then against the house, and, roused by the brilliantly lighted rooms, a moth was dashing itself between the candles and the colored fruits. The old man caught it in a crystal goblet, took it away, let it go into the darkness. For a hundred years and more, he had never killed anything.

Sometimes, he heard them laugh. The young man's laughter was at first too eloquent, too beautiful, too unreal. But then, it became ragged, boisterous; it became genuine.

The wind blew stonily. Vasyelu Gorin imagined the frail moth beating its wings against the huge wings of the wind, falling spent to the ground. It would be good to rest.

In the last half hour before dawn, she came quietly from the salon, and up the stair. The old man knew she had seen him as he waited in the shadows. That she did not look at him or call to him was her attempt to spare him this sudden sheen that was upon her, its direct and pitiless glare. So he glimpsed it obliquely, no more. Her straight pale figure ascending, slim and limpid as a girl's. Her eyes were young, full of a primal refinding, full of utter newness.

In the salon, Snake slept under his jacket on the long white couch, its brocaded cushions beneath his cheek. Would he, on waking, carefully examine his throat in a mirror?

The old man watched the young man sleeping. She had taught Vasyelu Gorin how to speak five languages, and how to read three others. She had allowed him to discover music, and art, history and the stars; profundity, mercy. He had found the closed tomb of life opened out on every side into unbelievable, inexpressible landscapes. And yet, and yet. The journey must have its end. Worn out with ecstasy and experience, too tired any more to laugh with joy. To rest was everything. To be still. Only she could continue, for only she could be eternally reborn. For Vasyelu, once had been enough.

He left the young man sleeping. Five hours later, Snake was noiselessly gone. He had taken all the cigarettes, but nothing else.

Snake sold the cigarettes quickly. At one of the cafés he sometimes frequented, he met with those who, sensing some change in his fortunes, urged him to boast. Snake did not, remaining irritatingly reticent, vague. It was another patron. An old man who liked to give him things. Where did the old man live? Oh, a fine apartment, the north side of the city.

Some of the day, he walked.

A hunter, he distrusted the open veldt of daylight. There was too little cover, and equally too great cover for the things he stalked. In the afternoon, he sat in the gardens of a museum. Students came and went, seriously alone, or in groups riotously. Snake observed them. They were scarcely younger than he himself, yet to him, another species. Now and then a girl, catching his eye, might smile, or make an attempt to linger, to interest him. Snake did not respond. With the economic contempt of what he had become, he dismissed all such sexual encounters. Their allure, their youth, these were commodities valueless in others. They would not pay him.

The old woman, however, he did not dismiss. How old was she? Sixty, perhaps—no, much older. Ninety was more likely. And yet, her face, her neck, her hands were curiously smooth, unlined. At times, she might only have been fifty. And the dyed hair, which should have made her seem raddled, somehow enhanced the illusion of a young woman.

Yes, she fascinated him. Probably she had been an actress. Foreign, theatrical—rich. If she was prepared to keep him, thinking him mistakenly her pet cat, then he was willing, for a while. He could steal from her when she began to cloy and he decided to leave.

Yet, something in the uncomplexity of these thoughts disturbed him. The first time he had run away, he was unsure now from what. Not the vampire name, certainly, a stage name—*Draculas*—what else? But from something—some awareness of fate for which idea his vocabulary had no word, and no explanation. Driven once away, driven thereafter to return, since it was foolish not to. And she had known how to treat him. Gracefully, graciously. She would be honorable, for her kind always were. Used to spending money for what they wanted, they did not balk at buying people, too. They had never forgotten flesh, also, had a price, since their roots were firmly locked in an era when there had been slaves.

But. But he would not, he told himself, go there tonight. No. It would be good she should not be able to rely on him. He might go tomorrow, or the next day, but not tonight.

The turning world lifted away from the sun, through a winter sunset, into darkness. Snake was glad to see the ending of the light, and false light instead spring up from the apartment blocks, the cafés.

He moved out on to the wide pavement of a street, and a man came and took his arm on the right side, another starting to walk by him on the left.

"Yes, this is the one, the one who calls himself Snake."

"Are you?" the man who walked beside him asked.

"Of course it is," said the first man, squeezing his arm. "Didn't we have an exact description? Isn't he just the way he was described?"

"And the right place, too," agreed the other man, who did not hold him. "The right area."

The men wore neat nondescript clothing. Their faces were sallow and smiling, and fixed. This was a routine with which both were familiar. Snake did not know them, but he knew the touch, the accent, the smiling fixture of their masks. He had tensed. Now he let the tension melt away, so they should see and feel it had gone.

"What do you want?"

The man who held his arm only smiled.

The other man said, "Just to earn our living."

"Doing what?"

On either side the lighted street went by. Ahead, at the street's corner, a vacant lot opened where a broken wall lunged away into the shadows.

"It seems you upset someone," said the man who only walked. "Upset them badly."

"I upset a lot of people," Snake said.

"I'm sure you do. But some of them won't stand for it."

"Who was this? Perhaps I should see them."

"No. They don't want that. They don't want you to see anybody." The black turn was a few feet away.

"Perhaps I can put it right."

"No. That's what we've been paid to do."

"But if I don't know—" said Snake, and lurched against the man who held his arm, ramming his fist into the soft belly. The man let go of him and fell. Snake ran. He ran past the lot, into the brilliant glare of another street beyond, and was almost laughing when the thrown knife caught him in the back.

The lights turned over. Something hard and cold struck his chest, his face. Snake realized it was the pavement. There was a dim blurred noise, coming and going, perhaps a crowd gathering. Someone stood on his ribs and pulled the knife out of him and the pain began.

"Is that it?" a choked voice asked some way above him: the man he had punched in the stomach.

"It'll do nicely."

A new voice shouted. A car swam to the curb and pulled up raucously. The car door slammed, and footsteps went over the cement. Behind him, Snake heard the two men walking briskly away.

Snake began to get up, and was surprised to find he was unable to.

"What happened?" someone asked, high, high above.

"I don't know."

A woman said softly, "Look, there's blood—"

Snake took no notice. After a moment he tried again to get up, and succeeded in getting to his knees. He had been hurt, that was all. He could feel the pain, no longer sharp, blurred, like the noise he could hear, coming and going. He opened his eyes. The light had faded, then came back in a long wave, then faded again. There seemed to be only five or six people standing around him. As he rose, the nearer shapes backed away.

"He shouldn't move," someone said urgently.

A hand touched his shoulder, fluttered off, like an insect.

The light faded into black, and the noise swept in like a tide, filling his ears, dazing him. Something supported him, and he shook it from him—a wall—

"Come back, son," a man called. The lights burned

up again, reminiscent of a cinema. He would be all right in a moment. He walked away from the small crowd, not looking at them. Respectfully, in awe, they let him go, and noted his blood trailing behind him along the pavement.

The French clock chimed sweetly in the salon; it was seven. Beyond the window, the park was black. It had begun to rain again.

The old man had been watching from the down-stairs window for rather more than an hour. Sometimes, he would step restlessly away, circle the room, straighten a picture, pick up a petal discarded by the dying flowers. Then go back to the window, looking out at the trees, the rain and the night.

Less than a minute after the chiming of the clock, a piece of the static darkness came away and began to move, very slowly, toward the house.

Vasyelu Gorin went out into the hall. As he did so, he glanced toward the stairway. The lamp at the stair-head was alight, and she stood there in its rays, her hands lying loosely at her sides, elegant as if weight-less, her head raised.

"Princess?"

"Yes, I know. Please hurry, Vassu. I think there is scarcely any margin left."

The old man opened the door quickly. He sprang down the steps as lightly as a boy of eighteen. The black rain swept against his face, redolent of a thousand mem-ories, and he ran through an orchard in Burgundy, across a hillside in Tuscany, along the path of a wild gar-den near St. Petersburg that was St. Petersburg no more, until he reached the body of a young man lying over the roots of a tree.

The old man bent down, and an eye opened palely in the dark and looked at him.

"Knifed me," said Snake. "Crawled all this way."

Vasyelu Gorin leaned in the rain to the grass of France, Italy, and Russia, and lifted Snake in his arms. The body lolled, heavy, not helping him. But it did not matter. How strong he was, he might marvel at it, as he stood, holding the young man across his breast, and turning, ran back toward the house.

"I don't know," Snake muttered, "don't know who sent them. Plenty would like to—How bad is it? I didn't think it was so bad."

The ivy drifted across Snake's face and he closed his eyes.

As Vasyelu entered the hall, the Vampire was already on the lowest stair. Vasyelu carried the dying man across to her, and laid him at her feet. Then Vasyelu turned to leave.

"Wait." she said.

"No, Princess. This is a private thing. Between the two of you, as once it was between us. I do not want to see it, Princess. I do not want to see it with another."

She looked at him, for a moment like a child, sorry to have distressed him, unwilling to give in. Then she nodded. "Go then, my dear."

He went away at once. So he did not witness it as she left the stair, and knelt beside Snake on the Turkish carpet newly colored with blood. Yet, it seemed to him he heard the rustle her dress made, like thin crisp paper, and the whisper of the tiny dagger parting her flesh, and then the long still sigh.

He walked down through the house, into the clean and frigid modern kitchen full of electricity. There he sat, and remembered the forest above the town, the torches as the yelling aristocrats hunted him for his theft of the comfit box, the blows when they caught up with him. He remembered, with a painless unoppressed refinding, what it was like to begin to die in such a way, the confused anger, the coming and

going of tangible things, long pulses of being alternat-
ing with deep valleys of nonbeing. And then the agonized impossible crawl, fingers in the earth itself,
pulling him forward, legs sometimes able to assist,
sometimes failing, passengers which must be dragged
with the rest. In the graveyard at the edge of the
estate, he ceased to move. He could go no farther. The
soil was cold, and the white tombs, curious petrified
vegetation over his head, seemed to suck the black sky
into themselves, so they darkened, and the sky grew
pale.

But as the sky was drained of its blood, the fore-
taste of day began to possess it. In less than an hour,
the sun would rise.

He had heard her name, and known he would
eventually come to serve her. The way in which he
had known, both for himself and for the young man
called Snake, had been in a presage of violent death.

All the while, searching through the city, there
had been no one with that stigma upon them, that
mark. Until, in the alley, the warm hand gripped his
neck, until he looked into the leopard-colored eyes.
Then Vasyelu saw the mark, smelled the scent of it
like singed bone.

How Snake, crippled by a mortal wound, bleeding
and semiaware, had brought himself such a distance,
through the long streets hard as nails, through the
mossy garden-land of the rich, through the colossal
gates, over the watery, night-tuned plain, so far,
dying, the old man did not require to ask, or to be
puzzled by. He, too, had done such a thing, more than
two centuries ago. And there she had found him,
between the tall white graves. When he could focus
his vision again, he had looked and seen her, the most
beautiful thing he ever set eyes upon. She had given
him her blood. He had drunk the blood of Darejan
Draculas, a princess, a vampire. Unique elixir, it had

saved him. All wounds had healed. Death had dropped from him like a torn skin, and everything he had been—scavenger, thief, brawler, drunkard, and, for a certain number of coins, *whore*—each of these things had crumbled away. Standing up, he had trodden on them, left them behind. He had gone to her, and kneeled down as, a short while before, she had kneeled by him, cradling him, giving him the life of her silver veins.

And this, all this, was now for the other. Even her blood, it seemed, did not bestow immortality, only longevity, at last coming to a stop for Vasyelu Gorin. And so, many many decades from this night the other, too, would come to the same hiatus. Snake, too, would remember the waking moment, conscious another now endured the stupefied thrill of it, and all that would begin thereafter.

Finally, with a sort of guiltiness, the old man left the hygienic kitchen and went back toward the glow of the upper floor, stealing out into the shadow at the light's edge.

He understood that she would sense him there, untroubled by his presence—had she not been prepared to let him remain?

It was done.

Her dress was spread like an open rose, the young man lying against her, his eyes wide, gazing up at her. And she would be the most beautiful thing that he had ever seen. All about, invisible, the shed skins of his life, husks he would presently scuff uncaringly underfoot. And she?

The Vampire's head inclined toward Snake. The dark hair fell softly. Her face, powdered by the lamp-shine, was young, was full of vitality, serene vivacity, loveliness. Everything had come back to her. She was reborn.

Perhaps it was only an illusion.

The old man bowed his head, there in the shadows. The jealousy, the regret were gone. In the end, his life with her had become only another skin that he must cast. He would have the peace that she might never have, and be glad of it. The young man would serve her, and she would be huntress once more, and dancer, a bright phantom gliding over the ballroom of the city, this city and others, and all the worlds of land and soul between.

Vasyelu Gorin stirred on the platform of his existence. He would depart now, or very soon; already he heard the murmur of the approaching train. It would be simple, this time, not like the other time at all. To go willingly, everything achieved, in order. Knowing she was safe.

There was even a faint color in her cheeks, a blooming. Or maybe, that was just a trick of the lamp.

The old man waited until they had risen to their feet, and walked together quietly into the salon, before he came from the shadows and began to climb the stairs, hearing the silence, their silence, like that of new lovers.

At the head of the stair, beyond the lamp, the dark was gentle, soft as the Vampire's hair. Vasyelu walked forward into the dark without misgiving, tenderly.

How he had loved her.

CHIHUAHUA FLATS

Michael Bishop

Michael Bishop is one of the most acclaimed and respected members of that highly talented generation of writers who entered SF in the 1970s. His renowned short fiction has appeared in almost all the major magazines and anthologies, and has been gathered in four collections: *Blooded on Arachne, One Winter in Eden, Close Encounters with the Deity,* and *Emphatically Not SF, Almost.* In 1981, he won the Nebula Award for his novelette *The Quickening,* and 1983 he won another Nebula Award for his novel *No Enemy but Time.* His other novels include *Transfigurations, Stolen Faces, Ancient of Days, Catacomb Years, Eyes of Fire, The Secret Ascension, Unicorn Mountain,* and *Count Geiger's Blues.* His most recent novel is the baseball fantasy *Brittle Innings,* which has been optioned for a major motion picture. Bishop and his family live in Pine Mountain, Georgia.

In the sly and sardonic story that follows, he shows us that love, even Unearthly Love, is where you *find* it, even if you find it in the most unlikely of places . . . and in the most unlikely of *forms.* . . .

Chihuahua Flats

In a dusty panel truck with a slack transmission and no spare, Dougan bumped into the cactus-lapped verges of Chihuahua Flats. He came nudged by a fitful Texas sirocco, desperate to expand his territory. Behind him, in the cargo bay, a dozen or more economy-size bags of N.R.G. Chunx in slick double-lined red paper, the dog food itself dry as potsherds and frangible as old biscuits.

Even over the engine's banging and backfires, Dougan, his good ear cocked, could hear a deranging insect rustle in two or three of the bags. Well. So what? How much could the blamed roach borers eat?

About a block from the kennel, he began to brake. He rode the rubberless pedal or else he fiercely pumped it. The truck squealed in the gust-driven desert blow, jounced in a perpetual sand scour; when it shuddered to a rolling ebb, Dougan wrestled it into the crazed adobe driveway of the kennel to which he had pointed it these past howevermany hours. Dead on the ground, Dougan's truck neither sighed nor swayed.

A sign in the yard—a huge red-cedar shake on oily chains, its letters heat-gouged out and dyed in char—said MILLICENT T. CHALVERUS / CHIHUAHUA FLATS KENNELS / BOARDING * GROOMING * BREEDING * SALES. It bucked and twisted, its chains glinting, its face sun-shellacked.

The sprawling house had a whitewashed mission look. Behind it, cockeyed on the rattlesnake-peopled steppe, blazed a three-story concrete run with a roof of terra-cotta macaroni halves.

Dougan pushed the door buzzer and got back through the wall a liazardly metallic hiss. The sweat-plastered hair on his nape struggled to stand, giving him an almost pleasant chill—so he buzzed again, and then again, leaning with his decent ear hard to the doorframe.

Come around! You got to come around! said a speaker unit next to him, a grill like an Aztec medallion.

Miss?

Come around! This so piercingly that Dougan nigh-on to stumbled off the porch. He recovered, though, and circled on a hurried limp to the fenced-in compound out back.

I'm Millie Chalverus, said the woman at the gate. Who are you? Whaddayawant? N why should I care?

She had green eyes bracketed by hard-to-see laugh lines, skin like coffee-colored suede, and, shoehorned into a pair of ebony-and-gold-embroidered pedal pushers, a haunch like a ripening matador's. A velvety black haltertop crossed her upper torso. Her toenails peered up at Dougan from her scuffed huaraches like lacquered violets. Ankles, midriff, shoulders, arms: continents of glistening suede.

Talk to me, lover. I got stuff to do.

Dougan said, Vernester Dougan, Kennel Supplier.

Zatso?

Yes, Miss. Outta Lubbock. Specializin in high-protein, super-vitaminized bugproof feed. Not to mention assordid n sundree groomin, trainin, n recreational products.

How you do talk. What you got beyond a downpat spiel?

Miss? Dougan's eyes bounced. A bowel south of

his navel went slack and took on a windy cargo of doubt. So much skin. Such lakegreen eyes. A mouth you could press a kiss on thout ever quite reachin her teeth.

By the way, Dougan. It's mam, not miss. I got a little too much age on me to truckle to miss.

Sorry, Dougan said.

Yeah. Well. Don't sweat it.

Beneath him, a quick yip and a helium-high growl. A dog no bigger than a heifer's stool had reared up against the chain-link gate. It had raised its paltry brindle hackles, and the fudge pools of its eyes stuck out like a mantis's. Dougan could have snapped off those eyes and sent the dog on a looping field-goal arc by slamming his boot against the gate. Except for Millie Chalverus, he would have surrendered to the idea and launched the mutt.

Instead he said, Nice dog.

He don't like you, Dougan. Thet's a fac.

He don't know me. I only jes got here.

Conchos has a built-in sense bout folks. You don't tickle his fancy cep mebbe crosswise n backards.

Conchos, huh? Hey, Conchos, howya doin? Dougan knelt in front of the dog. He moved a forefinger toward Conchos with a thought to rubbing his nose through the mesh, but Conchos leapt against the gate, snarling and pogo-sticking. Dougan fell over sideways.

Chalverus chortled. Dougan brushed himself off.

Guess if Conchos don't like me, *you* don't either, he said. Guess I got as much chanst to sell you on my bidnus as I do to drop me a baby nex Friday.

Don't give up so quick.

Mam?

Conchos cain't judge character worth a sue. Why, he'd bite Mother Teresa on the tush n lay a sloppy wet one on a liar like Ollie North.

Dougan blinked in the magnesium glare of the sun.
To the northwest, a hawk floated between Chalverus's
stockade and the salmon and mint ridges of a distant
rampart. Below Dougan's left eye, a tic began to cycle.

If Conchos don't like you, you must be okay.

No shit? Dougan turned crimson. His last word
rang in the air like a bell. No *lie*. I meant, no lie.

No lie, Chalverus said. Whynt you show me what
you got?

Dougan recovered. Currying combs? Choke chains?
Bugproof feed? Jes name it n I'll go gitter.

Whynt we try some food? Conchos ain't gonna
come round to you, honey, for no choke chain or metal
brush.

Food it is. Good choice. *Great* choice. N.R.G.
Chunx're flat-out worth their weight in Taos silver.

Dougan broke into a pebble-skittering trot. Thank
God Conchos didn't like him. Stupid pile of crap. Why'd
anybody own a chihuahua? Why'd a gorgeous gal like
Millie Chalverus *breed* the bat-eared midgets?

In the oven of his cargo bay, Dougan wrestled with
the dog-food bags. He scrutinized them all for punc-
tures, tears, and bore holes, then selected out a bag as
glossily seamless as the Messiah's robe. This one he
toted in a Groucho Marx crouch back to the kennel.

As soon as the Chalverus woman let him in,
Conchos seized his trouser cuff, snarling through
clenched teeth and flapping like a pennant on his instep
until they reached a feeding area under a wide green
plastic awning. All along the three-tiered run next to
it, a chorus of unseen caged chihuahuas whimpered
and yipped.

Chalverus cried, Let go, Conchos. *Let go!*

Conchos released Dougan's cuff, reared like
Trigger, and scuttled holus-bolus away, fussing without
relent. Grateful, Dougan lowered the dog-food bag and
bent over it like a soldier over a gutshot buddy.

Thanks, he said. Much bliged. It jes gits hotter. As if to prove this remark, clammy drooping semicircles had bloomed under his workshirt's arms, big cancerous splotches. He split the bag with his pocketknife and doled out onto the concrete a handful—a prodigal double handful—of N.R.G. Chunx, brick red pellets craggy as owlcasts and burly as paperweights. Conchos pricked his ears, tilted his head, scented the spill, skipped from foot to foot like a balsawood puppet. Several chihuahuas on the tiers, also smelling the food, began to yammer and bay, a doggy munchkin chorale.

Awright, Dougan told Conchos. Come git yore picnic.

Conchos looked at Dougan, then at Chalverus, then at the mound of N.R.G. Chunx. Go on, Chalverus said. I don't mind. Have yoreself a go. So Conchos tiptoed over and tried to mouth a chunk, but not one in the pile was less than half the size of his head. Conchos could not even crack a piece with a forepaw on it to hold it down. Stymied, he danced a bemused do-si-do, looking up again at Chalverus.

You must feed these boulders to Saint Bernards, she said. Or starvin African pachyderms.

We give you a lot for yore money.

Well. It's useless to me if Conchos n his sort cain't eat it. N it shore as shivers looks like they cain't.

Wait, said Dougan. Jes you wait. Outside the run, he saw a stepping stone long and wide as a breadloaf. Gimme a minit, okay? He wedged himself through the kennel gate while holding it ajar with an outstretched leg, prised up the stone, and eased back through the gate with it before him at groin height, an honest-to-Jesus threat to herniate him. See, he said. See, now. He dropped the stone on the N.R.G. Chunx, picked it up, dropped it again. He put one boot sole on the stone and ground it from side to side. There. See. He nudged the stone aside, disclosing a pile of rubbly fragments and a scatter of brick red powder.

Conchos pitter-pattered up and fell to. He chewed what he could, cracking the kibbles in his jaw teeth, and licked what he couldn't. He did a little jig as he ate.

The put-up-or-shut-up test, Dougan said. The taste test. I think this stuff's done passed it. Don't you?

Looks thet way, Chalverus said. But am I myself gonna have to pulverize ever bag I decide to buy?

Nome. No way. Place you a long-term order n I promise you plenty of prepulverized N.R.G. Chunx whenever you ast.

Deal, Chalverus said.

She and Dougan shook hands. Her palm and fingers, Dougan noted, had a breezy dry silkiness. Even her calluses had a well-cared-for feel, as if she refused to allow the desert any tyrannical say-so over the expression of her womanhood. What a find, thought Dougan.

On Christmas Eve, four months later, Dougan married Millie Chalverus in a Catholic ceremony in the den of her house on the outskirts of Chihuahua Flats. About seven years back, she had lost her previous husband, Joseph Worrill, to an oilfield fire between Midland and Odessa, Texas. Starting up Chihuahua Flats Kennels had rescued her from the blues and maybe even poverty, for the biggest part of Mr. Worrill's insurance money had gone to cover a slagheap of outstanding debts. Dougan cared nothing for the petty facts of Chalverus's past life, particularly her marriage and any earlier romances—except insofar as her past, sprouting up as memory or as unfinished business, derailed her happiness or blighted his and her itemhood. Even today, the rolling gravel in her laugh and

her skin's swarthy flush could make Dougan swoon
standing up.

I do, Chalverus had said, keeping her own name,
as she had kept it with Mr. Worrill (for business purposes and to feed her soul). Anyway, at that *I do*,
Dougan had begun to live—to live in sweet truth—for
the first time since his release from Dooly Correctional
Institution in Unadilla, Georgia, where he'd spent five
years on a DUI unlawful-death conviction. (Driving
blotto on cheap corn liquor in Macon, he had fender-
glanced with his pickup an old woman walking home.
Except for a vicious bump to his right ear, he had
killed her without half noticing.) Even operating his
own shoestring kennel-supply business in Lubbock
had failed to drain from Dougan a melancholy unease,
and this subtly toxic ache had poisoned him on every
long-distance haul through the panhandle or across
the hot alkaline flats of the Jornada del Muerto. But
one *I do* had changed that, nullifying the poison.

Dougan abandoned Lubbock. He threw over his
kennel-supply business. Chihuahua Flats Kennels had
work enough for two, and Millie Chalverus, now his
beloved wife, had no objection to his coming aboard
and shouldering a man-sized moiety of the labor. He
toted bags of chihuahua chow, hosed down the runs,
patched gaps in the chain link, replaced fallen roof
tiles, and haggled at the doorstoop with jewelry-
freighted high-pressure salesguys besotted with their
own stale hormones and decades of worn-out macho
propaganda. And so, in many ways, the union of
Vernester Dougan and Millie Chalverus seemed to
Dougan the recipient of a sure-nough heavenly blessing.

Conchos, though, never came around. He despised
Dougan. He yapped whenever Dougan entered the
house. He tried to guard the master bedroom against
Dougan's certain arrival. Failing that, Conchos fell back
to protect the bed itself, an immense two-layer wheel

under a spread of the same embroidered fabric from which Chalverus had made the pedal pushers in which Dougan had first beheld her delectable croup.

Yip yip yip, went Conchos, yap yap yap, meanwhile snarling his outrage and prancing in strategic if hopeless retreat. Dougan wore heavy suede gloves to deal with Conchos and always picked him up and moved him aside whenever such run-ins took place. It annoyed him, Conchos's implacable hatred along with all the silly-ass threats, but Dougan never—not once since the day of his first N.R.G. Chunx delivery—felt the least urge to strangle Conchos, drop-kick him into orbit, or render him unpeelable roadkill. Dougan had resolved not to hurt Conchos because Chalverus loved Conchos and what Chalverus loved Dougan respected unconditionally.

I love you, Chalverus told Dougan on their wedding night, but—

But what, babe?

But my soul—my deepest privatest heart—is tucked away in thet little dog. I jes cain't help it.

You don't have to, Dougan said. I respec whatsoever you love n'll try to love it myself n hope thet one day Conchos'll take to me too.

Although Dougan heard the nobleness of this pronouncement, he found that in town for his weekly haircut he had a hard time being faithful to it. Pete Mosquero, his barber, liked to rag him about Conchos:

You don look to me like a chihuahua esorta guy. No?

No. I jess refuse to blieve you *like* em.

I don't, Dougan said, but—

You see, I magine you an espringer espaniel esorta guy or mebbe a golden retriever.

Thanks, but—

As I esee em, chihuahuas are estupid popeyed prisses, n you got too much class to be messin widdem.

They've got their points.

Yeah. On the eends of their ears. Mosquero laughed at his own joke, sclipping his scissors to punctuate it.

Back out at the kennels, Conchos's despisal of Dougan went unallayed. The dog chewed holes in his jockey shorts, shat in his Sunday oxfords, peed on the mahogany valet that Chalverus had given him as a wedding gift, and either strewed about the house or punctured irreparably every foil-wrapped condom in a box of three dozen that Dougan had bought at Best Buy Drugs. Conchos scrabbled at the bedroom door every time Dougan and Chalverus grew amorous. When they declined to admit him and made love to spite him, Conchos stood in the hall baying like a plangently deflating balloon. If they did admit him, Conchos straddled Dougan's back and aimed penetrating nips at his nape and shoulder blades. This misbehavior had earned Conchos the sharpest scolding he'd ever got in Dougan's hearing and a quick exile to the utility room.

Couldn't we jes kennel him when we git frisky? Dougan said.

Why?

I lose concentration.

I don't. Mmm. Mmm mmm *mmm*.

S different for a man.

Yeah? Howso?

But Dougan could think of no explanation that did not imply that he might surrender total focus on her even in the throes of climactical passion. So Conchos remained indoors, if not in their bedroom, even when Cupid attacked.

Outside the boudoir, Conchos played other games. He sat on the couch between Chalverus and Dougan. He guarded his daily allotment of N.R.G. Chunkletz— chihuahua-sized pieces that the company had begun producing for smaller breeds—as if fearful that Dougan might hijack it and eat it himself. Conchos

never carried any of his rubber squeak toys or his
leash to Dougan, and on early-morning winter walks
through the cacti he refused to take a dump until
Dougan's lips had visibly blued and his bladder had
grown as taut as a volleyball. Often, once Dougan had
unzipped and made steam, Conchos would give in
and unload, eyeballing him from a crayfishing squat
that only a smart aleck could have choreographed.

Little dog, Dougan would say, you make me sad.

But not sad enough to go back to the bottle. And,
setting aside the hatred of one muleheaded chihuahua,
he viewed his new life with Chalverus as charmed.

I have a new idea for our bidnus, Vernester.

Yeah. Like what?

Races.

Whaddaya mean, *races*? Dougan stood baffled,
transfixed by the applegreen fire in Chalverus's eyes.

Chihuahua races. Daily doubles. Trifectas. The whole
everlovin pari-mutuel schmeer.

Ha ha.

S no joke, honey. It's legal for greyhounds, idnit?
Why not for my little Toltec babies?

I don't know why not, Dougan said.

So they built it. Or, nigh-on to single-handedly,
Dougan did, a track not much bigger around than the
public swimming pool in Tucamcari, with two sets of
seven-tiered bleachers on the eastern side so that paying spectators would not have to peer like nuclear-test
observers into a blazing sun when the evening races
started and the first nine to twelve chihuahuas broke
like windup toys from the miniature gates.

From the beginning, business at Chihuahua Flats
Raceland boomed, even if the dogs themselves failed in
heat after heat to have a like impact on the sound barrier. Breeders from across the country fell upon Dougan

and Chalverus's little town to strut their dogs and place flashy wagers. By mid April, sometimes as many as two hundred people occupied the stands; and on that red-letter night in early May when the one-thousand-and-first chihuahua hit the track for its maiden handicap, the raceland noted the event with a barrel drawing, a cowboy band from Portales, and a videocassette giveaway.

Dougan announced. As the bell rang to start each heat, he intoned over the public-address system, *"There . . . goes . . . Ricky!"* and the mechanical rat that paced the chihuahuas on a mobile pole lurched out to a herky-jerky lead, heading around the track via a concatenation of twitches and fits. Maybe a dozen times since the raceland's opening, the lead chihuahua had caught, or caught up to, Ricky, but owing to the rat's size—it stood almost as high at the withers as the pursuing dogs, else even patrons with binoculars would have had a hard go seeing it—no dog had yet halted Ricky or dragged Ricky off its jerkily advancing lever. Dougan thought it unlikely that even a *pack* of chihuahuas, cooperating as stranger dogs almost never did, could pull down Ricky and turn a decent money heat into a yelping group feed.

Dougan enjoyed calling the races, updating the odds, and introducing such celebs as the owner of the biggest local car dealership, the latest homecoming queen, and the weatherman at the NBC affiliate in El Paso. But Conchos, the winner of four tiptop stakes races and a first or second runner-up in several others, liked Dougan no better. Floodlamps burned through half their nights, and Chalverus often seemed distracted by success, drunk on the picayune details of public relations, concessions stocking, and the twelve thousand applicable state and federal tax laws. Such crap made Dougan long for the desert serenity of Chihuahua Flats before the boom. Sometimes, then, he took a beer; sometimes, even, a hit of the hard stuff.

Chalverus throve. An interviewer from a TV news magazine asked her questions against the backdrop of the sawdust track and its electronic toteboard, the hubbub of spectators, touts, bettors, and boozy hangers-on counterpointing the audio:

What led you to open a chihuahua track, Ms. Chalverus?

The chihuahuas. What else?

Why not cocker spaniels or miniature poodles?

I knew when my first hubby died thet whatever I did had to have a really cheerful grounding in my own selfhood. It also had to like start with the Chalverus sound. Thet was my first true ch-ch-ch-challenge.

Challenge?

To myself. To my womanly Chalverus spirit. At first, you see, I figgered chinchillas. A chinchilla ranch. For the furs n the cheap cheeky glamour.

Okay. What killed that idea?

Havin to kill the chinchillas. Also, you cain't cuddle em. They have a odor n they bite. You have to kill em to git any use from em. The pelts don't come off thout you brain the varmints then flat-out strip off their skins.

So you turned to chihuahuas?

Didn't want to cherry-pick. Or charm rattlesnakes. Or try out for cheerleader. N chow dogs're too danged mean.

Tell us, Ms. Chalverus, who's your little friend?

Oh. Him? Thisere's Conchos. Say hello to all the folks, Conchos.

Dougan, standing back, watched his wife take Conchos's paw and wave it at the nation.

Cute dog, said the interviewer.

Thanks. My soul lives in this little dickens. Him n me're jes like this. She crossed her fingers. So to speak.

How does your new husband and business partner feel about the colossal upheaval in your lives, Ms. Chalverus?

Dougan? Dougan honestly loves me. Whatsoever I love, even a persnickety n possessive little booger like Conchos, well, he tries hard to love, himself.

So he's *happy* with a thousand-and-one chihuahuas aswarm in your backyard?

Shore. Who *wouldn't* be? We're doin what we love n gittin royally flush in the doin.

But Dougan wasn't happy, and he didn't love Chihuahua Flats Raceland, and Conchos's spitefulness gnawed like a true *ratón* (rat) at his bruised and tender *alma* (soul). This condition was so painful, and yet so inward, that it billy-clubbed him when Chalverus, less than a week after her interview, received a medical diagnosis of inoperable pancreatic cancer. Before he could chew up and swallow this news, she had to start a series of radiation and chemical treatments in Las Cruces. Her hair let go. Her skin turned sallow and squamous. Her eyes played daily host to floating gray-green clouds.

By the end of summer, Chalverus was so sick that it hardly mattered, except to her, in which venue, public or private, she forsook the struggle and died. So Dougan brought her home. PR guys, gamblers, and uninformed chihuahua breeders still stopped by occasionally, but all racing activity had long since ceased, and Dougan knew in his bones that Chalverus had contracted her terminal disease as an apology to him and a huge unrepayable gift. He said as much, in rougher words, as Chalverus lay abed amidst the air-conditioner drone and the brittle night hush of the desert.

Nonsense, she said. Thet's all pure nonsense.

It ain't, babe. It purely ain't.

Lissen, you. I had to've had this damn ol cancer *before* we even begun our raceland. *Had* to've. If I hadn't, I wouldn't be this far along to . . .

She stopped, not for her benefit but his. They both

knew *dying* was the missing fill-in-the-blank word, and even unspoken it dropped between them like a wall.

You think I got sick apurpose?

Dougan sat with his long hands holding the insides of his knees and his long eyes downcast in craven abashment. Even so, he managed a mortified nod.

Sick apurpose? To give us cause to undo the nightly to-do round here? S thet what you think? Tell me.

Yessum, I do.

I got me a cancer to make you happy?

Yessum. You're like selfless thet way.

Awright then. Let me ast you. You happy?

Course not. How could I be? You think I'd trade off my precious wife dead jes for some lousy quiet?

Chalverus rolled her face toward Dougan on her pillow and smiled. No, she said. I never thought thet off the top of my brain or deep down in its kinks, neither one. Which shorely orter tell you somepin, lover.

Dougan began to cry. He kept looking down, though, and his tears plunked the backs of his dangling hands like beads of hot candlewax.

On the bed beside Chalverus, Conchos fought to his feet, peeled back his whiskery lip, and growled at Dougan in pitiable quivering disdain. Chalverus took Conchos's snout between her thumb and forefinger, tugged on his papier-mâché skull, and in spite of her weakness easily rolled him over.

Hush thet disrespecful noise. You silly cur you.

Dougan swept a forearm across his eyes and looked over at Chalverus with a question or maybe just a thanks.

Take care of Conchos when I go, she said. Do what you want with them others, but save Conchos to home. Promise?

Babe, you know me. You *know* me.

Thet's right. I do. I shorely do. N the Lord'll repay.

A week later, eased through at least a stint of her going by old Eddie Arnold songs and a morphine drip, Millie Chalverus forsook the struggle and died.

Conchos, sitting on her sheeted midriff, lifted a long bittersweet howl.

Dougan sold most of the chihuahuas in the kennel's runs and shut down its top two floors. He remained in Chihuahua Flats. He remained in his late wife's house. He fed and watered Conchos, who went on eyeing him askance, hitching growly rides on his trouser cuffs, eating his socks, and awakening him from dreams of Chalverus with vampire nips at his earlobes, fingers, and groin. But Dougan forbore, in obedience to the deathbed charge, Take care of Conchos.

One evening a month after the funeral, Chalverus appeared to Dougan in the kennel yard as he played hose water over the concrete in slate-thin tides. In haltertop, pedal pushers, and a wavery cape, she hovered three feet off the ground between a storage shed and the multilevel runs. Her image had so little substance, so little hue, that it looked to have faded from a hard medium like china onto a flimsy one like rice paper or old silk. It rippled as it hung, melting and remanifesting in the twilight like a Jornada del Muerto mirage.

Dougan, she said. Dougan.

This voice—no question that it was hers—sounded distant and tinny, like Franklin Delano Roosevelt on the radio. The voice startled him, though, even more than had the apparition. It startled him so much that he unwittingly put his thumb over the hose's nozzle and sprayed the floating eidolon of his wife with a piercing burst. Chalverus billowed backward, dissolving on the fusillade, and then came together again, wavering, much dimmer than before.

Babe, I'm sorry, he cried. Real real sorry.

I cain't stay, she said. I ain't got the strenth. But I'm with you always anyways n won't ever wholly depart.

Like Jesus? he said.

Lissen, honey, I love you. Even if, as thisere proclaimin shade, I've got to fade off to Lethe. So to speak.

You only jes got here. You cain't go.

Don't beg me, now. I'm leavin you with a comforter.

It's too danged hot for a comforter. Dougan flung the hose aside and trotted wet-faced toward the melting spectral figment that was, or had been, Millie Chalverus.

Adios! she called in her fading cathedral-radio voice. To God, my darlin!

When Dougan went inside that night, Conchos stood guarding the circular bed. The dog growled, feinting forward and back. Dougan opened the top drawer in his chest-of-drawers, found his gloves, pulled them on.

Hush, you popeyed rat, he said. Then he picked Conchos up, carried him in outstretched hands to the bedroom door, set him down gently in the hall, and, ashamed for even considering such an act, slammed the door on him with a bang that shook windows and toppled bric-a-brac. He slept soundly, though, a dreamless slumber of scouring purity.

In the morning, Conchos greeted Dougan with a wriggly butt, a toothy chihuahua grin, and an ecstatic four-footed jig. When Dougan walked to the kitchen, Conchos followed at heel, yipping in excitement and homage rather than in provocation or spleen. Outdoors, Conchos took care of business in two minutes flat and returned to the utility room for breakfast. When Dougan poured N.R.G. Chunkletz into his bowl, Conchos licked Dougan's hands; when Dougan pivoted to leave, Conchos reared up and begged for a noggin rub.

What in heavenly rip's got into you?

Mmm, Conchos whined. Mmm mmm *mmm*.

And Dougan knew. Chalverus had sent him a comforter. He let Conchos finish eating, then scooped him up, perched him in the crook of his arm, and took a reminiscent stroll through every room in the house and across every sandy stretch of his and Chalverus's arid acreage, however Gila-monster-haunted or booby-trapped with cacti. As they went, Dougan murmured sweet nothings to the dog, and Conchos rode like a raj in a howdah, lordly as all get-out. From that day forward, in fact, Conchos went everywhere with Dougan.

Even to the barbershop.

Esorry bout your loss, Mosquero said, trimming Dougan's hair as Conchos sat upright one swivel chair away.

Thanks, Dougan said. But the dead can do things the livin cain't.

Mosquero had no reply to this epigram. He clipped and snipped. Eventually he said, I never esaw you as a chihuahua esorta guy.

You didn't, huh?

Course not. They're aw like that one. Mosquero waved at Conchos with his comb. Ugly little rats. Deesgustin popeyed prisses. You musta had to take him to the vet or esomepin, eh?

Mmm, said Dougan.

That one, he's an especial laugh, eh? No more hair than a piglet. Legs like crippled finger bones. A face like one of them pickle-jar abortions. I mean, it's—

Dougan knocked Mosquero's hand away and jumped from the chair. No more insults! he cried. Not another nasty word! Or I'll danged shore deck yore ass!

Easy, Mosquero said, conducting a calm-down symphony with his open hands.

Easy? We're sick of yore insults!

I'm jess talkin, hombre. It's jess my esame ol hair-cuttin esorta way of time-passin.

Well, don't do it like thet no more!

Okay. O*kay*. You got my esolemn word.

Dougan and Mosquero held a long wary look. Conchos perched attentively in his swivel chair, a lop-sided grin on his snout. Dougan sat again, and Mosquero resumed cutting his hair with a sharp *sclip!* of the scissors.

A little later, taking care to say it behind Dougan's bad ear, Mosquero whispered, But he's *estill* ugly.

THE TWO-HEADED MAN

Nancy A. Collins

Nancy A. Collins is a native of Arkansas who now lives in New York City. Her first novel, *Sunglasses After Dark*, became one of the most widely acclaimed vampire novels of recent years, and in 1989 it won the Bram Stoker Award given by the Horror Writers of America. It was followed by a sequel, *In the Blood*, and by the unrelated novel, *Tempter*. Her most recent book is a werewolf novel, *Wild Blood*. For the past few years, Collins has been writing *Swamp Thing* for DC Comics, and has recently created a new graphic novel series for DC, *Wick*.

In the bizarre, compassionate, and intensely erotic story that follows, one of the strangest encounters with Unearthly Love in this entire anthology, she shows us that even in a remote and nearly deserted truck stop in a tiny sleepy town on a back-country road, the door may suddenly open and Mister Right may walk in—or Misters Right, as the case may be. . . .

The Two-Headed Man

It was going on midnight when the two-headed man walked into Kelly's Stop.

The short-order cook glanced up when the short burst of cold air rifled the newspaper spread across the Formica serving counter. The man stood in the diner's doorway, the fur-fringed hood of the parka casting his face in deep shadow. He tugged off his mittens and stuffed them into one pocket, flexing his fingers like a pianist before a recital.

"You're in luck, buddy," said the cook, refolding the newspaper. "We was just about ready to call it an early night."

The waitress stabbed out a cigarette and pivoted on her stool to get a better look at the stranger. She tugged at her blouse waist, causing her name, LOUISE, to twitch over her heart.

"Car had a flat . . . up the road . . . ," came a voice from inside the shadow of the parka's hood. "We don't . . . have a spare. . . . "

The cook shrugged, his back to the stranger. "Can't help you there, bub. Mike Keckhaver runs the Shell station down the road a piece, but he don't open up 'til tomorrow morning."

"Then we'll . . . have to wait."

"We?" Louise moved to the front window and peered out between the neon Miller Hi-Life and Schlitz signs. The gravel parking lot fronting the diner was empty. "You got somebody with you, mister?"

"Yes . . . You could say that," answered the stranger as he unzipped the parka and tossed back the hood.

Louise gasped and clamped a hand over her mouth, smearing lipstick against her palm. The cook spun around to see what was going on, butcher knife in hand: late-night truck-stop robberies were not uncommon along Highway 65.

The stranger had two heads. One was where heads are supposed to be. And a damn fine one at that. It was the handsomest head Louise had ever seen this side of a TV screen. The stranger's hair was longish and curly and the color of winter wheat. It framed a face designed for a movie star; straight nose, strong and beardless chin, high cheekbones, and eyes bluer than Paul Newman's.

The second head looked over the stranger's left shoulder, perched on his collarbone like a parrot. It wasn't a deformed or even an unsightly head—just average. But its extreme proximity to such masculine perfection made it seem . . . repulsive. The second head was dark where the other was fair, brown-eyed where the first was blue. It regarded Louise with a distant, oddly disturbing intelligence then turned so its lips moved against its fellow's left ear. The stranger laughed without much humor.

"Yeah, guess I *did* scare 'em some. . . . " The stranger shrugged off his coat. "Sorry, didn't mean to startle you like that."

Now that the parka was all the way off they could see that the stranger really didn't have two heads. A padded leather harness, like those worn by professional hitchhikers, was strapped to his shoulders and midsection. But instead of a bedroll and an army surplus dufflebag, he carried a little man on his back.

The stranger seated himself on one of the stools, leaning slightly forward under the weight of his burden.

"What is he? A dwarf or somethin'?" The cook ignored the look Louise shot him.

The man did not seem at all insulted. "Nope. Human Worm."

"Huh?"

"Carl's got no arms . . . or legs."

"That so? Was he in Vietnam?"

"No. Just born that way."

"How about that. Don't see that every day."

"No, you don't," he agreed amiably. The Human Worm leaned closer and whispered into his ear again. The stranger nodded. "Okay. Why not, long as we're here. We'll have two orders of bacon and eggs . . . one scrambled . . . one sunny-side up . . . two orders of toast . . . and two coffees. Got that?" The stranger pulled a cloth hankie out of his pants pocket and draped it over his left shoulder.

"Uh, yeah. Sure. Comin' right up."

"Name's Gary. This here's Carl," the stranger jerked a thumb to indicate his piggyback passenger.

"Pleased t'meetcha," the cook grunted.

Carl bobbed his head in silent acknowledgment.

Louise stood near the end of the serving counter, debating on whether she should try to talk to the handsome stranger with the freak tied to his back.

Talking to the various strangers that found their way into Kelly's Stop was one of the few perks the job had to offer. The trouble with the locals was that she knew what they were going to say before they even opened their mouths. She hated living in a pissant little town like Seven Devils.

She envied the strangers she met; travelers from somewhere on their way to someplace. She liked to pretend that maybe one of them would be her long-awaited Dream Prince and take her away from Kelly's

Stop—just like Ronald Coleman rescued Bette Davis in *Petrified Forest*. But if her Prince was going to put in an appearance, it was going to have to be pretty damn soon. Her tits were starting to sag and the laugh lines at the corners of her eyes were threatening to become crow's feet.

She studied the two men as they waited to be served. It was sure as hell a *weird* setup. But that face . . . Gary's face . . . was the one she'd pictured in her fantasies. It was the face of the Prince who would deliver her from a lifetime of bunions, corn plasters, varicose veins, and cheap beer.

The more she thought about it, he wasn't really *that* strange. It was kind of sweet, really, the way he carried the crippled guy on his back. It wasn't that much different than pushing a wheelchair.

The cook plopped the eggs and bacon onto the grill, slammed twin slices of bread into the toaster, and returned his attention to the spitting bacon.

"Louise! Get th' man his coffee, willya?" The command made her jump and she scurried over to the Mr. Coffee machine.

"How you like it?" she asked, hoping she didn't sound shrill. Her hands were shaking. She took a deep breath before she poured.

"Black. Cream and sugar."

She slid the cups across the counter and located a sugar dispenser. She felt his eyes on her as she moved to get the cream from the cooler, but she wasn't sure which one of them was doing the looking.

Gary picked up the cup of black coffee with his left, blew on it a couple of times, then lifted it over his shoulder. Carl lowered his head and noisily sipped from the lip of the cup while Gary stirred his coffee with his right hand.

"Wow. Neat trick." She kicked herself the minute she said it. What a *hick* thing to say!

Gary shrugged, causing Carl to bounce slightly. "Helps if you're ambidextrous."

"Ambiwhat?"

"Carl says that's being good with both hands," he explained, gesturing with a piece of bacon. Carl leaned forward, grasping the proffered strip with surprisingly white, even teeth before bolting it down like a lizard.

Louise watched as Gary fed himself and his rider, both hands moving with unthinking grace. He acted as if it was as natural for him as breathing. Carl wiped his mouth and chin, shiny with grease and butter, on the hankie draped over his companion's shoulder. His eyes met Louise's and she hastily looked away.

There was something hot and alive in those eyes; something hungry and all too familiar. Her cheeks burned and she dropped a bouquet of clean flatware onto the floor.

"Look, mister, I'm gonna be closin' shop real soon. Like I said, the Shell station don't open 'til seven or eight. There's a motel up the road a bit, the Driftwood Inn. You shouldn't have no trouble findin' a place there. They're right off th' highway, so they're open all night. I'd give you a lift but, uh, my car's in the shop an' I live in town, so. . . ." The cook fell silent and returned to cleaning his grill.

The two-headed man sat and drank coffee while Louise and her boss busied themselves with the ritual of closing. Louise mopped the floor faster than usual, trying not to look at the stranger and his freakish papoose.

"Well, lights out, folks," the cook announced with a forced smile. The two-headed man stood up and began shouldering themselves back into the parka. "Uh, look, Louise. . . . Why don't you lock up for me, huh? Laurie's waitin' up on me and you know how she gets."

Louise certainly did. Laurie had had enough of

waiting up for her husband three years back and joined
the others who'd abandoned Seven Devils, Arkansas.
She nodded and watched him flee the diner for the
safety of a nonexistent wife.

Gary pulled the parka's hood over his head and
zipped up. All she could see was his face—that achingly
handsome face—with its baby-smooth jaw and electric
blue eyes.

It was bitterly cold outside, their breath wreathing
their heads. The hard frost had turned the highway
into a strip of polished onyx. Gary stuffed his hands
into his mittens, gave Louise a nod and a half-wave,
and began to walk away, the parking lot's gravel
crunching under his bootheels. The lump under his
parka stirred.

*Do something, girl! Say something! Don't just let him
walk off!*

"Hey, mister . . . er, misters!"

He turned to smile at her. She felt her bravado
slip. *Dear God, what am I getting myself into?* But it was
two in the morning and everyone in Choctaw County
was asleep except for her and the blue-eyed stranger . . .
and his traveling companion.

"I've got a place 'round back. It's not much, but
it's warm. You're welcome to stay . . . I hate to think
of you walking all the way to the motel and then it
turn out to be full-up."

Gary stood there for a moment, his hands in his
pockets and his head cocked to one side as if he was
listening to something. Then he smiled.

"We'd be delighted."

The frozen grass crunched gently under their feet. The
dark bulk of Louise's trailer loomed ahead of them,
resting on its bed of cinderblocks.

"Where are we . . . . exactly? We've no real idea . . . "

"You're in Choctaw County."

"That's the name of this place?"

"No. Not really. This here's Seven Devils. Or its outskirts, at least. Not much to it, except that it's th' county seat. This used to be a railroad town, back before the war. But now that everything's shipped by trucks, there ain't a whole lot left. What makes you want to drive around in this part of Arkansas in the first place? There's nothing down here but rice fields, bayous, and broke farmers."

"We like the old highways . . . we meet much nicer people that way . . . "

Louise stopped to glance over her shoulder as she dug the house key from her coat pocket. Had it been Gary's voice she'd heard that time? All she could see was shadow inside the parka's hood. She stood on the cinderblock that served as her front stoop and fussed with her key chain. She could hear him breathing at her elbow.

"Welcome to my humble abode! It ain't much, but it's home. It used to belong to the boss. I keep an eye on the place for him."

Why was she so anxious? He certainly wasn't the first man she'd invited back to her trailer before. She'd known her share of truckers and salesmen, and hitchhikers tricked out in their elaborate backpacks. Some of them she'd even deluded herself into thinking might be her Prince in disguise.

Each time there had been the meeting of tongues, the grunts in the dark as groins slapped together, and the cool evaporation of sweat on naked flesh. Each time she woke up alone. Sometimes there'd be money on the dresser.

She flicked on the lights as she entered the trailer. The tiny kitchen and shoebox-sized den emerged from the darkness.

"Like I said; it ain't much."

He stood on the threshold, one hand on the door-knob. "It's nice, Louise."

She shivered at the sound of her name in his mouth. She moved into the living room, hoping for a chance to compose herself. She needed to think.

"Close the door! You're lettin' the cold air in!" her voice unnaturally chirpy.

Gary closed the door behind him. She felt a bit more secure, but she couldn't help notice how worn and tacky everything looked: the sofa, the dinette set, the easy chair. . . . For a fleeting second she was over-whelmed by a desire to cry.

Gary removed his parka, carefully draping it over the back of the easychair. He was wearing faded den-ims and a flannel shirt and he was so beautiful it scared her to look at him. He was so perfect she could almost ignore the Human Worm strapped to his back.

"Get you a drink?"

"That would be . . . nice."

She hurried past him and back into the kitchen. She retrieved her bottle of Evan Williams and a cou-ple of highball glasses. She poured herself two fingers, knocked it back, then poured another two before preparing a drink for her guest. She returned to the liv-ing room—he was standing in the exact same spot—and handed Gary the glass.

"Skoal."

"Cheers," he replied, lifting the glass to Carl's lips.

While his partner drank, Gary's eyes met and held hers. "We know why you invited us here, Louise . . . "

Her heart began to beat funny, as if she'd been given a powerful but dangerous drug. She wanted this man, this gorgeous stranger. She wanted to feel his weight on her, pressing her into the mattress of her bed.

" . . . but there's one thing you ought to know before we get started . . . and that's Carl's got to go first."

She stood perfectly still for a second before the words her Dream Prince had spoken sank in. She was keenly aware of Carl's eyes watching her. Her face burned and her stomach balled itself into a fist. She felt as if she'd awakened from a dream to find herself trapped in the punchline from a dirty joke.

"What kind of *pervert* do you think I am?" The tightness in her throat pitched her voice ever higher.

"I don't think you're a pervert, Louise. I think you're a very sweet, very special lady. I didn't mean to hurt you." There was no cynicism in his voice. His tone was that of a child confused by the irrationality of adults.

She felt her anger fade. She gulped down the rest of her drink, hoping it would fan the fires of her indignation. "I expected *something* kinky out of you—like maybe letting th' little guy *watch* . . . But not, y'know . . . "

"I see."

Gary moved to retrieve his parka. Before she realized what she was doing, she grabbed his arm. She was astonished by the intensity of her reaction.

"No! Don't leave! Please . . . it's so lonely here. . . . "

"Yes, it *is* lonely," he whispered. His eyes would not meet hers. "Go stand over there. By the sofa. Where we can see you."

Louise did as she was told. Everything seemed so far away, as if she was watching a movie through the wrong end of a pair of binoculars. Her arms and legs felt so fragile they might have been made of light and glass.

Carl whispered into Gary's ear. His eyes had grown sharp and alive while Gary's seemed to lose their focus.

"Take off your blouse. Please." The words came from someplace far away.

She hesitated, then her hands moved to the throat

of her blouse. The buttons seemed cold and alien, designed to frustrate her fingers. One by one they surrendered until her shirtfront fell open, revealing pale flesh. She shrugged her shoulders and the blouse fell to the floor.

Carl once more whispered something to Gary, never taking his eyes off Louise. "The skirt. Take it off."

Her hands found the fastener at her waist. Plastic teeth purred on plastic zipper and her skirt dropped to the floor, a dark puddle at her ankles. She took a step forward, abandoning her clothes.

Carl murmured into Gary's ear. She unhooked her bra, revealing her breasts. Her skin was milky white and decorated by dark aureole. Her nipples were painfully erect and as hard as corn kernels.

On Carl's relayed command she skinned herself free of her panty hose. When the cool air struck her damp pubic patch, her clitoris stirred.

Gary moved towards her, bringing Carl with him.

She gasped aloud when Gary's hands touched her breasts. His thumbs flicked expertly over her nipples, sending shudders of pleasure through her. Then one hand was between her legs, teasing her thatch and gently massaging her.

Louise felt her knees buckle and she grabbed hold of Gary's shoulders to keep from falling backwards. Her eyes opened and she found herself staring into Carl's dark, intense eyes. She felt a brief surge of shame that her orgasm had become a spectator event, then Gary worked a finger past her labia and sank it to the second joint. Louise groaned aloud and all thoughts of shame disappeared.

He moved swiftly and quietly, wrapping her in his powerful arms and lifting her bodily. She felt a different form of pleasure now, as if she was once more within her father's safe embrace. He moved down the narrow hall, past the cramped bathroom alcove, and into the tiny bedroom at the back of the trailer. He lowered her trembling body onto the bed, draping her legs over the edge of the mattress.

His left hand continued to trace delicate patterns along her exposed flesh while his right loosened the harness that held Carl in place. He only halted his exploration of her body when he moved to free his burden.

Louise saw that Carl was dressed in a flannel shirt identical to Gary's, except that the empty sleeves had been pinned up and the shirttail folded back on itself and fastened shut, just like a diaper. Gary removed the shirt and Louise swore out loud.

Even on a normal man's body Carl's penis would have been unusually large. It stood red and erect against the thick dark hair of his belly. Louise was so taken aback she scarcely noticed the smooth lumps of flesh that should have been Carl's arms and legs.

Gary positioned Carl's naked torso between her spread thighs. His gaze met and held her own so intently Louise almost forgot the absurd perversity of what they were doing.

"We love you," said Gary and shoved Carl on top of her.

Louise cried out as Carl penetrated her. It had been a long time since she'd last been with a man, and she had never known one of such proportions. She involuntarily contracted her hips, taking him in deeper. Gary's right hand kneaded the flesh of her breasts. His left hand helped Carl move. She could also feel something warm and damp just below her breasts. She suddenly realized it was Carl's face.

Gary's face was closer to hers now, his eyes mirroring her heat. She snared a handful of his hair, drawing him closer. His mouth was warm and wet as he clumsily returned her kiss. She felt the quivering that signaled the approach of orgasm and her moans became cries, giving voice to an exquisite wounding. Her hips bucked wildly with each spasm, but Carl refused to be unseated. As she lay dazed and gasping in her own sweat, she was dimly aware of him still working between her legs. Then there was a deep groan, muffled by her own flesh, and she felt him stiffen and then relax.

Louise rarely experienced orgasms during intercourse. She had been unprepared for such intensity; it was if Gary had stuck his finger in her brain and swirled everything around so she was no longer sure what she thought or knew.

No. Not Gary. Carl.

The thought made her catch her breath and she raised herself onto her elbows, staring down at the thing cradled between her thighs. Carl's face was still buried in her breast. She touched his hair and felt him start from the unexpected contact. It was the first time since their strange rut had begun that she'd acknowledged his presence.

She felt Gary watching her as she moved back further onto the bed. Carl remained curled at the foot of the mattress, his eyes fixed on her. Gary stood in the narrow space between the bed and the dresser, his hands at his side.

"What about you? Aren't you interested?" Her voice was hoarse. Gary did not meet her gaze as he shifted his weight from foot to foot.

"What's the matter? Is it me?"

His head jerked up. "No! It's not you. You're fine. It's just . . . " He fell silent and looked to Carl, who nodded slightly.

Gary took a deep breath and loosened his belt buckle. His manner had changed completely. His movements had lost their previous grace. Biting his lower lip and tensing as if in anticipation of a blow, he dropped his pants.

Gary's sex organs were the size of a two-year-old

child's. They lay exposed like fragile spring blossoms, his pubic area as smooth and hairless as his face. His eyes remained cast down.

Louise's lips twisted into a wry smile. She had willingly serviced a freak in order to please her long-awaited Prince, only to find him gelded. Yet all she could feel for the handsome near-man was sorrow.

"You poor thing. You poor, poor thing." She reached out and touched his hand, drawing him into the warmth of her arms. Surprised, Gary eagerly returned her embrace. To her own surprise, she reached down to pull Carl toward her. The three of them lay together on the bed like a nest of snakes, Louise gently caressing her lovers. After a while Gary began to talk.

"I've known Carl since we were kids. My mama used to cook and clean for his folks and I kept Carl company. His mama and daddy were real rich; that's how they could afford to keep him home. At least his mama wanted him home. Carl's daddy drank a lot and used to say how it wasn't *his* fault in front of Carl. I knew how he felt. About having your daddy hate you because of the way you was born. Maybe that's why me and Carl made such good friends. You see, I can't read so good. And I'm really bad with math and things like that. My daddy got mad at my mama when they found out what was wrong with me and ran away. I never really went to school. When Carl was five, his daddy got real mad and started kickin' him. And Carl hadn't even done anything bad! He kicked Carl in the throat and they took him to the hospital. That's why Carl can't talk too good. But he's real smart! Smarter than most people with arms and legs! He knows a lot about history and math and important stuff like that. Carl tells me what to say and how to act and what to do so people don't know I've got something wrong with me. If people knew I wasn't smart they'd be even meaner to us." He exchanged a warm, brotherly smile with the silent man and squeezed him where his shoulder should have been. "Carl looks after me. I'm his arms and legs and voice and he's my brain and, you know." He blushed.

"You're lucky. Both of you. Not everyone is as . . . whole."

"But we're not!" He folded her hands inside his own. "Not really. That's why we've been travelling. We've been trying to find the last part of us. The part that *will* make us whole."

Louise did not know what to say to this, so she simply kissed him. Sometime later they fell asleep, Carl's torso curled between them like a dozing pet.

The alarm went off at eight-thirty, jarring Louise from a dreamless sleep. She lay there for a moment, staring at Gary then Carl. She should have felt soiled, but there was no indignation inside her. She gently shook Gary's beautiful naked shoulder.

"It's morning already. The filling station must be open by now. You can get your tire fixed."

"Yes." His voice sounded strangely hollow.

She got out of the rumpled bed, careful to keep from kicking Carl, and put on a housecoat. Now that it was daylight she felt embarrassed to be naked. She hurried into the kitchen and made coffee.

Gary emerged from the bedroom, dressed, with Carl once more harnessed to his back. She handed him two mugs, one black and one with cream and sugar, and watched, a faint smile on her lips, as they repeated their one-as-two act.

After they'd finished, Gary picked his parka up and laid it across one arm. He glanced first at her then angled his head so that he was as close to face-to-face with his passenger as possible. After a moment's silent communion, he once more turned to look at her, and his eyes lost their focus. Carl's lips moved at his ear and Louise could hear the faint rasping of his ruined voice.

Gary spoke, like a man reading back dictation.

"Louise . . . you're a wonderful woman . . . I know you're not attracted to me, that's understandable . . . but I see something in you that might, someday . . . respond to *me* too. . . ."

As Gary continued his halting recitation, Louise's gaze moved from his face to Carl's. For the first time since she'd met them, she really looked at *him*. She studied his plain, everyday face and his brown eyes. As she listened the voice she heard was Carl's and she felt something inside her change.

"We'll stop back after we get the tire repaired. . . . It's up to you. . . . We shouldn't be more than a hour at the most. Please think about it."

Gary began to put his parka on, but before the jacket hid Carl completely she darted forward and kissed both of them. First Gary, and then, with great care, Carl. They paused for a second and then smiled.

Louise stood in the middle of the trailer, hugging herself against the morning cold, as she watched her lovers leave. Funny. She'd always imagined her Prince having blue eyes. . . .

THE JOY OF HATS

Mike Resnick &
Nicholas A. DiChario

Mike Resnick is one of the best-selling authors in science fiction, and one of the most prolific. His many novels include *The Dark Lady*, *Stalking the Unicorn*, *Paradise*, *Santiago*, *Ivory*, *Soothsayer Oracle*, *Lucifer Jones*, *Purgatory*, and *Inferno*. His award-winning short fiction has been gathered in the collection *Will the Last Person to Leave the Planet Please Turn Off the Sun?* Of late, he has become almost as prolific as an anthologist, producing, as editor, *Inside the Funhouse: 17 SF stories about SF*, *Whatdunits*, *More Whatdunits*, and *Shaggy B.E.M. Stories*; a long string of anthologies coedited with Martin H. Greenberg, including *Alternate Presidents*, *Alternate Kennedys*, *Alternate Warriors*, *Aladdin: Master of the Lamp*, and *Dinosaur Fantastic*, among others; and two anthologies coedited with Gardner Dozois, *Future Earths: Under African Skies* and *Future Earths: Under South American Skies*. He won the Hugo Award in 1989 for "Kirinyaga," one of the most controversial and talked-about stories in recent years. He won another Hugo Award in 1991 for another story in the Kirinyaga series, "The Manumouki." His most recent books include the novel

A Miracle of Rare Device; the anthologies *Alternate Outlaws* and *Alternate Worldcons; Deals with the Devil* (coedited with Martin H. Greenberg and Loren D. Estleman); and *By Any Other Fame* and *Sherlock Holmes in Orbit* (both coedited with Martin H. Greenberg).

Nicholas A. DiChario is a new writer whose work has appeared in *The Magazine of Fantasy & Science Fiction* as well as in anthologies such as *Alternate Kennedys, Alternate Warriors, Alternate Outlaws, Christmas Ghosts, By Any Other Fame, Dinosaur Fantastic,* and *Tales from the Great Turtle.* He has been a Campell Award nominee, and his story "The Winterberry" was a finalist for the Nebula Award and the World Fantasy Award.

Here they join forces in an ingenious little story that shows us that sometimes it *is* proper for a gentleman to keep his hat on in the presence of a lady. . . .

The Joy of Hats

Stress.

Stress could literally kill a man. That's what Haggerty's physician, a part-time stand-up comedian, had told him between acts over a bourbon and Coke at the Club Punch Drunk in Manhattan: "If you don't take a nice relaxing vacation to some quiet out-of-the-way place, you're likely to take a *permanent* vacation to some place so damned quiet you can hear the grass sprouting new roots in your skull bone. Get it?"

"You're never going to make it out of these cheap dives," Haggerty had told him, "unless you can learn to tell a joke without saying 'Get it?'"

Why did he have to come to the middle of the Adirondack Mountains to relieve stress, when his physician got to stand up and shoot his mouth off in front of hundreds of hecklers in the heart of the city? Haggerty missed his doctor's impenetrable optimism and lousy jokes. He missed his investments, his clients, Wall Street. He missed crunching numbers. He missed Louie, his morning cabdriver, to whom he still owed 212 bucks because he'd stuck with the Mets even longer than the mayor of New York.

Outside of Aunt Ida's Hat Boutique, a warm, sun-drenched, June morning crept in over the towering pine trees and mountain slopes. Sparrows fluttered and chirped. Ida's hat shop rested in the center of a small town, between a diner and a hardware store, across the street from Sam's Grocery. He'd spent a few summers here as a boy. He had fond, if vague, memories of the hat shop and the surrounding hills and valleys. As far as he could tell, nothing but the seasons had changed in over thirty years.

Well, that wasn't exactly true. The people had changed; they'd grown old. That was one of the first things Haggerty had noticed. His aunt, now stooped with arthritis, couldn't remember things like what time her favorite TV shows came on, and she'd stopped counting birthdays when she turned eighty. Sam, the grocer, had to be pushing ninety, and he still walked to work every morning, dragging his foot along behind him more out of habit, it seemed, than for any other reason. He had a seventy-year-old son who did all of the hard labor. In the city, most people died or moved out before they grew old. If you had any intentions of aging, you didn't belong in New York; if you couldn't handle the pressure, you didn't belong either.

Haggerty opened the door to Ida's hat shop and let in the mountain air. Welcome to God's country. Over a hundred summits graced the Adirondack Preserve, ranging from one to five thousand feet in height. Gneiss, granite, and gabbro steeples formed a watershed between the Hudson River and the majestic St. Lawrence. The Great North Woods, the locals called it, a nickname that traced all the way back to the 1700s. Haggerty could feel the wilderness swarming around him, its rich blue lakes, its ore and timber, its sprawling Catskills. If not for the thin, winding roads that cut through the heart of the mountains, a scant reminder of civilization, Haggerty might have expected to see the tepees of the Algonquin or the Iroquois Indians nestled in among the trees.

The hat shop had been closed for almost two months now. Ida couldn't get around much anymore, and she was tired, so one day she'd decided not to open for business, and she hadn't been back since. It hurt her, Haggerty knew. He could see it in the dullness of her pale blue eyes, and she'd mentioned more than once how much she missed her hats.

If it wasn't for Haggerty showing up a couple of days ago, the shop probably would have stayed closed until Ida died and someone had to come by and throw everything away. She had no customers left—absolutely none—and hadn't made a penny's profit in at least twenty years, ever since her husband died and left her a small fortune in land she'd sold to the state of New York. But she had friends. Her friends would stop by and talk and drink coffee or just sit around and do nothing. Now, instead of gathering at Ida's shop, they gathered at Ida's home.

So Haggerty came here to get his peace and quiet, to sit among the men's hats and stare out at the trees. (Ida didn't have any women's hats in the shop. She'd sold out a dozen years ago and never bothered to order new merchandise.) The shop, converted from a turn-of-the-nineteenth-century house, looked every bit its age—warped floors and crooked windows, small rooms little more than nooks by today's standards, lots of narrow passages and doorways (although all but a few of the doors had long since been removed). Ida had a couple dozen hat racks set up, some shelving, and two glass display cases. There was a cash register on a counter that had to be as old as she herself was.

Haggerty snatched a gray fedora off one of the shelves and put it on his head. He'd always hated hats. They were clumsy things. They matted and killed your hair. They were difficult to match with coats and suits. Worst of all, they were not fashionable in New York, hadn't been for decades, unless you condescended to wearing the ubiquitous New York Mets baseball cap. There was a time, though, when hats were all the rage, and a man wouldn't be caught dead without one. He looked at himself in the mirror. He rather liked the gray fedora. He was not a handsome man, but the hat flattered him, complimented his neatly trimmed beard and mustache, hid his bald spot. And it felt comfortable, as if it had been made to fit his head.

During the day, he dusted hats and polished lamps and straightened racks and worried—the stress had not magically disappeared—about the work he'd left behind in New York City and the precious time he was losing (not to mention the money). And the more he tried to put all this out of his head, the more he worried about it.

Haggerty took out the thermos of coffee he wasn't supposed to be drinking and popped a Cordizan. Relax, he told himself. Forget about the world. Take the comedian's advice. Catch a nap, for God's sake.

At dusk, he closed up shop and walked into the back room. There was an old mattress on the floor where Aunt Ida used to lay down when she got tired, with a nice soft pillow, surrounded by empty hat boxes, a broom and a dustpan, some buckets and rags and sponges. He thought he'd lay down for a half hour before heading back to Ida's small house in the woods.

"Hi."

The voice startled Haggerty—a young woman's voice. He didn't know where it came from at first. He'd been alone in the shop all day. Not a single customer had happened by in the two days he'd been there, and who knew for how many years prior to that? But he saw the girl sitting on the mattress in the corner. He reached for the light switch.

"Don't turn on the light," she said. "I love this time of day. It's so beautiful here in the mountains, when the sun is setting. It reminds me of dreams, good dreams."

"Who are you?" said Haggerty. "How did you get in here?"

"You look very handsome in that hat," she said.

"Thank you." He moved to take it off.

"No," she said hastily. "Don't take off the hat. Leave it on. If you leave it on, I'll stay."

"What do you mean, you'll stay?" He stepped deeper into the room. He saw that she had the blanket gathered around her. It got chilly in the mountains at sunset.

"I'll stay here . . . with *you.*"

She lowered the blanket to her waist. She was at least half naked, and Haggerty suspected more.

"Miss, what in the *world* do you think you're doing?"

"Take your shirt off," she answered, "and I'll show you."

Of course Hagerty *wanted* to take off his shirt, *and* his pants, and everything else. This was a fantasy screw waiting to happen. A young, homely girl from the Adirondacks hears about the big shot from New York staying on at his aunt's place, and all of a sudden she gets the urge to play loose. Maybe she hates her life with the mountains boys. Maybe she's just curious to see if city men have the same parts as mountain boys. Maybe Haggerty is in the right place at the right time for once. The only problem is, she's got a husband who's six feet four inches tall, weighs two-eighty, and knows how to kill a wolf with his bare hands. Or she's got a papa and twelve brothers with a gun collection that could fill a museum. Or she turns out to be your distant cousin.

Haggerty was no fool. He'd gone through his midlife crisis, and he'd been around enough to know what he could and could not have. He was overweight and his forehead was too tall and he had a fleshy face. Money could buy him some women for a little while. His power on Wall Street could get him others, until they decided to move on, or up. Fantasies were not his style. Besides, this girl was not in the least bit homely.

She had the most beautiful skin he'd ever seen, long, dark hair that shone like fine silk, round eyes that sparkled like sapphires, a trim waist, and full, firm breasts. What the hell was she doing here? With *him?* He closed his eyes. Women like this disappeared when men like Haggerty blinked. When he opened his eyes, she still sat on the mattress.

"Your shirt," she said. "Take it off."

Haggerty unbuttoned his shirt.

It was the kind of lovemaking a man is capable of only in his dreams. She bent to his every need, and he knew exactly when and where to touch her, and how to kiss her. She had a tongue of velvet, lips of satin. She moaned when he licked between her legs, and shook and cried out when he entered her, and when he came, she came too. And then they did it all over again, mingling like honey and whiskey and milk, sweet and hard and smooth, arms and legs synchronizing as if they'd known each other for generations—yet the sex as raw and heated as lovers joining for the first time. After they exploded together a third time, they clung to each other, panting and sweating, hungrier than ever.

"I must go," she said.

"No." He couldn't believe he wanted more, but he did.

"I must." She rolled to her knees.

He sighed and took off the gray fedora. When he reached for her, she slipped through his fingers and disappeared.

Literally, *literally,* she'd slipped through Haggerty's fingers and disappeared, leaving a hint of warm mist like dew after a summer's rain.

A ghost.

She could *not* have been a dream. They'd done it three times, and he'd used muscles he hadn't used in years, and he felt it the next day—felt his middle age—and he knew that a dream never would have gone as long or as hard or as far as it had last night. Where had she come from? More importantly, how could he get her *back*? Haggerty fussed with the gray fedora, studying himself in the mirror. Today the hat did not look so good, did not fit quite as neatly as it had the day before. He wore it anyway. The ghost girl had liked the hat. She had made him wear it while they'd made love, and, remarkably, it had stayed on his head the whole time, even when his head was buried between her legs. The hat was the key, definitely. He wore it even though it kept slipping off his head and it seemed as if it did not *want* to be worn.

Throughout the day, he kept looking for her in the back room, and when she didn't come, he thought that maybe he would only be able to find her when the sun was setting. He waited and waited for the slow Adirondacks clock to tick-tock toward dusk. He was not a religious man, but he found himself praying for the girl to be there when he stepped into the back room.

She was not.

Damn! He had been *sure* it was the fedora that had linked him to the girl. What else could it have been? What had he done wrong? Maybe he'd fussed with the hat too often. Maybe he'd been too conscious of it. He would wear it again tomorrow. He would do better with it. He *must*.

But the next day, Haggerty was even more troubled by the lay of the hat. The first day, it had fit perfectly; the day after, it had troubled him; today, it was the most uncomfortable thing he'd ever put on his head. Maybe the fedora was the problem rather than the solution. He picked another hat, a nice comfortable Panama, white with a black band. It looked good on him, and it felt right. He wore it the entire day without even noticing it was on his head. Toward the end of the day, his palms began to sweat and his heartbeat quickened (probably not what his comedian had had in mind as a stress reliever). But Haggerty wanted that girl, wanted her more than anything he'd ever wanted in his life, and he could almost *feel* her presence in the hat shop. She was near. She had to be. *Come to me,* he thought. *Please.*

At dusk, he opened the door to the back room.

"Hello," the woman said.

"You're here. I was hoping—"

"I know. So was I."

"It was the hat, wasn't it? I needed to pick a different hat."

"I think so. I wanted to come to you last night, but I couldn't. Tonight I could."

Haggerty reached for the light switch.

"No, please—no light!"

"Why not? I want to look at you."

"You can see me just fine," she said. "Take your shirt off."

He did. He wasn't about to argue. He was so excited his entire body shivered as he undressed. When he reached for the hat she said, "No. Keep it on."

Of course, of course.

And the sex was just as hot and desperate and loving as it had been their first night together. She smelled of wildflowers in a burgeoning emerald forest, she smelled of wood and pine. He did everything within his power to burrow deeper and deeper inside her, and she wrapped her legs around him and pulled him in. He was a better and stronger lover than he had any right to be. His need was so real it threatened to consume him, and he was driven as much by the terror of losing her at the end of the night as by the undeniable feel of her flesh as he moved within her. Haggerty was addicted. The more he gave, the more he took; the more he needed, the more she seemed to need him too.

"*I must go,*" she said.

"*Stay a little longer. Watch the sunrise with me.*"

"*I can't. It's time.*"

"*Who are you? What's your name?*"

"*I don't think you're supposed to know.*"

"But you know, don't you? Tell me."
She rolled to her knees. . . .
And again she slipped through Haggerty's fingers. He flopped back on the mattress. The hat slipped off his head.

The next day, the white Panama did not fit him at all. Haggerty had expected this. He did not bother to fuss with it. He slipped on a lightweight sun hat, taupe, with stitched eyelets, the type of hat you might see tucked on the brow of some old man deep-sea fishing in south Florida. It fit like a dream.

He had all sorts of theories about the girl, and all sorts of time to think about them. The hats had somehow forged a connection between Haggerty and the girl. The hats had opened a spiritual gateway. The girl, lured by the hats, had been called back to the land of the living to answer her unfulfilled sexual desires. Once he wore a hat, he couldn't use it again to call her back. The gray fedora had taught him that lesson.

At dusk, he went into the back room and found her waiting there, and again they took each other, wild and passionate, until it was time for her to go.

In the days that followed, Haggerty wore a homburg, an Irish walker, a hard bowler, a soft trilby, and a sombrero. He wore a plaid tam, a black beret, a Stetson, a top hat, and a *yarmulke*. He wore a sailor's cap, an olive green porkpie, and a kepi. He was delighted by the number of hats his aunt had acquired over the years, wondered how she'd accumulated such a collection, but didn't really care as long as the girl kept coming back to him.

Each day, a different hat; each night, the girl would come to him, and they'd make love until they could barely breathe, until they collapsed from total exhaustion.

Each night, Haggerty tried to find out something more about her, if not her name, then where she'd lived, or how she'd died, or why she kept coming back to the hat shop. But all she would say was that she didn't think he was supposed to know any of that, and that it didn't matter as long as they were together. And this, he felt, was true. Their togetherness was the most important thing in their worlds—hers a strange world of temporary permanence, his a permanence nothing more than temporary.

So Haggerty kept wearing hats. One day he wore what he was certain was an eighteenth-century tricorne that probably belonged in a museum. The next day he wore a tall, brimless hat that sprouted black feathers, something that might have looked fashionable on a sixteenth-century aristocrat. He didn't care how ridiculous he looked; no one ever came into the shop anyway. Without shame, he wore a cavalier's hat adorned with a thick brass buckle worthy of a pirate, a beaver-pelt hat with a long tail, and something that looked like Manchu headgear.

Still she came to him. Every night.

She came to him until he wore the rust brown fedora.

He couldn't understand it. He hadn't worn the hat before. He'd carefully separated those hats he'd worn from those he hadn't, because he didn't want to make a stupid mistake and miss her, not even for one night. Maybe there was just something about that particular rust brown fedora she didn't like.

He tried another hat the next day—a stiff, navy blue derby. But that night, although he was sure he felt the girl's presence, they could not find each other in the back room.

A horrible thought struck him then. He had assumed if he wore a hat, that specific hat would not call the girl back a second time. He knew that eventually he'd run out of hats, but there were so many of them he'd chosen not to think about that for a while. But what if the same held true for a particular *style* hat? He'd already worn a derby and a fedora. Did that mean no more derbies or fedoras would call the girl?

Haggerty panicked. He went crazy looking for more hats. He tore up the back room. He checked the musty cellar. Nothing. There was a padlock on a door that led upstairs. He found a crowbar and ripped the plate clean off the wood. The upstairs was empty except for cobwebs and spiders and dead flies, an old desk and chair, and a rolled-up carpet. Haggerty went downstairs and sat behind the counter, staring at the hats, his Aunt Ida's beautiful hats. He was soaked in cold sweat. He'd used every last style in the shop. He'd never get her back, never see her again. He hunched over and started to cry. He hadn't even had a chance to say good-bye. What was her name? He didn't even know her name!

Haggerty felt a different kind of fear then, a mad crimping of his body and mind, a sense of isolation that threatened to forever lock him outside the real world, alone, a hollow Haggerty. He wept until no more tears would come, and then he decided to do something about it.

"Aunt Ida, please *think*! Don't you recall anyone who might have looked like that?"

"Oh, no, Nephew, I'm sure I would have remembered a girl that attractive."

Aunt Ida always called him "Nephew." She hated his name. So did Haggerty, come to think of it. "Maybe she wasn't a regular customer," he suggested. "She might have just stopped in one day, really taken with the place, and maybe she bought a couple of hats . . . I don't know." He knew how ridiculous he must sound. How could he expect his aunt to remember a day like any other day in the past eighty years of her life just because some gorgeous girl might have walked into her shop? *Might* have. He couldn't even be sure of that.

Aunt Ida dabbed at her lips with a tissue. Her hair was steel gray. She needed help getting in and out of chairs these days. Soon it would be a wheelchair. "How are my hats?" she said. "I miss them, you know, I miss them very much."

"Your hats are fine." He paused, wondering if he dared ask the next question. But of course he dared; feeling foolish was a small price to pay for getting *her* back. "Do you remember any stories of a spirit or a ghost of a young girl haunting the area? Anything like that?"

"My goodness, Nephew! No, nothing like that ever happened around here. Why do you ask?"

How could that be? Not even one lousy ghost story? No mountain lore whatsoever? Haggerty bit at his knuckles. "What about a girl who may have died young, in her twenties, a horrible accident or something?"

Aunt Ida shook her head.

"Did anyone ever live in the room above your hat shop? Did you ever rent it out?"

"No. Your uncle spent a lot of time up there. He used it as an office." She stared at him. "You don't look so good, Nephew. What's the matter? Aren't you getting any rest at the shop? Your doctor was right. You need to relax."

It was clear that Aunt Ida was not going to be of any help. "Yes, well, I've been trying." He got to his feet. "I think I'm going to visit the cemetery. I'll be home later this afternoon."

"Maybe you could bring me down to the shop one day," she said; her hands were fluttering more and more, he noticed, with each passing day.

"One day, maybe, if you're feeling up to it."

"I love my hats," she said.

"Me too," answered Haggerty.

*   *   *

He spent most of that day at the cemetery. He had decided not to leave any stone unturned. He started at one end and read the names and dates on each gravestone. He cleared away grass and moss and leaves and branches from several stones. He'd brought a small gardening shovel and a pair of gloves specifically for that purpose. In the 1800s, Haggerty found a lot of dead babies. In the 1900s, the old folks had begun to pile up. There were some young men from the wars, but only a few young women, none of them the right one. He would have been able to tell if he'd come across his girl's grave. Somehow he would have felt her there. He didn't.

Haggerty returned to Aunt Ida's Hat Boutique and walked through the shop. Soon it would be dusk. He could still sense the girl's presence, but it was weaker now. He was in danger of losing her forever. He went into the back room.

"Where are you?" he said. "I can't find you! I'll do anything! Help me! *Please*!"

But she could not.

Haggerty pawed through the hats again, hoping against all odds he'd missed one. That's when it came to him—a possibility!

He dashed out of the shop and ran all the way back to Aunt Ida's house. She was asleep on the couch, the television blaring loud enough to be heard all the way to Lake Champlain. He sprinted up to the attic. Boxes, boxes everywhere. He began ripping them open, discovering old dishes and silverware wrapped in newspapers, old dresses and shoes, old books and *Life* magazines and 78 rpm records. More boxes, more junk. Candlesticks, doilies, toasters, coffeepots, cookie cutters, fishing lures, rods and reels, photo albums, lanterns, and a hatbox—*a hatbox*! His hands shook as he tore off the lid.

A *fez*! He hadn't yet worn a fez!

He put the fez on his head and ran back to Ida's hat shop as the sun began to creep below the tree line. By the time Haggerty closed the door behind him, his lungs gulped for air. He decided that if he were to suffer a heart attack, that would be all right, yes, perfectly fine by him. Life without the ghost girl wasn't worth living. She was a part of him now, and he a part of her. No matter what it took, he would figure out a way for them to be together. He straightened the fez on his head and walked into the back room.

"I'm afraid, I'm so afraid," she said.

"Don't worry, I'm here." He went to her. She was cold all over, and trembling. Haggerty held her to him.

"I couldn't find you—I tried everything—I searched for you—I was so alone—"

"It's all right," he said, cradling her. "*Shhh.* I'm here now."

"Yes, I can feel you. It's the last hat, isn't it? You've brought the last one."

"I'm so sorry. I don't know what to do."

"It's all right," she said, wiping the tears from her cheeks. "I can feel something happening already—a sense of peace."

"But how am I going to get you back? We have to talk about this. We have to figure out a way. I'm afraid to make love to you. What if I never see you again?"

"No, this is the way it was meant to be, don't you see?"

And then their lips joined, and he sank into her kiss and was instantly lost. She ripped off his shirt and tore at his pants. He scrambled urgently out of his clothes. There was no stopping this. He had known, had always known, that there would be one last time. Haggerty kissed and clawed and thrust into her with a savage lust he'd yet to unleash. He pushed himself beyond all human limits, hoping that each orgasm would bring with it his last earthly breath.

"I'm whole!" she cried, as she rode him for the last time.

"I'm free!" weeping, moving over him, slick with buttery sweat. "Thank you—thank you!"

And her breasts shrank and turned to leather under Haggerty's fingers, and her body grew shriveled and gnarled, and her skin withered and became dry and ancient, and her silky hair lost its luster and became as white as snow, all of this in a moment, in less time than it took to lose one's breath.

"I've made love to all my hats," she moaned, an old, old woman now, dying, dying right in front of his eyes. "I can rest now. Thank you so much, Nephew—now I can rest in peace!"

Still Haggerty clutched her. "I won't let you go!" he screamed. "Take me with you! Take me!"

But one cannot hold the dead.

She turned to dust. And was gone.

The fez slipped off Haggerty's head. He collapsed on the mattress.

"Dear God!" he whispered. "Aunt Ida!"

Aunt Ida died twice that night. Once in Haggerty's arms, and once when she went to sleep in front of the television and never woke up. Folks from all over the Adirondacks came to her funeral. Her hat boutique had gained quite a reputation throughout the Great North Woods area, with people as far away as the Mohawk River Valley and Lake Ontario having visited the shop at least once during their lifetimes. Old men filled Haggerty's ears with tales of her legendary beauty.

Later, when Haggerty went through the attic, he found some old photographs of her, and he cried over them until it didn't hurt anymore.

When he told his story over the phone to his physician in New York, even that impenetrable optimist tried to talk him out of his decision:

"You're staying there for all the wrong reasons," he said. "You feel guilty because you had several truly obscene sexual fantasies about your eighty-year-old

Aunt Ida. Christ, that's enough to terrify *anybody!*
Stress can play all sorts of dirty tricks on the mind—in
your case, downright filthy!"

"No, it's not like that," Haggerty said. "I don't feel
guilty. Hell, I set her *free.* She'd always loved her hats
and I gave her the chance to really, physically, love
them—otherwise her spirit might never have passed on.
As far as I'm concerned, that's something to be proud of.
And I'm staying because I want to remain close to her."

"That's *sick*! Take it from me, I'm a *comedian*. Look,
I think you're suffering withdrawal symptoms. I was
wrong about the peace and quiet, I see that now. Your
unstable personality can't handle it. Come back to
New York. I have a very good friend who's a psychia-
trist. He's booked from now till the end of the century,
but he owes me a favor and—"

"Let me tell you something," Haggerty interrupted.
"When I asked my aunt if she remembered a young
beautiful girl who might have lived in this area, when I
described the girl, do you know what my aunt said to
me? She said no—she said she definitely would have
remembered a girl that attractive. It never even crossed
her mind it might have been her, and it never crossed
my mind, either."

"All right, I'll bite. What are you driving at?"

Haggerty thought about it for a moment. He took
the phone over to Aunt Ida's kitchen window and
gazed into the woods. "I look out the window here,
and what do you think I see? I see an oak tree that has
probably lived for centuries, so thick you couldn't even
wrap your arms around it. I see a stream trickling with
clean, fresh water. I see squirrels in the forest and birds
in the sky, deer running through the thatch, dark blue
mountains reaching up to the clouds."

"You could see all that on the Discovery Channel."

"When I wake in the middle of the night, it's dark
and quiet. When I breathe, I smell the pine trees and

the summer flowers, not a trace of carbon monoxide. What I'm trying to say is, there's a rare beauty here that has no idea that it *is* rare or beautiful. Do you have any idea what that does to a man's soul? I'm lucky that I lived long enough to experience it. And I'm not damnfool enough to give it up now."

"You're starting to sound like John Denver. You're mad as a hatter, my friend. I mean, you're talking through your hat. Get it?"

"I get it. Good-bye." He hung up the phone.

Just a few more calls to make—transferring funds, cashing in some stocks and bonds, closing accounts, that sort of thing—and Haggerty, too, would be free. But all of that could wait a day or two, or even a week. Time meant nothing here. *Feeling* was what mattered. The song in a man's heart and the big country surrounding it gave one a different perspective. In the Adirondacks, you could love a sparrow you might never see again. You could love the sound of a small animal, forever unknown to you, scuttling through fallen leaves. You could love hats for no other reason than what they'd come to mean over the course of a lifetime. And you could love a memory.

Hats.

Haggerty put a white trilby on his head, a soft felt hat with a tapered crown, and tapped it into place. A perfect fit.

He decided he would take some of his money and order a brand-new line for the ladies. That would make Ida happy, he thought, even though he was sure none of the hats would sell. Why should they?

He stepped out into the bright morning and walked in the shadow of the mountains to Aunt Ida's Hat Boutique.

Once again open for business.

THE FIRE WHEN IT COMES

COMES

Parke Godwin

Here's a poignant, compelling, and passionate story that suggests that, to paraphrase the old saying, life is too precious to be wasted on the *living*. . . .

Parke Godwin is perhaps best known for the Arthurian epics *Firelord* and *Beloved Exile*, although his other novels include three written with Marvin Kaye, *The Masters of Solitude*, *Wintermind*, and *A Cold Blue Light*. His short fiction has been assembled in the collection *The Fire When It Comes*, and the novella of the same name, which follows, won the World Fantasy Award in 1982. His most recent book is another Arthurian novel, *Robin and the King*. He lives in Auburn, California.

The Fire When It Comes

For Betty H.—wherever

Got to wake up soon.

I've been sick a long time, I mean really sick. Hard to remember why or how long, but it feels like that time I had a 103 fever for a week. Sleep wasn't rest but endless, meaningless movement, and I'd wake up to change my sweaty nightdress for a clean one, which would be soaked by sunup.

But this boring, weary dream has gone on for ages. I'm walking up and down the apartment trying to find the door. The furniture isn't mine. People come and go, replaced by others with even tackier sofas in colors loud enough to keep them awake, and I flutter around and past them on my own silly route as if I'd lost an earring and had to find it before I could get on with life. None of it's very real, murky as *cinéma vérité* shot in a broom closet. I have to strain to recognize the apartment, and the sound track just mumbles. No feeling at all.

Just that it's gone on so long.

All right, enough of this. Lying around sick and fragile is romantic as hell, but I have to get it together, drop the needle on the world again and let it play. I'm—

Hell, I am out of it, can't even remember my name, but there's a twinge of pain in trying. Never mind, start with simple things. Move your hand, spider your fingers out from under the covers. Rub your face, open your eyes.

That hasn't worked the last thousand times. I can't wake up, and in a minute the stupid dream will start again with a new cast and no script, and I'll be loping up and down after that earring or the lost door. Hell, yes. Here it comes. Again.

No. It's different this time. I'd almost swear I was awake, standing near the balcony door with the whole long view of my apartment stretching out before me: living room, Pullman kitchen, the bedroom, bathroom like an afterthought in the rear. For the first time, it's clear daylight and the apartment is bare. Sounds are painfully sharp. The door screams open and shuts like thunder.

A boy and a girl.

She's twenty-two at the outside, he's not much older. He looks sweet, happy, and maybe a little scared. Nice face, the kind of sensitive expression you look at twice. The girl's mouth is firmer. Small and blond and compact. I know that expression, tentative only for a moment before she begins to measure my apartment for possibilities, making it hers.

"Really a lot of room," she says. "I could do things with this place if we had the money."

My God, they're so *loud*. The boy drifts toward me while she bangs cupboard doors, checks out the bathroom, flushes the toilet.

"The john works. No plumbing problems."

"Al, come here. Look, a balcony."

"Wow, Lowen, is that for real?"

Of course it's real, love. Open the door, take a look and then get the hell out of my dreams.

"Let's look, Al." He invites the girl with one hand and opens the balcony door. He's in love with her and doesn't quite know how to handle it all yet. They wander out onto my tiny balcony and look down at

Seventy-seventh Street and out over the river, where a
garbage scow is gliding upstream. It's a lovely day. Jesus,
how long since I've seen the sun? Kids are romping in
the playground across Riverside Drive. Lowen and Al
stand close together. When he pulls her to him, her
hand slips up over his shoulder. The gold ring looks new.

"Can we afford it, Lowen?"

"We can if you want it."

"If? I never wanted anything so much in my life."

They hold each other and talk money as if it were
a novelty, mentioning a rent way over what I pay. The
frigging landlord would love to hang that price tag on
this place. Lowen points to the drainpipe collar bed-
ded in a patch of cement, monument to my epic battle with that bastard to clear the drain and anchor it so
every rain didn't turn my balcony into a small lake.
Lowen's pointing to letters scratched in the cement.

"GAYLA."

That's right, that's me. I remember now.

They look through the apartment again, excited
now that they think they want it. Yes, if they're careful with their budget, if they get that cash wedding
present from Aunt Somebody, they can work it. I feel
very odd; something is funny here. They're too real.
The dream is about them now.

Hey, wait a minute, you two.

The door bangs shut after them.

Hey, wait!

I run out onto the balcony and call to them in the
street, and for the first time in this fever dream, I'm
conscious of arms and legs that I still can't feel, and a
fear growing out of a clearing memory.

Hey, hello. It's me, Gayla Damon.

Lowen turns and tilts his head as if he heard me, or
perhaps for one more look at where he's going to live
with Al-short-for-Alice. I can't tell from his smile, but I
lean to it like a fire in winter, out over the low stone

parapet—and then, oh Christ, I remember. For one terrible, sufficient flash, the memory flicks a light switch.

If I could cry or be sick, I'd do that. If I screamed loud enough to crack the asphalt on West End Avenue, nobody would hear. But I let it out anyway, and my scream fills the world as Lowen and Al stroll away toward Riverside Drive.

As if they could actually see me hunched over the balcony edge, head shaking back and forth in despair. They could will their real bodies to stop, real eyes lift again to a real, vacant balcony.

Because they're real. I'm not. Not sick or dreaming, just not.

You died, Gayla baby. You're dead.

The last couple of days have been bad. Panic, running back and forth, scared to death or life, I don't know which, trying to find a way out without knowing where to go or why. I know I died; God, am I sure of that, but not how or how to get out.

There's no fucking door! Lowen and Al sail in and out unloading their junk, but when I try to find the door, it's Not, like me. I'm stuck here. I guess that's what frightens all of us, because you can't imagine Not. I never bought the MGM version of heaven. For me, being dead was simply not being, zero, zilch, something you can't imagine. The closest you can come is when a dentist knocks you out with Pentothal or how you felt two years before you were born.

No. I don't end, you say. Not me, not the center of the universe. And yet it's happened and I'm stuck with it, no way out, trying to hack the whole thing at once, skittering back and forth from the bedroom to the living room, through the kitchen with its new cream paint, crawling like cigarette smoke in the drapes, beating my nothing-fists against the wall sometimes, col-

lapsing out of habit and exhaustion into a chair or bed
I can't feel under me, wearing myself out with the only
sensations left, exhaustion and terror.

I'm not dead. I can't be dead, because if I am, why
am I still here. Let me out!

To go where, honey?

There's a kind of time again. Al's pinned up a Japanese
art calendar in the kitchen, very posh. This month it's
a samurai warrior drawing his sword; either that or
playing with himself. I can't see it that well, but the
date is much too clear. 1981. No wonder the rent's
gone up. Seven years since I—

No, that word is a downer. Exited is better. Just how
is still a big fat blank wrapped in confusion. All I remember is my name and a few silly details about the apartment. No past, no memory to splice the little snippets of
film that flash by too swiftly to catch. Not that it matters,
but where's my body? Was I buried or burned, scattered
or canned in memoriam in some mausoleum? Was
there a husband, a lover? What kind of life did I have?

When I think hard, there's the phantom pain of
someone gone, someone who hurt me. That memory
is vaguely connected with another of crying into the
phone, very drunk. I can't quite remember, just how
it made me feel. Got to organize and think. I've worn
myself out running scared, and still no answers. The
only clear thought is an odd little thing; there must
have been a lot of life in me to be kept so close to it.

Don't ask me about death. The rules are all new. I
might be the first of the breed. It's still me, but unable
to breathe or sleep or get hungry. Just energy that can
still run down from overuse, and when that happens,
Lowen and Al grow faint.

Everything we do takes energy. A step, a breath,
lifting an arm. Because it takes so little, we never

notice until we're sick with something like a raging case of flu. That's when we're reminded of the accounting department. Take a step and pant. Take another and stop to rest. Try to walk faster and feel your body straining to function on a fraction of its usual energy. That's all there is to me now, energy, and not much of that. I have to conserve, just float here by Al's painfully correct window drapes and think.

Does anyone know I'm here? I mean, Anyone?

A few more days. Al and Lowen are all moved in. Al's decor works very hard at being House Beautiful, an almost militant graciousness. Style with clenched teeth. And all her china matches; hell yes, it would. But let's face it: whatever's happening to me is because of them. When they're close, I get a hint of solid objects around me, as if I could reach out and touch tables and chairs or Lowen, but touching life costs me energy. The degree of nearness determines how much of my pitiful little charge is spent. Like being alive in a way. Living costs. I learned that somewhere.

Just got the hell scared out of me. Al has a mirror in the bedroom, a big antique affair. Sometimes when she brushes her hair, I stand behind her, aching out of habit to get that brush into my own mop. Tonight as I watched, I saw myself behind her.

I actually jumped with fright, but Al just went on pumping away with the brush while I peered over her head at Gayla Damon. Thirty-three—I remember that now—and beginning to look it. Thank God that won't bother me anymore. Yes, I was tall. Brownish black hair not too well cut. Thin face, strong chin, eyes large and expressive. They were my best feature, they broadcast every feeling I ever had. Lines starting around my mouth. Not a hard mouth but beginning to turn down around the edges, a little tired. Hardness would have helped, I guess. Some of Natalie Bond's brass balls.

Nattie Bond: a name, another memory.

No, it's gone, but there was a kind of pain with it. I stared at the mirror. Cruddy old black sweater and jeans: was I wearing them? You'd think I could check out in something better. Hey, brown eyes, how did they do you for the curtain call? Touch of pancake, I hope. You always looked dead without it. Oh shit . . .

A little crying helps, Even dry it's something.

I watch Lowen more and more, turning to him as a flower follows the sun, beginning to learn why I respond to him. Lowen's a listener and a watcher. He can be animated when he's feeling good or way down if he's not. Tired, depressed or angry, his brown eyes go almost black. Not terribly aggressive, but he does sense and respond to the life going on around him.

He likes the apartment and being quiet in it. He smokes, too, not much but enough to bother Al. They've worked out a compromise: anywhere but the bedroom. So, sometimes, I get a surprise visit in the living room when Lowen wakes up and wants a smoke. He sits for a few minutes in the dark, cigarette a bright arc from his mouth to the ashtray. I can't tell, but sometimes it seems he's listening to pure silence. He turns his head this way and that—toward me sometimes—and I feel weird; like he was sifting the molecules of silence, sensing a weight in them. Sometimes in the evening when he and Al are fixing dinner, Lowen will raise his head in that listening way.

It's a long-shot hope, but I wonder if he can feel *me*.

Why has he brought me back to time and space and caring? All these years there's been only blurred shadows and voices faint as a radio in the next room. Real light and sound and thought came only when he walked in. When Lowen's near, I perk up and glow; when he leaves, I fade to drift, disinterested, by the balcony door.

Lowen Sheppard: twenty-four at most, gentle, unconsciously graceful, awkward only when he tries to be more mature than he is. Don't work at it, lover, it'll come. Soft, straight brown hair that he forgets to cut until Al reminds him, which is often. She's great on detail, lives by it. Faces this apartment like a cage of lions to be tamed, a little scared of it all. Perhaps it's the best she ever had.

Lowen seems used to this much or maybe better. Mister nice guy, not my type at all, and yet I'm bound to him by a kind of fascination, bound without being able to touch his hair or speak to him. And it's no use wondering why, I'm learning that, too. Like that old Bergman flick where Death comes to collect Max Von Sydow. Max says, "Tell me what eternity is like." And Death says, "Who knows? I just work here."

Don't call us. We'll call you.

Well, dammit, *someone* is going to know I'm here. If I can think, I can do, and I'm not going to sit here forever just around the corner from life. Lowen and Al are my world now, the only script left to work with. I'm a part of their lives like a wart on the thigh, somewhere between God and a voyeur.

Wait, a memory just . . . no. Gone too quick again.

If I could touch Lowen somehow. Let him know.

Lowen and Al are settled in, place for everything and everything in its place, and Al daring it to get out of line. Lowen works full-time, and Al must do some part-time gig. She goes out in the early afternoon. The lights dim then. Just as well; I don't like what she's done with my apartment. Everything shrieks its price at you, but somehow Al's not comfortable with it. Maybe she never will be. That mouth is awful tight. She wanted to keep plastic covers over the sofa and chairs, the kind that go *crunkle* when you sit on them

and make you feel like you're living in a commercial.
But Lowen put his foot down on that.

"But, Al, they're to use, not just to look at."

"I know, but they're so nice and new."

"Look, I wear a rubber when we make love. I
don't need them on the furniture."

She actually blushed. "Really, Lowen."

Son of a—she makes him—? Do guys still wear those
things? Whatever happened to the sexual revolution?

It's indicative of their upbringing the way each
eats, too. Al sits erect at the table and does the full
choreography with her knife and fork, as if disapproving Momma was watching her all the time. Cut the
meat, lay the knife down, cross the fork to her right
hand, spear, chew, swallow, and the whole thing over
again. Left hand demurely in her lap.

Lowen leans slightly into his plate, what-the-hell
elbows on the table. More often than not, he uses the
fork in his left hand, placing things on it with his
knife. The way he handles them both, he's definitely
lived in England or Europe. Not born there, though.
The fall of his speech has a hint of softness and mid-
South nasal. Virginia or Maryland. Baltimore, maybe.

Perhaps it's just plain jealousy that puts me off Alice.
She's alive. She can reach out and touch, hold, kiss what
I can only look at. She's the strength in this marriage,
the one who'll make it work. Lowen's softer, easier, with
that careless assurance that comes from never having to
worry about the rent or good clothes. He's been given to;
Al's had to grab and fight. Now he's got a job and trying
to cut it on his own for the first time. That's scary, but Al
helps. She does a pretty fair job of supporting Lowen
without letting him notice it too much.

She has her problems, but Lowen comes first. She
gets home just before him, zips out to get fresh flowers
for the table. A quick shower and a spritz of perfume,
another swift agony at the mirror. And then Lowen is

home and sitting down to dinner, telling her about the
day. And Al listens, not so much to the words but the
easy, charming sound, the quality she loves in him, as
if she could learn it for herself. She's from New York,
probably the Bronx. I remember the accent somehow.
Petite and pretty, but she doesn't believe it no matter
how much attention Lowen gives her. Spends a lot of
time at the mirror when he's gone, not admiring but
wondering. What does she really look like? What type
is she, what kind of image does she, should she, project, and can she do it? Lipstick: this shade or that? So
she fiddles and narrows her eyes, scrutinizing the
goods, hopes for the advertised magic of Maybelline
and ends up pretty much the same: more attractive
than she thinks, not liking what she sees.

Except she doesn't see. She's carried it around all her
life, too busy, too nervous and insecure to know what
she's got. Stripped down for a bath, Al looks like she never
had a pimple or a pound of fat in her life, but I swear she'll
find something wrong, something not to like.

Don't slop that goo on your face, girl. You're great
already. God, I only wish I had your skin. The crap I had
to put on and take off every night, playing parts like—

Parts like . . .

My God, I remember!

I was an actress. That's what I remember in quick
flashes of hard light. The pictures whiz by like fast
cars, but they're slowing down: stage sets, snatches of
dialogue, dim faces in the front rows. Bill Wrenn giving me a piece of business to work out. Fragments of
me like a painting on shattered glass. I grope for the
pieces, fitting them together one by one.

Bill Wrenn: there's a warm feeling when I think of
him, a trusting. Where did I meet him? Yes, it's coming back.

Bill directed that first season at Lexington Rep.
Gentle and patient with a weariness that no longer

expected any goodies from life, he always reminded me of a harried sheepdog with too many sheep to hustle. Forty years old, two marriages and struck out both times, not about to fall hard again.

But he did for me. I made it easy for him. We were out of the same mold, Bill and I. He sensed my insecurity as a woman and found ways to make it work for me onstage, found parts in me I'd never dream of playing. With most men, my whole thing began in bed and usually ended there. Bill and I didn't hurry; there was a love first. We enjoyed and respected each other's work, and theater was a church for us. We'd rehash each performance, sometimes staying up all night to put an extra smidge of polish on business or timing, to get a better laugh, to make something good just a hair better. We started with a love of something beyond us that grew toward each other, so that bed, when it came, was natural and easy as it was gorgeous.

I made him love me, my one genuine conquest. We even talked about getting married—carefully skirting around a lot of ifs. I seem to remember him asking me one night in Lexington. I *think* he asked then; there's a thick haze of vodka and grass over that night. Did I say yes? Not likely; by that time the old habits were setting in.

It was too good with Bill. That's not funny. Perfection, happiness, these are frightening things. Very few of us can live with them. After a while, I began to resent Bill. I mean, who the hell was he to take up so much of my life? I began to pick at him, finding things not to like, irritating habits like the nervous way he cleared his throat or dug in his ear when he was thinking out some stage problem; the way he picked his feet in bed and usually left the bathroom a mess. Just bitchiness. I even overreacted when he gave me notes after a performance. All bullshit and panic; just looking for a way out. How dare you love me, Bill Wrenn? Who asked you? Where did I get that way, where did it begin?

When Nick Charreau came into the company, he was tailor-made for me.

He was alone onstage the first time I saw him, a new cast replacement going through his blocking with the stage manager. Everything his predecessor did, Nick adjusted to show himself in a better light. He wasn't a better actor, but so completely, insolently sure of himself that he could pull off anything and make it look good, even a bad choice. Totally self-centered: if there were critics in the house, Nick lit up like a sign, otherwise it was just another working night in the sticks.

Nick was a lot better looking than Bill and eighteen years younger. Even-featured with a sharp, cool, detached expression. Eyes that looked right through you. He could tell me things wrong with myself that would earn Bill Wrenn a reaming out, but I took it from Nick. He didn't get close or involved all the way down. Perhaps that's why I chose him, out of cowardice. He wouldn't ever ask me to be a person.

When he finished the blocking session, I came down to lean on the stage apron. "You play that far back, you'll upstage everyone else in the scene."

"It's my scene. I'm beautifully lit up there." Nick's smile was friendly with just the right soupçon of cockiness. A little above us all, just enough to tickle my own self-doubt and make me want to take him on. I can handle you, mister. You're not so tough.

But he was. There was always part of Nick I couldn't reach or satisfy. I started out challenged, piqued, to cut him down to size in bed and ended up happy if he'd just smile at me.

Looking over Al's shoulder in the mirror, I know it's not what we're born but what we're made into. The game is called Hurt me, I haven't suffered enough.

I needed a son of a bitch like Nick. You don't think I'd go around deserving someone like Bill, do you?

Call that weird, Alice? You're the same song, different verse. You have that wary, born-owing-money look yourself. You handle it better than I did—you knew a good man when you saw one—but you still feel like a loser.

The fights with Bill grew large, bitter and frequent. He knew what was happening and it hurt him. And one night we split.

"When will you grow up, Gayla?"

"Bill, don't make it harder than it has to be. Just wish me luck."

Dogged, tired, plopping fresh ice cubes into his drink. "I care about you. About you, Gayla. That makes it hard. Nick's twenty-two and about an inch deep. He'll split in six months and you'll be out in the cold. When will you learn, Gay? It's not a game, it's not a great big candy store. It's people."

"I'm sorry, Bill."

"Honey," he sighed, "you sure are."

I still hovered, somehow needing his blessing. "Please? Wish me luck?"

Bill raised his glass, not looking up. "Sure, Gay. With Nick you'll need it."

"What's that mean?"

"Nothing, forget it."

"No, you don't just say things like that."

"Sorry, I'm all out of graciousness."

"What did you mean I'll need it?"

Bill paused to take a swallow of his drink. "Come on, Gay. You're not blind."

"Other women? So what."

"Other anybody."

"Oh boy, you're—"

"Nick swings both ways."

"That's a lie!"

"He'd screw a light socket if it helped him to a part."

That was the nastiest thing Bill ever said about anyone. I felt angry and at the same time gratified that he made it easier to walk out mad. "Good-bye, Bill."

And then he looked up at me, showing what was hidden before. Bill Wrenn was crying. Crying for me, the only person in this fucking world who ever did. All the pain, anger, loss, welling up in those sad sheep-dog eyes. I could have put my arms around him and stayed . . . no, wait, the picture's changing. I'm here in the apartment. *Get him out of here, Nick*—

No, it goes too fast or I will it to go. I can't, won't remember that yet because it hurts too much, and like a child I reach, cry out for the one thing I could always trust.

Bill-l-l—

Not a scream, just the memory of sound.

Lowen looks up from his book, puzzled. "Al? You call me?"

No answer. It's late, she's asleep.

Once more Lowen seems to listen, feeling the air and the silence, separating its texture with his senses. Searching. Then he goes back to his book, but doesn't really try to read.

He heard me. He heard *me*. I can reach him.

Sooner or later he'll know I'm here. Bust my hump or break my heart, I'll do it. Somehow. I've got to live, baby. Even dead it's all I know how to do.

I've hit a new low, watched Lowen and Al make love. At first I avoided it, but gradually the prospect drew me as hunger draws you to a kitchen; hunger no longer a poignant memory but sharp need that grows with my strength.

I've never watched lovemaking before. Porn, yes, but that's for laughs, a nowhere fantasy. One of the character men in Lexington had a library of films we used to dig sometimes after a show, hooting at their ineptitude. They could make you laugh or even horny now and then, but none of them ever dealt with reality. Porn removes you from the act, puts it at a safe distance.

Real sex is awkward, banal, and somehow very touching to watch. It's all the things we are and want: involvement, commitment, warmth, passion, clumsiness, generosity or selfishness, giving and receiving or holding back, all stained with the colors of openness or fear, lovely—and very vulnerable. All that, and yet the words are inadequate; you can't get any of that from watching. Like the man said, you had to be there.

Rogers and Astaire these two are not. It's all pretty straight missionary and more of an express than a local. Lowen does certain things and Al tries a few herself, sort of at arm's length and without much freedom. I don't think Lowen's had much experience, and Al, though she needs sex, probably learned somewhere that she oughtn't like it all that much. She's the new generation; she's heard it's her right and prerogative, but the no-no was bred in early, so she compromises by not enjoying it, by making it uphill for both of them. She inhibits Lowen without meaning to. He has to wait so long for her to relax and then work so hard to get her going. And of course at the best moment, like an insurance commercial in the middle of a cavalry charge, he has to stop and put on that stupid rubber.

I wonder if Al's Catholic, she never heard of a diaphragm? Or maybe it's money. That's not so far out. Maybe she's uptight about getting pregnant because she remembers how it was to grow up poor. Maybe it's a lot of things adding up to tense ambivalence, wondering why the bells don't ring and the earth shake like she read in *Cosmopolitan*. I seem to remember that trip.

She doesn't give herself much time to relish it afterward, either. Kiss-kiss-bang-bang, then zip with the

Kleenex and pit-pat into the shower as if someone might catch them. Maybe that's the way it was before they married, a habit that set before either of them realized it.

But I've touched Lowen. God, yes, for one galvanized split second I felt his body against me. I paid for it, but it had to be.

It was after they made love and Al did her sprint from bed through the shower and into her nightie-cocoon. Lowen went into the bathroom then. I heard the shower running and drifted in after him.

His body looked marvelous; smooth light olive against Al's blue flower-patterned bath curtains, the soap lather standing out sharp white against the last of his summer tan. Not too muscular; supple like Nick. It'll be a while before he has to worry about weight.

Lowen soaped and rinsed, and I enjoyed the shape of his chest and shoulders when he raised his arms over his head.

You're beautiful, Mr. Sheppard.

I had to do it then. I moved in and kissed him, *felt* his chest, stomach, the bulge of his cock against the memory of my pelvis. Only a second, a moment when I had to hold him.

The sensation that shivered through me was like a sudden electric shock. I pulled back, frightened and hurt, hovering in the shower curtain. Lowen jerked, grabbing for the towel rack, taut, scared as myself. Then, slowly, the fear faded and I saw that listening, probing attitude in the lift of his head before the instinctive fear returned. Lowen snapped the water off, stumbled out of the tub, and just sat down on the john, dripping and shaking. He sat there for minutes, watching the water drying on his skin, runneling down the sides of the tub. Once he put a hand to his lips. They moved, forming a word I couldn't hear.

You felt me, damn you. You know I'm here. If I could just talk to you.

But the exhaustion and pain ebbed me. We slumped at opposite ends of the small bathroom, Lowen staring through me, not hearing the sob, the agony of the pictures that flashed into life. Touching him, I remember. After the shock of life comes the memory, filling me out by one more jagged fragment, measuring me in pain.

Al, Al, frowning at your mirror, wondering what magic you lack—I should have your problem. The guys probably lined up around the block when you were in school. Not for Gayla Damon; hell, that wasn't even my real name, not for a long, hard time. First there was big, fat Gail Danowski from the Bronx, like you, and at seventeen what you men prayed for and likely never got, I couldn't give away.

Why do I have to remember that? Please, I tried so hard to get away from it. My father who worked for the city as a sandhog, my dumpy mother with her permanent look of washed-out disgust, both of them fresh off the boat in 1938. My sister Sasha, who got married at seventeen to get away from them. Big change: all Zosh did after that was have kids for that beer-drinking slob husband of hers. Jesus, Charlie disgusted me. Sunday afternoons he'd come over and watch football with my father, swill beer and stuff potato chips. Every once in a while he'd let out a huge belch, then sigh and pat his pot gut like he was so goddam pleased with himself. For years, while Zosh's teeth went and her skin faded to chalk delivering five kids.

And me growing up in the middle of it, waiting for the big event of the day in the South Bronx, the Good Humor truck out on the street.

"Mommy, Mommy, the goojoomer's here! C'n I have a dime for the goojoomer?"

"Y'fadda din leave me no money."

Urgent jingling from the Good Humor, ready to leave and take excitement with it. "Mommy!"

"Geddouda here. I ain't got no dime, now shaddup."

I used to think about that a lot: a lousy dime. So little and so much to a kid. Go to hell, Momma. Not for the dime, but for a whole beauty you never had and never missed. You weren't going to keep me from it.

It wasn't much better in high school. I was embarrassed to undress for gym because of the holes in my underwear. And the stains sometimes because I had to use Momma's Kotex and she didn't care if she ran out. I could have used Tampax; virgin or not, I was a big, healthy ox like her and Zosh. I could have conceived an army. When Momma found the Tampax I bought, she slapped me halfway across the room.

"What's this, hah? *Hah?* I ain't got enough trouble, you started already? You sneakin around, you little bitch?"

No such luck, Momma. They didn't want me. The closest I got to boys was talking about them. Sitting in a coffee shop over the debris of my cheap, starchy lunch, the table a garbage dump of bread crusts, spilled sugar, and straw wrappers, shredding food bits and paper ends like our envious gossip dissected the girls we knew and the boys we wanted to know.

I never had any sense about men or myself. That happens when you're five foot seven in high school and still growing. A sequoia in a daisy bed, lumpy and lumbering, addicted to food, my refuge when I lost the courage for school dances. I fled home to the icebox and stayed there, eating myself out of my clothes, smearing my acne with Vis-o-Hex, or huddled for hours in a movie, seeing it twice over to pretend I was Hepburn or Bacall, slim, brittle and clever. Or Judith Anderson tearing hell out of *Medea*. I read the play and practiced the lines at my mirror with stiff approximations of her gestures.

But it was *A Streetcar Named Desire* that changed my life. I hardly spoke for days after seeing it. The play stabbed me deep and sparked something that was going to be. I bought more plays and devoured them. Fewer trips to the movies now and more downtown to Broadway and the Village. Live theater, not unreeling on a spool, but happening the moment I saw it.

I was still a lump, still 150 pounds of un-lusted-after virgin bohunk, and nobody was going to star Gail Danowski in anything but lunch. I walked alone with my dreams while the hungers grew.

You can go a little mad with loneliness, past caring. Virginity? I couldn't give it away, Momma; so I threw it away. No big Zanuck production, just a boy and a party I can't picture too clearly. We were drinking and wrestling, and I thought, all right, why not? Just once I'm gonna grab a little happiness even if it's just getting laid, what am I saving it for? But I had to get drunk before he fumbled at me. If there was pain or pleasure, I barely felt them, only knew that at last I tasted life where it sprang from the fountain. A meager cup, the cut version, the boy pulling at his clothes afterward, distant, disgusted.

"Shit, whyn't you tell me, Gail?"

Tell you what, lover? That I was a virgin, that by accident you were the first? Is that a guilt trip? Whatever I lost, don't mourn it. Cry for the other things we lose in parked cars and motel beds because we're too drunk or there's too much guilt or fear for beauty. It was the beauty I missed. Be first anytime, score up a hundred stiff, clumsy girls, say the silly words, break a hundred promises, brag about it afterward. But leave something of yourself, something of beauty. Only that and you part with a blessing.

He didn't.

The next morning, hung over and miserable, I looked at that frazzled thing in the mirror, had clean through and down to rock bottom, and knew from here on out I'd have to be me or just another Zosh. That day I started to build Gayla Damon.

I graduated an inch taller and thirty pounds lighter, did hard one-week stock as an apprentice. Seventeen hours a day of walk-ons, painting scenery, fencing, and dance classes. Diction: practicing for hours with a cork between my teeth—

"Baby, the word is dance. DAAnce, hear the A? Not de-e-ance. Open your mouth and *use* it when you speak."

—Letting my hair grow and moving down to Manhattan, always running away from that lump in the mirror. I never outran her. She was always there, worrying out of my eyes at a thousand auditions, patting my stomach and thighs, searching a hundred dressing room mirrors, plastering pancake on imagined blemishes, grabbing any man's hand because it was there. The years just went, hurrying by like strangers on a street, trailing bits of memory like broken china from a dusty box: buses, planes, snatches of rehearsal, stock, repertory, old reviews.

Miss Damon's talent is raw but unmistakable. When she's right, she *is* theater, vivid, filled with primordial energy that can burn or chill. If she can learn to control . . . she was superbly cast as . . .

—a self-driven horse record-time sprinting from nowhere to noplace. Life? I lived it from eight to eleven o'clock every night and two matinees a week. For three hours each night, I loved, hated, sang, sorrowed enough for three lifetimes. Good houses, bad houses, they all got the best of me because my work had a love behind it. The rest was only fill and who cared? Season after season of repertory, a dozen cities, a dozen summer towns barely glimpsed from opening night to closing, a blur of men and a lot of beds, flush or broke, it didn't matter. Zosh caught a show once when I was playing in

Westchester. Poor Zosh: pasty and fat as Momma by
then, busting out of her dresses and her teeth shot. She
came hesitantly into my dressing room, wondering if
someone might throw her out. The first stage play she
ever saw. She didn't know really what to make of it.

"Oh, it was great and all. You look good, Gail. God,
you really got some figure now, what size you wear? I
never knew about plays. You know me'n school, I
always got my girlfriend to write my reports."

She barely sipped the scotch I poured her. "Charlie
never buys nothin but beer." I wanted to take her out
for a good dinner, but no, she had a sitter at home and
it was expensive, and Charlie would yell if she came
home too late when he was out bowling.

"Let the dumb fuck yell. You're entitled once in a
while."

"Hey, you really gettin a mouth on you, Gail."

"Speaking of that, doesn't Charlie ever look at
yours? Doesn't he know you need a dentist?"

"Well, you know how it is. The kids take it out of
you."

I gave Zosh a hundred dollars to get her teeth
fixed. She wrote that she spent it on the house and
kids. *There was the gas bill and Christmas. You cant com-
plain theres nobody on the other end of the phone. Ha-ha.
My friends all want to know when your on TV.*

Are you still around, Zosh? Not that it matters.
They buried you years ago. No one was going to do
that to me.

And then suddenly I was thirty, that big, scary number. Working harder, running harder without knowing
where, doing the where-did-it-all-go bit now and then
(while the lights caught her best, most expressive angle).
Where are you now, Bill? You must be pushing fifty. Still
a great lay, I hope. Did you find someone like me or just
the opposite? I wouldn't blame you.

And how about you, Nick?

He'll split in six months. You'll be out in the cold.

When Bill said that, I remember thinking, hell, he's right. I'm thirty-two and after that comes thirty-three. Fourteen years, seven dollars in the bank, and where the hell am I?

But I was hung up on Nick's eyes and Nick's body and trying to please him. Perhaps there were other, unspoken things that have nothing to do with loving or sex. You get used very early to not liking yourself. You know you're a fraud, someday they'll all know. The Lump hiding inside your dieted figure and with-it clothes knows you haven't changed, no matter what. The Lump doesn't want to like you. How can she tolerate anyone who does? No, she'll sniff out someone who'll keep her in her lowly place.

Crimes and insanities. Hurting Bill was a very countable sin, but I knew what I needed. So it was Nick, not Bill, who moved in here with me.

And where are you this dark night, Nick? Did you make the big time? I hope so. You're almost thirty now. That's getting on for what you had to sell. Your kind of act has a short run.

My mind wanders like that when Lowen's not around.

Energy builds again, the lights fade up. I drift out onto the balcony, feeling that weight of depression it always brings. My sense of color is dimmed because the kids are asleep. Seventy-seventh Street is a still shot in black and white. Not a soul, not even a late cab whispering up Riverside Drive.

Hey, look! There's a meteor, a falling star. Make a wish: be happy, Bill Wrenn.

And listen! A clock tower. Even with Lowen asleep, I can hear it. Two-three-four o'clock. Definitely, I'm getting stronger. More and more I can feel and some-

times see my legs when I walk, less like floating in a
current. I move back through the apartment to hover
over Lowen as he sleeps. Wanting. Wondering.

After all this time, why should it be Lowen who
wakes me? He felt me in that shower, and we both
wonder how, why? Nothing's clear but that I can touch
life again with him. If that's wrong, I didn't write the
script. Name any form of life you want. A cold germ is
just a bug trying to make a living in the only way it
knows, in a place it doesn't understand, and it only
takes a little out of the place trying. That's me, that's all
of us. I'll take what I need to live. If there's air to
breathe, don't tell me I can't. That's academic.

Al sleeps tiny and still beside Lowen, hardly a
bump under the covers. It must be wonderful to sleep
like that. I could never stay out more than two hours
at a time. No, wait: here she comes up out of it with a
sigh and turnover that barely whispers the covers. She
slides out of bed and pit-pats to the bathroom. Bladder
the size of an acorn, up three times a night like I was.

When the john flushes, Lowen stirs and mumbles,
flops over and sinks again. The bathroom door creaks,
Al slips back in beside him. She doesn't settle down yet,
but rests on one elbow, a momentary vigil over Lowen,
a secret protecting. I'll bet he doesn't know she watches
him like that. Then she slides under the covers very
close, one arm over him, fingers spread lightly on his
skin where his pajama top is unbuttoned.

To lie beside Lowen like that, to touch him simply
by willing it. If that were my hand resting on his skin.
What wouldn't I give for that?

The idea is sudden and frightening. Why not?

If I could get inside Al, stretch out my arm through
hers, wear it like a glove; just for a moment move one
real finger over Lowen's skin. It couldn't hurt her, and
I need it so.

I wait for Al to fall asleep, scared of the whole

notion. It could hurt. It hurt to touch Lowen before.
Maybe it's against some natural law. They're flesh, I'm
a memory. Lots of maybes but I have to try. Slow and
scared, I drift down over Al and will what shape there
is to me into the attitude of her body. There's no shock
when I touch her, but a definite sensation like dipping
into swift-running water. So weird, I pull away and
have to build up my nerve to try again, settling like a
sinking ship as the current of Al's healthy young life
surges and tingles around me, and her chest rises and
falls like a warm blanket over cozy sleep. My breasts
nestle into hers, my arm stretching slowly to fill out
the slim contour of her shoulder, elbow, wrist. It's
hard and slow, like half-frozen syrup oozing through
a hose. My fingers struggle one by one into hers.

So tired. Got to rest.

But I feel life, I *feel* it, humming and bubbling all
around me. Jesus, I must have sounded like a steel mill
inside, the way I drove myself. The power, such a wonder. Why did I waste so much time feeling miserable?

The electric clock glows at 5:03. More minutes
pass while each finger tests itself in Al's, and then I try
to move one on Lowen's skin.

The shock curdles me. I cringe away from it, shriv-
eling back up Al's arm, all of me a shaky little ball in
her middle. Just as in the shower, I felt skin against
skin, even the tiny moisture of pores, but it drains me
as if I've run five miles.

Rest and try again. Slow, so slow, so hard, but my
fingers creep forward into Al's again. Same thing: the
instant I let myself feel with Al's flesh, there's a bright
shock and energy drains. If that's not enough, those
delicate fingers weigh ten pounds each. I push, poop
out, rest, try again, the hardest battle of my life, let
alone death, and all in dogged silence broken only by
their breathing and the muted whir of the clock.

6:32. The dark bedroom grays up to morning. I can

see Lowen's face clearly now: very young, crumpled with sleep. He can't hear my soundless, exhausted panting like the heartbeat of a hummingbird.

6:48. Twelve minutes before the clock beeps the beginning of their day, one finger, one slender thread binding me to Lowen . . . moves. Again. I go dizzy with the sensation but hang on, pouring the last of my strength into one huge effort. The small hand flexes all five fingers like a crab, sliding over the sparse hair on Lowen's chest. A flash-frame of Bill, of Nick, and a thrill of victory.

Hi, baby. I made it.

Then Al stirs, moves *don't, please, wait!* and flips over on her other side, unconcerned as a pancake. I let go, used up, drifting out to nowhere again, barely conscious of space or objects, too burned out even to feel frustrated after all that work.

But I did it. I know the way now. I'll be back.

Night after night I kept at it, fitting to Al's body, learning how to move her fingers without burning myself out. Stronger and surer, until I could move the whole hand and then the arm, and even if Lowen pressed the hand to his mouth or nestled his cheek against it, I could hold on.

And then I blew it, the story of my life. Klutz-woman strikes again. I tried to get in when they were making love.

I said before they're not too dexterous in bed. Al gets uptight from the start, and I can see her lying there, eyes tight shut over Lowen's shoulder, hoping he'll come soon and get it over with. Not always; sometimes she wants it as much as him, but the old hang-ups are always there. She holds back, so he holds back. It's usually one-sided and finished soon.

But that evening everything seemed perfect. They

had a light supper, several drinks rather than the usual one, and Lowen didn't spare the vodka. They just naturally segued to the bedroom, not rushed or nervous, undressing each other slowly, enjoyably, melting into each other's arms. Al brought in a candle from the supper table. Nice touch: Nick and I used to do that. They lie there caressing each other, murmuring drowsily. Lowen looks gorgeous in the soft glow, Al like a little Dresden doll. And me—poor, pathetic afterthought—watching it all and yearning.

Jesus, Al, act like you're alive. That's a man. Take hold of him.

Damn, it was too much. The hell with consequences. I draped myself over Al with the ease of practice, stretched my arms and legs along hers. Foolhardy, yes, but at last *my* arms went around Lowen, smoothing, then clawing down his back.

Love me, baby. Love all of me.

My mouth opened hungrily under his, licking his lips and then nipping at them. I writhed Al's slim body under his, pushed her hands to explore him from shoulders to thighs. I never had much trouble in bed. If the guy had anything going and didn't run through it like a fire drill, I could come half a dozen times, little ones and big ones, before he got there.

With Lowen it was like all the best orgasms I ever had. The moment before you start to go, you want to hold back, prolong it, but you can't. I was dependent on Al's chemistry now. Her body was strangely stiff as I hauled her over on top of Lowen. Something new for her. She went taut, resisting it.

"Lowen, wait."

He can't wait, though I'm the only one who sees the irony and the lie. Lowen is coming, I certainly want to, but Al is out of it. I want to *scream* at her, though I should have guessed it long before this. She always times her cries with his, as if they came together.

But it's a lie. She's faking it. She's learned that much.

My God, you're alive, the greatest gift anyone ever got. Does a past tense like me have to show you how?

With a strength like life itself, I churned her up and down on Lowen, hard, burning myself out to tear Al's careful controls from her emotions. She moaned, fighting me, afraid.

"Lowen, stop. Please stop."

You don't fake tonight, kid.

"Stop!"

No way. Go . . . *go!*

Lowen gripped her spasmodically, and I felt his hips tremble under mine/hers. He couldn't hold back any longer. With the last ounce of my will, I bent Al's body down over his, mouth to mouth.

"Now, Lowen. Now!"

Not Al's voice but mine, the first time I've heard it in seven years. Deeper, throatier than Al's. In the middle of coming, an alien bewilderment flooded Lowen's expression. Al stiffened like she was shot. With a cry of bleak terror, she tore herself loose and leaped clear off the bed, clawing for the lamp switch, big-eyed and terrified in the hard light.

"Oh God. Oh Jesus, what's happening?"

Confused, a little out of it himself now, Lowen sat up to stare back at her. "Al, what's the matter?"

She shuddered. "It's not me."

"What?"

"It's not *me.*" She snatched up her bathrobe like the last haven in the world. Lowen reached for her instinctively, comforting.

"It's all right, honey, it's—"

"No. It's like something hot inside me."

He went on soothing her, but he knew. I could see that in his eyes as he pulled Al down beside him. He knew: the last thing I saw, because the lights were going down for me, their last spill playing over memory fragments before fading. A confused montage: Nick putting on his jacket, me fumbling for the phone, then pulling at the balcony door, and the darkness and the silence then were like dying again.

I've had some hangovers in my time, mornings of agony after a messy, screaming drunk. Coming back to queasy consciousness while the night's party repeats in your mind like a stupid film loop, and you wonder, in a foggy way, if you really spilled that drink on somebody, and—oh no—you couldn't have said *that* to him, and if you're going to be sick right then or later.

Then the smog clears and you remember. Yeah. You spilled it and did it and you sure as hell said it, and the five best Bloody Marys in the world won't help.

I blew it good this time, a real production number. Now they both know I'm here.

December 23. I know the date because Al's carefully crossed the days off her calendar where she never bothered before. I've been turned off for days. Almost Christmas, but you'd never know it around here. No holly, no tree, just a few cards opened and dropped on the little teakwood desk where they keep their bills. When Lowen brushes one aside, I can see a thin line of dust. Al hasn't been cleaning.

The kitchen is cluttered. The morning's dishes are still in the sink. Three cardboard boxes stand on the floor, each half full of wrapped dishes and utensils.

So that's it. They're moving. A moment of panic: where do I go from here, then? All right, it was my fault, but . . . don't go, Lowen. I'm not wild about this script myself, but don't ask me to turn out the lights and die again. Because I won't.

There's a miasma of oppression and apprehension all through the apartment. Al's mouth is tighter, her eyes frightened. Lowen comes out into the living room, reluctant and dutiful. Furtively he tests the air as if to feel me in it. He sits down in his usual chair. 3:13 by the miniature grandfather clock on the bookcase. The lights and sound come up slowly with Lowen's nearness. He's home early this afternoon.

Al brings out the Waterford sherry set and puts it on the coffee table. She sits down, waiting with Lowen. The whole scene reminds me of actors taking places before the curtain rises, Al poised tensely on the sofa, revolving her sherry glass in white fingers, Lowen distant, into his own thoughts. The sound is still lousy.

" . . . feel silly," Lowen ventures. " . . . all this way . . . time off from . . . just to . . . "

"No! . . . live here like this, not with . . . " Al is really shook; takes a cigarette from Lowen's pack on the coffee table and smokes it in quick, inexpert puffs. "You say you can feel her?"

Lowen nods, unhappy. He doesn't like any of this. "I loved this place from the first day."

"Lowen, answer me. Please."

"Yes."

"Where?"

"Somewhere close. Always close to me."

Al stubs out the cigarette. "And we sure know it's *she*, don't we?"

"Al—"

"Oh hell! I loved this place, too, but this is crazy. I'm *scared*, Lowen. How long have you known?"

"Almost from the start."

"And you never told me."

"Why?" Lowen looks up at her. "I'm not a medium; nothing like this ever happened before. It was weird at first, but then I began to feel that she was just *here*—"

"What!"

"—and part of things like the walls. I didn't even know it was a woman at first."

"Until that time in the shower," Al finishes for him. "Bitch."

Thanks a lot, kid. At least I know what to do with him.

"Look, Al, I can't tell you how I know, but I don't think she means any harm."

Al gulps down her sherry and fills the glass. "The—hell—she—doesn't. I'm not into church anymore. Even if I were, I wouldn't go running for the holy water every time a floor creaked, but don't tell me she doesn't mean anything, Lowen. You know what I'm talking about." Her hands dry-wash each other jerkily. "I mean that night, the way we made love. I—always wanted to make love to you like that. That . . . free."

The best you ever had, love.

Al gets up and paces, nervous. "All right, I've got these goddamned problems. You get taught certain things are wrong. If it's not for babies, it's wrong. It's wrong to use contraceptives, but we can't afford a baby, and—I don't know, Lowen. The world is crazy. But that night, it wasn't me. Not even my voice."

"No, it wasn't."

"All right." Her voice quavers a little as she sits back down. "I loved this place, too. But even if I'd been screwing since I was six, I couldn't live with that."

Lowen must be way down, depressed, because my energy is wavering with his, and sound fades in and out. There's a muffled knock at the door. Lowen opens it to a bald little man like a wizened guru in a heavy, fur-collared overcoat.

Wait, I know this guy. It's that little weasel Hirajian, from Riverside Realty. He rented me this place. Hirajian settles himself in a chair, briefcase on his knee, declining the sherry Al offers. He doesn't look too happy about being here, but the self-satisfied little bastard doesn't miss Al's legs, which make mine look bush-league in retrospect.

I can't catch everything, but Hirajian's puzzled by something Al's saying. No problem about the lease, he allows, apartments rent in two days now, but she's apparently thrown him a curve.

Al now: " . . . not exactly our wish, but . . . "

"Unusual request . . . never anything . . . "

Now Al is flat and clear: "Did you find out?"

Hirajian opens his briefcase and brings out a sheet of paper while I strain at his through-the-wall mumble.

"Don't know why . . . however, the tenants . . . before you . . . " He runs through a string of names until I make the connection. The tenants who came after me, all those damned extras who wandered through my dreams before Lowen.

Lowen stops him suddenly. He's not as depressed as Al; there's an eagerness in the question. "Did anyone die here?"

"Die?"

"It's very important." Al says.

Hirajian looks like an undertaker's assistant now, all professional solemnity and reluctance. "As a matter of fact, yes. I was getting to that. In 1974, a Miss Danowski."

Lowen's head snaps up. "First name?"

"Gail."

"Anyone named Gayla? Someone cut the name Gayla in the cement on the balcony."

"That was the Danowski woman. Gayla Damon was her stage name. She was an actress. I remember because she put that name on the lease and had to do it again with her legal signature."

"Gayla."

"You knew her, Mr. Sheppard?"

"Gayla Damon. I should, it's awfully familiar, but—"

"Single?" Al asks. "What sort of person was she?"

Hirajian cracks his prim little smile like a housewife leaning over a back fence to gossip. "Yes and no, you know show people. Her boyfriend moved in with her. I know it's the fashion nowadays, but *we*"—evidently Riverside and God—"don't approve of it."

There's enough energy to laugh, and I wish you could hear me, you little second-string satyr. You made a pass when you showed me this place. I remember: I was wearing that new tan suit from Bergdorf's, and I couldn't split fast enough. But it was the best place yet for the money, so I took it.

Dammit, how did I die? What happened? Don't fade out, weasel. Project, let me hear you.

Al sets down her sherry glass. "We just can't stay here. It's impossible."

Don't go, Lowen. You're all I have, all there is. I won't touch Al, I promise never again. But don't go.

Of course there were promises, Nick. There's always a promise. No one has to spell it out.

I said that once. I'm starting to remember.

While Hirajian patters on, Lowen's lost in some thought. There's something in his eyes I've never seen before. A concern, a caring.

"You mean he didn't come back even when he heard Gayla was dead?"

I love the way he says my name. Like a song, new strength.

"No end of legal trouble," Hirajian clucks. "We couldn't locate him or any family at first. A Mr. . . . yes, a Mr. Wrenn came and made all the arrangements. An old boyfriend, I suppose."

You did that for me, Bill? You came back and helped me out. Boy, what I had and threw away. Sand through my fingers.

"Gayla. Gayla Damon." I grow stronger as Lowen repeats my name, stronger yet as he rises and takes a step toward the balcony door. I could touch him, but I don't dare now. "Yes. Just the name I forgot. It's hard to believe, but it's the only thing I can believe."

Such a queer, tender look. Al reads it, too. "What, Lowen?"

He strides quickly away to the bedroom, and the lights dim a little. Then he's back with a folded paper, so deep in some thought that Al just stares at him and Hirajian is completely lost.

"The things we learn about life," Lowen says. "An English professor of mine said once that life is too random for art; that's why art is structured. Mr. Hirajian, you said no one else ever complained of disturbances in this apartment. I'm not a medium, can't even predict the weather. But I'm beginning to understand a little of this."

Will you tell me, for Christ's sake?

He hands the paper to Al. It looks like an old theater program. "You see, Mr. Hirajian, she's still here."

He has to say it again, delicately as possible. Hirajian pooh-poohs the whole notion. "Oh really, now, you can't be sure of something like that."

"We know," Al says in a hard voice. "We haven't told you everything. She, it, something's here, and it's destructive."

"No, I don't think so." Lowen nods to the program. I can't see it too well. "Eagle Lake Playhouse, 1974. I saw her work."

You couldn't have. You were only—

"She played Gwendolyn in *Becket*. That's her autograph by her name."

Where the hell is Eagle Lake? Wait a minute. Wait—a—minute. I'm remembering.

"My father was taking me back to school. I spent my whole life in boarding schools all the way through college. Dad thought for our last night together, he'd take me to an uplifting play and save himself making conversation. My parents were very efficient that way.

"Gayla only had one scene, but she was so open,

so completely translucent that I couldn't take my eyes off her."

I did play Eagle Lake, and there's a faint memory of some double-breasted country-club type coming back for an autograph for his kid.

"I still remember, she had a line that went: 'My lord cares for nothing in this world, does he?' She turned to Becket then, and you could see a *line* in that turn, a power that reached the other actor and came out to the audience. The other actors were good, but Gayla lit up the stage with something—unbearably human."

Damn right. I was gangbusters in that role. And you saw me? I could almost believe in God now, though He hasn't called lately.

"I was sixteen, and I thought I was the only one in the world who could be so lonely. She showed me we're all alike in that. All our feelings touch. Next day I hitch-hiked all the way back to the theater from school . . . " Lowen trails off, looking at Al and the apartment. "And this was her place. She wasn't very old. How did she die?"

"Depressing," Hirajian admits. "Very ugly and depressing, but then suicide always is."

What!

"But as regards your moving out just because—"

The hell I did, no fucking *way*, mister. No. No. NO! I won't listen to any more. Don't believe him, Lowen.

Lowen's on his feet, head tilted in that listening attitude. Al puts down her glass, pale and tense. "What is it?"

"She's here now. She's angry."

"How do you know?"

"Don't ask me how, dammit. I know. She's here."

No, Lowen. On the worst, weakest day of my life, I couldn't do that. Listen. Hear me. Please.

Then Al's up, frightened and desperate. "Go away, whoever you are. For the love of God, go away."

I barely hear her, flinging myself away from them

out onto the balcony, silent mouth screaming at the frustration and stupid injustice of it. A lie, a lie, and Lowen is leaving, sending me back to nothing and darkness. But the strength is growing, born of rage and terror. Lowen. Lowen. Lowen. Hear me. I didn't. *Hear me.*

"Lowen, don't!"

I hear Al's voice, then the sudden, sharp sound of the balcony door wrenching open. And as I turn to Lowen, the whole uncut film starts to roll. And, oh Jesus, I remember.

Eagle Lake. That's where it ended, Lowen. Not here, no matter what they tell you. That's where all the years, parts, buses, beds, the whole game came to an end. When I found that none of it worked anymore. Maybe I was growing up a little at last, looking for the *me* in all of it.

Funny, I wasn't even going to audition for stock that summer. Bill called me to do a couple of roles at Eagle Lake, and Nick urged me to go. It was a good season, closing with *A Streetcar Named Desire*. The owner, Ermise Stour, jobbed in Natalie Bond for Blanche Du Bois, and I was to be her understudy. Nattie's name wasn't smash movie box office anymore, but still big enough for stock and star-package houses. She'd be Erm's insurance to make up whatever they lost on the rest of the season.

Erm, you tough old bag. You were going to sell that broken-down theater after every season. I'll bet you're still there, chain-smoking over a bottle of Chivas and babying that ratty poodle.

Ermise lived in a rambling ex-hotel with a huge fireplace in the lounge. We had all our opening-night parties there with a big blaze going because Eagle Lake never warmed up or dried out even in August.

At the opening party for *Becket*, all of us were too

keyed up to get drunk, running on adrenaline from the show, slopping drinks and stuffing sandwiches, fending off the local reviewers, horny boy scouts with a course in journalism.

Dinner? No thanks. I've got a horrible week coming up, and it's all I can do to shower and fall into bed. Bill, let's get *out* of here. Thanks, you're a jewel, I needed a refill. Gimme your sweater. Jesus, doesn't it ever get warm in this place? You could age beef in our dressing room.

Nick was down for a few days the week before. Bill rather pointedly made himself scarce. He was still in love with me. That must have hurt, working with me day after day, keeping it inside, and I didn't help matters by dragging Nick everywhere like a prize bull: hey, look what I got! Smart girl, Gayla. With a year's study, you could be an idiot.

But Nick was gone, and we'd managed to get *Becket* open despite failing energy, colds, frayed nerves, and lousy weather. It was good just to stand with Bill against the porch railing, watching moths bat themselves silly against the overhead light. Bill was always guarded when we were alone now. I kept it light and friendly, asked about his preparations for *Streetcar.* He sighed with an Old Testament flavor of doom.

"Don't ask. Erm had to cut the set budget, first read-through is tomorrow morning, and Nattie's plane won't get in until one. I'm going to be up all night and I'll still only be about five pages ahead of you people on blocking."

"Why's she late?"

"Who the hell knows? Business with her agent or something. You'll have to read in for her."

Good. One more precious rehearsal on my Blanche, one more time to read those beautiful words and perhaps find one more color in them before Natalie Bond froze it all in star glitter. That was all I had to look forward to now. The fatigue, the wet summer, lousy houses, all of it accumulated to a desolation I couldn't shrug off. I had a small part in *Streetcar*, but understudying Natalie Bond meant watching her do my role, never to touch the magic myself. Maybe her plane could crash—just a little—but even then, what? Somehow even the thought of Nick depressed me. Back in New York he'd get in to see the right agents where I couldn't, landing commercials, lining up this, grabbing that, always smarter at business than me.

That night before the party I sat on my bed, staring glumly at the yellow-green wallpaper and my battered Samsonite luggage, and thought, *I'm tired of you. Something's gone. There's gotta be more than this.* And I curled up in my old gray bathrobe, wallowing in self-pity. Nick, you want to get married? Bring me the towel and wash my back? Baby me a little when I feel rotten, like now? There's a big empty place in me wants to be pregnant with more than a part. Tired, negative, I knew Nick would never marry me. I was kidding myself.

So it was good to have Bill there on the porch for a minute. I leaned against him and he put an arm around me. We should have gone to bed and let it be beautiful one more time. It would have been the last.

"Tired, Gay?"

"I want to go home."

Except I never in my whole life found where it was.

Natalie Bond came and conquered. She knew her lines pretty well going in and crammed the rest with me in her room or the restaurant down our street. No one recognized her at first with her hair done just the right shade of fading dishwater blond for Blanche, most of her thin face hidden behind a huge pair of prescription sunglasses. She was nearsighted to blindness; some of her intensity on film must have come from trying to feel out the blocking by braille. But a pro she was. She soaked up Bill's direction, drove herself and us, and I saw the ruthless energy that made Nattie a star.

I saw other things, too. Nattie hadn't been on a live stage for a lot of years. She missed values left and right in Blanche, and didn't have time to pick them up on a two-week stock schedule. Film is a director's medium. He can put your attention where he wants with the camera. Stage work takes a whole different set of muscles, and hers were flabby, unused to sustaining an action or mood for two and a half hours.

But for the first time that season, we were nearly sold out at the box office. Erm was impressed. Bill wasn't.

"They're coming to see a star. She could fart her way through Blanche and they'll still say she's wonderful."

Maybe, but life wasn't all skittles for Nattie. She had two children in expensive schools and got endless phone calls from her manager in California about taxes.

"I gotta work, honey," she told me over black coffee and dry toast. "The wolf's got my ass in his chops already."

She meant it. Another phone call, and that same afternoon between lunch and rehearsal call, Nattie Bond was gone, and I was sitting in Ermise's living room again while Erm swore back and forth across the worn carpet, waving her drink like a weapon, and Bill tried to look bereaved. He always wanted me for Blanche. He had me now.

"Fucked me from the word go." Ermise sprayed ashes over the rug and her poodle. "She knew this when she signed and never said a goddam word."

The facts filtered through my rosy haze. Natalie's agent had a picture deal on the coast so close to signing that it was worth it to let Ermise sue. They'd just buy up her contract—if she could be in Los Angeles tomorrow.

Ermise hurled her cigarette into the trash-filled fireplace, gulped the last of her drink, and turned a mental page. Nattie was one problem, the show another. "You ready to go, Gayla?"

"In my sleep, love."

I was already readjusting the role to the Blanche in my ear and not as sorry for the box office as Erm. Screw 'em all, they were going to see ten times the Blanche Nattie Bond could give them on the best day she ever worked.

"Bill wants me to give you a raise," Ermise said. "Wish I could, Gay, but things are tight."

I pulled the worn script out of my jeans, grinning like a fool back at Bill, who couldn't hide his glee anymore. "Just pay on time, Erm. Keep out of my hair and don't clutter up my stage. Bill, let's go to work."

From my first rehearsal, the play convulsed and became a different animal. The whole cast had to shift gears for me, but no longer suffused by Nattie's hard light, they began to find themselves and glimmer with life. I ate and slept with the script while Blanche came sure and clear. Hell, I'd been rehearsing her for fourteen years. It wasn't hard to identify with the hunger for love half appeased in bed-hopping and sexual junk food and what that does to a woman. The blurred, darkening picture of a girl waiting in her best dress to go to the dance of life with someone who never came.

Play Blanche? Hell, I *was* Blanche. And Stella with her stupid hots for Stanley, Roxane on her silly balcony, loving the wrong guy in the dark for the wrong reasons. I was Ophelia, fucked up and used and never knowing why or how; Alice falling on her butt through the Looking Glass, hunting for a crown on the eighth row that some son of a bitch sawed clean off the board. Man, I was all of them, the whole reamed-out world looking up at God and wondering where it all went with nothing to show. I paid my dues.

Then, just as it seemed to be coming together, it went flat, deader than I am now. But out of that death came a beautiful, risky answer.

Blanche Du Bois is a bitch of a role and demands a powerhouse actress. That's the problem. Like the aura that surrounds Hamlet, the role accumulates a lot of star-shtick and something very subtle can get lost. I determined to strip away the layers of gloss and find what was there to begin with.

"The part's a trap, Bill. All those fluttery, curlicued lines reach out and beg you to *act* them. And you wind up with dazzle again, a concert performance."

"Cadenzas," he agreed with me. "The old Williams poetry."

"Right! Cadenzas, scales. No, by God! I've played the Deep South. There's a smothered quality to those women that gets lost that way. The script describes her as a moth. Moths don't dazzle. They don't glitter."

"Remember that night on the porch," Bill said thoughtfully. "They don't glitter, but they do need the light."

And that was it. Blanche aspired to the things she painted with foolish words. A dream of glitter seen by a nearsighted person by a failing candle. The lines are ornate, but just possibly Blanche is not quite as intelligent as she's been played.

A long artistic chance, but they're the only ones worth taking. If you don't have the guts to be wrong, take up accounting.

So my Blanche emerged a very pathetic woman, a little grotesque as such women are, not only desperate for love but logical in her hopes for Mitch. For all of Belle Reeve and the inbred magnolias, she's not that far above him. Bill gave me my head, knowing that by finding my own Blanche, even being wrong for a while, I'd find the play's as well. On my terms and with my own reality.

I had three lovely labor-pained days of seeing her come alive. On the third day, I was sitting in a corner of the stage with coffee and a sandwich, digging at the script while the others lunched. When Sally Kent walked in, I snapped at her.

"Where's the rest? It's two o'clock. Let's go."

"They want you over at the office, Gay."

"What the hell for? I don't have time. Where's Bill?"

"At the office," Sally admitted reluctantly. "Natalie Bond is here. She's back in the show."

The kiss of death. Even as I shook my head, no, Erm wouldn't do this to me, I knew she would.

Ermise hunched in a chair by the fireplace, bitter with what she had to do, trying not to antagonize Bill any further. He poised on the sofa, seething like a malevolent cat.

"Nattie will do the show after all," Ermise said. "I have to put her back in, Gay."

I couldn't speak at first; sick, quivering on my feet with that horrible end-of-the-rope hollowness in my stomach. No place to go from here. No place . . .

"When we pulled her name off the advertising, we lost more than a third of our reservations." Erm snorted. "I don't like it. I don't like *her* right now, but she's the only thing'll keep my theater open."

Bill's comment cut with the hard edge of disgust. "You know what this does to the cast, don't you? They've readjusted once. Now they have to do it again and open in two days. They were coming beautifully, they were an ensemble with Gayla. Now they're the tail end of a star vehicle."

Bill knew it was already lost, but he was doing this for me.

Ermise shook her head. "Gay, honey, I can't afford it, but I'm gonna raise you retroactive to the first week of your contract." Her hands fluttered in an uncharacteristically helpless gesture. "I owe you that. And you'll go back in as Eunice. But next season—"

I found my voice. It was strange, old. "Don't do this to me. This role, it's mine, I earned it. She'll ruin it."

"Don't look at me," Bill snapped to Ermise. "She's right."

Ermise went defensive. "I don't care who's right. You're all for Gay. Fine, but I can't run a theater that way. Lucky to break even as it is. Nattie's back, she plays and that's the end of it. Gay's contract reads 'as cast.' She's Eunice. What else can I say?"

I showed her what else. I ripped the *Streetcar* script in four parts and threw them in the fireplace. "You can say good-bye, Ermise. Then you can take your raise and shove it." I was already lurching toward the door, voice breaking. "Then you can put someone in my role, because I'm leaving."

I meant it. Without Blanche, there was no reason to stay another minute. Finished. Done.

Except for Natalie Bond. I found her in her hotel room, already dressed for rehearsal and running over the script.

"Come on in, Gayla. Drink?"

"No."

She read my tension as I crouched with my back against the door. "All right, hon. Get it off your chest."

"I will."

I told the bitch what I felt and what I thought and didn't leave anything out. It was quite a speech for no rehearsal, beginning with my teens when I first knew I had to play Blanche, and the years and hard work that made me worthy of it. There wasn't a rep company in the East I hadn't worked, or a major role from Rosalind to Saint Joan I hadn't played. To walk out on the show like she did was pure shit. To crawl back was worse.

"Right," said Nattie. She faced me all through it, let me get it all out. I was crying when I finished. I sank down on a chair, grabbing for one of her Kleenex.

"Now do you want a drink?"

"Yes, what the hell."

She wasn't all rat, Nattie. She could have put me

down with the star routine, but she fixed me a stiff gin
and soda without a word. I remember her fixing that
drink: thick glasses and no makeup, gristly thin. She
had endless trouble with her uterus, infection after
painful infection and a work schedule that never
allowed her to heal properly. A hysterectomy ended
the whole thing. Nattie's face was thinner than mine,
all the softness gone, mouth and cheeks drawn tight.
No matter how sincere, the smile couldn't unclench.

And this, I thought, is what I want to be? Help
me, Nick. Take me home. There's gotta be a home
somewhere, a little rest.

"Know what we're like?" Nattie mused. "A little
fish swimming away from a big, hungry fish who's
just about to be eaten by a bigger fish. That's us,
honey. And that's me in the middle."

She screwed Ermise but someone shafted her, too.
The picture deal was big fat fake. The producer wanted
someone a little bigger and hustled Nattie very plausi-
bly to scare the lady into reaching for a pen.

"I'm broke, Gayla. I owe forty thousand in back
taxes, my house is on a second mortgage, and my kids'
tuition is overdue. Those kids are all I have. I don't
know where the hell to go from here, but Ermise
needs me and I sure as hell need the job."

While I huddled over my drink, unable to speak,
Nattie scribbled something on a memo pad.

"You're too good to waste, you're not commercial,
and you'll probably die broke. But I saw your rehearsal
this morning."

I looked up at her in weepy surprise. The smile
wasn't quite so hard just then.

"If I can do it half that well, Gay. Half."

She shoved the paper into my hand. "That's my
agent in New York. He's with William Morris. If he can't
get you work, no one can. I'll call him myself." She
glanced at her dressing-table clock. "Time, gotta run."

Nattie divined the finality in my shoulders as I sagged toward the door. "You going to play Eunice?"

"No. I'm leaving."

Pinning her hair, she shot me a swift, unsmiling appraisal through the mirror. "Good for you. You got a man in New York?"

"Yeah."

"Get married," she mumbled through a mouthful of pins. "It's not worth it." As the door closed, she raised her voice. "But call my agent."

My bags were packed, but I hadn't bothered to change clothes. That's why my permanent costume, I suppose. Who knew then I'd get very tired of black? Bill insisted on driving me to the airport. When he came for me, I must have looked pathetic, curled up on the bed in one more temporary, damp summer room just waiting to eject me. No love lost; I got damned sick of yellow-green wallpaper.

Bill sat on the edge of the bed. "Ready, Gay?"

I didn't move or answer. Done, finished. Bill put aside the old hurt and lay down beside me, bringing me into his arms. I guess something in him had to open in spite of his defenses. He opened my heart gently as a baby's hand clutched around something that might harm it, letting me cry the last of it out against his shoulder. The light faded in the room while we lay together.

We kissed good-bye like lovers at the departure gate. Bill was too much a part of me for anything less. Maybe he knew better than I how little was waiting for me.

"Be good, Gay."

"You too." I fiddled with his collar. "Don't forget to take your vitamins, you need them. Call me when you get back."

He hugged me one last time. "Why don't you marry me sometime?"

For a lot of reasons, Bill. Because I was a fool and something of a coward. The stunting begins in the seed when we learn not to like ourselves. The sad thing about life is that we usually get what we really want. Let it be.

Funny, though: that was my first and last proposal, and I kissed him good-bye, walked out of his life, and four hours later I was dead.

There was time on the plane to get some of it together. Natalie was a star, at the top where I wanted to be, and look at her: most of the woman cut out of her, flogged to work not by ambition but need. Driven and used. She reminded me of a legless circus freak propelling herself on huge, overdeveloped arms, the rest of her a pitiful afterthought cared for by an expensive gynecologist. I thought, at least when I get home there'll be Nick. Don't call him from the airport, let it be a surprise. We'll get some coffee and cold cuts from Zabar's, make love, and talk half the night. I needed to talk, to see us plain.

Get married, Nattie said. It isn't worth it.

Maybe not the way I chased it for fourteen years. I'd call her agent, keep working, but more New York jobs with time left over to be with Nick, to sit on my balcony and just breathe or read. To make a few friends outside of theater. To see a doctor and find out how tough I really am, and if everything in the baby box is working right, so that maybe—

Like she said, so maybe get married and have kids while I can. A little commitment, Nick, a little tomorrow. If the word sounds strange, I just learned it. Give me this, Nick. I need it.

The light was on in our living room as I hauled my suitcase out of the cab and started up. Hell, I won't even buzz, just turn the key in the lock and reach for him.

I did that.

There was—yes, I remember—one blessed moment of breathing the good, safe air of my own living room as I set down the luggage. I heard a faint stirring from the bedroom. Good, I've surprised him. If Nick was just waking from a nap, we'd have that much more time to touch each other.

"It's me, baby."

I crossed to the bedroom door, groping inside for the light switch. "I'm home."

I didn't need the switch. There was enough light to see them frozen on the torn-up bed. The other one was older, a little flabby. He muttered something to Nick. I stood there, absurd myself, and choked, "Excuse me."

Then, as if someone punched me in the stomach, I stumbled to the bathroom, pushed the door shut, and fell back against it.

"Get him out of here, Nick!"

The last word strangled off as I doubled over the john and vomited all the horrible day out of me, with two hours left to live, retching and sobbing, not wanting to hear whatever was said beyond the door. After a short time, the front door closed. I washed my face, dried it with the stiff, clumsy movements of exhaustion and got out to the living room somehow, past the bed where Nick was smoking a cigarette, the sheet pulled up over his lean thighs.

I remember pouring a drink. That was foolish on an empty stomach, the worst thing I could have done. I sat on the sofa, waiting.

"Nick." The silence from the bedroom was the only thing I could feel in my shock. "Nick, please come out. I want to talk to you."

I heard him rustle into his clothes. In a moment Nick came out, bleak and sullen.

"Why are you back so early?"

"No, they—" My reactions were still disjointed, coming out of shock, but the anger was building. "They put Nattie Bond back in the show. I walked out."

That seemed to concern him more than anything else. "You just walked out? They'll get Equity on you."

The delayed reaction exploded. "*Fuck* Equity! Never mind about Equity, what are *we* gonna do?"

"What do you mean?" he asked calmly.

"Oh, man, are you for real?" I pointed at the door. "What was that?"

"That may be a Broadway job." He turned away into the kitchen. "Now get off my back."

"The hell I—"

"Hey look, Gayla. I haven't made any promises to you. You wanted me to move in. Okay, I moved in. We've had it good."

I began to shake. "Promises? Of course there were promises. There's always a promise, nobody has to spell it out. I could have gone to bed with Bill Wrenn plenty of times this summer, but I didn't."

He only shrugged. "So whose fault is that? Not mine."

"You bastard!" I threw my glass at him. He ducked, the thing went a mile wide, then Nick was sopping up whisky and bits of glass while I shook myself apart on the couch, teeth chattering so hard I had to clamp my mouth tight shut. It was all hitting me at once, and I couldn't handle half of it. Nick finished cleaning up without a word, but I could see even then the tight line of his mouth and the angry droop of his eyelids. He had guts of a kind, Nick. He could face anything because it didn't matter. All the important things were outside, to be reached for. Inside I think he was dead.

"The meanest thing Bill ever said to me," I stuttered. "When I left him for you, h-he said you played both sides of the fence. And I c-called him a goddam liar. I couldn't believe he'd be small enough to— Nick, I'm falling apart. They took my show, and I came home to you because I don't know what to do."

Nick came over, sat down, and held me in his arms. "I'm not, Gayla."

"Not what?"

"What Bill said."

"Then w-what was this?"

He didn't answer, just kissed me. I clung to Nick like a lost child.

Why do we always try to rewrite what's happened? Even now I see myself pointing to the door and kissing him off with a real Bette Davis sizzler for a curtain. Bullshit. I needed Nick. The accounting department was already toting up the cost of what I wanted and saying, *I'll change him. It's worth it.*

I only cried wearily in his arms while Nick soothed and stroked me. "I'm not that," he said again. "Just that so many guys are hung up on role-playing and all that shit. Oh, it's been said about me."

I twisted in his lap to look at him. "Nick, why did you come to me?"

The question gave him more trouble than it should. "I like you. You're the greatest girl I ever met."

Something didn't add up. Nothing ever bugged Nick before; he could always handle it, but he was finding this hard.

"That's not enough," I persisted. "Not tonight."

Nick disengaged himself with a bored sigh. "Look, I have to go out."

"Go out? Now?" I couldn't believe he'd leave me like this. "Why?"

He walked away toward the bedroom. I felt the anger grow cold with something I'd never faced before, answers to questions that gnawed at the back of my mind from our first night. "Why, Nick? Is it him? Did that fat queer tell you to come over after you ditched the hag?"

Nick turned on me, lowering. "I don't like that word."

"Queer."

"I said—"

"Queer!"

"All right." He kicked viciously at the bedroom door with all the force he wanted to spend stopping my mouth. "It's a fact in this business. That's why I get in places you don't. It's a business, cut and dried, not an *aht fawm* like you're always preaching."

"Come off it, Nick." I stood up, ready for him now and wanting the fight. "That casting-couch bit went out with Harlow. Is that how you get jobs? That and the cheap, scene-stealing tricks you use when you know and I know I played you against the fucking wall in Lexington, you hypocritical son of a bitch."

Nick threw up a warning hand. "Hey, wait just one damn minute, Bernhardt. I never said I was or ever could be as good as you. But I'll tell you one thing." Nick opened the closet and snaked his jacket off a hanger. "I'll be around and working when nobody remembers you, because I know the business. You've been around fourteen years and still don't know the score. You won't make rounds, you don't want to be bothered waiting for an agent to see you. You're a goddam *ahtist*. You won't wait in New York for something to develop, hell no. You'll take any show going out to Noplaceville, and who the hell ever sees you but some jerkoff writing for a newspaper no one reads. Integrity? Bullshit, lady. You are *afraid* of New York, afraid to take a chance on it."

Nick subsided a little. "That guy who was here, he produces. He's got a big voice where it counts." Again he looked away with that odd, inconsistent embarrassment. "He didn't want to sleep with me, really. He's basically straight."

That was too absurd for anger. "Basically?"

"He only wanted a little affection."

"And you, Nick? Which way do you go basically? I mean was it his idea or yours?"

That was the first totally vulnerable moment I ever saw in Nick. He turned away, leaning against the sink. I could barely hear him. "I don't know. It's never made much difference. So what's the harm? I don't lose anything, and I may gain."

He started for the door, but I stopped him. "Nick, I need you. What's happened to me today—I'm almost sick. Please don't do this to me."

"Do what? Look." He held me a moment without warmth or conviction. "I'll only be gone a little while. We'll talk tomorrow, okay?"

"Don't go, Nick."

He straightened his collar carefully with a sidelong glance at the mirror. "We can't talk when you're like this. There's no point."

I dogged him desperately, needing something to hang on to. "Please don't go. I'm sorry for what I said. Nick, we can work it out, but don't leave me alone."

"I have to." His hand was already on the door, cutting me off like a thread hanging from his sleeve.

"Why!" It ripped up out of the bottom, out of the anger without which we never love or possess anything. "Because that fat faggot with his job means more than I do, right? How low do you crawl to make a buck in this business? Or is it all business? Jesus, you make me sick."

Nick couldn't be insulted. Even at the end, he didn't have that to spare me. Just a look from those cool blue eyes I tried so hard to please, telling me he was a winner in a game he knew, and I just didn't make it.

"It's your apartment. I'll move."

"Nick, don't go."

The door closed.

What did I do then? I should remember, they were the last minutes of my life. The door closed. I heard Nick thumping down the carpeted stairs, and thank God for cold comfort I didn't run after him. I poured a straight shot and finished it in one pull.

A hollow, eye-of-the-storm calm settled on me and then a depression so heavy it was a physical pain. I wandered through the apartment drinking too much and too fast, talking to Nick, to Bill, to Nattie, until I collapsed, clumsy, hiccuping drunk on the floor with half an hour to live.

Another drink. Get blind, drunk enough to reach . . . something, to blot out the Lump. Yeah, she's still with you, the goddam little loser. Don't you ever learn, loser? No, she won't ever learn. Yesterday did this day's madness prepare. What play was that and who cares?

I tried to think but nothing came together. My life was a scattered Tinkertoy, all joints and pieces without meaning or order. A sum of apples and oranges: parts played, meals eaten, clothes worn, he said and I said, old tickets, old programs, newspaper reviews yellowed and fragile as Blanche's love letters. Apples and oranges. Where did I leave anything of myself, who did I love, what did I have? No one. Nothing.

Only Bill Wrenn.

"Christ, Bill, help me!"

I clawed for the phone with the room spinning and managed to call the theater. One of the girl apprentices answered. I struggled to make myself understood with a thickening tongue. "Yeah; Bill Wrenn, 'simportant. Gayla Damon. Yeah, hi, honey. He's not? Goddammit, he's *gotta* be. I *need* him. When'll he be back? Yeah . . . yeah. Tell'm call Gayla, please. Please. Yeah, trouble. Real trouble. I need him."

That's how it happened. I dropped the phone in the general vicinity of the hook and staggered to the pitching sink to make one more huge, suicidal drink, crying and laughing, part drunk, part hysteria. But Bill was going to bail me out like he always had, and, boy, ol' Gay had learned her lesson. I was a fool to leave him. He loved me. Bill loved me and I was afraid of that. Afraid to be loved. How dumb can you get?

"How dumb?" I raged mushily at the Lump in the mirror. "You with the great, soulful eyes. You never knew shit, baby."

I was sweating. The wool sweater oppressed my clammy skin. Some sober molecule said take it off, but no. It's cooler out on my balcony. I will go out on my beautiful, nighted balcony and present my case to the yet unknowing world.

I half fell through the door. The balcony had a low railing, lower than I judged as I stumbled and heaved my drunken weight behind the hand flung out to steady myself and—

Fell. No more time.

That's it, finished. Now I've remembered. It was that sudden, painless, meaningless. No fade-out, no end-title music resolving the conflict themes, only torn film fluttering past the projector light, leaving a white screen.

There's a few answers anyway. I could get a lump in my throat, if I had one, thinking how Bill came and checked me out. God, let's hope they kept me covered. I must have looked awful. Poor Bill; maybe I gave you such a rotten time because I knew you could take it and still hang in. That's one of the faces of love, Mr. Wrenn.

But I'd never have guessed about Lowen. Just imagine: he saw me that long ago and remembered all these years because I showed him he wasn't alone. I still can't add it up. Apples and oranges.

Unless, just maybe . . .

"Lowen!"

The sound track again, the needle dropped on time. The balcony door thunders open and slams shut. Al calls again, but Lowen ignores her, leaning against the door, holding it closed.

"Gayla?"

His eyes move searchingly over the balcony in the

darkening winter afternoon. From my name etched in the cement, around the railing, Lowen's whole concentrated being probes the gray light and air, full of purpose and need.

"Gayla, I know you're here."

As he says my name, sound and vision and my own strength treble. I turn to him, wondering if through the sheer power of his need he can see me yet.

Lowen, can you hear me?

"I think I know what this means."

I stretch out my hand, open up, let it touch his face, and as I tingle and hurt with it, Lowen turns his cheek into the caress.

"Yes, I feel you close."

Talk to me, Lowen.

"Isn't it strange, Gayla?"

Not strange at all, not us.

"When I saw you that night, I wanted to reach out and touch you, but I was just too shy. Couldn't even ask for my own autograph."

Why not? I could have used a little touching.

"But I hitched all the way from school next day just to catch a glimpse of you. Hid in the back of the theater and watched you rehearse."

That was Blanche. You saw that?

"It was the same thing all over again. You had something that reached out and showed me how we're all alike. I never saw a lonelier person than you on that stage. Or more beautiful. I cried."

You saw Blanche. She did have a beauty.

"Oh, Gayla, the letters I wrote you and never sent. Forgive me. I forgot the name but not the lesson. If you can hear me: you were the first woman I ever loved, and you taught me right. It's a giving."

I hear Al's urgent knock on the other side of the door. "Lowen, what is it? Are you all right?"

He turns his head and smiles. God, he's beautiful.

"Fine, Al. She loves this place, Gayla. Don't drive her away."

I won't, but don't go. Not now when I'm beginning to understand so much.

He shakes his head. "This is our first house. We're new, all kinds of problems. Parents, religion, everything."

Can you hear me?

"We were never loved by anyone before, either of us. That's new, too. You pray for it—"

Like a fire.

"—like a fire to warm yourself."

You *do* hear me.

"But it's scary. What do you do with the fire when it comes?" Lowen's hands reach out, pleading. "Don't take this away from her. Don't hurt my Al. You're stronger than us. You can manage."

I stretch my hand to touch his. With all my will, I press the answer through the contact.

Promise, Lowen.

"Don't make me shut you out. I don't know if I could. Go away and keep our secret? Take a big piece of love with you?"

Yes. Just that I was reaching for something, like you, and I had it all the time. So do you, Lowen. You're a—

I feel again as I did when the star fell across the sky, joyful and new and big as all creation without needing a reason, as Lowen's real fingers close around the memory of mine.

You're a *mensch*, love. Like me.

Lowen murmurs: "I feel your hand. I don't care what anyone says. Your kind of woman doesn't kill herself. I'll never believe it."

Bet on it. And thank you.

So it was a hell of a lot more than apples and oranges. It was a giving, a love. Hear that, Bill? Nattie? What I called life was just the love, the giving, like kisses on the wind, thrown to the audience, to my work, to the casual men, to whom it may concern. I was a giver, and if the little takers like Nick couldn't dig that, tough. That's the way it went down. All the miserable, self-cheating years, something heard a music and went on singing. If Nattie could do it half as well. If she was half as alive as me, she meant. I loved all my life, because they're the same thing. Man, I was beautiful.

That's the part of you that woke me, Lowen. You're green, but you won't go through life like a tourist. You're going to get hurt and do some hurting yourself, but maybe someday . . .

That's it, Lowen. That's the plot. You said it: we all touch, and the touching continues us. All those nights, throwing all of myself at life, and who's to say I did it alone? So when you're full up with life, maybe you'll wake like me to spill it over into some poor, scared kid. You're full of life like me, Lowen. It's a beautiful, rare gift.

It's dark enough now to see stars and the fingernail sliver of moon. A lovely moment for Lowen and me, like the night with Bill a moment before we made love for the first time. Lowen and I holding hands in the evening. Understanding. His eyes move slowly from my hand up toward my face.

"Gayla, I can see you."

Can you, honest?

"Very clear. You're wearing a sweater and jeans. And you're smiling."

Am I ever!

"And very beautiful."

Bet your ass. I feel great, like I finally got it together.

One last painful, lovely current of life as Lowen squeezes my hand. "Good-bye, Gayla."

So long, love.

Lowen yanks open the door. "Al, Mr. Hirajian? Come on out. It's a lovely evening."

Alice peeks out to see Lowen leaning over the railing, enjoying the river and the early stars. His chest swells; he's laughing and he looks marvelous, inviting Al into his arms the way he did on their first day here. She comes unsurely to nestle in beside him, one arm around his waist. "Who were you talking to?"

"She's gone, Al. You've got nothing to be afraid of. Except being afraid."

"Lowen, I'm not going to—"

"This is our house, and nobody's going to take it away from us." He turns Al to him and kisses her. "Nobody wants to, that's a promise. So don't run away from it or yourself."

She shivers a little, still uncertain. "Do you really think we can stay. I can't—"

"Hey, love." Lowen leans into her, cocky and charming but meaning it. "Don't tell a *mensch* what you can't. Hey, Hirajian!"

When the little prune pokes his head out the door, Lowen sweeps his arm out over the river and the whole lit-up West Side. "Sorry for all the trouble, but we've changed our minds. I mean, look at it! Who could give up a balcony with a view like this?"

He's the last thing I see before the lights change: Lowen holding Al and grinning out at the world. I thought the lights were dimming, but it's something else, another cue coming up. The lights cross-fade up, up, more pink and amber, until—my God, it's gorgeous!

I'm not dead, not gone. I feel more alive than ever. I'm Gail and Gayla and Lowen and Bill and Al and all of them magnified, heightened, fully realized, flowing together like bright, silver streams into—

Will you look at that *set*. Fantastic. Who's on the lights?

So that's what You look like. Ri-i-ght. I'm with it now, and I love You, too. Give me a follow-spot, baby.

I'm on.

Copyrights

GARDNER DOZOIS has been honored with the Hugo Award for Best Editor six times and has twice received the Nebula Award for his own short fiction. He is the editor of *Asimov's Science Fiction* magazine and lives in Philadelphia, Pennsylvania.